Home T

Sylvie Short

After many years in the teaching profession, Sylvie has retired to East Anglia to concentrate on writing full time.

Home To Roost

HOME TO ROOST

By

Sylvie Short

Best wishes,

Sylvie

Home To Roost

Dedication:

For Margaret whose story inspired this
family saga

Acknowledgements - I am indebted to:

My solicitor, Elizabeth Morris, for advising me
about Power of Attorney;

Dr. Paul Williams for sharing his knowledge of
Dimercaprol with me;

Michael Farrell for his book 'Poisons and
Poisoners' from which I obtained information
about the toxic effects of arsenic in paint;

Tony Waters for his knowledge of financial
policies and procedures within the United
Kingdom banking system;

Helen Short for the cover photographs;
Paul Haresnape for cover configuration

Home To Roost

THE BABY 1944

The room felt cold, so cold – stark, bare and empty and that's how she felt too, drained and empty and freezing cold in spite of the beads of sweat on her forehead and upper lip. She could feel it trickling down her back – cold and wet. She lay back on the clammy sheets, exhausted, gasping for breath and was conscious of the wet stickiness between her legs. Swiftly and efficiently the doctor was finishing his job. The room was silent; the bundle had gone. Then through a sea of mist a face swam into view just above the end of the bed. She tried to sit up, but couldn't; she stretched out her hand,

"Please….please…."

The face at the end of the bed was stony and without expression; the mouth twitched,

"No. We all agreed. You know it's for the best."

She sank back sobbing, tears mingling with the sweat on her cheeks. Then another face; soft and kind and wet with tears.

"Here. Just for a moment."

And she struggled to sit up as the bundle, tiny and warm and white was thrust into her arms. She looked at the screwed up face, the mouth making small sucking movements and the eyelids like tiny translucent shells. The fingers – minute and perfect

– crawled in the air; she looked back at the face and suddenly the eyes opened wide and looked into hers. Green, so green – the greenest green she had ever seen. Then she felt it – a rush of purest love, a love that almost stopped her breath. With shaking fingers she pushed the little packet deep into soft folds of cloth unseen by the woman standing by the bed looking anxiously over her shoulder,

"You'd better give her back."

Gently she took the bundle and the woman sank back onto the bed and turned her face to the wall. She sobbed – a silent, retching sound – until there was nothing left.

PART ONE

Home To Roost

CHAPTER ONE

1953

Crystal could feel the bubble of excitement, tiny at first, then swelling, slowly but surely, getting bigger and bigger the nearer they drew to Savron Pinder. She peered out of the windows of the old Hillman as it bumped and rattled along the narrow fen roads, first to the left and then to the right, marvelling at the strange beauty of the flat landscape. She opened the car window and felt a warm wind on her cheeks; it was sweeping across the land picking up dust and bending the few sparse trees down to meet soil as black as soot. She gazed upwards to where clouds were scudding across huge skies then looked back to the surrounding countryside at old grey buildings squatting like toads on the fields – golden, green, black, green again – criss-crossed by dykes and drains.

"We're nearly there, my love. Watch for the sign, it comes all of a sudden as you go round a bend."

Marjorie had turned to smile at her excited daughter who bounced forward and looked out between the front seats at the road ahead, straining her eyes for her first sight of the village that was to be their new home.

"There it is. Look."

Mother and daughter leaned forward as the small white sign came into view, clapping their hands as they passed it then looking from right to left as the car started to wind its way along the village street. Crystal stared up at the huge Church to the right and then immediately looked to the left as her mother pointed to a small, low building, set back from the road and almost hidden by a wall.

"That's the school."

Crystal twisted round to look back at it through the rear window of the car and felt the bubble of excitement wobble a bit. Would she be happy there? Would she make friends? Before she had time to think about it anymore she felt the car slowing down and begin to turn slowly up a little sloping drive.

"This is it; Maple Cottage."

Her dad, who had been smiling indulgently at the excited exclamations, now wrenched on the handbrake, turned off the engine and looked at his wife and daughter.

"Well?"

His eyes were on Crystal as she gazed at the cream-coloured cottage criss-crossed by thick black beams. Marjorie was looking at her too and smiling. She and George had already fallen in love with the place and wanted to see if it would weave its magic spell on their daughter too.

"Oh it's lovely," she breathed, stepping slowly out of the car and moving towards her new home as if caught in a dream.

The rest of the day was lost in a haze of unpacking boxes and trying to restore enough order to make a simple meal and at least get their beds sorted for the night. Crystal kept walking through the rooms, dusty with neglect, and imagining how they would look when her mum and dad had lovingly redecorated and restored them.

"Nothing that a dab of paint and a bit of loving care can't sort out," George exclaimed cheerfully as if Marjorie or Crystal needed reassuring – which they didn't.

That night she lay in her tiny bed under the sloping roof and listened to the house martins scratching in their nests just under the eaves. She had been leaning on the windowsill earlier watching them swooping and diving until the sun had gone down, painting glorious colours across the sky with sweeping strokes, and the first stars of the evening had appeared. She turned over to sleep and was aware of the strangest feeling – she had come home.

CHAPTER TWO

The sun was hot on their backs as the two girls lay silently on top of the barn roof. Scarcely daring to breathe, they slithered to the edge and watched as the huge horses, some grey and some dark chestnut, leapt forward and galloped across the grass, kicking their heels in an ecstasy of celebration – they were free. For a few hours the collars wouldn't chafe their shoulders as they strained to pull heavy loads of hay, straw or manure along the village streets. Then the man appeared; iron-grey hair sticking out beneath an old cloth cap, tattered waistcoat over his collarless shirt and trousers tied at the knee with string. He stood, hands on his hips, watching the horses, and the girls lowered their heads right down to the roof, trying not to giggle, fearful that he would turn, see them and shout at them for trespassing. Minty lifted her head first then put her nose right over the edge of the barn,

"It's OK he's gone," she whispered and they both slid back down the roof, jumped lightly into the soft, scratchy straw then raced out of the yard and down the road. They didn't stop until they reached the orchard where they collapsed under one of the apple trees, rolling around and laughing. Minty sat up first and pulled some pieces of straw out of Crystal's hair – a tumble of bright, dark red curls that framed her pale skin and fell in a shining mass about her shoulders. Then she stood up and bent over to shake the dust and chaff from her own hair, short, dark brown and coarse.

"Who do the horses belong to?" Crystal asked; keen to get to know more about the village that had become her home.

"The Lynton-Bells at Manor Farm, most stuff around here belongs to them; though the Elliotts at Savron Pinder House own a lot of the land. You sometimes see old Squire Elliott riding round the village on a bike. I don't know who he thinks he's kidding 'cos everyone knows he's got fancy cars, including a Rolls Royce. He likes to stop and talk to people; pretend he's one of us and not a toff. Come on, let's go and get a drink."

The girls raced out of the orchard and round to the back door of the farm house where they let themselves into the kitchen. They clattered over the old flagstones and wrinkled their noses at the sweet, sticky smell of fruit that greeted them. Minty's gran, her stick-thin body wrapped in a flowery apron, was standing at the Aga stirring a large, bubbling pot. She turned towards them and continued stirring as she pushed a wisp of hair back from her forehead and tucked it under a clasp. It was thick and coarse like Minty's and hung, dead straight, to just below her jaw where it was cut in a line round the back of her neck. It swung a little as she turned back towards the pot,

"Now what do you two want? Something, I'll be bound for that's the only time we ever do see you."

Minty climbed onto one of the chairs at the huge oak table that ran almost the whole length of the kitchen, so Crystal did too. She cleared a space by pushing away the pile of toys strewn across the dark, shiny surface and spoke in a wheedling voice directed at her gran's back

"We're thirsty, gran, can we have a drink?"

"I made some lemonade this mornin'. It's in the fridge; you'll have to get it yourself as I gotta keep a stirring this 'ere jam."

Minty jumped down, selected two glasses from a cupboard and hauled open the door of the massive fridge that stood humming quietly in the corner of the kitchen.

She smiled at Crystal as the pale, cloudy liquid splashed into the glasses then stuck in two white straws and the girls drank, making small slurping sounds as they sat quietly side by side. Shouts and laughter drifted in through the open window and Crystal could see Hannah, Minty's aunt, playing on the lawn with her two small children. Timmy, the three year old was throwing a coloured ball in the air and chasing it, laughing and shouting to his mother to watch him; while Lottie, the baby, gurgled and kicked on a blanket in the sunshine.

Crystal looked back at her friend and remembered the time, only six weeks ago, when she had first seen her sitting in a pool of sunlight at her desk in the village school. She had felt nervous and held on tightly to her mum's hand while Mrs. Dean, the Head Teacher, had talked to them and proudly showed them around the school. She was a middle-aged woman, dressed smartly in a burgundy suit with a pale pink chiffon scarf lying in soft folds around her neck. Bristling with energy, she had swept them along through three class rooms – two in use, one for the infants and one for the juniors while the third in between them was kept for music and movement. Her dad had asked questions but Crystal had kept quiet, peeping shyly up from under her lashes as thirty pairs of infant and then junior eyes silently stared. There were murmurs as they turned to go and Crystal knew they were talking about her hair. Everyone did. It was a cross she had to bear and she was learning that there was absolutely nothing she could do about it. They had stopped near the door and Mrs. Dean seemed puzzled about something. She turned and looked at Crystal and then started muttering again to her dad. Crystal leaned towards her mum and whispered,

"What's the matter?"

"I think she's having trouble deciding where to put you, dear – the infant or the junior room."

Crystal felt indignant. She was nine years old and in the big town school she had just left she certainly wasn't an infant any more. She found her voice.

"Mrs. Dean….I have just started pounds, shillings and pence takeaways." She spoke clearly and Mrs. Dean turned towards her. She looked relieved,

"Have you dear? – Well that decides it then; into the junior room with you!"

Crystal said goodbye to her mum and dad and left her coat in the cloakroom. Standing next to Mrs. Dean in the junior room, she had felt gawky and awkward again, then, glancing up, she had seen this girl, quite plump with short, brown hair – the sort of hair she would have loved to have instead of her dark red corkscrew curls that marked her out as different – sitting in a shaft of sunlight that streamed in through the class room window. The girl smiled and a huge dimple appeared in each cheek. Mrs. Dean seized the moment,

"Araminta, will you look after Crystal, dear. There's a good girl – and I know the rest of you will do all you can to make our new pupil feel welcome." Twenty nine blank faces nodded obediently as Crystal made her way to where Minty was clearing a place at the desk next to her.

They both finished their lemonade at the same time, giggling as the straws made little gurgling noises in the bottom of the glasses.

"Have you made any hedgehogs, gran? We love your hedgehogs; don't we love gran's hedgehogs, Crystal?"

"Yes….we do."

Minty was grinning as her gran turned, raised her eyes to heaven and indicated the tin on a nearby sideboard.

"Only one each, mind. I'll not have you spoiling your suppers."

"Thanks gran. You know I love you."

The old woman tutted and raised her eyes to heaven again as she turned back and resumed her vigorous stirring of the jam. She shook her head but Crystal noticed there was a smile playing around her lips. Minty jumped down from the table and, carefully prising the lid off the tin on the sideboard, she took out one of the chocolate sausage-shaped cakes. She beckoned to Crystal who joined her and helped herself then, with a surreptitious glance over her shoulder; Minty took another one and motioned to Crystal to do the same.

"Just going upstairs gran. Won't be long."

The two girls lay across Minty's bed licking the coconut off the outside of their hedgehogs then chewing the delicious chocolaty bits inside. Crystal loved coming to Pook's Farm where cats, chickens and pigs roamed around scratching or just lolling about in the mud and dust. It was a small holding, managed well by Hannah's husband, Ed, and there was always a relaxed atmosphere about the place. She knew from the other children at school that Minty's mum had died from something called Leukaemia when she was just three years old, but Minty never talked about it. She was remembered by the people in the village as a refined, gentle woman, dearly loved by her husband Matthew, a ruggedly handsome man who also never talked about the loss of his beloved wife. His younger sister, Hannah and his mother, Martha, helped him with the daunting task of bringing up his mischievous daughter and, as there was plenty of room in the sprawling farmhouse, the family rubbed along tolerably well together. Minty licked her lips;

"Guess what! I'm going riding on Saturday."

"Oh you lucky pig. Where?"

"Monk's Manor; I'm going with my dad. I don't really want to, but I have to"

Of course; Crystal should have guessed that was where her friend would be going. She lay back and stared at the ceiling wondering what it must be like not to want to go riding on a pony. She longed to, but hadn't so far managed to find a way of asking. Minty's dad was the head groom at Manor Farm, home of the Lynton-Bells, and occasionally, because the two manors were so closely linked by family ties, he was asked to work at Monk's Manor as well. While exercising the thoroughbreds from Manor Farm he was required to take Minty down to Monk's Manor where she rode the pony belonging to Giles Cowper as he was away at boarding school. His mother, Eleanore, was the daughter of Isobel Lynton-Bell of Manor Farm.

Minty leaned up on her elbow,

"Hey, I've got an idea. Why don't you come too? I've just remembered; dad was talking on the phone to Mr. Geoffrey and I'm sure I heard him say that Mrs. Cowper has bought another pony for Giles. I couldn't hear what Mr. Geoffrey was saying, but I think he was being rude about his sister. Dad was laughing and saying things like, 'it takes me all my time to persuade her to come with me to exercise one, never mind two.' I think they were implying that Mrs. Cowper hadn't really thought it through but had just bought another pony on impulse.

"But I haven't got the right clothes." Crystal's heart was beating fast; she didn't dare allow herself to hope that she might go riding with Minty and her dad. Minty knelt up at the window.

"I thought so, here comes dad. Let's go and ask him."

"But, Minty, I haven't…"

Minty swung round with one hand on the door knob and tapped her head with the fore finger of the other,

"Don't worry - another idea!"

"Hello, Mints." Matthew Graham ruffled his daughter's hair while at the same time throwing a bridle down onto the cluttered surface of the kitchen table where it clattered amongst the mess of toys, crayons and half finished pictures. Martha, his mother, tutted and swooped like an angry little sparrow, gathering it up and hanging it on a hook by the huge fire place while giving her son a disapproving look. He saw, and aimed a swipe at her skinny bottom as she passed him on her way back to the aga where the cauldron of jam was cooling a little before being tipped into the waiting jars; she dodged and they both laughed.

He was a big man, tall and muscular with legs that had become bowed from riding horses for most of his adult life. His jodhpurs were greasy and worn and his leather jerkin hung loosely about his shoulders. His skin was tanned and weather beaten; his neck, the colour and texture of leather, rose out of a surprisingly white collar and his brown face accentuated the whiteness of his teeth. When he smiled, it was a smile that lit up his whole face and Crystal noticed that he seemed to fill the room with his presence. He removed his cap and ran his hand through his thick, brown curls as he turned towards their visitor.

"Hello you. Have you moved in with us?"

Crystal blushed.

"Ignore him, Cryssie, he thinks he's a comedian; wants to go on this new television thing everyone's talking about if it really catches on."

Minty tried to pinch her dad's bottom but the hard shiny material of his jodhpurs wouldn't allow her to get a grip. Matthew turned and hugged his daughter then kissed the top of her head,

"You can move in if you want, Crystal. You might teach my tomboy daughter some of your lady-like ways."

He smiled at Minty as he said it and they all knew he wouldn't change a thing about his beloved child – even though her mischievousness nearly drove them all crazy at times. Matthew flung himself down in the armchair by the huge fireplace and let out a sigh, pleased to be home at the end of a hard day. Minty climbed onto his lap and glanced over to where Crystal was leaning on the doorpost then back to her dad.

"Dad"

"Yes, what do you want?"

Minty looked at him in surprise.

"How do you know I want something?"

There was a bark of laughter from the aga where gran, having transferred the hot, sticky jam from the iron pot to a jug was carefully pouring it into warm, gleaming jars immediately turning them red. Minty ignored her and turned back to her dad,

"Well…. I heard you talking to Mr. Geoffrey and I worked out from what you said that Mrs. Cowper has bought another pony for Giles…."She sat up straight and spoke very quickly, "and I just wondered if Crystal could come with us on Saturday and ride it. Please dad."

She flung her arms round his neck and buried her head in his shoulder. He smiled, rubbing his hand gently up and down her back, but his face was serious when he looked at Crystal.

"Have you ever ridden before, Crystal?"

Minty sat up,

"No, she….."

Matt. Graham held up a finger at his daughter,

"Be quiet, Minty. Let her speak."

Crystal swallowed and cleared her throat; the room was quiet apart from the ticking of the grandfather clock in the corner and from somewhere deep in the house she could hear the sounds of Hannah and her children. Suddenly the baby started to cry.

"No….I've never had the chance." She hesitated and then looked straight at him, "but I would love to, Mr. Graham. I would so love to ride."

Matt. looked back at the pretty girl facing him across the cluttered kitchen, her green eyes shining, her skin pale and delicate with a slight flush to her cheeks all framed by that mass of extraordinary hair and he thought, not for the first time, that Minty's new friend was going to be a beauty.

"Do you have anything to wear?"

Crystal looked down and Minty, afraid of being silenced again, spoke quietly and respectfully to her father,

"She doesn't dad, but I have an idea."

She jumped down from Matt's lap and knelt up at the table where her gran was now popping little circles of greaseproof paper onto the filled jars.

"Gran…"

The old woman looked up and made a face at her granddaughter,

"Yes, Minty, I was wondering when I would become useful in your plans. Now let me guess.

19

You've remembered that I used to ride and that I still have all my stuff up in the wardrobe in the back bedroom. And with Crystal being a little skinnimalink like me your busy brain was putting two and two together and you was going to ask me if she could borrow it." Gran looked over to Crystal and continued, "of course you can wear it, m' dear. It's doing no good hanging in the cupboard." Minty's mouth fell open and she regarded her grandmother, who had read her mind so perfectly, with a new respect.

"Am I right or am I right?"

"Yeah. Thanks Gran." Minty reached over to scoop up a blob of jam with her finger and gran smacked her hand lightly with a wooden spoon before clattering it into the sink with the other utensils.

CHAPTER THREE

The material of the jodhpurs felt stiff and a little scratchy and the boots squeaked as Crystal walked briskly down the drive with Matthew and Minty Graham. The black jacket fitted beautifully as did the black velvet hat, already firmly on her head. Minty was carrying hers as she skipped along beside her father, but Crystal and her mum had decided that it was best to cram Crystals deep red curls up into a net and under the hat before she set out. Marjorie knew her daughter would never manage it on her own.

She and George had been only too pleased to let Crystal go riding at Monk's Manor. From her chats with the ladies at the Women' Institute Marjorie knew that the family was well regarded in the village, though they kept themselves very much to themselves, only emerging to put in token appearances at village events. They did occasionally host the annual fayre and had once held a barbecue in one of their barns – an event that was talked about for many years afterwards.

'….And, of course they can be relied upon for generous donations to any charitable causes and for mulled wine and mince pies when we go Carol singing at Christmas.'

Even before the house came into view, Crystal found herself wondering again about the Cowper family at Monk's Manor. She knew that Eleanore was the daughter of the old lady who lived at Manor Farm; that she had married a doctor, who worked mainly on dead bodies, and that they had three children, Clive, Rosemary and Giles. Because they had all gone to prep. schools in Cambridge and then on to boarding school – Giles, of course was still there – the village people didn't know a great deal about them and Crystal was to learn that, in a village, what you don't know you invent.

The doctor's name was William and the general consensus seemed to be that it was a good job he worked with the dead as he was completely without charm and had no patience at all with the living. She had heard him described as a 'miserable git' by some of the men who worked on the gardens there. His eldest son, Clive, was apparently no better and had been referred to by one old boy as a 'nasty piece of work', though Crystal had no idea why. She had asked Minty about him one day when they were lolling about in her bedroom and, glancing round to make sure the door was firmly closed so that gran couldn't hear her, she had replied,

"He's an arsehole."

It was obvious that she was repeating something she had heard and it suddenly sounded so funny, hanging there in the air, that they had both got the giggles and fallen off the bed onto the floor with such a thud that gran had shouted up the stairs for them to make less noise. Rosemary, the daughter, was generally considered to be alright, though Crystal had heard one of the cleaning ladies from Monk's Manor talking in the village shop about the forthcoming Debutante's Ball in London at which Rosemary was due to be presented to the Queen. She was telling Mrs. Willis, the shop keeper's wife, who was busy weighing sugar into a blue bag, that the dress hanging up in one of the bed rooms was beautiful,

"....It's just a pity that Rosemary's got a face like a horse's backside," the woman concluded as she paid her money, picked up the small blue bag and turned to leave the shop. Mrs. Willis had laughed.

"You're right there, dear. All their money doesn't buy them looks – though she does, of course, take after her father not her mother."

Before Crystal had time to think about Eleanore, Rosemary's mother, or the youngest son, Giles, they rounded a bend in the drive and she saw the Manor for the first time. She gasped at the sight then looked along the path nervously, hoping that Minty and her dad were far enough in front not to have heard. She was afraid they might think her foolish to be so enraptured by something they must have seen so many times. She needn't have worried; Minty was chatting away non-stop and Matt was trying to listen attentively to his daughter, so Crystal was free to continue gazing with her mouth open at the most beautiful house she had ever seen. It was a Tudor building – real, not mock Tudor like the ones in the avenue where she used to live, and it sort of nestled into its grounds, a beautiful sloping lawn surrounded by trees. The building itself was painted a deep cream colour with lots of thin brown beams running both vertically and horizontally over its surface. The roof was made of small, dark red tiles and huge chimneys rose up against the sky.

"Come on, slow coach." Minty had half turned and was jumping along with a sideways movement, beckoning to Crystal and trying to keep up with her father at the same time. Crystal held on to her hat and ran to join them just as they reached the gate to the stable yard.

"Minty, for crying out loud will you stop being so bone idle and rise to the trot. You look like a sack of potatoes."

"But I want to canter."

"No. You wait until we get to the end of this road; the track is much straighter and the ground more even. The last thing I want is a pony with a broken leg or a daughter with a broken neck. Now do as you're told and rise to the trot – AND KEEP THOSE KNEES IN TO THE SADDLE!"

Matt. was shouting instructions to his daughter while holding Crystal's pony, a pretty little mare called Poppy, on a leading rein along side Swallow, the hunter that he was riding. Maxi, Minty's mount, was still trotting ahead and Minty was now rising up and down in the saddle as instructed.

Crystal was in heaven. From the moment she had arrived in the tack room she had been enraptured. She had loved the smell of leather and saddle soap, the feel of Poppy's rough coat as she had brushed her to make sure that there was no dirt on her back that could irritate her skin under the saddle, and the smoothness of the saddle as Matt. had shown her how to throw it over the pony's withers and slide it into place on her back.

The three of them had been quite alone in the stable yard at first then Crystal had heard a woman's voice calling and whistling. Two black Labradors had bounded into the yard and started jumping all over them then the woman had appeared.

"Come here you two. Ben, Bonny, HEEL!" She had grabbed the dogs, "Hello, Matt. Sorry about that. Hello, Minty."

Matt gave a small nod of his head, "Miss Cowper."

She'd looked at Crystal then back at Minty,

"Aren't you going to introduce me to your friend?

"Miss Cowper, this is Crystal; Crystal, this is Miss Cowper."

Crystal held out her hand and it was firmly shaken by the woman standing before her who smiled and immediately looked as though she had too many teeth. Her hair was scraped back into a pony tail which made her large nose look even larger.

"I'm very pleased to meet you, my dear. I hope you have a lovely ride."

Her voice sounded so much like the new Queen, who Crystal had heard a few times on the radio that she wondered for a minute whether she should curtsy, but Rosemary had already turned and was deep in conversation with Matt. about the horses. At that moment Minty had sidled up and, nudging her ever so gently, had hissed,

"Don't look now, but there's horrible Clive."

Crystal waited for a moment as Minty wandered away from her then she looked up casually just in time to see a tall, lean man with jet black hair walking towards the back of the house. His shoulders stooped as he picked his way across the cobbles and before he opened the door he turned for a moment and looked towards the group near the stables. His mouth was a thin line and, even though he was some distance away there was something – perhaps the coldness of his eyes – that made Crystal shudder. Then she was shown how to mount and they were off; she felt, for the first time, the strange sensation of the pony moving beneath her, its head pulling gently away with every step.

She would love to have turned and looked again at the beautiful house as they made their way back up the drive, but she was concentrating hard remembering to hold the reins as Matt had shown her and gripping with her knees. If she had turned, she might have just glimpsed the shadow at the window, the beautiful woman watching them, with the fingertips of her right hand resting lightly on her throat.

CHAPTER FOUR
1958

The old brown and white bus bumped its way along the country roads and Crystal stared out of the window at the now familiar landscape. Her friends had already got off at stops in their respective villages and she was alone for the last part of the journey each day. She looked at her watch, twenty past five, home in ten minutes; then she looked back to where the fields and trees were gradually disappearing, swallowed by the early evening dusk of October.

"Clocks go back this weekend,"

Her dad had reminded them that morning just before he set off to work at the factory on the outskirts of Cambridge. He was a manager in the sales department and always liked to be on time.

Crystal thought about her mum and dad and how hard they had both worked to make the cottage into a home, not that she was there much with all the riding she was doing these days up at Manor Farm. And when she was there, homework seemed to take up a lot of her time; she groaned – that was the price you paid for passing the dreaded eleven plus. She thought about Minty and smiled. Minty had had no intention of doing anything as daft as passing the test at eleven which was supposed to separate the clever kids from the others. She firmly believed that it was much cleverer not to pass so that she could spend her time doing what she wanted instead of sticking her nose into books every waking minute.

There were times, on those increasingly rare occasions these days when she managed to visit Pook's Farm, that Crystal thought she may have a point. Minty had started breeding rabbits and keeping a few chickens of her own, so her summer evenings were spent in happy contentment tending her animals instead of wrestling with Algebra, English Grammar and the causes of the Seven Years War. She also had a boyfriend and Crystal didn't; but Crystal had a secret. It was hers alone and she kept it buried very deeply inside her. She didn't dare breathe it to anyone in case it wasn't real, in case the telling of it should make it disappear. She hugged her arms hard against her chest, closed her eyes and thought about him now.

It had happened the very first moment she had seen his photograph on the grand piano in the drawing room at Monk's Manor; a black and white photograph of a boy sitting with his right side facing the photographer but looking over his shoulder directly into the camera. He had curly brown hair and a smile so warm that it lit up his face; but it was when Crystal looked into his eyes that she experienced a strange sensation, like a squeezing in her chest. She had turned away from it quickly, feeling embarrassed, and glanced up at Rosemary to see if she had noticed but she was busy arranging the cups and saucers so Crystal had let her eyes roam again round the drawing room resting here and there on comfortable chintz-covered chairs, ancient furniture, that had been polished until it shone like conkers, and beautiful old blue and white lamps and vases.

Finally she looked back at Rosemary and wondered again why she had been invited into the drawing room for tea. Rosemary had simply said that she had something important to ask her and was now sitting on the sofa pouring tea from a large, flowered tea-pot. Crystal sat on the edge of her chair and waited until Rosemary looked up and asked, in a matter of fact way as though it were quite an ordinary request, if she would like to show one of the little thoroughbred mares for Mr. Geoffrey at Manor Farm.

"You see, my dear, Matt. has been singing your praises to uncle Geoff who made it his business to watch you one day when you were out riding and he liked what he saw – so how about it then?" Rosemary's clipped speech, the words too perfectly formed, cut through the air between them as she handed Crystal a dainty flowered cup full of tea and smiled showing her huge teeth.

To Crystal the invitation was far from ordinary and she was so excited that she had to put the cup and saucer gently down on the table in front of her to stop them rattling in her shaking hands. She had raced home to ask her mum and dad if it would be OK and had walked on air for the rest of the evening when, after much discussion and sincere promises from Crystal that her homework wouldn't suffer as a result, they had consented.

It wasn't until much later when she was lying in bed unable to sleep that the boy in the photograph swam back into view and she drifted into sleep wondering if he was Rosemary and Clive's younger brother, Giles. Was he as good-looking as his photograph? What was he like and would she ever meet him?

And that was how Crystal's association with the family at Manor Farm first began. She was in awe of the strange quartet who inhabited the huge, grey, manor house on the edge of the village. Geoffrey was the first one she met. Sensing her nervousness, Matt. had been there when she arrived at the stables to meet and ride Bluebell for the first time,

"You'll be alright, sweetheart. Just remember they're different from ordinary folk; it's all that breedin' – they're a bit high-strung, like their 'orses."

She had smiled feeling reassured by Matt's solid presence and then she stiffened again as a tall, gaunt-looking man in jodhpurs and a pale green jacket walked quickly towards them across the stable yard.

"Mr. Lynton-Bell, this is Crystal; Crystal, Mr. Geoffrey Lynton-Bell."

Nervously she stretched out her hand and remembered how she had thought for a long time that his surname was Geoffrey, not realising that calling him 'Mr. Geoffrey' was just the village people's way of distinguishing him from his brother, 'Mr. Claude,' who managed the farm. Geoffrey was in charge of the horses. He held her hand and looked her up and down. She noticed that his eyes were a sort of greeny-brown colour and his nose rather long and hooked. He didn't smile and she took her hand back; then, hearing the sound of horse's hooves on the cobbles behind her, she turned and watched Bluebell being led out of the stable by one of the grooms. She looked so beautiful and as Crystal turned back to smile at Matt she heard Mr. Geoffrey murmur,

"Nice little filly."

He was looking at her and Matt was frowning.

Geoffrey Lynton-Bell spent a lot of time putting Crystal and Bluebell through their paces before he thought they were ready for their first show. He was a hard task master, who rarely smiled and expected instant obedience from both horse and rider; but Crystal was keen to learn and her diligent perseverance earned his respect. Gradually, during the course of her instruction, she became aware of the other members of this strange household.

Mr. Claude, a thickset man with iron grey hair and a coarse, bushy moustache was occasionally to be seen striding up the drive towards the farm buildings. There was an older sister, Evelyn, who had some connection with a hospital in Cambridge; Crystal sometimes saw her getting out of her car as she arrived back home. She was gaunt, thin and unsmiling like Geoffrey and barely acknowledged the girl her brother was training to ride his precious new horse.

But most mysterious of all was the old lady who lived on the first floor of the huge, grey building. Even before she started going there Crystal had heard tales of old Mrs. Lynton-Bell, the mother of Evelyn, Geoffrey and Claude, who hadn't been seen out in the village for years. While she was still at the village school, Crystal had heard some of the stories that the other children made up –

"….I did hear tell that she died years ago and it's really her ghost what lives at the top of that old house."

"….Well my mum told me that, as she never eats nothin', she's as thin as a piece of paper and that if she tried to come down them old stairs she'd crumble to bits…"

Crystal had laughed as the tales got wilder, but even after she'd been going to the Manor for several months she'd still never seen the old lady. She did, however, learn a little more about the connection with Monk's Manor. Eleanore Cowper was Geoffrey, Claude and Evelyn's sister and, like her mother, was also somewhat of a recluse; she rarely left Monk's Manor, but no-one knew why.

The Elliott family at Savron Pinder house remained a complete mystery. All Crystal knew about them was that their house was very big, the grandest in the village, and that the 'Squire' business was something that was gradually petering out as the old man was rarely seen about on his bike any more. At Christmas time Carol Singers ventured down the long, winding drive in the hope of getting a glimpse of 'Old Squire and his Misses,' the descriptions of whose state of health would be worth a few pints at The White Hart, but they were usually disappointed. The mulled wine and mince pies were there alright as always, but served by Alice, Vera and Nelly; it wasn't like the old days when Squire and Mrs. Elliott would be there chatting and laughing with them..

Crystal jumped down from the bus and shrugged her satchel up onto her shoulder for the short walk home in the gathering dusk. She had no way of knowing that this evening she would be told something so shattering to her world that it would, for a while, drive out all thoughts of the strange families in the two manors at opposite ends of the village.

CHAPTER FIVE

Crystal tapped her pencil and looked up from the homework on the desk in front of her. The room was quiet apart from the clicking of her mother's knitting needles and the rustle of the newspaper which her dad was reading. They sat one each side of the old stove, which threw out enough heat for the whole room, absorbed in their tasks and bathed in the circles of light from the old oil lamps they had successfully converted to electricity. Crystal smiled. How she loved and appreciated her parents. She had even stopped minding about not having any brothers or sisters. When she had been younger she had so wanted not to be an only child, but Marjorie's response when she had mentioned having a little brother or sister had been enough to silence her on the subject for ever. It was when she was about six years old and she was helping her mother to pick gooseberries in the garden; Crystal was thinking about a girl at school called Molly who, although she already had two brothers and a sister, said that her mum was getting them another one.

"How do you know?" Crystal had asked, wide-eyed and wishing it was her mum.

"Because she said she's going back to look under the old gooseberry bush in the summer and she knows there'll be another one there."

Crystal had stopped picking the hairy green fruit and stared under the bushes. She carefully lifted one or two of the thin, leafy branches until she pricked her finger on one of the savage thorns and yelped. Her mother had smiled,

"I told you to be careful. What are you doing? You won't find any fruit under the bushes – if it does fall it won't be fit to eat as it's soft fruit and goes bad very quickly."

She moistened her hanky and dabbed the little drop of blood on her daughter's finger.

"I was looking for a baby. Molly's mum is getting them another one from under their gooseberry bushes soon and I thought we might find one here."

Crystal saw her mother's face go very white. She stopped dabbing and held her daughter's fingers tightly then, looking away, she swallowed hard and took several deep breaths. She spoke very softly,

"I'm sorry, my love, but I can't get you any brothers or sisters. I'm sorry….."

And to her horror Crystal saw that her mother's eyes had filled with tears. She started crying too and flung her arms round her mum's neck,

"Mummy, it's alright. Please don't cry. It doesn't matter really…" she sobbed and Marjorie held her tightly then stroked her hair and whispered,

"You are our special only one, darling; our precious Crystal."

Crystal looked back down at her history homework. The Tudor Family Tree; how very complicated it was and their history teacher, Miss Stanwell, thought it would make the subject more interesting if the girls all researched their own family histories and had a go at producing a family tree. She looked again at her mum and dad still sitting peacefully by the fire. As yet they had no television set like some of the other girls in her class, so she was able to sit at the old Davenport desk at the back of the lounge to do her homework instead of being banished to her bedroom.

Her family tree; she thought about her dad's mum, Granny Morris – Granddad Morris had died when she was a baby, but they often visited Granny Morris who lived on her own in a remote Norfolk village. Marjorie's parents, Grandma and Grandpa Bates, lived at the seaside in a place called Eastbourne on the South Coast. She loved seeing Granny Morris who had taught her how to boil an egg, bake a sponge cake and tell the time. Because she lived quite close, Crystal was allowed to go and stay sometimes without her parents and Granny Morris spoilt her. Visiting Grandma and Grandpa Bates was different. They all went together as it was their summer holiday and she loved everything about it – the smell of the sea, the rock pools where she looked for tiny creatures, lying on the beach in the sun and the fish and chip suppers eaten in the restaurant where she had felt very grown up as she was allowed to stay up late and eat with the adults.

She put down the pencil and sat back in her chair,

"Mum, I've got to do a family tree," Marjorie looked up quickly and the needles stopped.

"You know, one of these." Crystal held up the Tudor tree as an example. "I've got to do some research into my family history. Can you help? I thought I might talk to the grandparents too. Miss Stanwell says you never know what strange secrets you might unearth once you get going. She says…." Crystal stopped speaking and noticed that her father, who had finished reading his newspaper, folded it and had been getting up from his chair, quietly sat back down again while she had been speaking. He and Marjorie were looking intently at each other and it was as if, without any word being spoken, a decision had been made. Marjorie carefully put her knitting down on the floor beside her chair and Crystal saw that she had gone white, just like that day all those years ago when she had asked about a brother or sister.

"What....what is it? What have I said?" Crystal felt panicky as she looked at her mother and then at her father who was again rising from the chair. He looked quickly across at Crystal then, without a word, left the room, quietly closing the door behind him.

Marjorie sat up straight in the arm chair and asked Crystal to come and sit opposite her in the chair her father had just left. With her heart hammering inside her chest, Crystal did as she was asked. She had no real idea why she should feel so terrified; it was as if she somehow knew that after her mother had spoken life would never again be the same. Marjorie leaned forward,

"Crystal, I think now is the time that I have to tell you something very important. There is no easy way to say this and I want you always to remember how much your father and I love you." Her voice and face were so serious that a fresh wave of panic swept over Crystal. Was she terminally ill? Was dad?

"Mum, please, just tell me." She couldn't keep the fear out of her voice and Marjorie continued quickly before her courage failed her.

"You are our beloved, darling child; the reason we live, but.....we adopted you. George and I are not your real mum and dad."

When she thought about this moment afterwards – which she did, many times – Crystal was struck by the strangeness of the things she noticed. Her world had turned upside down but nothing moved. Her mother sat as still as stone in the chair opposite, her eyes, full of sympathy, never leaving her daughter's face. The fire hissed and the flames flickered and danced on one of the copper pans hanging on the wall. Marjorie waited to see how the news, how this staggering truth which could no longer remain a secret, would affect her.

"But...but I don't understand." She had heard the words, but her mind just wouldn't take it in. Her mum and dad were....her mum and dad. Up to that point in her life it was one of those things, like the sky, earth and sun being in their right places which was beyond question or doubt. But it wasn't. And if Marjorie and George were not her mum and dad, then who...? She felt stunned, completely numb. She had to ask the question even though she wasn't sure she wanted to know the answer.

"If you are not my mum and dad....then who are they?"

The words hung in the space between them and Marjorie continued to look at her daughter, her face full of concern and sympathy. She spoke very quietly.

"I have no idea, no idea at all. One of the conditions of the adoption was that we would not – ever – be told anything about your parents and we should not investigate. We signed an agreement to that effect.

"So my real mum didn't want me…" Crystal's voice broke as she heard the words she was speaking and Marjorie crossed the small space between them; she knelt down and took her daughter's hands,

"Darling, I don't know…..but what I do know is that we did want you and we still do; we chose you. You are our beloved daughter – the greatest gift we could ever have been given, the best thing that ever happened to us. We chose you and we couldn't love you more than we do."

Crystal held on to Marjorie's hands. Of course nothing had changed….but it had. Everything had changed. She felt confused, overwhelmed by the revelation.

"Why didn't you tell me before? Why have you waited until now?"

"We just didn't know when would be the right time. There isn't really any guidance for a situation like this; dad and I decided that there would come a time when it would seem appropriate and we both felt tonight that that moment had arrived. You have a right to know but…." Marjorie didn't know how to continue. She would have done anything to save her daughter from the pain of this discovery and could only say again and again that she and George loved her more than anything in the world.

"Although I can't give you any information about your family, there is something I have to give you; something that has been carefully put away waiting for this moment."

She went to the back of the room and, lifting a small blue and white jar that stood on the windowsill, removed a tiny key from underneath it. She lifted the lid of the davenport desk and unlocked a little drawer right at the back. Carefully she lifted something out, locked the drawer, returned the key and sat down again by the fire. Crystal saw that she was holding a small, blue velvet bag,

"This was found in the folds of the shawl which was wrapped around you when you were handed to us. It must have been put there by your mother and no-one else knew it was there or I'm sure it would have been removed. It belongs to you."

She handed the soft blue bag to Crystal who was still struggling with the strangeness of a world that had suddenly extended; with her mum referring to someone else as 'your mother.'

She undid the silky blue cord at the top of the bag and turned the contents out into her hand. It was a piece of carefully folded, white tissue paper with something hard inside. It rustled as, slowly, she unfolded it and gasped at the large crystal pendant which lay there gleaming in the lamplight. It was the most beautiful thing she had ever seen. She picked it up and let it hang from its exquisite silver chain. Her inheritance; the only thing she possessed from a mother who had borne and, for some reason, rejected her.

"So…this is why you called me Crystal."

"Yes."

For a while Crystal pushed the whole thing to the back of her mind. She didn't care. What did it matter? She had a lovely mum and dad who wanted her – why should she worry, or even think about, someone who had rejected her. She did enough history homework to satisfy Miss Stanwell using information gleaned from her adoptive family and she just carried on as before. She had a good life and wasn't going to let it be spoilt by something that wasn't her fault and over which she had no control

Gradually, however, in those quiet moments, usually just before sleep, she found herself wondering; and in spite of her determination to ignore the shattering revelation, her mind wandered and she couldn't help thinking about who she might be and where she came from. Where was her real family? What were they like? And did she – could she possibly - have brothers and sisters somewhere?

She asked Marjorie again why they had decided to tell her on that particular evening and her mum told her that she and George had decided long ago that they didn't want to risk Crystal getting into a situation where she might start to wonder about her birth. They never wanted to tell her half truths. When she said she was investigating the family tree they didn't know how in depth that would be. Would she, for instance, discover that no-one anywhere in the family had her extraordinary hair – the bane of her life, but the envy of all who saw her. Crystal could see what Marjorie meant and respected her parents for their thoughtfulness. And even though she pushed it to the back of her mind it was always there now. It couldn't be denied; like toothpaste, it wouldn't go back neatly where it came from. The secret, now known, couldn't be unknown again. And she did, in spite of herself, wonder about her real family.

CHAPTER SIX

1961

Crystal felt the familiar tingle of nerves as she waited. Bluebell felt it too. She pawed the ground, shook her head and chewed the bit in her mouth making little white flecks of spit appear at the corners.

"Sssshhhh," Crystal soothed her, gently stroking the velvet nose and pulling her twitching ears. Then it was her turn; she was up in the saddle and they were off. The first two jumps were easy and she and Bluebell soared over them and on to the third – a little more tricky, but they made it and then the fourth and fifth in quick succession. Crystal reined Bluebell in and turned her ready for the sixth.

"Come on…..come on beauty….."

She urged her forward towards the wall, knowing that this was the one the little mare would like the least. But they were over…it was close, so close she was sure that the tip of Bluebell's hoof just touched the wall but they had made it. Then the seventh….on to the eighth and they were clear! Crystal fell on Bluebell's neck laughing and patting the taut, sweaty skin. They had done it! They had won the coveted Fairfax Trophy at the Peterborough show. She pulled on the reins and Bluebell responded so that together they made a dignified exit with the applause of the crowd and snatches of the commentary following them out.

"...what a fantastic round for Crystal on Bluebell........the only clear round....a mare from the Lynton-Bell stable....a very good season...."

She took her place in front of the other horses and riders then proudly led them back into the ring where Bluebell had a red rosette pinned to her bridle and Crystal bent down to receive the prestigious trophy. It was heavy and hung with red ribbons but it felt as light as a feather as she held it high above her head and smiled over to where Geoffrey and some of the other family members were leaning against the railing and cheering her. A lap of honour followed then they left the ring.

Geoffrey lifted her down and gave her a hug. He was smiling and Crystal blushed with pleasure at the praise she was receiving.

"Well done, my dear. That was spectacular." He gave her shoulders a final squeeze then turned and patted Bluebell's neck. Rosemary came panting up, the epitome of upper class, horsy lady in headscarf, riding mac and green boots, and added her congratulations then the three of them started walking back towards the enclosure where the horse boxes were parked.

It wasn't until they were nearly there that she saw him. He was standing with two other young men and they were laughing at something, throwing their heads back as they shared the joke. He had his back to her so she didn't recognise him at first and she could only see the faces of the other two – both dark haired and with that air of assurance worn by the wealthy and privileged. They stopped laughing and stared as the trio approached with Bluebell and it was then that the other young man turned to follow their gaze. She knew immediately that it was him. She was staring straight into the eyes of the young man in the photograph. He was older but it was definitely him. As they stood looking at each other, Rosemary glanced up,

"Crystal, this is my brother Giles. He rarely graces us with his presence on these occasions, but today we are honoured."

Giles had stepped forward and now held out his hand. Crystal took it and felt a shock – something strange, like recognition – in the warm, firm grip. He was smiling at her,

"Well done, that was fantastic. No wonder Uncle Geoff is so pleased with you." He turned towards his friends, "this is Percy and Jeremy."

Crystal nodded towards the two young men who still hung back. She was nervous and could feel herself blushing. To cover her feelings of insecurity she did, without thinking, what she always did immediately after leaving the ring and just before attending to Bluebell. She took off her hat and hair net and shook out her hair. She looked up. Giles and the other two were staring at the mane of shiny, red curls that had tumbled on to her shoulders.

"I wouldn't mind a ride on that." Percy whispered to Jeremy; at least it was trying to be a whisper, but his usual tones were so strident that he had no idea how to moderate his voice so that he couldn't be heard. Crystal blushed furiously as she realised he wasn't referring to Bluebell. Geoffrey and Rosemary hadn't heard as they were deep in conversation with each other; Jeremy sniggered. Crystal glanced at Giles – was he going to turn out to be just another Hooray Henry? But he turned, glared at his friend and hissed,

"Shut up, perve."

Crystal took Bluebell's bridle and turned away, smiling quietly to herself as she walked off to find the groom.

There was a red sky. Crystal looked up and saw the vibrant colour splashed all over a pale blue background. She remembered the old saying about red sky at night being a shepherd's delight as she hurried across the cobbles towards the stables.

What a day! Had she really won that trophy at last? The one she had been trying to win for the last two years; and had Giles really been there to see it? Thank goodness she hadn't known he was there, she would have been twice as nervous as she was. She smiled at herself. What a silly fantasy, it really was time she let go of it after all these years, but today she had met him – was she disappointed? No…stop. She dismissed all thoughts of him and reached out to open the door of the tack room. She just wanted to collect a carrot and say goodnight to Bluebell before hurrying home to tell the good news to Marjorie and George. What a pity they hadn't been there to see it, but George had an eye appointment in Cambridge and Marjorie had gone with him. Never mind.

She pushed open the tack room door and immediately heard the whistling – a slow and quite tuneful rendering of 'making whoopee.' She smiled; one of the grooms was obviously just finishing up for the day. The interior of the tack room was quite dim as late afternoon began to slip into twilight but she decided not to bother with a light. She walked towards the carrot bin and the whistling got louder, then she saw him sitting on the old wooden table that was used to soap the saddles. She jumped and instinctively put a hand to her throat; he jumped down,

"Sorry, I didn't mean to startle you. That's why I was whistling." Giles smiled a sort of lop-sided apologetic smile.

"I thought it was one of the grooms," Crystal had recovered herself and smiled back.

There was an awkward silence as they looked at each other.

"I just wanted to apologise for Percy. He's OK really but…he shouldn't have said what he did."

"It doesn't matter." Crystal suddenly felt mischievous and quite bold. She looked straight at Giles,

"How did you know I'd be here?

"I overheard Uncle Geoff talking to Uncle Claude. He said you always give Bluebell a carrot and say goodnight before you go. He was concerned that you may leave it too late and have to walk home through the village in the dark. They were wondering if one of them should give you a lift, but then saw that the sky is still quite bright – all that red." He paused and took two steps towards her. "You seem to have made quite an impression on my family – brought out a sort of caring side in those two crusty old men."

Crystal could feel that she was blushing again and was furious with herself; luckily she was sure that Giles couldn't see her red cheeks in the gloom of the tack room. Was she blushing at what he had said or was it his proximity that was causing this feeling of self-consciousness. Surely at seventeen she should be over this sort of thing. And where was the boldness of a moment ago? To cover her confusion she babbled,

"Well...what are you doing here anyway?" And immediately felt even more embarrassed. What on earth had it got to do with her? He was family and had more right to be there than she had. He smiled, feeling more sure of himself in the light of her nervousness.

"Do you mean here in the tack room? Here at Manor Farm, instead of Monk's Manor with Ma and Pa? Or here, as in not at Oxford where I should be in the middle of June?"

Crystal turned away and walked a few steps to put some distance between her and Giles. That assurance! They're born with it. Well two can play at that game. She turned back towards him and slowly folded her arms.

"Well, now let me see. We've dealt with the first one as we've established that you came here to find me, so let's take the other two in order – if you want to tell me, that is."

Giles was clearly intrigued by her sudden self-possession and, leaning back against the table, said,

"OK. I'm here at Manor Farm because it's Grandma Isobel's seventy-fifth birthday tomorrow and all the family have been summoned. We have to make an occasion of it in case the old girl doesn't get to eighty. To help me through the ordeal, I have been allowed to bring a couple of mates with me – which explains the presence of Jem and the 'orrible Perce. We are staying here for the night as my Aunt Bette is also coming to celebrate and will stay at Monk's Manor with Ma, Pa, Rosie and Clive. Ma insisted on it as she and Bette are thick as thieves – always have been ever since they were girls – from what I can gather. As Bette has two little girls we've been kicked out, so to speak, to make space for them and are staying here where there's loads of room." He paused. "Come to think of it that pretty well answers question three as well – released from Oxford for the weekend to attend celebration for aging relative."

Crystal was intrigued. So there really was an old lady living at Manor Farm. And who was Bette? She had had no idea that there was yet another sister for Evelyn, Eleanore, Geoffrey and Claude. Family; some people were so fortunate.

"You are so lucky to have such a big family." She spoke from the heart, without thinking, and Giles snorted,

"Do you think so?" He paused. "I think maybe the notion of a big happy family is an illusion clung to by those who don't have it. For us on the inside there are too many skeletons clattering around in too many cupboards for us to be truly happy."

"But your folks always seem so….." Crystal hesitated then decided – yes she would say it, "…so sure of themselves somehow……..as if they would never encounter a situation they couldn't cope with. I must say it does seem strange, though, that your Aunt Evelyn, Uncle Geoff and Uncle Claude have never married."

Giles smiled.

"There you are, you see. Listen. Can you hear them?"

"What?"

"Those skeletons starting to rattle. Who said Claude and Geoffrey have never been married?"

Crystal was amazed and Giles was clearly pleased at the effect he was having on her,

"Tell you what. I'll be home for the summer in a couple of weeks. Come out for a drink with me and I'll tell you more about my relatives."

"OK."

Crystal tried to sound matter of fact and hoped he couldn't hear the sound of her heart beating as though it was about to break out of her chest. She turned towards the door,

"I must go. The light will be fading soon." She made her way to the door and Giles followed.

"Do you want me to come with you?

"No it's OK. I do this all the time. But thanks anyway." She smiled at him once more then turned and walked up the drive.

Crystal clattered along the village street in her riding boots, walking, running and jumping. What a day. What a fantastic day. Had all that really happened? She composed herself as she reached the door of Maple Cottage, ready to re-live the excitement and receive hugs and congratulations from Marjorie and George.

Later, as she lay in her bed, she allowed herself to think about Giles. He really was lovely, quite unpretentious and so handsome with green eyes, like hers, and soft, light brown curly hair, just like the photograph. She had never met him before for, of course, as soon as he had come home from boarding school for the holidays she had not been needed to exercise his ponies as he had ridden them himself. Then when he went to Oxford, the ponies had been sold and she was involved with Bluebell and Manor Farm by then. 'Oh damn, I forgot to take Bluebell her carrot,' she thought just before drifting into sleep.

CHAPTER SEVEN

The evening sun was warm on Crystal's shoulders and danced on the water; she leaned back and, with eyes closed, lifted her face to the warmth.

"Here we are."

Squinting up she saw Giles' face. He was smiling and handed her a drink; as she took it he dropped down beside her and they both looked out onto the water of the River Cam to where an immaculate white boat was ploughing its way upstream creating waves that made little splashes against the grassy bank.

They had chosen to drive to a river-side pub near Cambridge, partly because it was a beautiful day so they could sit outside by the water, partly because they didn't really want to encourage any gossip in the village and partly because Giles wanted to show off his new toy to Crystal. It was his birthday on July 1st and he had been given a sports car. She was duly impressed by the shiny red machine and smiled at Giles' boyish enthusiasm as he put it through its paces, revving the engine and taking the corners just a little too fast. Crystal gasped and put her hand over her mouth, pretending to be a bit scared, but in reality feeling more excited than she had ever felt before. This was even better than soaring over the jumps on Bluebell and she was almost sorry when they had arrived at the pub.

"So, you want to know more about my crazy family." Giles licked the foam off his upper lip and turned towards her.

"I am quite curious, I must admit,"

"OK here goes. Grandma – Isobel Hunter, as she was – and John Lynton-Bell fell madly in love, but for some reason his family didn't approve – I have no idea why as I haven't uncovered that particular skeleton yet – but they got married anyway. Rumour has it that Evelyn was already on the way by the time the wedding took place. It was a quiet affair in Scotland and John was lucky as an uncle, who did approve of the marriage, gave the couple Manor Farm here in East Anglia as a wedding present.

Apparently they were very happy and after Evelyn, Eleanore – my Ma – Claude, Geoffrey and Bette followed in quick succession. John was a good man and a good farmer and Claude was always set to follow in his footsteps so he stayed at home and learned the ropes. However, he disgraced himself in John and Isobel's eyes by falling in love with – and marrying – one of their house-keepers. It just wasn't done, so he had to move out to a cottage in the village, but still worked on the farm. I must say it seems strange to me that if Isobel and John had had to fight for their love, they should be so intolerant of their son falling for 'the wrong sort,' but maybe there was more to it than that. Anyway there were no children and, after about five years, she left him. He sold his cottage and moved back into the Manor where he's been ever since.

Geoffrey has always worked with horses and in the course of buying and selling new stock he met and fell in love with a beautiful French woman. After a whirlwind romance they married and had a son, Philippe. He brought them back to Manor Farm but Marianne hated it. She loathed village life and because Geoffrey adored her and would have done anything to make her happy, he hired a nanny to look after Philippe and paid for her to go back to Paris to study art.

What he couldn't have foreseen, poor chap, was that she would fall in love with an artist and never come back." Giles paused, "Well, that's not strictly true. She came back for long enough to collect her clothes and Philippe and then walked out of his life for ever leaving him with a broken heart.

I think for both of my uncles their first foray into the world of matrimony was enough and neither of them has shown any sign of wanting to repeat the experience. Instead they live on the top floor at the farm, have totally separate responsibilities and making a success of these seems to be sufficient for them. They get on well enough as long as they don't encroach on each other's territory."

"Phew," Crystal felt shocked by these revelations and both men, whom she'd previously assumed to be bachelors, had suddenly acquired new personas following these revelations.

"What about Evelyn, your parents and Bette?" she leaned forward, eager to learn more. Her glass was empty and Giles had just gulped down the last of his beer. She shivered a little and noticed the sun had gone down and a light breeze ruffled the water. He took her glass,

"Tell you what. I'll drive you home and we'll talk about you, I'll even tell you a bit about me – if you're interested," he gave her a sideways glance, grinning, "Then, if you really want to know any more about my folks, you'll just have to come out with me again."

So that's what they did; and driving home much more slowly in the cool of the evening she learned that Giles was reading Archaeology at Oxford, but wanted to farm when he left. She told him a little about herself, about Marjorie and George and that she had once aspired to be a teacher. She didn't tell him at this early stage of their relationship that she was adopted and that the discovery of this fact had rocked her world to the extent that, for some strange reason, she no longer wanted to go into teaching. In fact she had no idea what she wanted. At least she hadn't until that drive home under the early evening stars with Giles Cowper. They were just entering the village when he told her about his ambition to have his own farm and she suddenly had this vision of being there with him. She saw horses, beautiful creatures that she could train and show; she even heard the laughter of children.

"Penny for them." The car had stopped outside Maple Cottage and Giles was looking at her. She felt her face go crimson as she thought how awful it would be if he could read her mind and see the little scenario that had lodged itself there a moment ago.

"Oh, nothing. I...I wasn't thinking anything," she lied and the lie made her blush even more.

"I don't know many girls who do that."

"What?"

"Blush like you do."

"Oh...." She turned away, still blushing. How stupid! Of course, the girls he knew at university were most probably much more sophisticated. She started to open the door.

"I must go."

"No wait. I like it. It's nice. I wasn't criticising." Giles looked serious,

"When can I see you again?"

"When do you want to see me again?"

"Tomorrow."

Crystal laughed and they settled on the following Saturday. They would go for a picnic if it was fine and to the pictures if it rained. By the time she pulled the bedclothes up under her chin that night, tried to sleep and couldn't, Crystal Morris knew that she was already more than a little bit in love with Giles Cowper.

They saw a lot of each other over the next three weeks and during this time Crystal learned more about the families living in the two farms at opposite ends of the village. Evelyn had never married, but had worked as a nurse at a famous hospital in London until she had come home to Manor Farm where her main task was to look after her mother. She did some voluntary, part time work at Addenbrookes Hospital which got her out of the house for a while every week and seemed to be acknowledged by the family as a life line for her. Apparently the old lady could be very difficult.

Giles thought the world of his mother, Eleanore, and didn't really know why she was becoming reclusive, like his grandma. He wondered if it had something to do with, his father, William, quite a cold, remote man who didn't relate well to people at all. He had always got on well enough with his sister, Rosie, but thought his brother Clive 'a very odd fish.' His Aunt Bette, the baby sister of the family, he described as 'magical.'

"….always full of fun and laughter. She really is wonderful. I remember when I was small she would think of games for us to play and give us treats and all sorts of good things to eat. We always loved it when Aunt Bette was around as everyone seemed happier and the house rang with laughter. She reminded everyone that we were children and needed to have some fun. Her husband, Tommy, is nice too; he's an officer in the army and has to go away a lot, but Aunt Bette doesn't let it get her down, even though they are devoted to each other."

One day Giles and Crystal went riding together. They set off separately so as not to arouse suspicion; they had been very discreet as, so far, for some reason as yet unspoken between them, they were both reluctant to let anyone know they were seeing each other. For Crystal, although she could barely have acknowledged it to the extent of framing the words, she felt somehow that a magic spell would be broken if their growing feelings for each other became known. Giles wasn't sure why he didn't say anything to his family; he wasn't ashamed of Crystal, of that he was quite sure, and he knew his family liked her, it was just something instinctive. There was no way they could know that the events which would follow the revelation of their feelings for each other meant that their instincts for secrecy had been right. The storm that was about to break would change the course of their lives for ever in a way that neither of them could have imagined.

CHAPTER EIGHT

"It's my 'do' and I want you there." Giles kissed her again and Crystal gently pushed him away so that she could answer. She was hot and trembled with joy; she loved being kissed by Giles but needed to think about what he had just asked her. She couldn't believe it. The birthday at the beginning of July had been his twenty first and he had told her that the family were holding a big party for him at a hotel in Cambridge in two weeks time. They had had to wait until the middle of August to get the whole clan together and now Giles was asking her to go.

"Please come, darling. It'll be such a lovely surprise for everyone. I'll tell them that I'm bringing a girl friend and they'll expect someone from Oxford. Imagine how thrilled they will be when they see that it's you. It'll be the perfect time to show them that we are together." He paused, "we are together, aren't we, Crystal?" He drew away from her so that he could see her face clearly and she saw that he looked very serious as he held her eyes, waiting for an answer.

"Yes….oh yes we are together."

He held her face gently in his fingers,

"You do know that there aren't any girls from Oxford, not now; not since I first saw you standing there between my sister and my uncle, holding

Bluebell, your lovely face flushed with the success of winning that trophy." He pushed his fingers deep into her shining red curls, "then when I saw these tumble down around your shoulders I was lost. " He buried his head in her hair and kissed her neck. Crystal held his face close to hers,

"I was smitten first." She whispered.

"No you weren't. " He tried to kiss her again, but she told him quietly about the photograph.

He leaned back and laughed,

"Good grief! That goofy old school-boy pic; well, what do you know. So have I lived up to expectations?"

"You're doing OK," Crystal said mischievously and Giles squeezed her waist and tickled her until she screamed.

"Sssshhhh," he covered her mouth with his hand and glanced up through the car window to Maple Cottage. It was in darkness, but he was sure George must have heard the little sports car pull up and was expecting Crystal to go into the house before very much longer.

"So will you come to my twenty first bash?"

"I'd love to." She smiled, gave him one more kiss, then slipped out of the car and up the drive. Giles started the engine and watched her go, noting with a smile, that the light had come on in her parents' bed room.

Crystal stood in front of the mirror in the ladies' powder room and shivered with excitement. She was pleased with her appearance; the pale blue dress that she and Marjorie had chosen together looked lovely and fitted perfectly. It was her first really grown up dress and she felt very glamorous in it. She moved from side to side and watched the light sparkle off the tiny stones sewn onto the bodice. It had a V neck and showed just a glimpse of her small, firm breasts then came right in to emphasise her tiny waist. The skirt hugged her hips and then splayed out in a sort of fish tail as it reached her knees and made a swishing sound as she moved. She pulled on her long white gloves, picked up her pale blue bag then paused to look again at the finishing touch Marjorie had fastened round her neck just before she had left the house.

"It's yours, darling. Wear it if you want to."

The crystal sparkled like a giant diamond in the light and looked perfect nestling at her throat with the red curls falling all around. She had twirled for George just before Giles had arrived to pick her up and then hugged him as she saw the tears in his eyes that prevented him from speaking. She hugged Marjorie too knowing that they had both spent far more than they could afford on the outfit she was wearing for this special occasion.

They knew about Giles and were delighted. George had been wary at first knowing that his family were from a very different level of society, but he had gradually warmed to the sincere young man who seemed unpretentious and, most important of all, trustworthy. Crystal may be his adopted daughter, but he couldn't possibly love her any more than he did and he wasn't prepared to stand aside and see her hurt by some member of the local gentry. He could see, however, that Giles and Crystal had fallen deeply in love and he was sure that he wouldn't hurt her. He enjoyed Giles' visits to the house as the young man was keen on cars and would often help George to sort out problems with the Rover 75, the car that had replaced the old Hillman when he got promoted to general manager. Yes, all in all, he liked Giles; good luck to them. He just hoped that the other family would feel the same.

Crystal walked down the stairs very carefully, unaccustomed to the feel of high heeled shoes. They were pale blue like the dress and also encrusted with tiny stones. She saw Giles waiting at the bottom in the hallway near the door; he had his back to her and was chatting to some friends, just like the first time they had met. He was greeting them as they came in and there was a lot of hugging, shouting and back-slapping. Crystal saw him glance up a couple of times, looking for her, but there were other people on the stairs and his attention was pulled back each time by exuberant friends before he could locate her. She could feel herself smiling and couldn't wait to see his face when he saw her. Marjorie had also bought her a pale blue, full length satin cape which fastened at the throat and had a huge hood trimmed with white fur; she had managed to slip that on before they had let Giles in to the cottage and she had hugged it round her.

"Come on, let's see the frock," Giles had said, impatiently and Crystal, Marjorie and George had burst out laughing.

"Frock? Frock! – What a quaint old-fashioned word," and Crystal had swept past him to the door, "no you can't," she had said pertly, "wait till we get there." Then blowing a kiss to both her parents, she spluttered with laughter again as the sound of them repeating the word 'frock' followed her out into the darkness. She had linked arms with Giles and pecked him on the cheek, pleased that, for the first time, she had had the satisfaction of seeing him blush.

At last he turned and saw her. He watched as she stepped daintily down the last few stairs and walked towards him. His gaze said it all; it was what she wanted, what she had been waiting for; it made everything worthwhile. She came very close and kissed him lightly on the lips then smiled as he still looked completely dazed.

"Don't you know it's rude to stare?"

"You look wonderful."

A chorus of "....Cor, lucky beggar..." "....Who's that then...?" and low whistles followed them as he took her arm and led her proudly towards the door of the ball room to meet his parents.

The room was beautiful and full of light sparkling from the huge chandeliers that hung down along the whole length of the high ceiling. The thousand crystal drops made her remember her special jewel and she touched it as Giles led her towards a couple standing in the centre of the room. She recognised Dr. Cowper as she had seen him briefly once or twice when she had gone to ride Giles' ponies. He had dark, crinkly hair and the sort of face that looked as though the features had been squashed in to a space that was just a little too small for them. Both Rosemary and Clive resembled him but in different ways; Rosemary had his rather coarse, heavy features and stocky build, whereas Clive, although thin, was dark with the same swarthy complexion. Crystal saw him out of the corner of her eye as he glanced shiftily in her direction, his slicked down black hair giving him more the look of a spiv rather than the son of a prominent family. His features were pinched and pointed and his eyes too close together; they moved shiftily from side to side as he looked at the world down his over-large and slightly hooked nose.

Rosie was standing with him and her mouth fell open with surprise and pleasure as she saw who her little brother was leading across the room to meet her parents. She smiled and waved and Crystal felt grateful to know that they had her support; Rosemary had been the one with whom she had always had the most contact since the time she had first started going to Monk's Manor. She held tightly on to Giles' arm, feeling confident that nothing could spoil this evening or indeed the rest of her life.

They had almost reached the spot where his parents were standing surrounded by a crowd of friends all laughing and talking, when Dr. Cowper, who had his back to them, shifted to one side to hear better what was being said by the person on his right. Crystal gave a little gasp as she found herself looking straight at one of the most elegantly beautiful women she had ever seen. She was wearing a shimmering black, lacy dress, long black gloves and round her neck were several strands of pearls caught in a silver and pearl clasp at her throat. Her dark hair had been pulled back from her face and arranged in coils on her head and she wore a pair of exquisite pearl earrings. Crystal stopped in front of her and stared into her emerald green eyes as Giles reached out his hand and gently touched her arm.

"Ma, this is Crystal." He glanced back at her as he said it but before he could turn back to his mother, even as Crystal was reaching out to shake hands, the woman's eyes closed and she sank to the floor.

"Oh my God! Get some water someone." Dr. Cowper was bending down over his wife and cradling her head. "Would you all move back, please, and give her some air."

A large group of the guests who had crowded round shuffled backwards and suddenly Evelyn appeared with a glass of water. She took charge and ordered Giles to raise his mother's legs off the floor so that they were higher than her head. She removed the pearl necklace and ordered someone to open a window.

Eleanore moaned softly and her eyes opened. Someone appeared with a chair as she started to try and get up. Evelyn, all thin efficiency, ordered her to lie still and motioned to Giles to keep holding her legs. The room had gone silent, but now people started murmuring again as it became clear that Eleanore had only fainted. She wasn't injured; in fact she hadn't even bumped her head as she had slithered down against the legs of the man standing behind her at the time.

After a few more minutes Evelyn ordered Giles to lower her legs and she allowed her sister to sit up. Eleanore was very pale and put her hand to her head as one of the waiters appeared with a cold, wet towel.

"About time," Evelyn scolded and the young man looked embarrassed as she frowned at him before taking the cloth and laying it on her sister's forehead.

"How silly of me.....how very stupid." Eleanore muttered as she sat holding the white cloth to her head, and all around there were murmurs of

"....poor thing..." ".....it was rather hot in here....." "......not used to coming out, you know....."

Evelyn and William Cowper helped Eleanore to get up and she sat on the chair taking deep breaths and looking very pale. Evelyn whispered something to her brother in law and he immediately left the room. He returned a few minutes later and nodded to Evelyn over his wife's head. They bent down and gently helped Eleanore to her feet.

"Hotel's giving us a room where she can lie down for a bit." William spoke a little too loudly, sharing his wife's embarrassment and, as he paused, Eleanore reached out and took Giles' hand,

"I'm so sorry, darling. I hope I haven't spoilt your evening." She lowered her voice, "please find Aunt Bette and ask her to come to wherever they're taking me."

Held between her sister and husband, Eleanore was helped from the room. Giles looked round for his Aunt Bette, but she was nowhere to be seen. He turned to Crystal,

"I'll bet I know where she is. Come on." And he led her out of the ballroom and into the dining room where a magnificent buffet had been spread along a huge table waiting for the arrival of the guests. Half way down the room a petite, blond woman was walking slowly, surrounded by a group of excited children. She was carrying a small boy and they were all gasping with delight at the array of delicious food. Crystal watched as she reached into a fruit bowl and popped a tiny grape into each child's mouth. Suddenly she saw Giles and Crystal approaching and her smile broadened then she laughed with delight.

"Ah, now then children, we have a treat. Here comes the handsome prince, the star of the evening. And how do we know he's a prince?" She looked down to where the little group of upturned faces were gazing at her ecstatically, waiting for her to tell them. She put the little boy carefully down and reached forward with both her hands,

"We know because he has with him a young girl so beautiful that she must be a princess." The little boy clung to her skirt as she took both of Crystal's hands and pulled her forward. She hugged her and kissed her on both cheeks before holding her at arms length again. Then she turned to Giles,

"And how is my darling favourite nephew?" She hugged him and he bent down and kissed her. Bette kept hold of Giles with one hand and reached again for Crystal with the other while the little boy, refusing to relinquish his place near his own fairy princess clung on to her skirt and almost disappeared amongst their legs.

"Giles, why haven't you introduced me to this exquisite creature? Do so at once."

Giles was smiling as, Crystal thought later, it was impossible not to around this amazing person so full of vitality. He could have pointed out that she hadn't exactly given him a chance to say anything, but he just continued to smile as he introduced Crystal to his favourite Aunt. Crystal wondered how three sisters could all look so different: Austere Evelyn with her thin lips and bony body; exquisite, dark-haired Eleanore and now Bette – tiny and blond with twinkling blue eyes and a smile that lit up her whole face. Any further thought was impossible as she was being kissed again and introduced to each one of the children. Two of them, both girls, both blond and both very pretty turned out to be Bette's daughters. They were pulled forward for special attention by their proud mother and Crystal shook hands with first the elder of the two, Charlotte, who must have been about sixteen and then Daisy, who was about twelve. Bette chatted and laughed all the while, clearly completely unaware of the drama that had been played out in the room next door.

Giles waited for a lull then quietly asked if he could have a quick word.

"Of course, my dear. Children stay here with Princess Crystal. I won't be a moment and when I get back we'll see what else we can find on the table." She winked at them then allowed Giles to lead her a little way away where he spoke softly enough for them not to hear him.

As he explained, the pretty face grew serious and Crystal saw Bette's hand fly up to her mouth.

"Oh, the poor darling." Bette turned and beckoned to the children, "Come along now, my pets, we must go and find your parents," She put her arms round her two daughters, clearly giving them instructions to look after the little ones and, with them all trailing behind her, she swept out of the room, hurrying to find her beloved sister.

Crystal put her hand on Giles' arm. He looked distracted, staring down at the floor, frowning. He started and looked up as he felt her touch him then pulled her towards him, kissing her lightly on the forehead.

"Sorry about Ma. Not quite the meeting I had imagined."

"Oh, don't worry about me. I just hope she'll be OK. Has she often fainted before?"

Giles thought for a moment,

"Not that I can remember. She does have the occasional bouts of depression when she seems to withdraw from life – the doc. in the village gives her tablets for those. I think that's why she likes Aunt Bette's company – seems to lift her right back up again."

He looked very serious and Crystal realised there was a strong bond between him and his mother. Suddenly he smiled.

"Come on, this is a party – and mine at that! Let's go and have some fun; after all, Ma only fainted, no real harm's done and she'll be OK now that Bette's with her."

He grabbed Crystal's hand and led her back into the ballroom where they were soon surrounded by friends and family, all apparently delighted with

Giles' choice of girl friend. Only Clive stood by himself at the edge of the room, drinking too much whisky, smoking too many cigarettes and scowling through the curling smoke towards his younger brother with the beautiful girl at his side.

Upstairs in a dimly lit hotel bed room Eleanore clung to her younger sister and wept as though her heart would break.

CHAPTER NINE

The next day Marjorie and George wanted to know all about the party and Crystal was more than happy to oblige. She described the beautiful room, delicious food and the way that everyone had made her feel so welcome. She told them about Eleanore's faint, but said that it hadn't spoilt the evening – which it hadn't as several members of the family, including Giles, had gone up at regular intervals to check on her. She didn't come down again, but some food was taken up and the message relayed to all the concerned guests was that she was feeling better and wanted everyone just to get on and enjoy the party.

Crystal told her mum and dad about the different members of the family whom she had now seen in a new light. Geoffrey, looking stiff and starchy at first in the unfamiliar evening clothes, had soon undone his bow tie and relaxed, leaning on the bar and swapping horsy stories with several old friends. Claude had sat quietly, beaming at everyone, his moustache twitching and his cheeks getting more flushed with every passing hour as people stopped to talk to him, making sure his glass was topped up before they moved on.

Their many old friends present on this special occasion knew only too well why these two men had been unlucky in love. Geoffrey, with his eye for beautiful creatures, had been passionately committed to his stunning French wife, loving deeply and only once; hurt beyond description by her desertion. Claude, amiable and easy going, had become the prey of an ambitious woman who saw him as her passport into a prestigious family. When it became clear that they wanted nothing to do with her, she showed herself in her true colours and, having nagged the poor man nearly into his grave, she left him. He had maintained, for a while, the air of sobriety that he felt was warranted by such an occurrence, pretending to be upset. In truth, he was greatly relieved to be rid of her and only too happy to move back in and share the top floor of The Manor with his brother; only too pleased to continue the life he loved, ambling around the fields and managing the farm without having to carry the burden of an unloving wife.

Evelyn didn't change all evening; she looked the same as always – stiff, remote and unsmiling – and Crystal found herself intrigued by this strange woman. What sort of life had she led? It certainly wasn't one that had brought her much joy that was for sure. But by far the most intriguing character of all was Giles' Grandma, old Isobel Lynton-Bell. She was dressed in a black satin two-piece, the top of which was sewn with shiny, jet black beads. Her white hair was wound up on top of her head and she had sat at the edge of the ball room, watching everything and everybody. It seemed to Crystal that nothing escaped those button-bright eyes as her head darted around this way and that. She sat very straight and all her movements, as she ate and drank, were quick and light like a bird. She was never without attention; waiters buzzing round as family members constantly ensured that her every need was satisfied, only then could they attend to themselves and other guests.

Crystal could see that she had once been beautiful and indeed was still striking to look at with a face both strong and full of character. She was hoping that she might meet the old lady, but she seemed to disappear from the party at about the same time that Eleanore fainted and Crystal didn't see her for the rest of the evening.

Bette had returned from her sister's bedside and continued to sparkle, though Crystal thought there was something a little forced about her gaiety, something that hadn't been there when they had first met. She put it down to the concern she must be feeling for her sister, though she was a bit surprised when, as she and Giles passed her on the way to the dance floor, Bette had suddenly grabbed her arm, looked into her eyes and kissed her gently on the cheek. Giles had laughed and squeezed Crystal's hand,

"Well you've certainly made a hit with Aunt Bette."

Crystal had smiled, but for a moment was disturbed by something she had seen in the older woman's eyes – was it pity? She dismissed it from her mind as Giles swept her on to the dance floor.

She didn't tell George and Marjorie about the drive home and the way Giles had kissed her before she got out of the car. He had told her he loved her and that their next date would be very special as he had something important to ask her.

"I'll call you tomorrow, my darling," he had whispered as she had slipped quietly out of the little red car and, blowing him a last kiss, disappeared up the drive in a swirl of blue satin.

As it was Sunday she sat quietly in her bed room all afternoon doing her homework, but was finding it hard to concentrate as she was waiting and listening for the phone to ring. At six o'clock when Marjorie called her for tea it still hadn't rung. She thought it was strange but realised that he had probably been besieged by well-wishing relatives all day long. It was a lovely evening and she wanted to go for a walk, but stayed in instead to wait for Giles' call.

She smiled as she sat in the sitting room with her parents, pretending to read, knowing that at any moment the phone would ring and he would be apologising for leaving it so long.

"Crystal, why do you keep picking up the phone, darling?"

"Oh….just checking that it's OK. It hasn't been out of order at all today has it?"

"No it hasn't been out of order. I used it earlier to ring Madge."

George smiled and glanced at Marjorie. The look that passed between them said 'young love!' and they raised their eyes to heaven – making sure that Crystal didn't see them.

'Oh, bother.' Crystal felt cross. Of course. Now she knew what had happened; Giles had obviously tried to ring while her dad was on the phone to his sister. She would ring him and apologise. Feeling relieved to have a logical explanation for the silence, she jumped up,

"OK if I ring Giles?"

"Of course," her parents said in unison and hid their smiles from their daughter as she bounded towards the door.

It was Aunt Bette who answered,

"Oh Crystal……hello." She sounded strange, not at all like the bubbly, vivacious woman that Crystal had met the previous evening.

"No, I'm sorry. He's not here," she said when Crystal asked if she could speak to Giles.

"Well….can I ring later?" She paused, feeling very confused then blurted out, "When will he be back?"

"I'm not at all sure, dear. I….I'll get him to ring you. Goodbye" She sounded uncomfortable and desperate to get off the phone. What on earth had happened to the Bette she had met the previous evening? Where was Giles and why hadn't he rung?

He didn't ring later or on Monday or Tuesday. After a wretched day at school on Wednesday, Crystal got home, flung her satchel in the corner and marched purposefully up to the phone. It was Rosemary who answered and told her, in a matter of fact sort of voice that Giles had gone to stay with Aunt Bette in Dorset for the rest of the holiday and would go back to Oxford from there.

CHAPTER TEN
1962

From a bale in the barn doorway where she sat chewing a piece of straw, Crystal watched Minty stroking a huge grey rabbit that squatted on her lap, eyes closed and long ears flat against its silky back.

"That's the trouble with the toffs – only after one thing!"

Crystal coloured at Minty's candour which hadn't changed over the years."

"As a matter of fact, it wasn't like that."

"You mean he didn't…..you know."

"No he didn't. In fact if you must know it was him who stopped, not me. I would have. ….."

She found herself blushing as she remembered the time she had really wanted Giles to make love to her, but he wouldn't as he had said he wanted to show her that, for him, she was special.

"Well, good job you didn't isn't it, considering he cleared off without a word."

"Minty, if you carry on like that I shall wish I hadn't told you anything!"

Crystal spoke sharply and Minty looked up; her hand stopped the rhythmic stroking and her fingers dug into the rabbit's soft fur.

"Sorry Crys. It's just that it makes me so mad. How dare he treat you like that?" Her genuine anger on her friend's behalf made her dig her nails into the rabbit's back just a little too hard causing the indignant creature to jump down and hop lazily away across the yard where chickens were clucking and scratching in the July sunshine.

Minty went to retrieve the rabbit and Crystal closed her eyes. It had been more than a year ago yet the memories were still as painful as ever; it seemed she was compelled to re-live them over and over again, hoping, as people said, that time would eventually prove to be a healer and the pain would stop. As yet there was no sign of this happening. She remembered, as if it were yesterday, the numbness, the feeling of disbelief, on being told by Rosemary that Giles had gone to Dorset. It simply hadn't seemed real. He couldn't have done. She had tried to hide her feelings from her parents but her father had quietly knocked on her door and asked very gently why she had been crying. She had broken down again then and told him what had happened. He had sat with his arms round her until her sobbing had subsided then went down stairs to tell Marjorie.

"Come down when you're ready, darling, and we'll have a cup of tea."

She had heard them talking softly and, although she couldn't hear what was being said, she had a pretty good idea that George was sharing with his wife some murderous thoughts towards Giles. How could he have got it so wrong? How come he hadn't seen through the veneer of sincerity to the duplicity and cavalier attitude which must have been lurking just beneath the surface? How could he have let his daughter down?

"If I could get my hands on the little……." He had raged, quietly, to Marjorie, moving his hands together in a wringing movement.

By the time Crystal felt able to go downstairs, some self-possession had returned. She sat with her parents drinking tea and calmly made George promise not to go anywhere near Monk's Manor or Manor Farm.

"I must sort this out on my own, pops…..you can see that, can't you?"

Reluctantly George had agreed and secretly both he and Marjorie admired their daughter for this decision.

By the weekend Crystal had a plan. She went to ride Bluebell as usual and noticed that Geoffrey was just the same with her as always. After the session he praised her for her performance and she listened quietly before looking straight at him and asking,

"Geoffrey, do you know why Giles has gone to Dorset?"

"Has he, my dear? No I don't know why – didn't even know he'd gone. I expect he'll be writing to tell you all about it before long. He always liked to go and stay with Bette, but with you here I should have thought.......oh well, bound to be an explanation, you'll see."

Before going home she went to find Claude and asked him the same question. He stroked his moustache,

"Dashed if I do, my dear. Gone to Dorset, you say, what to stay with Bette? Well, I never." He paused and looked at Crystal with a twinkle in his eye, "I'll say this though, my girl, if he's got any of our red blood in his veins, he'll be back to see you before you know it." Crystal smiled in spite of herself and started up the drive for home.

She was met with a similar response when she plucked up the courage to go to Monk's Manor, steeling herself to confront whoever she might see there. Everywhere was quiet; there was nobody in the yard and nothing moved inside the house as she marched up to the door and knocked loudly. She was relieved when Rosemary answered; she hadn't really relished the thought of talking to Clive or his father.

"I wondered if you could tell me when Giles will be back." She tried to sound more confident than she was feeling and Rosemary looked blank.

"I can't say I can. He just went off with Bette and the kids the day after his party. He'd had a long talk with Ma, then packed his bags and went. I thought it a bit strange, but I must say, it never occurred to me that you didn't know he was going. Look there must be a simple explanation – I'm sure he'll write to you and tell you what's going on. We were all delighted when we saw that you and he were…..do you want to come in for some tea?"

Crystal said no thank-you and walked slowly back up the drive. She didn't look back or she might have caught a glimpse of a slick of dark hair and pair of shifty eyes watching her intently from just inside one of the stables. As she disappeared round the bend in the drive, Clive slunk back into the dim interior and lit a cigarette.

She sobbed herself to sleep for the next two weeks and was first up each morning, waiting eagerly to see what the postman would bring. There was nothing.

At the end of the first month she made a decision and wrote a letter to Geoffrey telling him that, owing to the pressures of studying for her 'A' levels, she would no longer be able to ride Bluebell for him. He wrote back and tried to persuade her to change her mind, but she was adamant. It was just too painful to keep going to the place where she had had her first real conversation with Giles. Every time she went into the tack room she kept hoping, foolishly, that he would be there, sitting on the soaping table whistling a silly tune. She just couldn't bear it.

The next month passed and when there was still no word from Giles she stopped crying and started to focus on her exams. She told herself that she would have to forget him – even though she knew she never would. He knew her address, he knew her telephone number and yet he had made no attempt to contact her. What had she done wrong? Had she said something to offend someone? If only she knew then she could at least try to put things right. But there was no way she could humiliate herself further by trying to contact him, so that was that. It was over and she must turn her face to a future that didn't include him.

She was resolute because she had to be, and inside she was aware of something a little like a stone, something hard that hadn't been there before she had fallen in love with Giles Cowper. She set her face to the future, but every so often what had happened bubbled up to the surface and she was mystified afresh, totally unable to find rhyme or reason as to why he had gone away suddenly and without explanation. It just didn't make any sense.

She went through the motions of living because she had to; there was no choice and she got down to her studies, forcing herself to go forward, each day, one step at a time. Marjorie and George were there for her, loving, supporting and encouraging. She realised how lucky she was to have parents like them and refused to think about who her real mother and father might be – whoever they were they couldn't possibly be have loved her better or given her more than George and Marjorie.

She got herself a Saturday job in a department store in Cambridge and resurrected her idea of being a teacher. It wasn't easy, but by sheer determination and will power she got through the autumn and winter; then spring came bringing warmth and sunshine. One sunny Saturday, while she was sitting by the river in the grounds of King's College eating her lunch time sandwiches and watching the punts drift lazily by; she became aware that she was smiling.

To someone who hadn't been through the heartbreak that she had endured, this would not seem significant. To Crystal it was a turning point. She put her empty sandwich bag into her pocket and strolled back to the store for the afternoon session. 'I can do this,' she thought and although the stone was still there, the hard knot inside her, and although she knew that she would never get over the pain of being rejected in such a cruel way, she became certain that she could cope.

Spring turned to summer and the dreaded 'A' levels were upon her. She took English, Art and

History and felt reasonably confident about all three. She was provisionally accepted by Homerton Training College on the understanding that she achieved reasonable grades in her exams. She had started seeing Minty again and had found some comfort in her friend's pragmatic approach to life.

She was still with Rob, her first and only boyfriend, who shared Minty's passion for breeding rabbits and chickens. Rob's dad had a small holding at the edge of the fen where his son already lived and worked and which he would one day inherit. It was Minty's dream to marry Rob, live there with him and, while he farmed in a very modest way, she would bring in a little money with her rabbits and chickens.

She already had a tiny diamond engagement ring that she wore on a chain around her neck as they both knew that their families would say they were too young to be engaged yet. They were biding their time and waiting for an appropriate occasion to announce their engagement. Rob was going to ask Matthew's permission to marry his daughter, an idea which made Minty giggle when she told Crystal, but she knew that her dad would be pleased by such a gesture.

"Just say if you don't want to talk about 'that' family, Crys, but I wondered if you had heard that Evelyn died?"

Jolted back to the present, Crystal looked towards Minty who had resumed her seat on the upturned half barrel and had the recaptured rabbit on her lap where he was allowing himself to be pacified by a piece of carrot and a few torn lettuce leaves.

"Yes…..yes, I read about it in the paper."

It had happened at the end of May. Crystal had seen the headline in the Cambridge Evening News – 'Daughter of Local Farming Family Dies of Heart Attack.' Underneath there had been a picture of Evelyn when she was younger, though she didn't look very different from the way that Crystal remembered her. The article was quite long and described all the good work she had done in her life, devoting herself to working with the down and outs in London, then nursing at Addenbrook's Hospital after the war. It was full of praise for such an upright citizen and finished by saying that, as she had never married and had no children, it was thought she had named various charities in her will to benefit from her estate. Crystal remembered thinking how strange it was that she had died while the old lady, her mother, Isobel, was apparently still alive and well.

Even though she had had no particular affection for Evelyn, Crystal's heart had turned over just at the sight of a member of the family. The family, of course would gather for the funeral; maybe Giles would phone…..maybe….her heart leapt, then she stopped herself abruptly. No – she had promised herself. No false hopes. She had shut the paper and pushed it to one side. On the day of the funeral George and Marjorie had taken her out for shopping and lunch so that there was no chance of her bumping in to any of the family members around the village.

Crystal got up from the straw bale and stretched in the late afternoon sun. She went over and kissed the top of Minty's head.

"What on earth was that for?" The rabbit's ears twitched and Minty looked surprised. Crystal ruffled her friend's spiky, brown hair.

"Oh…..just for being there for me….for being you. It's been a tough year. Anyway must go." She turned and started to walk towards the gate.

"Crystal," she turned back. "Take care." There was real affection in Minty's eyes and Crystal realised once again that she had a friend for life.

"Yeah, you too, rat-bag."

"And come and see me again, or I'll visit Maple Cottage in the middle of the night and put rabbit poo through the letter box."

"Charming!"

Crystal laughed and strode up the drive, waving to Matthew and Gran who were standing by the farm door.

As Crystal sauntered along the village street that Sunday in the late afternoon sunshine, Clive was, at that very moment, unearthing a piece of family history so staggering that it caused a smile to spread across his face and linger there for a very long time. Clutching the small, black book that was the source of his newly acquired knowledge very close to his chest, he crept stealthily out of the room at Manor Farm that had, until recently, been occupied by his Aunt Evelyn and made his way silently down the stairs.

His Grandmother Isobel dozed in her room a few doors away, his Uncle Geoffrey put a new thoroughbred through her paces out in the paddock and Claude leaned on a gate, surveying with satisfaction a field that was nearly ready to harvest. None of them could have guessed what their least favourite relative had in his possession as he clanked and rattled back to Monk's Manor in his sister's Morris Minor.

CHAPTER ELEVEN

It started off just like any other Saturday. Crystal took the bus into Cambridge and walked the short distance from the terminus to the shop. She helped to take the dust sheets off the counters then polished the glass with some special strong-smelling liquid cleaner to remove finger-prints from the previous day. High heels clicked on the floors and the air was filled with chatter about boyfriends, parties and the latest lip colour. Crystal kept quiet and felt a stab of envy at the apparently uncomplicated lives of the other girls.

The doors opened at nine o'clock, but it was a slow start, so the supervisor asked her to change some of the displays – a job that Crystal enjoyed and one she knew she was good at. She worked in the perfumery department and to make aesthetically pleasing displays in the glass cabinets below the counters she was allowed – encouraged in fact – to go to other departments and borrow beautiful scarves, gloves trimmed with fur and little ornaments in order to show off the pretty bottles to their best advantage.

At lunch time it was raining, just a light drizzle, but enough to discourage her from venturing far outside the store. She ate her sandwiches upstairs in the canteen then wandered through some of the other departments before going to a couple of nearby shops. She returned on time and walked back into the department to wait for afternoon customers. Pat, a young woman from Newcastle and full time employee, was just picking up her bag from behind the counter to go for her own lunch break. She stopped when she saw Crystal,

"Oh Crystal, a note came for you while you were out. Jenny's got it. Jenny…..Jenny give Crystal the note…you know, the one that weirdo delivered." She was calling another of the part timers, then turned to Crystal again,

"Honest to God, love, I wouldn't like to be meeting him on a dark night. Anyway he said it was very, very important and that we had to be sure to give it to you."

"– Practically made us sign for it in our own blood." Jenny had joined them and was handing Crystal a note. She pulled a face then wiped her hand on her pink overall after parting with the envelope, as if she was trying to eradicate all traces of the man who had delivered it.

"Oh….er…thanks." Crystal frowned. She wasn't expecting a note and she didn't know any weirdoes……Oh dear God, no. Suddenly, linked with the idea of weirdoes, a face flashed before her; pointed features…shifty eyes too close together… a slick of dark, greasy hair. Clive! Could Clive really have been here? What on earth could he possibly want with her? Pat click-clacked away for her lunch and Jenny leaned on the counter looking at Crystal, arms folded and one eyebrow raised,

"Aren't you going to open it?"

"Yeah, but I'd better go to the stock room…..just in case Mrs. Johnson's around….you know what she's like."

Crystal hurried to the little room nearby, pleased with her quick thinking. There was no way she was going to open the note in front of any one, even harmless, blond Jenny, and all the girls knew that the supervisor would take a dim view of anyone standing reading anything in working time. She turned back and spoke in a conspiratorial whisper,

"Cover for me if the dragon appears. I'll bring back some bottles of toilet water."

"'Course I will." Jenny smiled, obviously pleased to be included, and now certain that she would be told what the note contained.

Crystal closed the door quietly and looked at the plain, white envelope. Her name was scrawled on the front in black ink and in the bottom left-hand corner it said 'private and confidential.' She turned the envelope over, slit it open at the top and carefully unfolded the single piece of paper inside. The message was scrawled in the same untidy hand that had written her name on the front:

Crystal,

Meet me in the stable at the corner of the old paddock. Be there at 7 o'clock on Sunday; come alone and don't let anyone know where you are going. I have discovered something about you; it will affect your whole future and it's very important that you should be told. If you bring anyone I will leave and never tell you.

Clive.

She read it through twice and still couldn't believe it. What on earth could Clive know that would affect her? It had to be something to do with Giles, but then she looked again – it specifically said something about **her**. The hand holding the note dropped to her side and she could feel her heart beating very fast. Quickly she re-folded the piece of paper, put it into the envelope and stuffed it into her pocket. Grabbing a box of toilet waters she took a deep breath and went back out into the department.

Jenny scuttled up to her side as Crystal put the box onto the counter,

"Well?"

"Oh…you were right. Just some creep I met at a dance last week. I've already told him I'm not interested, but you know what it's like. Some just won't take no for an answer. I'll ignore him then he'll have to get the message."

"Oh, I know what you mean. Do you know the very same thing happened to me….." and Jenny launched into her own story about an unwanted admirer, while Crystal calmly arranged the toilet waters on the shelf. The account was curtailed by the simultaneous arrival of Mrs. Johnson and two customers.

"Byeee……byeee….see you next Saturday. And don't forget to kick creepo into touch if he tries to see you again."

"Yeah. You can do much better than that." And with a wave, Jenny and Pat went off in one direction while Crystal walked in the other towards the bus station.

There was very little sleep for Crystal that night. Cursing Clive for disrupting a life which she had just about managed to put successfully back on track, she tossed and turned. Of course she wasn't going to go…..it wouldn't be dark at seven o'clock in the middle of summer, but the thought of being alone with Clive even in broad daylight sent shivers down her spine. He was an idiot. He couldn't possibly know anything about her…..could he?

Confused thoughts whirled around in her mind until, just before dawn, she sat up in bed and hugged her knees.

'I will go. Why should I be afraid? What have I got to be afraid of? I'll take dad's old stick for protection and tell them I'm just going for a walk. I have to go, because if I don't this will be another question mark hanging over my head for ever.'

Having made the decision she slept, but it was a shallow sleep troubled by disturbing dreams in which she was running, trying to find something, but it was always out of reach, hidden round the next corner.

She propped the stick up against the outside wall, walked hesitantly into the old stable and looked slowly around; the floor was hard, dry mud, pressed down through years of use, and her feet brushed against the occasional wisps of straw. The inside was dim, a stark contrast to the evening sunshine she had just left behind and she blinked as her eyes adjusted to the change. The stable hadn't been used for a long time, probably not since she had taken Giles' ponies in there for their winter feed of chopped carrots and chaff, and she was conscious of a damp, musty smell. There was a rusty manger in the corner and a few bits of mildewed tack hanging against the walls on huge black nails.

Instinctively she stayed close to the door and stared straight ahead to where an opening led through to a second stable. Nothing moved, and as she waited she heard the Church clock strike seven.

It had been fairly easy to get away as she frequently went for walks on sunny evenings, so nothing odd about that, and George had seemed pleased that she wanted to take his stick.

"Don't go too far down the fen, darling. When can we expect you back?"

"Oh, in about an hour,"

And she had set off through the village, turned down the road towards the fen, then cut off left across the fields to the old paddock. She was quite certain that she hadn't been seen; the roads and fields had been completely deserted as she had hurried along, glancing furtively around as though it was she who had something to hide. 'Just the effect 'orrible Clive has on people,' she had thought as she reached her destination.

She held her wrist out in the sunlight and looked at her watch. Five past seven. She looked round the stable again. Still no sound and nothing moved; then her eye was held by one of the bridles hanging against the wall. She walked across and touched it – yes she was sure it was the very first one she had used on Poppy. She rubbed her forefinger on the mildewed leather, what a shame....

Suddenly a match flared in the darkness of the opening to the other stable. She whirled round and gasped with fright as she saw, illuminated there, two staring eyes and a large hooked nose. Clive lit a cigarette and threw the spent match onto the floor. He took two steps towards her and smiled – at least she thought it was meant to be a smile, but it was a sort of lop-sided leer and didn't reach his eyes.

"I hope I didn't alarm you, my dear."

"No, of course not. I mean what could possibly be alarming about someone suddenly appearing from the darkness without any warning at all!"

A combination of anger and fright made Crystal bold and she surprised herself by daring to speak to Clive in that way. A muscle in his cheek twitched as the pseudo smile vanished instantly from his face. He didn't like sarcasm unless he was using it; but he consoled himself with the fact that what he knew would soon topple little miss hoity-toity from her pedestal. He had been waiting for years to repay her for the snub she had given him. Admittedly, locking her in the stable once while she was tending to Poppy and he was joshing around with some mates was pretty stupid. But he had let her out after only a very few minutes and he had even apologised before asking her out. She had said no, quite rudely, and disappeared up the drive with her nose in the air; then, before he knew it, she was going out with his little brother. Who did she think she was…? Ah well…whoever she thought she was, he was pretty soon going to put her right on that one!

Crystal was also thinking about the time when Clive and his silly friends had locked her in the stable. She remembered them peering down through a small opening from the hay loft above the manger and giggling as she waited quietly by the door for at least one of them to come to their senses. She had heard the bolt being drawn back then walked past them as they stood sheepishly staring at her. She remembered only too well Clive following her up the drive, stammering a sort of apology then asking her out, and it was with great satisfaction that she had said, 'no Clive, not now, not ever,' before continuing on her way. She and Minty had laughed about it for hours and even pretended to make themselves sick by imagining what it must be like to be kissed by Clive.

And here he was, leering at her, apparently with something important to say. She could see that her boldness had made him angry and was almost amused at how hard he was trying to hide this.

"So what is it you have to tell me?" She looked straight into his eyes, challenging him to get on with the business, whatever it was.

Still on her high horse! By God he was going to enjoy this.

"Why don't we sit down?"

"On what?"

With an exasperated sigh, as though he was dealing with a small, slightly stupid, child, Clive indicated two old, wooden chairs in the corner which Crystal hadn't noticed before. She strode across, took one and placing it near the doorway, sat down. With her legs crossed she looked back at him and waited. He pulled the other chair out into the centre of the room and slowly sat down facing her. Her green eyes flashed and the evening sun, pouring in through the doorway, glinted on her dark, copper-coloured curls. 'What an amazing looking girl….and maybe after today, she might just look at me differently.' Crystal felt uncomfortable as she was aware of Clive staring silently and intently at her. She spoke clearly, confidently and slowly,

"Clive, will you please tell me why you have brought me here. I can't stay long as my parents are expecting me back soon and…."

"Your parents? Your parents you say are expecting you?"

"Yes!" Dear God this man was such a creep….

"Well, Crystal," he leaned forward, "I think we both know that it's not 'your parents' who are expecting you back at that little cottage in the village, don't we?"

Crystal felt herself go cold, as if all the warm blood in her body was draining away to her toes and being replaced by something icy.

"What....what on earth do you mean?" She stammered and she saw the muscle in Clive's cheek twitch again. He reached into his pocket and brought out a small, black book.

"I have here the evidence that your mother..." He leaned forward, "Your mother, my dear, was none other than my poor, dear departed Aunt Evelyn....God rest her soul, of course."

"Don't be ridiculous!" she was on her feet, shouting and waving her arms, "Don't be so bloody ridiculous, you stupid man. What are you talking about? Your Aunt Evelyn never married and had no children...."

Clive sat where he was, though he was a little startled by Crystal's sudden, spontaneous fury. Choking, she paced back and forth, and for a moment he thought she might hit him. He stood and went behind his chair where he leaned against the back of it.

"If you will allow me to finish, I will prove that what I'm saying is true." Crystal slumped back down in her chair, panting, resisting the urge to punch Clive hard in the face. Of all the meddling, lying bastards! How dare he?

"You bastard." She spat the word at him into the room and he leaned across the chair back, pointing a finger at her.

"No, my dear, I think you'll find it's you who's the bastard. Now calm down, shut up and listen." He sat back down and his voice was cold, low and menacing. He held up the black book.

"This is my Aunt's diary written in 1944. It makes fascinating reading, particularly because I am sure that no-one was ever supposed to see it. That always makes things more interesting, don't you think?" Crystal didn't trust herself to answer, but pressed her fist against her mouth and looked straight at Clive, waiting for him to continue.

"It seems that, while working in London, she was raped by one of the down and outs she was trying to help and she became pregnant. She didn't believe in abortion so she had the child – a little girl." Crystal tried to stifle a gasp, "Yes, a little girl, who none of us ever saw, so we can only assume she put her up for adoption."

Crystal took her hand away from her mouth and was now breathing more normally. Clive was, of course, insane.

"Clive I am very sorry for your Aunt Evelyn – and for the little girl – but there is nothing on earth to connect either of them with me…."

"Oh but there is! Yes, Crystal there is." There was a note of triumph in his voice as he continued, "You see, my dear, I overheard my mother and Aunt Bette talking together the night of my little brother's party. You remember how Ma fainted when she saw you – very odd I thought that was, so I went up to see what was going on. Well I was about to go inside when I realised that Aunt Bette was with her and I couldn't help hearing what they were saying. The door was only open a crack and Ma was clearly very upset, so I couldn't hear everything, but I definitely heard Ma say, '…so she is that little girl….it's the same girl….she's one of the family….You can see, can't you, that Giles can't possibly marry her…..' then Aunt Bette had asked if she was sure and Ma said she was, over and over again 'yes…..it's her.' And then I heard, '…don't tell Evelyn." I couldn't hear any more as Pa came up to see them and I had to pretend I was just coming out."

Sneaking about, hiding behind corners, listening at closed doors…..were there any depths to which this man would not stoop in order to uncover something nasty, something that would cause another person pain? Crystal had never felt hatred for anyone before, but knew that what she was feeling for Clive must come pretty close to it. Still clutching at straws she looked defiantly across the room at the man to whom, she realised with a sudden shock, she may be indeed related.

"Yes, but what made her think that little girl is me?"

"Now that I don't know, but she would hardly faint and make such a fuss if she wasn't sure, would she. Obviously I didn't know until I found Evelyn's diary then Ma's 'don't tell Evelyn' and the revelation in the diary fitted perfectly. Bingo the whole thing fell into place. And of course knowing you are adopted…."

Crystal blazed with anger,

"And how the hell do you know that?" She was shaking with fury. Giles….he couldn't have done, surely….Giles was the only person apart from her immediate family who knew about that. She had told him in the strictest confidence when she realised they were getting serious about each other and he had said it didn't matter at all. In fact he'd laughed and said it made her a woman of mystery. Surely he couldn't have told Clive of all people. She glared straight at him and could see that he had been wrong footed; he had slipped up and he stammered "I…..I….."

"Well come on spit it out. Did Giles tell you?"

For a split second he considered lying then thought better of it. What the hell did it matter?

"No....no, he didn't tell me; but he was foolish enough to leave his diary lying around where anyone could have found it."

'Yes, I'll bet!' thought Crystal. 'I wonder how deeply you had to dig to find it just 'lying around!' She sneered at him and he saw the contempt in her eyes. Suddenly and viciously he lunged at her, grabbed her wrist and jerked her towards him. She was caught unawares and found her self staring straight into his loathsome eyes, his tainted, smoky breath making her feel nauseous.

"Just accept it, my pet; it all adds up to you being the bastard daughter of my straight-laced old aunt and some guttersnipe – a ne'er do well, down and out who raped auntie and you were the result. Pretty, isn't it?"

He threw his cigarette butt down, stamped on it and grabbed her other wrist, "No wonder my little brother dropped you like a hot coal…. threw you away like a piece of rotten fruit." He pushed her roughly back against the wall, pinned her arms down by her sides and pushed his body hard against her, "but I'm not like that," he was panting, "oh no, there is no reason why cousins can't marry – better if they don't have children perhaps, but who cares about nasty, smelly little sprogs – you and I, my dear, what a couple we would make, eh?"

Crystal struggled and tried to scream, but he stopped it with his mouth and she felt his teeth grinding against hers. He had moved one hand up and held her chin in a vice-like grip as his tongue snaked into her mouth. She pushed and struggled, but he was too strong and she felt his right hand pulling at her clothes. Utterly terrified, she realised she couldn't push him off and cursed her stupidity for leaving the stick outside the door…she could hardly move or breathe…there was nothing she could do….Then suddenly it all stopped. He was off her and she was sliding down the wall, panting and gasping for breath. There was another voice, not Clive's,

"You evil sod…" then the sound of bone on bone – once, twice, three times and she saw Clive fall hard onto the earth floor. She looked up and found herself staring straight into Giles' eyes.

For a moment nothing and no-one moved and in the stillness Crystal could hear rasping sobs which she knew were hers. Giles bent down and reached towards her to help her up. She scrambled sideways, away from his hand, and pulled herself to her feet, almost in one movement,

"Get away! Don't you dare touch me!"

She circled warily around him, edging towards the doorway and trying to straighten her clothes at the same time. Giles took a step towards her,

"Crystal I…."

"No, I don't want to hear it! I don't want to hear anything from you….you cheating, lying bastard. You are no better than him." She pointed to Clive who was groaning and just starting to move as he re-gained consciousness.

"Go to hell, both of you," she yelled, then turned and ran out of the door and across the paddock, not stopping until she reached the fence. She didn't want to think, just to get home – to reach the safety and normality of Maple Cottage. She wiped her face, straightened her clothes and, once over the fence, walked up the fen road then steadily along the village street, hoping and praying that she wouldn't meet anyone she knew. She couldn't have coped with polite conversation, but was holding herself together, putting one foot in front of the other, with just enough self possession to reach home. At first the street was deserted then an old lady wearing a paisley headscarf and staring straight ahead, rode carefully past on her bicycle; an elderly couple strolled by arm in arm and some children chased each other on a small, walled patch of grass that served as a village green. The sun had gone down and swallows were swooping above her as Maple Cottage came into view.

Again she was praying that she could reach the safety of her bedroom or the bathroom without seeing George or Marjorie. She made her way to the back door and saw, with relief, that they weren't in the garden. Quietly she turned the handle and walked into the dining room. She could hear the sound of clattering dishes coming from the kitchen and a muffled tune on the radio in the sitting room. She took a deep breath and forced out a voice that sounded cheery and normal,

"Hello…I'm back. Just popping up to the toilet." And with that she flew up the stairs into the bathroom, locked the door, sat down on a small chair and, with her head in her hands, sobbed silently, letting the tears roll unchecked down her face and onto the floor.

At Monk's Manor Giles was about to enter his bed room when his mother came out of hers. She smiled at her son, her favourite child, and asked if he would like to have a drink with her.

"I think it's time, darling, that I told you the truth, as I promised I would." She looked more closely at him and, noticing he appeared a little shaken, she frowned and reached out to touch his arm. He drew away and looked at her coldly.

"There's no need, Ma, I already know."

"Oh," Eleanore's fingers flew to her lips. "And are you alright?"

"Yes. Go and lie down."

"I'll see you in the morning then."

"Yes."

In the morning she wrote hastily to her sister, Bette, from whose house Giles had just returned after staying for a week on his way down from Oxford for the holidays.

My darling sister,

Thank-you for caring for my son as though he were your own; thank-you for what you did for him. Thank-you for your help. I shall miss you so much while you are away and look forward to your return when we can spend some time together. Have a lovely time with Tommy; you both deserve it.

Yours ever, with love and affection,

Ellie.

She gave it to Rosemary to post, insisting it had to go immediately as Bette and the girls were about to fly out to join Tommy in Malta. He was half way through his tour of duty as Colonel of the 29th regiment and they were going to spend a few weeks on holiday with him before the start of the new school term.

Eleanore watched Rosemary stride up the drive with the dogs, practical, capable Rosemary; then thought again with gratitude of her younger sister. How typical of Bette to take the burden off her shoulders and tell Giles the truth. He seemed to be taking it well. As she had thought, they were young, and giving him a year to get over her before telling him….it had been a good idea. Best not to say anything more to Giles yet; they would have to talk, of course but not yet. He needed time to get over the shock of such a discovery, after all there was no doubt he had been very fond of Crystal. Crystal…yes….now she could think about Crystal. After all she was……

If the Cowper family had been better at communicating; if Eleanore had talked to her son properly; If only Giles had challenged his mother, told her what he had heard Clive saying and asked her why it was such a big deal, Crystal being his cousin. After all, as Clive had said, cousins could marry and the accident of her birth wasn't her fault. If only Bette had just picked up the phone and spoken to her sister instead of assuming that the thank-you was for having Giles to stay for a week. If only…if only…

They were to ask themselves many times in the future why they had done none of these things; because if they had, then the tragedy that was to follow could possibly have been avoided.

CHAPTER TWELVE

The following morning it was raining, quite usual for the fens in July, and Crystal was supposed to start work at the store full time for the holidays, but she was too ill to get out of bed. Marjorie fussed over her with hot drinks and she slept fitfully for most of the day. She was feverish and her dreams were disturbed by images of Clive's face, his mouth open as if he was about to swallow her, his stinking breath making her retch. She called out, waking herself up several times, panting and sweating, to see Marjorie with a thermometer and a worried frown on her face, bending over her. There were other dreams too; of Evelyn staring at her with a cold, unsmiling look, while she tried to say the word 'mother,' but it wouldn't come.

In the evening George came quietly up the stairs and sat by her bed. She was propped up on pillows feeling a little better and he held her hand.

"Poor Poppet; that certainly was a very nasty fall. How are you feeling now?"

Crystal told him truthfully that she was much better and didn't even feel guilty about the lie of the previous evening. She had managed to dry her tears and knew that she had to face George and Marjorie. She had looked at herself in the bathroom mirror and seen what a mess she was in, her blouse torn and all her clothes covered in dirt from the stable floor. Her lips were swollen and bleeding and her wrists bruised, with several grazes from where Clive had scraped them against the wall. She looked as though she had fallen down a bank and into a ditch, which was what she decided to tell George and Marjorie had happened. Luckily it had been a fairly dry summer so far so the fact that the 'ditch' had had no water in it sounded quite plausible.

George went downstairs and Marjorie appeared a few minutes later with a bowl of soup. Crystal thanked her and did manage to eat most of it before putting the tray carefully down onto the floor and sinking back into the pillows feeling exhausted.

"Curse Clive....curse him....curse the whole family." She felt tears stinging her eyes as she muttered softly to herself. She tried to sort out her thoughts, organise them into some kind of order but they just kept running in circles round her head.

'... Evelyn was her mother....Geoffrey and Claude were her uncles ....Eleanore and Bette were her aunts....there were cousins – Rosemary was her cousin.....Giles was her cousin.....Clive..... (Oh dear God, how horrible!) Clive was her cousin! The old lady at the Manor was her grandmother...and none of them would want to know she existed. She was the relative they didn't want to own because of the way she had been conceived – the product of a brutal rape and born only because her mother couldn't face an abortion. Abortion or adoption, either way it added up to her being unwanted. She turned her face to the wall to stifle a sob.

Evening became night; Marjorie and George made sure she was as comfortable as possible and had everything she needed before going to bed themselves. As they gently touched her cheek and stroked her hair after kissing her goodnight Crystal made up her mind about one thing. She wasn't going to tell them about her discovery. Evelyn was dead, the rest of the family didn't want her; there was nothing to be gained from upsetting the family she had, who loved and cared for her. As she turned over to sleep, feeling calmer than she had all day, she was too young to realise that the decision she had just made had taken her one very positive step nearer to growing up.

Crystal stayed at home for one more day to recover and by Wednesday felt fit enough to start her holiday job. She jumped out of bed and got ready to catch the bus, surprised by how positive she was feeling. 'I can cope with this,' she thought as she dressed, ate a light breakfast and reassured an anxious Marjorie that she was fine,

"Honestly, mum, I'm well enough to push a few toiletries over the counter," then giving her a kiss she ran out of the door, promising faithfully to catch an early bus home if she had a relapse during the day.

Both Wednesday and Thursday went well with Crystal feeling stronger all the time. The bruises were less painful and she was developing a healthy mental attitude to her situation. The most reassuring thing, and the one that she clung to, was that none of it was of her own making. It was not her fault that Evelyn had been raped or that she hadn't wanted to keep her. She had done nothing wrong and, in fact, felt that she had been rewarded by being given to George and Marjorie to bring up as their own. She would not even think about that other family – even Giles. He had abandoned and betrayed her; there was nothing more she wanted to say to him – ever.

It was therefore a shock, and the last thing in the world that she expected, when she looked up from the counter, where she had been studying a stock sheet, at just after eleven o'clock on Friday morning and saw him standing there in front of her. Everything inside her turned over as he looked steadily into her eyes.

"Crystal, may I take you out to lunch, please?" She couldn't believe what she was hearing.

"No, Giles, you may not. Please go away and don't ever come back."

She spoke very softly and could hear the tremor in her voice. Her fingers gripped the edge of the counter and she could see Pat watching her out of the corner of her eye as she served a customer further down the department. In the other direction, Mrs. Johnson was re-arranging boxes of cosmetics on the shelves that went all the way up to the ceiling on the back wall.

"I can't go away, Crystal. I simply cannot leave things as they are. You don't understand….."

"I understand perfectly. What's not to understand about being dumped because of who I am?"

"That's where you've got it so wrong. Please give me a chance to explain."

Whether it was because Giles looked so genuinely sorry, or because Crystal saw Mrs. Johnson click-clacking in her direction, one eyebrow rising steadily as she registered Crystal talking to an attractive young man, who was clearly not looking at perfume samples, with customers piling up behind him, she was not sure. But Crystal heard herself muttering,

"OK. Meet me outside here at 12.30." Relief flooded Giles' face as, with a smile playing around the corners of his mouth, he made a small bow and walked quickly out of the department.

Jenny, who had been for her coffee, now appeared round the corner and together they dealt with the customers. Mrs. Johnson paused and stared hard at Crystal, who was by then attending so solicitously to a foreign gentleman, confused by the array of perfumes and anxious to get just the right one for his wife, that she decided not to say anything and walked briskly out of the department.

There was a lull and the other two crowded round her,

"Now, that's more like it. What a dish!" Pat turned to Jenny, "honestly, Jen, you should have seen the gorgeous man who came in here while you were at coffee and chatted Crystal up. Where did you find him? And has he got any brothers?"

'If you only knew…,'Crystal thought, but said, in quite a matter of fact voice,

"Oh him! He's just an ex. We're still good friends, though." Pat looked excited and patted her short, dark hair,

"Well, if you've finished with him, introduce me. I certainly wouldn't mind…."

"Sorry, he's already taken – girl friend at Oxford."

"Oxford! Terrific looking and brains too! Well, let me know if they break up, I'll be first in line."

They sat on the grassy bank that sloped down to the river in the grounds of King's College. Behind them the west elevation of the magnificent Chapel soared up against the blue sky and all around people were laughing and chatting in the sunshine. Crystal looked out across the Cam towards the backs, also dotted with people enjoying a lunch time stroll, and waited for Giles to speak. He had bought some sandwiches and cold drinks and was carefully laying them out on the grass between them.

At that moment in time Crystal had no idea how she could ever forgive him – if indeed forgiveness was what he was seeking – and just wanted to hear what he had to say, then leave and never see him again. If she was really honest she would have acknowledged that, in her heart of hearts, she was more than a little disturbed by his presence in a way that she simply didn't want to be. She turned towards him, shielding her eyes from the sun,

"Well?" Had she not felt quite justified in sounding so cold, she would have hated herself for it. Giles cleared his throat,

"I don't quite know how to say what I've got to say because I know I come out of it very badly, but I have to try. Crystal, when I got home after my party last year, my mother was distraught. She and Aunt Bette talked to me for a long time and the gist of it was that there was a reason why I absolutely must not see you again. I couldn't understand it and asked them to tell me why." He paused and rubbed his hand over his face before continuing, "It was then that Ma asked me to be patient with her and said that she needed time. She begged me to wait for a year without seeing or contacting you at all. I couldn't believe it, but she stressed that I must give myself time to 'get over' you. I told her that I wouldn't and she said I absolutely had to. She promised that after a year she would tell me why and that I would understand. She said that in the light of 'the truth' I would be thanking her." He put his head in his hands.

"They were so insistent – Bette as well as my mother – that by Sunday they had worn me down and I gave my word – no contact at all for a year. Then, of course, I found out, by accident – overhearing my lunatic brother harassing you – that all the fuss was about the fact that you are my cousin!" He turned and looked at Crystal. "What must you think of me. I can't believe now that I did it; the only thing I can say is that Ma seemed very near the edge…..oh bloody hell. Crystal, I am so sorry, so very sorry that I threw away something so special. I know I can't ask you to forgive me – I can't expect that – but you had to know the truth." He paused and looked straight into her eyes, "I loved you then.....I love you now...... I always will."

There were tears in his eyes as he got to his feet and walked away from her along the bank towards the bridge that led to the road at the back of the college.

Crystal hugged her knees and stared after the retreating figure, trying very hard to hate him. He had put his mother before her. He could have contacted her without Eleanore knowing. Then, to her amazement, she found herself experiencing a sort of admiration for what he had done and for the fact that he hadn't broken his promise or gone back on his word in any way. 'What kind of a man behaves like that?' She asked herself and the answer that came was 'an honourable one.'

Yes, she had been heart-broken, but it was obvious that Giles had truly believed his mother's life was in danger. He had said she was close to the edge and what with Bette at him as well...He had made a mistake, but wasn't he now putting her first by seeing her and explaining what had happened? He'd heard the truth and decided it was all a fuss about nothing. So what did he want of her? He had said he loved her but was too upset to wait for her response; he had just assumed that she would never forgive him.

"Weak, mummy's boy!"

She tried again, muttering into her knee caps, but it was no good; it didn't have the ring of truth.

She thought of Marjorie. To what lengths would she go for that gentle woman who had cared for her all her life? She tried to imagine her mother close to the edge, in a state about something, and she couldn't. Dear, good, sensible, down to earth Marjorie, practical and capable, always sure of what to do in every situation. It was then that Crystal realised, with a shock, that she was, indeed, very different from her adoptive mother and deep down she had always known that she was different She thought, a little fearfully, about the strange family to whom she discovered she was, apparently, related. Was she 'highly strung' like Matt. had said they were just before she had met Geoffrey? Or maybe she had inherited something more down to earth from her 'guttersnipe' father – whoever he may be.

Giles was over the bridge now and heading for the road. She leapt up, grabbed the uneaten lunch which she threw into the nearest rubbish bin and ran along the path after him.

CHAPTER THIRTEEN

August

"Honestly, Minty, everything's happened so fast my head is absolutely spinning."

Crystal sat on her friend's bed with hands clasped and looked again at the tiny diamond ring on the gold chain hanging round her neck. Minty grinned,

"So it's really going to work out this time, is it?"

"Well, Giles has asked his mother and Aunt Bette to have drinks ready at seven tomorrow evening and all he has said is that he has something very important to tell them. Bette is arriving at about six – she got back from Malta last weekend and Giles' mother asked her to stay so that they can catch up with each other's gossip. Rosemary will be out; Giles is not sure about Clive, but since the business in the stable he steers pretty clear of his younger brother and will stay out of the drawing room if he knows he's not wanted."

"What about Giles' dad?"

"Away at a conference, so you see we think we've chosen the best time to make our announcement – first of all just to those two before we tell the rest of the family."

Crystal was glowing with happiness but Minty was still a bit doubtful about the whole situation. She had gasped with astonishment when she'd heard about Evelyn being Crystal's mother and was livid when Crystal told her, in the strictest confidence, about the way Clive had behaved in the stable.

"You nutcase! Fancy going down there to meet that perve on your own. You should have let me go with you, I'd have smacked him so hard in the balls with a stick he would never have bothered any woman ever again."

"Yes, thanks Minty. Graphic as ever."

There were things that Crystal hadn't told even Minty, like the way Giles had looked when she had caught up with him that day by the river and had told him that she loved him. They had both cried then, clinging together under the trees, just another pair of lovers in the sunshine.

In the days that followed Crystal knew she had some very serious thinking to do. Giles had told her that he couldn't imagine life without her and had asked her to marry him. She had said yes. They had discussed the fact that they shouldn't have children, but both agreed that it was a sacrifice they were prepared to make to be together. They had talked endlessly, working out how to handle the situation.

Giles had assured her repeatedly that nothing was now going to be allowed to stand in their way,

"You do believe me, don't you, darling, from now on I am putting us first." And she knew beyond all doubt that she could trust him.

Crystal had agonised over how to tell Marjorie and George. The turn of events meant that it was no longer possible to keep from them the truth about her parentage, but she had no idea how to go about telling them. She didn't want them to know about Clive's behaviour in the stable; George had been diagnosed as suffering from high blood pressure and she didn't want to do or say anything that would upset him. How would they feel about her being with Giles again, particularly in the new circumstances? Would they believe that he was trustworthy?

In the end she decided that she had to take the same risk as Giles; he was putting their love before everything else; she would do the same. So one Sunday evening at the end of July she had asked her parents to sit down in the lounge and quietly told them the whole story. She glossed over the business in the stable by saying that Giles' brother had taken the trouble to meet with her and had told her about Evelyn being her mother, producing the diary and some other papers as evidence. Marjorie had gone very pale at this point, but continued to listen in silence while Crystal told them about her reconciliation with Giles and the fact that they wanted to get married. She didn't say so, but she knew that Giles was going to see George formally and ask his permission to marry her as soon as the Cowper family had been put in the picture. George would like that. When she had finished Marjorie quietly thanked her for telling them the truth and said it was a pity she hadn't known all this while Evelyn was alive.

Crystal frowned and said nothing as one of the strangest things about the whole revelation was that she hadn't felt that at all. She simply couldn't think of Evelyn as her mother and was secretly glad that she hadn't had to acknowledge her in that role. George had asked when they wanted to get married and what they were going to live on. Proudly Crystal told them that Giles had already secured the position of manager on a farm in the next village. The owner was a gentleman farmer who had taken a fancy to Rosemary and was therefore only too pleased to lend a helping hand to her younger brother. They were a little disappointed that Crystal was no longer planning to go to college – her 'A' level results had been good and her place confirmed – but they understood that she and Giles wanted to be together and married as soon as possible,

"We will set the actual date after we have told his family," she said, brightly and hoped that, like George and Marjorie, no-one in the Cowper family would express disappointment that grandchildren would have to come from a source other than Giles and Crystal.

Giles was calling for her at 6.45. She dressed carefully, taming her long, red curls as best she could and watched with shining eyes while Marjorie fastened the crystal round her neck. She frowned.

"You don't think it's too much – you know – too flamboyant with this outfit?"

"No, darling, it looks lovely. Trust me." And Marjorie kissed the top of her head.

Giles was on time and they sped along the village street in his little red car.

"Ready?"

She smiled,

"Yes, I'm ready."

He ushered her gently through the front door and together they walked towards the drawing room.

Crystal knew she would never forget what happened next. The events, in perfect sequence, were destined to play in her head like a film until the day she died.

Giles lifted the latch then stood back to let her walk through first. She felt nervous as she took a step into the room, then Giles was at her side, his hand in hers, and she was looking straight at Eleanore who was by a drinks table on the other side of the room. As she saw Crystal, she went deathly white and froze to the spot; her mouth opened and the decanter she was holding slipped from her fingers and smashed into pieces on the polished wood floor. Bette flew to her side immediately, manoeuvring her swiftly into a nearby chair then she grabbed a folded cloth from the drinks tray and threw it over the splintered glass, successfully halting the progress of the widening patch of red that was seeping towards the edge of the carpet. Eleanore was gasping, as if trying to speak, but no words would come. Bette poured some water into a glass from a nearby jug and gave it to her sister who took a few sips and started to breathe more easily. She looked at her son,

"Giles, what are you doing?"

"Mother, please don't be so melodramatic. Crystal and I are together; we want to get……" Eleanore put her hands over her ears,

"Giles….Giles, you said you knew….you can't…." She spoke with difficulty and looked as though she couldn't believe what she was seeing.

Giles stood up very straight and spoke clearly,

"Don't start all that stuff again. I do know," he glanced at Crystal, "We both know all about Evelyn being her mother and that we are cousins. We know what that means and we still…"

"What on earth are you talking about? What are you saying?" In desperation Eleanore looked at her sister,

"Bette I thought you had told him."

"No, darling, I didn't tell him. I thought you were going to…."

"But, Giles, you said you knew the truth…" Giles looked a little less sure of himself but his voice remained steady.

"And I do. Clive found a diary in Evelyn's room all about the little girl she had and…"

Suddenly Eleanore's face went white with fury.

"Clive!"

She leapt to her feet, covering the distance between her chair and the door with remarkable speed. It had been left ajar and she threw it open, grabbed a retreating Clive by the shoulder and pushed him into the room. Crystal recoiled in disbelief and Bette gasped as Eleanore slapped her eldest son viciously twice across his face as hard as she could. He whimpered and slunk back, falling against the arm of a sofa as he clutched his stinging cheek. Eleanore lunged towards him again, but Bette stopped her.

"Of all the devious, mischief-making, evil-doers I have ever met, you are the worst. You have no idea how it grieves a mother to feel loathing towards a child she has borne and you do not yet know the damage you have done. Your sneaking around and poking into other people's business was always destined to do harm, but I never dreamt it would be like this."

She stopped and collapsed exhausted into a chair. Giles was unable to keep the tremor out of his voice as he asked,

"Mother what exactly is going on?"

Eleanore leaned back in the chair and sat quite still, breathing deeply, with one hand over her face. Without looking at him, she addressed her eldest son,

"Clive, leave the room. Get out. Go outside or upstairs, but do not listen outside this door. If you do," she looked up, "If you do, I will not be responsible for my actions."

Giving his mother a wide berth and keeping his eyes firmly fixed on the floor; Clive slid silently out of the room and closed the door.

Eleanore sat up and self possession settled around her shoulders like a mantle. She knew what she had to do and she faced the situation with admirable calm. She was about to inflict unbearable pain on the two people who meant more to her than they would ever know and there was nothing she could do to avoid it. It should have been told a year ago and couldn't be put off any longer. She motioned towards the sofa and Giles and Crystal sat down. Bette moved towards her sister and, standing behind her chair, reached down and took her hand. With immense dignity Eleanore looked at her beloved youngest son and the girl at his side and said,

"Giles, Crystal is not your cousin. She is your sister."

No-one moved. In the silence that followed Crystal was conscious of a solitary bird singing outside the window, and the ticking of a clock on the mantelpiece was so loud it filled the room. Giles' and Crystal's hands had been entwined and quietly, as if by some unspoken mutual agreement, they unclasped them. Crystal simply couldn't take in what she had been told. It was surreal. She sat as still as stone, aware of her heart thudding against her chest as if trying to escape. Giles stood up and looked at his mother,

"Where…how….? This can't be….mother, this cannot be true." He put both arms against the mantelpiece and his body sagged. Bette, sensing that her sister was in control, sat down and looked at the floor. Eleanore turned towards Giles' where he still stood slumped against the mantelpiece,

"Please sit down, Giles. I will tell you both everything."

Obediently he sat again on the sofa, but both he and Crystal were conscious of keeping a space between them. In that moment, with the uttering of four words, the world had turned upside down and changed for ever. Suddenly Crystal found her voice though she could manage no more than a hoarse whisper as she gasped,

"You cannot be my mother….you cannot…" she sobbed and looked down, putting her hands over her face. Eleanore's voice was steady,

"Crystal look at me." She waited, but Crystal kept her face covered.

"Please."

She looked up, into the face that she now saw was so similar to her own – the same green eyes, the same shape, the pale complexion.

"But my hair…..you haven't got my hair."

"I will tell you where you get that from. I will tell you the whole story. I am so very sorry. I would have done anything to prevent the pain that this revelation has caused. Bette please pour everyone a drink and I will tell you both the truth."

CHAPTER FOURTEEN

Eleanore's story

"Although I am your mother, my dear, William, my husband is not your father. Please believe everything I am about to tell you because it is all true. One of the reasons I asked you, Giles, to give me time was so that I could check and double check all the facts – and this I did. Part of me was full of joy to have discovered my lost baby daughter, but, because of the relationship between the two of you, I was praying that somehow it would turn out not to be true. This didn't happen. You are my daughter and your father is John Elliott, my childhood sweetheart and the love of my life. Yes, I'm sorry, Giles, it's true; William, your father is a good man but I married him on the rebound when I thought that I couldn't marry John, or Jack as we all called him. But I must start at the beginning.

The Elliott family lived at Savron Pinder House – some of them still do – and we lived at Manor Farm. When we were children we were often taken there to play as there are extensive grounds with a lake and woods. Generally speaking, we got on well, apart from the usual ups and downs that are normal when you are very young. Jack was a year older than me and the eldest of three, having two sisters, Mary and Emily. Because of our ages, it worked out that Evelyn, Jack, Claude, Mary and I played together while the three youngest, Geoffrey, Emily, and then Bette when she came along, toddled about on the lawn with the nannies most of the time, from what I can remember.

We had the most marvellous fun, rowing about on the lake in boats we had made ourselves, playing cowboys and Indians in the woods and making secret dens. We even made a tree house and were allowed to have picnics there or by the lake. It was a magical childhood and Jack was always the one who thought of the best things to do. He was the leader, the cleverest of us all; any boat that he made never sank and he was the one who designed the tree house. I adored him and followed him in everything he did. We were best friends and would often laugh and joke together, staying out later than the others, taking more risks and, of course, getting into more trouble. Evelyn, who was the eldest, used to get cross with us, but Jack could even charm her into not telling the grown ups where we were until we would magically appear, pretending to have been in the garden room, or somewhere equally innocuous, all the time.

Every year a fete was held at Savron Pinder House. It was a sort of hangover from Edwardian times when it was traditional for the people who owned the grandest house in the village to open the grounds for a bazaar which could be enjoyed by everyone. I particularly remember the one held in 1921. Jack was twelve and I was eleven and we were going round and taking part in everything – having a whale of a time. Jack was the star of 'tip the man off the log' – nobody could beat him – and as I was watching him whack his opponents with a pillow and knock them onto the straw, I glanced up and saw a strange looking girl staring at him. Evelyn told me that she was the daughter of the new estate manager that Mr. Elliott had just hired and that her name was Wendy Wetherall. Anyway she kept staring at Jack and she looked really odd with weird eyes, but then I thought no more about her as Jack retired unbeaten from the game and we flew off to try something else.

It was about half an hour later that we decided to go away from the crowds, down to the lake and check that our boat was alright. As we got near the water's edge we could hear screaming coming from the little wooded copse nearby. We ran to investigate and saw a group of village boys – four I think there were – threatening Wendy with sticks and calling her names. They were shouting things like, 'Windy Wetherall, come on Windy…let's see what colour knickers you've got on…..P'raps the ol' wind'll blow that skirt right up over yer 'ed….or I'll do it with me stick.' Wendy was cowering back against a tree, whimpering and screaming for help by turns. The boys thought they were quite safe as they were well away from the fair and they didn't think anyone could hear her for all the noise of the band and general merriment.

Jack didn't hesitate; he just marched in, grabbed the sticks from the startled lads and drove them away. He told them to clear off and said that if he saw them again that afternoon he would get his dad to call the police. And off they went. I hovered in the background as he picked Wendy up from where she was sitting, sobbing, against the tree with her head in her hands. He helped her to dust herself off and even gave her his hanky to blow her nose on. She stammered her thanks and for some reason felt compelled to tell him why they called her windy,

'They say I'm a windbag….a bossy windbag…but…. I…I'm not…I'm not…'

Years after I was told that she was sure she saw me laughing when she said this and it was from that moment she developed a huge crush on Jack – which actually became quite obsessive – and started to hate me with a passion."

Eleanore paused as Giles got up to refill his glass and his mother saw from his face that he was unable to understand why this incident from her childhood had any relevance to the current situation. She continued,

"Believe me, Giles, I will only include things which have a bearing on our predicament and Wendy Wetherall's feelings do contribute to the events that followed.

Our childhood idyll came to an end as the boys were sent away to school and we all, in our various ways, started to grow up. Inevitably we grew apart and would only meet on fairly formal social occasions. We were still friends but it was different; the innocence of childhood had gone and, of course, we saw each other differently.

Jack and I fell deeply in love and were planning to get married, but in January 1930 he was asked by his father to go with him to India where he had some business that needed attention. Jack didn't want to leave me, but knew that if he managed to help his father sort out the problem there would be a lot of money in it for him – enough for us to get married and set ourselves up here with a substantial estate. It made sense for him to go so, even though it was a wrench for both of us, he went, promising to write once a week at least. The day before he left he took me out and, after a wonderful dinner, put a blue velvet bag into my hand inside which was an exquisite crystal on a silver chain."

Crystal swallowed hard and fingered the jewel at her throat.

"He said it was a token of his love for me and that when he returned from India we would be together for ever.

The weeks passed and no letter arrived. Weeks turned to months; the months became nearly a year and a half and still there was no word from Jack, not even a post card. I would have spoken to his mother, but she had shut up the house and was travelling with her daughters. They were in London for the season, during which Mary came out, and then they travelled all over Europe. Arthur Elliott was still in India with Jack. I was distraught. There was no-one I could turn to.

It was a Saturday at the end of May 1931 when one of our maids knocked on my bedroom door and said there was a girl down in the kitchen who had some news that they both thought I ought to hear. I really wasn't very interested but said that I would be down in ten minutes and that she could be shown into the morning room. They stood there, side by side, our maid, Janice and her friend, who looked very nervous.

"Come along, Maud; tell Miss Lynton-Bell what you know."

The girl cleared her throat and began,

"Well, madam, my cousin works in London for a family what knows of the Elliott's what live 'ere in the village – when they aren't travelling that is." My heart turned over at the mention of the name and I urged the girl to tell me what she knew. She said that Mr Arthur and his whole family had been celebrating because Mr. Jack had got married to a beautiful girl that he had met in India. I froze and Janice ushered her friend out of the room. She returned a few minutes later, said how sorry she was and asked if there was anything she could do.

I was absolutely heart-broken. I grieved for a long time but then I knew I had to make a life for myself that didn't include Jack. On New Year's Eve in 1932 I was persuaded to go to a party where I met William Cowper. I found him very attentive, caring and sincere and in April I agreed to marry him. The wedding was in September and the following June 1933 Rosemary was born, then Clive arrived two years later. We were living in Oxford until the Second World War broke out, then we moved back here and bought Monk's Manor where you were born in 1940, Giles. I had lost contact with the Elliott family and Savron Pinder House was being used to accommodate the land girls, but someone in the village did say that Jack had joined the army.

Then in 1943 he came home. I hadn't seen him for thirteen years and suddenly there he was, standing in front of me. It was a hot July day; you were three years old, Giles, and I was taking you for a walk. You were pushing one of those stuffed animals on wheels that you had been given for your birthday and we had just reached the top of the drive when you tripped up. I bent down, wiped your grazed knees and dried your tears, then as I stood up I saw Jack just standing there looking at me. We were both speechless and then he asked, rather coldly, why I hadn't answered any of his letters. I couldn't believe what I was hearing and, of course, told him that I hadn't received any. He told me that he had written every week for two years until he received a letter from a 'well-wisher' telling him that I had married someone else. He looked at you, Giles, and said, 'I see that my information was correct.' I told him that I hadn't married for over two and a half years and then only because I was told that he had married a girl he had met in India. He looked at me and said, very quietly, that he wasn't married; that he had never married."

Eleanore took a sip of her drink and sighed before continuing,

"I will tell the rest of the story quite briefly. It turned out that the maid, Janice, was none other than Wendy Wetherall. She had changed her name

143

because of all the teasing and I didn't recognise the smart, rather severe looking young woman who applied to work for us as the same snivelling child from the day of the fete ten years before. She knew that Jack was in love with me and that she could never have him, but was determined that I wouldn't either; so she intercepted, read, and destroyed all his letters. She then bullied her friend into lying about his marriage and engineered the letter telling him of mine – even though I was still single at that point.

When Jack and I realised what had happened we were utterly devastated. Jack had to return to active service, but before he did we spent one glorious night together, the happiest of my entire life and you, Crystal, were the result." Eleanore paused again, close to tears, and Crystal took the opportunity to ask,

"Where is my father now?"

"I'm coming to that, my dear. When he returned to his platoon we didn't know that you were on the way, but we vowed that somehow we would be together when the war ended. Then I found out that I was pregnant and William knew it couldn't possibly be his as, after meeting Jack again, I wouldn't have my husband anywhere near me. He found out the truth and was absolutely furious; he hit me so hard that I fell to the floor then he said I was to go away and stay with Evelyn in London until after the baby was born. If I kept it I would never see my other three children again; if I had it adopted, I could return home but must never ever contact or have anything to do with the child. It was a terrible decision to have to make, but I was determined that somehow I would keep Jack's child and get my other children as well; when Jack returned we would work it out together.

Then the telegram arrived. Jack was killed in March 1944. The day after I heard that he was dead I went into labour and gave birth to you, Crystal, on the nineteenth of March knowing that I had no future unless I gave you away. With Jack gone my life had to be with my other three children."

Eleanore stopped speaking and Bette gave her a drink of water. She continued,

"Evelyn and Bette were both with me when you were born. I knew I had to part with you and it broke my heart. Evelyn was strong and decisive, of course, but Bette," she paused and smiled at her younger sister, "Bette brought you in so that I could hold you for a moment. I felt such love for you, Crystal. I managed to tuck the package containing the crystal into the folds of your baby garments before Bette took you away – the crystal you are wearing this evening.

There are one or two more twists to this sad tale then it's over. By the time we found out about

Janice's treachery she had been promoted to housekeeper at Manor Farm and then wormed her way into Claude's affections to the extent that he had married her. When my mother discovered what she was really like she threw her out of the house. Initially Claude went with her and they set up home together, but it didn't last.

I also found out after I had married William that he is Janice's brother. I didn't know this as their parents had split up and William had stayed with his mother, taking her name. There was no way that I could have connected the quiet, reserved man I married with Wendy Wetherall. Sadly I have to admit that Clive has inherited much of his aunt's character.

The information he unearthed from Evelyn's room was true. She was raped and she did have a daughter in the December of 1944 but the child was stillborn – a fact she had difficulty acknowledging and probably would not have written in the diary. I can only assume that the entries in the diary are ambiguous and that the references to losing her daughter were misinterpreted by Clive."

Eleanore rose stiffly and walked to a desk on the opposite side of the room. She opened a drawer and took out something that had obviously been hidden there under a pile of papers. She went over to Crystal and put a large piece of card in her hand. It was covered with a flap of tissue paper which Crystal lifted and gasped. It was the portrait of a beautiful woman with a pale complexion and a mass of dark red curls. Eleanore spoke again,

"That's Constance Elliott, Jack's mother, your grandmother; one of the most wonderful women I have ever met.

So there you have the full story; I am so, so sorry." She stopped speaking and sat back in her chair exhausted.

It was difficult to believe that less than an hour had passed since Eleanore had started telling her story. Outside it was still a summer evening and the birds were singing their last songs of the day. The sun had dipped down below the horizon and soon the sky would begin to darken. There was silence in the room as Giles sat forward on the sofa and looked at Crystal. She turned towards him and was startled by the expression she saw on his face. It was blank. There were no words to describe the shock they had both received, but she was deeply disturbed by the expression on the face of the man she loved…the man she must now learn to love as a brother. How could she do that?

Before she could think any more, Giles leaned towards her and kissed her on the cheek then looked long and hard into her face before getting up and walking out of the room.

The three women heard the engine start and a second later the sound of the little red sports car disappearing up the drive. It was Bette who spoke,

"Poor darling; he needs to be alone for a while."

Crystal was frozen to the spot. She wondered many times afterwards why she hadn't leapt out of her chair and jumped into the car with him, but she just sat, her heart pounding. Then she heard herself saying,

"I need to be by myself too."

She stood up and in spite of protests from Eleanore and Bette, insisted on walking home alone. Eleanore touched her arm,

"Take care, Crystal. I will telephone Marjorie in the morning. We must talk."

And so it was that Crystal, walking on her own through the village street in the twilight, heard, in the distance, the sound of a police car siren followed by the loud, clanging bell of an ambulance. It was almost midnight when the telephone rang in Maple Cottage. Unable to sleep, Crystal had gone down to answer it and it was Bette's voice on the other end. It was Bette who, sobbing so much she could hardly speak, told her that her brother, Giles, was already dead when he had been cut from the wreckage of his little red sports car.

CHAPTER FIFTEEN

Feverish…sweaty…cold…clammy…"Ican't breathe…I can't breathe…" Soothing words, kind faces, swimming about like huge jellyfish, bulging and distorted; rubber balls being squeezed…lost in a strange twilight, an underwater world of green darkness. Murmured voices…faces…eyes…"help me! Help me out!" A hand…then lost…down again…down, down, down. It's cold, murky…there's no way out…I can't get out. Floating…drifting…

For two weeks following Giles's death Crystal was confined to bed with a fever. She was lost to the world, trapped in a sea of pain and confusion, barely conscious most of the time, thrashing around, clammy with sweat and calling out in a sleep which was clearly deeply troubled. Marjorie and George hovered anxiously over her and James Robertson, the doctor, called several times.

"It's shock. There's only so much any human being can take and your daughter has been pushed beyond what she can endure. The body is simply shutting down to try and let her recuperate. I'll give her something to bring her temperature down, but there's really nothing more we can do. Just give her plenty of fluids and keep bathing her forehead with cold, wet towels. Call me day or night if she gets any worse."

Sick with worry, George and Marjorie took it in turns to sit by Crystal's bed. They managed to coax fluids into her and even, occasionally, a little soup but for most of the time she seemed unaware that they were there.

Then, quite suddenly, the fever left her. She sat up, feeling very weak, and Marjorie gently hugged her, handing her a drink which she sipped gratefully. She felt the cold liquid slipping down her throat like ice and tried to think. She couldn't remember anything; for a few blessed moments her mind was a blank and then...Oh God...Giles...Giles is... She spluttered and Marjorie quickly took the glass from her hand. Crystal's fingers scrabbled at the sheet in front of her and she started moaning softly, hot tears streaming down her face. Marjorie held her shoulders, so thin and frail, as she sobbed, her body shaking; then she lay back on the pillows, exhausted and Marjorie held her hand,

"My darling, I'm so sorry. I can't take any of the pain away. I can't make things better for you but I'm here when you want to talk."

But Crystal couldn't talk. She lay and stared at the wall for hours. Even when she became well enough to get out of bed and sit in a chair downstairs she still stared at the wall, tears streaming silently down her cheeks. She remembered the phone call, Bette's voice telling her what had happened, then she had passed out, sliding down the wall onto the tiled floor with the phone still in her hand. After that she remembered nothing until she woke up in bed a fortnight later.

She could, however, remember with crystal clarity, everything that had happened during the evening before the phone call. She saw it running before her like a film, sobbing and choking with the pain of it all; she cried until she couldn't cry any more each time she remembered again that Giles was dead. She saw the little car, mangled and broken, tortured herself with visions of Giles' body crushed in amongst the metal. Her head throbbed until she thought it would burst and she would go mad with the weight and pain of it all.

Gradually, very slowly Crystal began to recover her strength. College was out of the question; all she could manage for the first couple of months were short walks down the fens accompanied by a solicitous George or Marjorie and the rest of the time she spent sitting in a chair quietly reading. She didn't know it then, but George's blood pressure had become dangerously high. He was unable to work, but instead of burdening Crystal with the truth, he told her he had taken some holiday he was owed to help look after her.

She knew that Giles' funeral had taken place while she was ill in bed, but refused to allow herself to think beyond that fact. She was numb; simply couldn't feel anything at all. It was as if she had put Giles, Eleanore and everything to do with those families into a box and fastened down the lid. She refused to let them out, wouldn't acknowledge their existence. She stayed in a little world of her own, eating, sleeping, reading and walking, hugging it round her and shutting everything else out.

Christmas was uneventful and the Morris family slid quietly into a new year. The months of January and February in 1963 were very cold with bitter winds, iron-hard frost and snow billowing across the fens, drifting into huge white banks, making travel difficult. George struggled to work every day but he was clearly not well and decided to retire early on the grounds of ill-health. March and the first signs of spring saw George driving back from the factory on the outskirts of Cambridge for the last time and Crystal venturing out again into the world of work.

Two days after her nineteenth birthday she started working full time at the store in Cambridge where she had been employed as a Saturday girl. It wasn't much but it was a start. She took her place in the queue every morning then climbed onto the old brown and white bus. At first she made herself stare straight ahead when she passed the driveway leading down to Monk's Manor, then again a few hundred yards further on where the huge iron gates and high wall enclosed the grounds surrounding the palatial Savron Pinder House. She made herself think of something else, something prosaic – a bit of gossip from the other girls at the store, shopping, the evening meal – anything to stop her from thinking…wondering.

Gradually, however, her thoughts did begin to turn again to the family at Monk's Manor. Eleanore – beautiful, exquisite, elegant Eleanore – her mother. Crystal knew it was true; she felt it in a way she had never felt when Clive had said that she was Evelyn's daughter. She knew that the rather fragile, yet steely, Eleanore with the beautiful green eyes was her mother. And what of her father – the dashing Jack Elliott – handsome, brave, clever and strong – the leader of the group. What must he have been like?

It was with a shock that she realised she was the living link between the two most prominent families in the area. And what about Constance Elliott? Did she still live at Savron Pinder House? It was all surreal. She had two grandmothers, one grandfather and two aunts, Mary and Emily, whom she had never met. Geoffrey, Claude and Bette were her uncles and aunt, and Rosemary and Clive her half brother and sister. Giles, of course, was....no. She couldn't think about Giles.

She rammed her fist hard up against her mouth and stared out of the bus window. There was a lump inside her again, something shut off...she dared not let it out. She must not open that box...she couldn't think about Giles yet.

The brakes of the bus squealed and it jolted to a halt. Crystal ran down the stairs and jumped lightly out into the spring sunshine to begin another day serving customers with face creams and bottles of perfume; another day when she could put all thoughts of families back in a place where they wouldn't bother her.

It was in June that George died. It happened quite suddenly, a massive stroke while he was pottering about in his beloved garden. One minute he was bending over a tub of geraniums and the next Marjorie heard a crash as he fell, clutching his chest. He was already dead when she reached him and Crystal returned home from the shop to find George removed to the undertakers and Marjorie sitting by the window, crying quietly, waiting for the sight of the brown and white bus that would bring her daughter home.

The house was very quiet that evening as they sat and talked about the man who had been father to one and husband to the other. They sobbed and comforted each other by turns, remembering little things about this unremarkable yet irreplaceable man.

"He may not have been my father, Mum, you know, my real father, but he was my…my dad – the dad who brought me up."

"I know, darling. He was very special; a very gentle man."

The funeral took place a week later in the village Church attended by many friends and relatives. Granny Bates, living alone now as her husband had died two years ago, had been brought on the train all the way from Eastbourne by Marjorie's younger sister, Paula; while Granny Morris was driven across the fens in an ancient Standard Vanguard by George's sister, Madge. She was angry and upset by turns, one minute grieving for the loss of her beloved son before his time, then raging because she should have been taken first.

She clung to Crystal with claw-like fingers, noisily blowing her nose and ramming her black beret back down onto her head as it threatened to blow off in the high wind at the graveside and join her son's coffin in the earth below. Crystal loved this feisty old lady who had taught her so much, and she found that focusing on her grief helped her to cope with her own. Marjorie and Paula looked after gentle Granny Bates and it was afterwards, during the simple tea at Maple Cottage, that Crystal overheard the three of them discussing something that alarmed her.

"....so I really don't think I can afford to go on living here." Marjorie was speaking quietly, biting her lip, a worried frown creasing her brow. Paula and her mother exchanged glances and Marjorie knew what they were thinking. They each had a flat on the seafront quite close to each other, but both were small – too small to accommodate anyone else.

"I wish you could come and live with me but...."

Marjorie put her hand on her sister's arm,

"I know, dear, you haven't any room."

Her mother spoke next, clearly worried about her eldest daughter,

"Perhaps you could sell up and buy something near us." Marjorie continued to look worried,

"That would be nice, but this cottage is nowhere near paid for and even if I did sell I wouldn't have enough to buy on the South coast. The prices are so different from this area, I wouldn't even get a little one bedroom flat like yours. Then there's Crystal, I must think of her, she's had such a difficult time..." She stopped speaking as she caught sight of her daughter hovering nearby and went to her, concerned to see how she was coping.

Later, when everyone had gone, Crystal sat quietly by herself, thinking. She had been so wrapped up in her own grief, first for Giles and now for the man she had always known as the kindest father anyone could ever have, that she hadn't thought about Marjorie. What would her mum do? What did she want to do? And would she even consider her own wants or needs while she had Crystal to worry about and put first just as she had always done? She resolved to speak to Marjorie very soon about the future and with that resolve came strength.

She straightened her back and faced facts fairly and squarely. Giles was dead. She faltered a bit, but forced herself to go on. She had family in the village, blood relatives, but had no idea how they felt about her. She had a job which had only ever been a way of helping her to get out into the real world again. It wasn't a career and didn't pay enough money to help them stay at Maple Cottage. Even before talking to Marjorie she was fairly sure that George's illness and early retirement had meant they were not well off. She stopped thinking and sat back in her chair, realising that she had no idea how to help solve the problem of their future.

But help did come, and when it came it was from a source that shouldn't really have caused Crystal as much astonishment as it did. Three days after George's funeral a letter was hand delivered to Maple Cottage by a man who she recognised as one of the gardeners at Monk's Manor. He doffed his cap respectfully as Crystal answered the door and, having made sure of her identity, handed her a thick, white envelope.

"From the Manor, Miss, only to be given to Miss Crystal Morris. 'Tis from Mrs. Cowper and it's very important that you should have it."

Crystal thanked him as she took the envelope; her hand was shaking a little and her heart beating fast as the man touched his cap again then backed out of the porch before turning and crunching his way down the drive.

Marjorie was upstairs, just beginning the painful task of sorting through George's clothes. Crystal had been full of admiration for the fact that she could even think about facing this so soon, let alone make a start; but she should have known that Marjorie's down to earth approach to life wouldn't fail her even at a time like this.

"It has to be done, dear, and will get no easier with being put off – just the opposite, in fact."

She was so brave, but Crystal could see that it was with a heavy heart she had trudged purposefully up the stairs.

Crystal went into the sitting room and closed the door. She sat down and pulled the thick sheets of writing paper out of the envelope. Her hands were still shaking but, without giving herself time to think, she quickly unfolded the letter and started to read. The writing was firm, quite large and forward-sloping, the black ink a sharp contrast to the expensive, white paper:

My dear Crystal,

I have no idea how to begin writing this letter, but I know I must. There are things I have to say to you and I am aware that, by reaching out to you in this way, I am risking your rejection of me. I have to take that risk.

We have suffered the most terrible loss. Giles was a special son, increasingly precious to me in the light of the bad character displayed by his elder brother who has, since the evening of the terrible accident, taken it upon himself to disappear without trace. I shall not look for him. As I told you both on that last evening, I know what it's like to experience and lose a great love. I loved your father with a passion that I know would have sustained us through this life and beyond, but we were thwarted; it wasn't to be. And now your life has been blighted in the same way. I am guessing that you have been unable to think about Giles – that having cried until you are empty you have put him away inside you, afraid to think, afraid to go there for fear of what you will find, what it will do to you.

You will not thank me for saying this, Crystal, but I have to as I am your mother: Time will heal you. It has to. The wound will heal over, but it will never go away. There will always be a scar and you wouldn't have it any other way. That scar will be part of you for ever, but you will move on. I have met and seen you for such a short time, but I sense that you are a very strong person, much stronger than you can possibly know. You are the product of a great love and will have in you your father's courage and whatever few qualities I may possess.

I, too, am grieving and I'm in such pain at the loss of my darling son – a loss for which I feel so responsible; yet I have to try and tell myself that the circumstances were out of my control. I have searched my heart and it is important to me that you should know I do not in any way blame you for what happened.

Crystal, my dear girl, I cannot express in words the love I felt for you when your Aunt Bette put you in my arms for that brief moment on the day you were born. I felt my heart break when you were taken away, but I knew what I had to do. Life is like that sometimes – very, very hard. Not one day has gone past when I haven't thought of you and longed to see you. Never did I imagine that our meeting would be so tragic and cause the loss of one of the children I had to choose over you, or be the source of so much pain when all I ever desired was your well-being. What a cruel twist of fate. Your other mother, Marjorie, has kept me informed of your progress through the illness that struck you down following the tragedy; and now I understand you both have more pain to bear as your other father has died. I am so sorry, my dear. When I discovered who you were, I made it my business to find our more about your adoptive parents and I thank God that you were brought up by such lovely people.

Now I come to the practical part of this letter. Again I am partly guessing, but it may be that your adoptive father's death has left you both in difficult circumstances. Please don't look upon what I am about to offer you as charity – I can never repay Marjorie what I owe her for bringing you up, loving and nurturing you into the beautiful girl you are now. When I couldn't be anything to you, she was there and mere money can't pay for that – it is beyond price. But money happens to be what I have and I would deem it a great honour if you and Marjorie will allow me to help you now.

I made no contact with you on the occasion of your birthday in March as I knew you were still very fragile following your illness. I guessed you would not want to celebrate in any way and Marjorie confirmed this. However I would now like to make amends and offer you a birthday gift of a holiday in Italy. The Elliott family have a little house there near a beautiful beach and I happen to know that they will be delighted for you and Marjorie to use it. I have a lot to tell you regarding that side of your family and hope, if your reaction to this letter is favourable, to get the opportunity to talk to you before you go.

I shall speak to Marjorie, of course, but I wanted to know, first of all that you were not against the idea. If you do go, Maple Cottage will be well looked after in your absence and I would also like to talk to Marjorie about securing the cottage for her so that you can both stay there on your return with no financial worries.

Please, dear Crystal, allow me to do these things for you. I cannot reach back into the past and change anything that has happened. Please allow me to make things easier for you both now. I hope, and indeed pray, that this may be the beginning of us getting to know each other and I wait, in some anxiety, for your reply.

Your loving mother,

Eleanore Cowper.

Crystal let the papers fall into her lap and stared out of the sitting room window. She felt tears pricking behind her eyes and swallowed a lump that had risen in her throat, but she didn't cry. She read over and over again the words, 'your loving mother' and thought about the woman upstairs. Should she hate Eleanore for what had happened? But how could she? If it were not for Eleanore she wouldn't be here. If it were not for Eleanore and Jack, Marjorie and George wouldn't have had a daughter. How did she feel about the fact that Marjorie and Eleanore had been communicating with each other during her illness? She didn't really know anything much about Eleanore yet, but smiled to herself as she imagined Marjorie answering the phone and speaking to Eleanore, quietly talking, building bridges, thinking all the time at the back of her mind that she was doing it for her beloved daughter, the daughter that had been given in to her loving care perhaps only until her real mother came along.

'Marjorie Morris doesn't have a selfish bone in her body, so maybe it's time I started thinking about someone else instead of myself,' and with that thought Crystal went to the bottom of the stairs and called her mum.

CHAPTER SIXTEEN

The meeting at Savron Pinder House was strange indeed. Eleanore had been delighted when Crystal had phoned her and said yes she and Marjorie were interested in what she was proposing.

"That's wonderful news, my dear. I wonder....I mean....I hope it's not too soon to suggest another very important meeting for you." Eleanore waited, but in the light of Crystal's silence at the other end of the phone, she plucked up courage and continued,

"I know that Constance and Arthur Elliott would love to meet you. I have, in secret, kept in very close contact with them and – I do hope you don't mind, my dear – but I have told them all about you. They are absolutely thrilled to know that they have a granddaughter, that somehow, through you they have a part of Jack still living...Oh dear, I'm afraid that sounds very dramatic, but you see they have no other grandchildren and the way things are going...well..."

Eleanore stopped speaking, feeling she may already have said too much about a family Crystal didn't yet know.

Crystal hesitated, but only for a moment. Following the receipt of the letter she was determined not to run away from anything. She steeled herself to embrace her future whatever it might be and that meant facing up, fairly and squarely, to who she really was. If Arthur and Constance were her real grandparents then she would meet them; she had hesitated only because she was intrigued by Eleanore's use of the words 'in secret' in relation to her contact with the Elliott family. There was no time to ponder further on this as day and time of the meeting were agreed with Marjorie and there followed a quick call by Eleanore to Savron Pinder House. It was decided that they would go there for tea at three o'clock in the afternoon of the first Saturday in July. And it was with some trepidation on that day that Crystal and Marjorie set out to make the short journey through the village to the gates of the large house on its outskirts.

Arm in arm they walked down the long, winding drive then both stood stock still as the house came suddenly into view. The sun was shining on the cream-coloured stone and danced off the blue water of the lake that nestled nearby in the rolling grounds surrounding the building. The ends of the house were rounded and there were lots of windows along the front with a stone balustrade and a pathway from the centre leading down to the lake and woods – the lake where her mother and Jack had played….the woods where the seeds of Wendy

Wetherall's twin passions of love and hate were first sown and were to seal the fate of so many people.

It was the grandest house Crystal had ever seen and she was struck by the incongruity of such a magnificent building on the edge of the fens. The stone must have been imported at great expense and the gardens expertly landscaped to achieve the rolling effect on what was naturally flat ground. The two women looked at each other but said nothing as they continued their walk up to the front door. Crystal pulled a square piece of metal and a bell jangled somewhere inside the house. The door was opened by a young girl dressed in a black dress with a white cap and apron. She smiled,

"Mrs. Morris and Miss Crystal Morris?" She glanced from one to the other and Crystal nodded.

"Do come in. Mr. and Mrs. Elliott are expecting you."

She led them down a wide hallway and tapped lightly on a door leading off to the left.

"Your visitors, Sir….Ma'am," with a small curtsey she took one step to the side to allow Crystal and Marjorie to pass, then she left the room, closing the door quietly behind her.

The whole thing was like something from a bygone age and this impression was enhanced by the décor of the room which was the most exquisitely elegant Crystal had ever seen. Before she had the chance to look around and take it all in, her attention was caught and held by the tall, slim woman who had risen to her feet as they entered the room and was standing in front of her. Her hands were tightly clasped and she was holding herself very straight; thinking about it afterwards Crystal was sure that for a few seconds she had actually stopped breathing. She just stood, staring at Crystal, and then let out a long breath,

"Jack's daughter…"

An elderly man was struggling to lift himself up out of an arm chair and the woman standing, who Crystal knew must be Constance, motioned to him to remain seated, all the while keeping her eyes fixed on Crystal's face. He sank down again, puffing slightly, and it was then that Crystal saw Eleanore standing near the window, the sweep of lawn and distant, sparkling lake stretching out behind her. She stepped forward,

"Constance…Arthur this is Marjorie Morris and….Crystal….mine and Jack's daughter."

She had hesitated after Crystal's name and there was a catch in her voice as she finished the sentence in a hushed whisper, glancing anxiously at Marjorie, hoping, Crystal guessed, that her words were not causing her adoptive mum any pain. Marjorie

169

remained composed, her face without expression as she stepped forward to shake hands with Arthur and Constance. As their fingers touched she smiled and murmured,

"I'm very pleased to meet you."

"And I, you"

The old man looked down, still trying to regain his breath, but Constance's eyes only left Crystal's face for a moment as she greeted Marjorie. Then they were back, fixed on her granddaughter as though she wanted to drink in and memorise every tiny aspect of the girl who stood before her. As Constance dropped Marjorie's hand to move forward, Crystal saw the sun glinting on the coils of hair wound up on top of her head and in amongst the grey there were strands of shining copper. Green eyes looked deeply into hers and her hands were caught and squeezed in the older woman's long, slim fingers.

"Crystal….I can't begin to tell you what this meeting means to me…" There were tears in her eyes and she couldn't continue to speak. Eleanore took her gently by the arm,

"Some tea perhaps, Constance?" She said softly and the older woman recovered herself,

"Yes, of course, how rude of me." She walked across the room and pulled a piece of fabric that Crystal knew from watching old films would make a bell ring in the kitchen. They all sat down and a few minutes later tea arrived, the fussing with tiny sandwiches, teacups, milk and sugar providing a welcome diversion.

By the time they left, Marjorie and Crystal had accepted the invitation to go to the house in Italy at the beginning of August and stay for just over two months, returning to England in the middle of October. Eleanore had taken Marjorie quietly down to the other end of the room and, Crystal learned later, had insisted on buying Maple Cottage outright with the understanding that Marjorie would live there, at no expense, for the rest of her life.

The afternoon had a strange, fairytale quality about it as if they were all caught in a spell; it was a good feeling and it continued until just before Crystal and Marjorie stood up to leave. The door opened suddenly and a woman stood on the threshold. She was of stocky build with short, iron-grey hair and was dressed very plainly in a grey skirt topped by a pale lemon twin set. She kept a firm grip on the door handle as her eyes swept round the room, eyes that were hard and set in a face that wore a grim expression, the thin lips turned down at the corners betraying the fact that this was a fairly permanent look for these plain features.

"Am I to take it that we have guests for dinner, and if so why…?"

The voice was harsh and unpleasant and before she could continue Constance interrupted her,

"No, Mary. Our guests, who have just taken tea with us, are preparing to leave. If they were staying for dinner, you would, of course have been informed."

Constance's voice was firm and she looked straight at her daughter, her eyes glinting dangerously. For a moment there was silence then, in an attempt to lighten the atmosphere again she indicated Crystal and began,

"Mary, this is…"

"I know who she is," Mary threw the words rudely across the room at her mother, then, with a malevolent glance at Crystal, turned and walked out as abruptly as she had arrived.

There was a stunned silence as the door closed then Constance turned to her guests,

"I apologise for my daughter's rudeness. I am so sorry and hope it hasn't spoiled your afternoon."

Crystal's heart went out to this kind, gentle lady and she suddenly felt a bond with her grandmother; she could see why there was such a strong friendship between her and Eleanore. They both possessed fine qualities, the ability to act with dignity, remaining ladylike, yet not being phased or thrown by rough, rude behaviour. As she reassured Constance that the afternoon had been lovely and remained quite unspoilt she wondered if she too had been lucky enough to inherit this core of hidden strength. It was perhaps a good thing that she didn't know, at this point in her life, how much she was going to need it.

CHAPTER SEVENTEEN

August

The sun, large and red, sank slowly down into the water as the waves rippled onto the beach and the scent of pine needles filled the air. Crystal let the warm sand trickle through her fingers, drinking in the sights and sounds of early evening; the lapping of the water, insects buzzing, scraping and clicking – sounds impossibly large for such tiny creatures; lovers strolling; dogs splashing in and out of the foam, their tongues lolling and silly dog-grins on their faces.

Soon she would stroll back up the beach and along the sandy track to where the little wooden house nestled in amongst the pine trees. She knew that Marjorie would be on the balcony watching for her, trying not to seem anxious, bending her head quickly back over her knitting as soon as she saw Crystal as though she hadn't been looking down the track at all. The holiday was doing them both so much good, the heat of the sun helping to breathe warmth and life back into two women grieving for men they had loved.

The beginning of July had been significant for Crystal, not only because she had met her grandparents for the first time, but also because it had been Giles' birthday. On the actual day she had woken with a heavy heart and in the afternoon had made her way alone along the village street and up to the Church yard. It was the first time she had visited his grave and, taking a deep breath, she had walked steadily forward until she was staring down at the mound of earth. The headstone, almost hidden by a huge arrangement of flowers, referred to him as the 'beloved son of Dr. and Mrs. Cowper,' then there were dates and, right at the bottom, the words 'taken from us too soon.'

Crystal stared hard at these words and then, finally, forced herself to open the secret place inside that she had kept shut for so long. She made herself bring out a thought that had been lodged right at the back of her mind, scarcely acknowledged as it was so deeply troubling, a thought that had remained buried until now. She kept staring hard at the headstone as she mouthed the words, 'he wasn't taken….it wasn't an accident. Giles' death wasn't an accident. And he didn't commit suicide'

Tears poured down her face and she knew in her heart that what she said was true. She composed herself and made two vows as she stared at the earth, already sprouting whiskery grass. The first was that one day, when the time was right, she would make sure everyone knew the truth about Giles' death, even though she didn't yet know it herself, but she would….she would; and the second was that she would never marry. She felt sure that she could never love anyone as much as she had loved Giles.

The sun had gone but the air was still warm as Crystal left the beach and walked slowly along the dusty track. Although it was only dried mud and not made up into a road, it was wide enough for cars and was used by people with their own vehicles. Two things surprised Crystal as she rounded a bend and the pretty wooden beach house came into view. The first was the fact that the balcony was empty and the second was the presence, on the grassy area outside the door, of a long, shiny red car.

She frowned. They weren't expecting visitors and didn't know anyone with such a startlingly ostentatious machine. She quickened her pace and ran lightly up the steps then wrinkled her nose at the unpleasant smell of cigarette smoke that invaded her nostrils as she opened the door. She went quickly into the sitting room and saw Marjorie, thin-lipped and clearly ill at ease, handing a coffee cup to a woman perched on the edge of the sofa. Opposite her, on one of the chairs, sat a man, lounging back with his legs crossed and blowing smoke out into the room. The woman was also smoking, using a long, black cigarette holder, and Crystal could feel her eyes starting to smart. She blinked as they both turned towards her and Marjorie threw a look across the room which clearly indicated she was extremely pleased to see her daughter.

"Soooo….this is Crystal…." The woman spoke then paused for enough time to take a long pull on her cigarette and blow a curl of smoke out into the room. Her eyes, hard and cold, never left Crystal's face. "….This is our brother Jack's little sprog…..the only one of us to get Ma's hair….wouldn't you know it. He could do no wrong while he was alive and he still gets it right after he's dead."

The woman's voice was harsh, clipped and cold and her words formed with an exaggerated upper class drawl. Her lips, painted bright red, made the shape of a smile but this didn't reach her eyes, and the man gave a bark of laughter as though she had said something funny.

Whether it was the fact they had clearly upset Marjorie, their swaggering self assurance, what the woman had said about her dead father or even a combination of all three, Crystal wasn't sure; but she suddenly found herself shaking with fury. She knew who this woman was, but, keeping her voice as cold as ice, she said,

"Well, you obviously know who I am; perhaps you would be good enough to introduce yourselves,"

"Oh, sorry, dear, didn't I say? How remiss of me. I'm Emily Elliott – as was – Constance and Arthur's youngest daughter. This is Mickey, my husband – number three I'm afraid. They say you have to kiss a few frogs before you find your Prince and all that. Anyway that makes me Emily Fergusson as from a week ago. We're on our honeymoon, you see, aren't we Sweetie?" She glanced towards the man, who simpered in return, and then finished by looking back at Crystal and opening her eyes very wide,

"So there you are. Now you know."

The whole speech was delivered in a voice which ranged from the upper class drawl to a nasal twang and was accompanied by a supercilious look. The woman was wearing a tight, white dress that clung to her curvaceous body with a little black satin cape around her shoulders. There was a small, black patent bag on her lap and perched on the side of her head was a large white flower which she had stuck in her gingery coloured hair. Her features were quite coarse and lavishly coated with make-up giving her skin an orangey tinge. The whole effect was overpowering; she was obviously trying to look younger than she really was and failing miserably.

She was matched in the most extraordinary way by the man, Mickey, who wore black trousers, a black shirt, white tie and jacket and had a white trilby perched on his knee. He looked like a gangster from one of the films Crystal had seen in a cinema in Cambridge, an impression further reinforced by his hair, which was jet black, and the thin, black moustache on his upper lip.

While Crystal was thinking how odd and out of place this unreal duo would be in Savron Pinder, Emily continued,

"You must be wondering how we knew you were here. Well, my sister Mary, the poor dowdy old frump who stays at home to look after the house and the two wrinklies, wrote and told me that Ma had gone all gaga because you had turned up out of the blue and that she had let you have this God-forsaken little hut to use for a while. I wouldn't normally come within ten miles of the place – and the same goes for Savron Pinder – but as Mickey and I were 'tying the knot' so to speak in a nearby castle it seemed too good an opportunity to miss. I was curious, I suppose, to see what my brother had produced." She paused again, "I suppose there is no doubt, is there.......? No…. with that hair….." she took an angry pull on her cigarette and looked out of the window.

Crystal thought she had never before encountered such an overtly nasty person, apart from one, and, in a flash, knew why Emily was there and why she was agitated. This was a matter of inheritance. Eleanore had said there were no other children; Mary was unmarried and older than Emily, who must be about forty five, in spite of trying to look ten years younger. She was rattled in case her newly discovered niece was after her parents' money.

Her palms felt clammy as Crystal pressed her hands together and, cold with fury, she spoke,

"I don't know why you thought you could just arrive here, uninvited and unannounced. I don't really know what you want. Yes it is true that, through no fault of my own, I am your brother's child. It is also true that your mother, my grandmother, has been very kind to my mum and me." She glanced at Marjorie then continued, "It is none of your business, but I will tell you anyway, that I want nothing from my newly discovered family. I have asked for nothing and I expect nothing. The most I hope for is the pleasure of getting to know them a little better while there is still time. So now **you** know!" She walked to the door and opened it,

"You've seen your brother's little sprog, now I think it's time for you to go."

Crystal stood still, looking at Emily, who could see how furious she was,

"Well….I"

"No, don't say anything…we've heard quite enough. Just go. Both of you"

Emily stubbed out her cigarette and stood up, straightening her dress and tucking her bag under her arm with an angry flick.

"Come on, Mickey, We know when we're not wanted."

They swept past Crystal and it wasn't until they were safely on the other side of the door that Emily threw her parting shot,

"So the little cat's got claws. Of course you can't expect the breeding to be there on the other side of the blankets."

Coming from her, the dig was so ludicrous that Crystal almost laughed, but instead just closed the door and walked over to the window which Marjorie had flung wide open to let the smoke out. They both watched as Emily and Mickey climbed huffily into the red car, glancing up towards the window and muttering before banging the doors hard and roaring away, bumping and swaying down the track then disappearing in a cloud of dust.

"They look like book ends," said Marjorie and she and Crystal collapsed with laughter.

CHAPTER EIGHTEEN

Crystal was almost dry after her swim in the warm, blue sea. The sun was hot on her body and the sand a soft heated cushion beneath her towel. She sat up and, shading her eyes, waved to Marjorie who was sitting in a deck chair under the pine trees. It was only half past ten in the morning, but Crystal knew that it wouldn't be long before she would be driven to take refuge in the cool shade with Marjorie before they both wandered up to the house to escape the searing heat of the midday sun.

She turned over onto her front and, pulling an old straw hat over her red curls, thought again about the extraordinary visitation of the previous evening. After Emily and Mickey had left, she and Marjorie had talked about how different people can be even when brought up in the same way by the same parents. They could imagine how disappointed Arthur and Constance must be in their daughters, and how powerless they were to change things. In the circumstances, Jack's death had indeed been a bitter blow and no wonder they were so keen to see Crystal. What a strange world.

She raised her head and, pushing back the hat, rested her chin on her hands. Her eyes wandered along the stretch of pale, yellow sand and it was then that she saw him. The beach was not crowded;

just a few families, playing and sun-bathing; young bikini-clad girls trying to get a sun tan and some already bronzed young men, watching – while pretending not to watch – the girls. She had noticed him before, walking ankle deep in the water with a camera slung around his neck, taking snaps of people. He would then persuade them to take his card and buy the photographs which he would deliver to them in a few days.

Crystal noticed that he was tall and very good looking, then felt herself start to blush as she saw that he was making his way towards her. He drew level with a small group of pretty girls and was clearly enjoying their flattering attention and self conscious giggles. Crystal smiled as she watched him flirting with them, then turned quickly away when he started to walk in her direction again. He stopped in front her, suddenly crouching down and taking a photograph. He was right in front of her face and Crystal felt extremely irritated. She could just imagine how ghastly the photograph was going to look – a pair of huge sun glasses and a straw hat with red curls sticking out of the sides. The man smiled and handed her a card but she shook her head and scrambled to her feet.

"No thanks."

She grabbed her towel and, as she did so, some sand flicked from the end of it into his face. He leapt up and shook his head. Crystal had meant to turn and walk up to where Marjorie was sitting, but did feel a little concerned about what had happened.

"Sorry about that. Are you alright?"

He brushed a few remaining grains off his face.

"Yes, I am….very good."

He smiled and she was relieved to see that none had gone into his eyes. He held out the card again,

"You take this and I bring photograph in two days. Here on the beach."

Crystal had had no intention of having anything to do with the photographer, but her resolve was weakened by feelings of remorse for showering him with sand. She reached out and took the slip of paper.

"I see you here on the beach. Eleven o'clock. In two days."

He smiled again and walked off towards the water.

Marjorie tucked her knitting away in her bag as Crystal approached,

"What happened there?"

"The silly man took my photograph. I wasn't going to buy it but I accidentally showered him with sand so…I know it'll be dreadful. I shall throw it away."

Feeling agitated, she threw herself down on a carpet of pine needles and Marjorie looked out to sea.

Two days later he arrived on the beach with the photograph, which actually wasn't too bad, and as he handed it over he asked her if she would like to go for a drink with him. Crystal was taken aback and for a moment unsure of what to say. He stood waiting and she noticed again how good-looking he was, his skin naturally tanned, green eyes with flecks of hazel and dark hair which fell over his forehead in a most engaging way. She could imagine he had the pick of the girls on the beach during the summer and she decided that she didn't want to be one of them.

"No thanks."

He looked disappointed, "It would please me very much if you would…."

"No thank-you. I would really rather not…thanks anyway."

He shrugged in a very Italian way and ambled off up the beach, the camera round his neck swinging from side to side.

There were only two more weeks of the holiday left and Crystal saw the photographer again several times as she swam or sunbathed at the beach. One morning she heard one of the lads call him 'Mario' as he shouted something to him. Then, late in the afternoon on the day before they were due to fly back to England, Crystal was picking up her towel and about to leave the beach, when she saw him standing in front of her. He snapped and, before she could protest, he held up his hand,

"Please. This one for me, not for you to buy." And for a moment he just stood and stared at her. She was furious. What a cheek! She opened her mouth to tell him exactly what she thought of him, but he turned away,

"Goodbye beautiful English girl."

And with a wave of his hand he was gone. She watched him walk away up the beach and her anger gave way to sadness as she realised she would never see him again. He actually seemed very nice even though he was, inevitably, often surrounded by a crowd of pretty girls. Then she thought of Giles and remembered the vow she had made at his graveside. With a heavy heart she walked up towards the beach house to help Marjorie with the packing, unsure of what she would do back in England and completely unaware of the strange turn of events about to influence the course of her life.

CHAPTER NINETEEN

Christmas 1963

There were no brown and white envelopes in a heap on the floor making it difficult to open the door, something that Crystal always remembered from previous holidays. Instead the mail was piled neatly on the dining room table which shone as though it had recently been polished. She and Marjorie put down their bags and looked at each other in silence. This was it; this was the start of making a life that didn't include Giles or George.

"Tea, I think." Crystal moved positively towards the kitchen, then paused and turned to Marjorie,

"And you....through you go into the sitting room and put your feet up. It's been a tiring journey and we shall both have our tea before we even think of tackling the unpacking."

Marjorie smiled at Crystal and did what she was told. She was feeling very tired and sank gratefully into a comfortable chair.

In the kitchen Crystal was surprised to see the tea things already laid out with a white envelope, addressed to both of them, propped against the pot. She boiled the kettle, staring out at the garden, also surprisingly free of weeds with grass that had obviously been cut in the last few days. It seemed like a lifetime ago that they had left Torre de Mare, could it really have been only that morning? Was it only earlier that day when she had found herself peering out of the taxi window as they rounded the corner near the beach for the last time, realising with a shock that she was looking for Mario.

She smiled at herself. How foolish. Picking up the tray she carried the tea things through into the sitting room and put them down very quietly as Marjorie's eyes were already closed. They opened suddenly when Crystal sat down and the two women smiled at each other. Marjorie struggled to sit up,

"Oh dear me.....I must have nodded off." She looked a bit sheepish and Crystal laughed,

"That's OK. I said you were tired." She handed her the tea, "there you are, that'll make you feel better. There's nothing much we need do tonight as Eleanore, true to her word, seems to have looked after the place for us while we've been away – well, sent someone to do it anyway. I wouldn't be surprised if we find that our beds have been turned down for us. Look, this was leaning against the tea tray which was left all ready in the kitchen."

She held up the white envelope, then, putting down her cup, slit it open with her thumb.

Dear Marjorie and Crystal,

Welcome home.

I do hope you had a lovely time at the beach bungalow. Arthur and Constance used to enjoy the place so much, but they can't get over there any more. They very kindly let me borrow it a few times over the years and I absolutely fell in love with the place – so peaceful and relaxing.

I also hope you have found everything to your liking at Maple Cottage. I sent Margaret down once a week to clean and give the place a good airing and Stan from the village has kept the garden under control. I would love to see you both soon and will ring in a couple of days when you have had time to catch your breath,

With very best wishes,

Eleanore

"Oh that's nice." Marjorie looked genuinely pleased and Crystal marvelled again at how well things seemed to be working out between her two mothers. It could have been so different, but their reaction to each other was indicative of the calibre of these women, so different from one another yet thrown together in life through such strange circumstances. She thought that Marjorie was beginning to feel 'looked after' and part of a family, which was good as her own mother and sister were so far away. Crystal was also surprised at how natural it was beginning to feel for her to have this sudden, unexpected family extension in her life and did, as she had said to the unwelcome visitors at the beach bungalow, want to spend time getting to know them better.

The next morning, after a good night's sleep, Crystal and Marjorie tackled the pile of post. These were mostly letters from friends or circulars and Crystal was surprised to see there were no bills. She said as much to Marjorie who looked away and hesitated before replying,

"Eleanore meant what she said about 'no expense.' She insists on paying all the costs related to this cottage." Marjorie frowned and looked at Crystal, "Do you think I'm being too dependent, dear?"

Crystal took her mum's hand,

"No I don't. As Eleanore herself said, you have done something for her that mere money can never repay. Let her do this, mum and don't worry. Go out and enjoy the village life you love. There's no point in making a rod for your back."

Marjorie squeezed her hand, "What made you so wise?"

"Oh I don't know. Must be the way I was brought up!"

Crystal wrinkled her nose at Marjorie then continued to sort out letters into their respective piles. They were mostly for Marjorie, but one of the ones addressed to her was from the shop in Cambridge where she had worked up to the time she had left to go to Italy and hadn't really thought about whether she would return or not. The letter was asking if she wanted her old job back, at least until Christmas to help them over their busiest time.

"What do you think, mum?"

"It's up to you, dear. Do you want to do it?"

"To tell you the truth, I don't really know what I want yet."

And it was true. Crystal could see no clear path to her future. College could still be an option, but how keen was she? She wasn't sure, but she had to do something, though she didn't see herself working in a department store for the rest of her life.

"I think I will do it, mum. It gets me out there – for the time being anyway."

For the rest of October until Christmas, Crystal travelled to Cambridge every day and again became part of the bustle of a large department store. Pat and Jenny were delighted to have her back and she even went with them to several dances in the evenings. She got asked out more than once by some of the boys she danced with, but always said no, in spite of encouragement from her two new friends to say yes, particularly as most of the lads were very attractive. She just didn't feel ready for any sort of dating at that time and wondered if she ever would. She started to take more of an interest in fashion and, again encouraged by Pat and Jenny, treated herself to a few of the somewhat outrageous new clothes that were appearing in the shops. The swirly pink, orange and green materials looked amazing with her hair and she discovered a new self-confidence in her appearance.

It was also during that time that Eleanore became a frequent visitor to Maple Cottage and it was on one of these occasions that Crystal and Marjorie learned all was far from well between her and William. The re-appearance in her life of the 'baby', whose existence he had never wanted to acknowledge, together with the death of his youngest son had driven them even further apart. The rift would never be healed as he blamed Eleanore for Giles' death and finally faced the fact that she had never really loved him. Theirs was now a marriage in name only and Eleanore confided to Crystal and Marjorie that she felt sure he was only staying until Spring the following year when Rosemary was marrying her farmer,

"I've got a feeling he will leave after the wedding and go to live with his sister, Janice, in the next village, unless of course he has a mistress I know nothing about. Either way I'm afraid I don't really care. I do actually feel quite sorry for him as I know I haven't treated him well; it must be very hard to know that you have always been second best. But there's nothing to be done about it; we must simply go our separate ways in as dignified a manner as possible." Eleanore looked at Crystal, "I must face facts and be positive about the future and one of the good things is that, with William gone, you can come and visit me at Monk's Manor," she looked round to include Marjorie, "both of you can, in fact. I will also be able to spend more time with my mother at Manor Farm as well as continuing my visits to Savron Pinder House."

She looked a little guilty as she mentioned the last venue and Crystal remembered the word 'secret' that Eleanore had used in connection with her relationship with Arthur and Constance. She plucked up her courage and asked,

"Eleanore, is there some reason why you shouldn't be seeing the Elliotts?"

A flush crept slowly up Eleanore's cheeks and she hesitated before replying,

"It's an old family feud, Crystal, all very foolish as I am absolutely certain that my Ma, your

Grandmother Isobel, has got hold of the wrong end of the stick and just won't let go." She looked at her watch, "I must go. We dine at seven thirty and William and I are keeping up appearances while Rosie is still at home." She put on her coat and went to the door then turned back to Crystal.

"Tell you what. The first time you come and visit me at Monk's Manor in the Spring I will tell you all about it." She kissed them both and hurried off down the drive.

Later in the evening Crystal found herself wondering about the feud between the two families. She also wondered how her relatives at Manor Farm felt about her, particularly Grandmother Isobel, who so far seemed not to have acknowledged her existence. She must know, of course; the whole village knew of the strange revelations in connection with Crystal's birth. Luckily the advent of the liberal sixties seemed to have encouraged a more tolerant attitude towards illegitimacy, even in Savron Pinder. There was no way that these things could be kept secret in a small, close-knit community but everyone seemed to accept her – everyone that is except Grandmother Isobel. If, as it seemed, Grandmother Isobel did have some kind of grudge against Constance and Arthur, maybe she didn't want to have anything to do with a girl whose very existence linked the two families. And what about Geoffrey and Claude? Where did they stand in all this? What must have happened, she wondered, to cause this level of enmity which had apparently lasted for such a long time?

CHAPTER TWENTY

Marjorie and Crystal were not looking forward to Christmas. Madge and her family would have Granny Morris to stay in Norfolk and, although they had been invited to go there, it would not be possible as neither of them could drive and the villages were too remote for public transport. Madge said she would drive to Norwich and meet them at the station if they travelled there by train, but it was a long way from her home and Marjorie felt it would be unfair, particularly as no-one knew what the weather would be like. Going as far as Eastbourne to Granny Bates and Paula was out of the question, so they decided on a small chicken and a quiet day together – that was until a letter arrived from Savron Pinder House.

Crystal and Marjorie had both written letters to Arthur and Constance full of profuse thanks for their kindness in letting them stay at the beach bungalow. Neither of them mentioned the visit they had received from Emily and Mickey, as they could see no point in upsetting the elderly couple, and intuitively felt that they wouldn't be hearing about it from Emily herself. They had received very nice letters in reply and it was obvious that Arthur and Constance wanted them to visit again, but no actual date was mentioned. Crystal thought that this was most likely to have something to do with Mary's hostility towards her, and the letter received at the beginning of December seemed to confirm this. It arrived on Saturday and, as Crystal wasn't working that day, she read it out to Marjorie as they finished their breakfast cups of tea.

Dear Marjorie and Crystal,

The year has flown by so fast it doesn't seem possible that Christmas is almost upon us again, but it is, and we have been thinking about how to spend it. Mary has informed us that she will be going to stay with her sister, Emily, who married again recently in Italy and now lives with her husband in London where, we understand, he owns and runs nightclubs. Although Arthur and I were somewhat taken aback by Mary's announcement as our two daughters are very different and have not, in the past, got on too well together, we were pleased to think that they are at last making an effort to be friends.

It does, however, leave us here on our own in a large, empty house, so we wondered if you would like to come and spend Christmas with us. We considered this carefully before writing to you as we feel sure you must already have made other arrangements. If, however, you are free and would like to come to Savron Pinder House, we would deem it a great honour and be absolutely delighted to have you. Please let us know as soon as possible so that, if your reply is positive, suitable arrangements can be made.

Sincerely yours,

Constance Elliott.

"Do you want to go?" Marjorie looked across the table as she spoke.

"Why not?"

Crystal found that the idea immediately appealed to her. She had taken an instant liking to the elderly couple, particularly Constance, and they were, after all, her grandparents, so if Marjorie didn't mind....

"What do you think, Mum? I'll only go if you want to."

"Actually, Crystal I think it has to be the other way round. I have no problem with accepting the invitation as long as it's what you want to do."

And that was how Crystal and Marjorie found themselves sitting in one of the large drawing rooms at Savron Pinder House, sipping pre-dinner sherry the night before Christmas Eve. They had been picked up from Maple Cottage by Mr. Bowman, the chauffeur/handyman/gardener in a beautiful Rolls

Royce which purred its way through the village and down the drive, sweeping round to the front door of the house and crunching to a halt on the gravel.

Arthur and Constance had greeted them as though they were visiting royalty and they had been shown up to adjoining bedrooms, each with its own bathroom. Their bags were brought in by Mr. Bowman and Constance hovered, hands clasped, anxious to know that the rooms were to their liking. They reassured her that everything was perfect.

"Well, just ring the bell when you are ready and Vera will bring you down. We're in the blue drawing room this evening."

Crystal and Marjorie had walked round their rooms gently touching the exquisite fabrics and marvelling at such luxury. They had dressed for dinner before leaving the cottage so, after quickly tidying their hair and applying some lipstick, they were ready to go down and nervously pulled the piece of fabric near the door in Crystal's room. A few minutes later the maid, Vera, appeared and they followed her downstairs and into the drawing room.

The huge fire was banked up with logs brought in earlier by Mr. Bowman, and the blue and gold curtains had been drawn against the cold. Constance, looking the model of upper class elegance in a beautifully tailored outfit, ushered them both to armchairs near the fire, while Arthur, who had leapt to his feet as they entered the room, stood nervously in the background, stroking his moustache. As they sat, so did he, bolt upright in his starched white shirt, green tweed jacket, cavalry twill trousers and mustard coloured waistcoat. They had obviously both made quite an effort for their visitors, but Crystal guessed that Constance was more accustomed to dressing up these days than her husband was.

They ate a delicious dinner in the dining room, also heated by a roaring log fire, and all the while during the meal, Arthur and Constance kept up a continuous flow of conversation, obviously delighted to have their only granddaughter with them for Christmas. They drank wine and when the cheese was passed around Arthur asked for some port.

"Be careful, my dear," Constance murmured, looking a little worried.

"Nonsense, woman; stop fussing." He held up his glass and the ruby liquid sparkled in the light of the chandelier, "this is a time for celebration – a very special occasion."

He looked at Crystal and she was touched to see that his eyes had filled with tears. Next moment he was telling them another amusing story about the old days and they were laughing again.

At the end of the meal Constance led them all back to the drawing room and on the way whispered to Crystal,

"Honestly, my dear, I haven't seen him like this for years. You've breathed new life into him." She squeezed her granddaughter's arm, "into both of us, in fact."

Crystal felt very touched,

"I wonder if I might be excused for a moment. I'd like to get a breath of air."

"Yes, of course, but don't get cold."

Slipping on her coat, she stood outside and looked up at the moon and stars shining brightly in the dark, night sky, the little pin-pricks of light multiplying even as she stared. The air was clear and cold and frost sparkled thickly on grass, huge stone urns and bushes cut into the shapes of cones and balls. Her gaze travelled down to the gleaming, silvered lake and woods where bare trees were thrown in silhouette against the moonlit sky. She sighed, her breath pluming out in the cold air, and wondered what it must be like to live in such a place. Suddenly she was aware of someone behind her and, turning saw Arthur standing there in his thick, sheepskin coat.

"It's stunning isn't it – the old place? Connie and I love it. I'll show you round in the morning;" then, his voice tinged with sadness, he added, "mind you, it's nothing like it used to be. We do our best, but can't quite keep it up to scratch like the old days."

Crystal hesitated, then asked the question that had been puzzling her,

"I was wondering about the grounds," she waved her hand in front of her to indicate the rolling landscape, the lake with small hillocks and waterfalls in the distance, "it's just so unusual for the middle of the fens."

"Yes I know, my dear. It was the work of my father, old Charles Elliott. He was quite an eccentric man who had too much time on his hands and enjoyed spending money. He did it for his wife who had a fondness for the Lake District. Lovely, though, isn't it?"

"Beautiful," Crystal breathed, gazing out again over the extraordinary landscape."

"He was quite odd in other ways too…but enough of that for now," he squeezed her shoulder, "Come on, m'dear, Vera's got some coffee for us," and Crystal followed him back into the blue drawing room, wondering, and curious to know more about her eccentric great grandfather.

Vera was serving the coffee and suddenly, above the tinkling of spoons and crackling logs, Crystal heard singing. She looked up and saw that the others had heard it too. Arthur struggled to his feet,

"It's the Carol Singers. Vera get the mulled wine ready and heat up the mince pies. Come on let's go and make them sing for their supper."

Constance raised her eyes to heaven, but there was a smile on her face as they all followed Arthur, who was rubbing his hands with boyish enthusiasm. Vera frowned and whispered to Constance,

"The pies and wine are all ready, Ma'am. I gets them ready at this time every year."

"I know you do, my dear. Take no notice of Mr. Elliott. It's a long time since he's turned out for the Carol Singers or paid any attention to them at all, but he's very happy this year."

Vera was placated and hurried off to the kitchen to perform the annual ritual of serving hot pies and wine.

Lanterns glowed on ruddy faces as the familiar Carols rang out in the night air. Constance brought out warm coats for everyone and her eyes shone as she placed one around Crystal's shoulders and insisted that she do it up. Crystal smiled, understanding that this small service was part of what grandparents did for their grand children; what Constance, up to now, had been denied. She looked at the sea of faces, muffled in coloured scarves, the knitted hats bobbing up and down, and recognised a few of her old primary school class mates. Then, to her delight, she saw Minty and Rob standing together with shining faces, singing under a shared lantern. As the Carol finished and Arthur welcomed everyone inside, Crystal rushed forward to her friend,

"Hi ya, toff,"

"Hello Peasant."

They hugged each other then Crystal reached up and gave Rob a kiss on his cold cheek. Arm in arm the two girls walked into the brightly lit kitchen where steaming cups of wine and home-made mince pies were already being handed round. Constance was walking about, chatting to people and putting them at their ease; she reached her granddaughter's side and looked enquiringly at the two friends she was talking to in such an animated fashion. Crystal turned and, without thinking, said,

"Grandmother, this is my friend, Araminta Graham – but we always call her Minty – and this is her boyfriend, Rob."

Constance didn't reply and, looking back at her, Crystal saw a strange expression on her face; but, almost immediately, she recovered herself and shook hands with Minty and Rob.

"I'm very pleased to meet any of my granddaughter's friends," she put her arm round Crystal; "my husband and I are so delighted to have her here with us." She paused for a moment looking at Minty, "Graham...you must be....no, I mustn't say any more," she squeezed Crystal's waist, "mustn't spoil one of your surprises – and this is one that your grandfather wants to tell you about." She turned back to Minty and Rob,

"Lovely to meet you both. I hope I shall see you again," and she moved on to talk to someone else. Crystal frowned,

"She's fab, isn't she? But she did look a bit odd when I introduced you."

"Well, you called her 'grandmother' didn't you, lamebrain – I bet you haven't done that before – and she was in Seventh Heaven." Minty made a face at her friend and Crystal realised she was right. She looked across the room to where Constance was smiling and listening to one of the other Carol Singers, and felt they had somehow turned an important corner in their relationship.

Minty hugged Crystal again then joined the rest of the singers who were making their way noisily back out into the cold night. Ramming a red bobble hat onto her head, she turned back to where her friend stood with arms folded, stamping her feet on the doorstep

"Come and see me, Cryssie – can you manage the day after Boxing Day? Only we've got a lot to talk about; that's if you haven't become too grand to be my bridesmaid next year."

Crystal ran out and grabbed her again,

"Oh, fab, Mints. Thank-you. Yes, yes, yes!!"

"Of course the whole colour scheme will have to be built around that blessed hair of yours."

Crystal aimed a kick at her friend's retreating backside but missed, then turned back to the house to join her family on the doorstep.

Next morning breakfast was eaten in the dining room with bright sunlight from a perfect blue sky streaming in through the windows and shining on the frost-white world outside. Arthur, impatient to get on with the day, hurriedly finished his second cup of coffee then, throwing down his napkin, pushed back his chair and stood up,

"Come on Crystal – things to see and do…"

"Arthur for goodness sake let the poor girl finish her breakfast."

Crystal and Marjorie were amused by his boyish enthusiasm, but Constance spoke quite sharply and Arthur halted in his rush for the door, realising that his behaviour could be seen to be bordering on rudeness. Somewhat more quietly he said,

"Tell you what, I'll go and chivvy up Bowman – make sure he's got the tree sorted out as we'll be decorating it this afternoon. That'll give you time to finish your breakfast." He turned to Marjorie, "You will, of course be welcome to come with us. I'm going to show Crystal round the old place, particularly the stable block."

Crystal could see that Marjorie was trying to find a polite way to refuse the outing and Constance came to the rescue,

"I've promised Marjorie that we'll go looking for knitting patterns and wool, I've got loads put away somewhere."

"Oh well, no matter. See you outside the front door when you're ready, Crystal."

And he bounced out of the room, shouting for Bowman as he made his way down the passage.

Crystal was in Heaven as she walked with her grandfather round the grounds of the most beautiful place she had ever seen in her life. They crunched over frosty grass and stood by the lake where reeds at the edge were sticking stiffly up like sugar-coated sentinels from the thick layer of ice that stretched far out, becoming black and brittle in the middle.

"A few more degrees of frost and we could skate on that, you know. We've got plenty of spare skates in the boot room." Arthur paused and his eyes took on a far away look.

"We used to have the most wonderful parties….crowds of us here….All the children from the Manor and…ah well….. times change. Come on."

They walked past the boathouse, through the woods, where Crystal tried to imagine Wendy Wetherall pinned against a tree, and then up towards the stable block. This hadn't exactly fallen into disrepair but it was clearly underused and, as if reading her mind, Arthur explained,

"Used to be all of a bustle, this place, room for twenty horses; and their grooms would sleep in the quarters above."

He took her into the tack room where there were still quite a number of saddles and bridles stored along the walls.

"Do you have any horses here now?" Crystal asked.

"Only a couple of old favourites; they have the run of the fields and come in to a nice warm stable in weather like this. Their working lives are over but they were good point to pointers in their day and deserve a happy retirement. Pensioned off like Connie and me."

He gave a bark of laughter and Crystal saw two horses' heads peering over the tops of two of the stable doors. She stroked their noses,

"Oh, they're lovely," she breathed softly into their nostrils in turn and they nuzzled her.

"Yes, they're gentle creatures. If Connie ever fancies a hack, she feels quite safe on old Bella there. I used to ride Danny, but can't get up on him now. We have a lad who looks after them….should be here somewhere. Jimmie….Jim…where the devil are you?"

A young man, whistling and carrying two buckets, appeared from round the corner of the yard. He was tall, about Crystal's age, and she recognised him from her days at the village school.

"Ah, Jim, this is Miss Crystal…..come to look at the horses."

They both said hello, trying to keep straight faces at the 'Miss' and Crystal turned back to rub Bella's nose in case she burst out laughing. Jim had put down the buckets and was being led aside by Arthur who was whispering something to him. Crystal could just make out the words, "….everything ready then….? You know…" and she heard Jim say, 'yes,' but couldn't hear what they were talking about. Arthur looked flushed and happy, like a little boy with a secret, as they said goodbye to Jim and made their way back to the house for lunch.

The midday meal was a simple affair of home-made soup and cheese and when they had finished Constance explained that Arthur usually took a short nap at this time of day. He looked horrified,

"Nap! Good grief woman, we're too busy for a nap today! The very idea, with a ten foot tall, bare Christmas tree standing in the red room waiting to be decorated." He winked at Crystal then slapped his sides, hopping from one foot to the other, impatient to be off. He looked much fitter and livelier than when Crystal had first seen him the day they had come to tea. He was well-built and, even in old age, radiated energy that would have made him very attractive when younger. She realised that, in the nicest possible way, he was showing off to her, 'playing to the gallery' George used to call it. Constance and Marjorie disappeared to the kitchen to help Mrs. Bowman with her preparations for the following day; Constance seemed to relish the prospect of working in her own kitchen and Marjorie was interested to learn new recipes for stuffing and Christmas pudding.

Delighted to have his granddaughter to himself again, Arthur led the way to the red room and Crystal was warmed by the thought that her presence should give anyone such a sense of purpose. He stopped by the door,

"Now in here, as well as the tree, is one of my surprises,"

He turned the knob and beckoned her in. The room was cosy and, as the name suggested, decorated predominantly in red. Once again there was a roaring fire and, in one corner, the biggest Christmas tree Crystal had ever seen. But it was to one of the corners by the fireplace that Arthur directed her attention, and she saw there a very elegant television set, obviously one of the most expensive ones available. Arthur opened the polished wooden doors in front of the screen,

"What do you think, m'dear? Do you like watching the television?"

"I don't really know. We…we've never had one."

"Well this evening after dinner we shall all come in here and see if there is a programme on that will make us laugh eh? Now let's get decorating."

They walked over to where several boxes had been placed near the tree and started to take out the motley collection of coloured ornaments that twinkled in the firelight. As these were held aloft and examined to see if they were still fit to be used there were exclamations from Arthur of,

"Good Lord, didn't know we still had that….Bless my soul, Mary made that… thought it had been thrown out years ago…"

Which made Crystal think that maybe it was a long time since Arthur and Constance had even bothered with a tree at Savron Pinder House.

When it was finished they sat back and gazed at the glorious creation, multi-coloured and sparkling in the fire-light. Arthur went to the door,

"I'll get the girls to rustle up some tea and cake and bring it in here, what a surprise for them, eh?

You sit here by the fire and enjoy looking at our handiwork."

The tree glowed softly, flames flickered and danced, making shadows on the ceiling; and Crystal stared again at the myriad of tiny ornaments. She thought about the fact that most of them would have been touched by her father, Jack, and felt a strange sensation, a link with the past, with this – her family – stretching back through time.

Constance and Marjorie were enchanted by the tree; they gazed and gasped as tea was poured and cake sliced, then everyone settled down round the fire for a well-earned rest.

That evening there was supper of soup, cold ham, salad and tiny new potatoes, minted and buttery, followed by television round the fire in the red room. Marjorie was impressed by the quality of the ham and the way it had been stuck with cloves then glazed with honey and brown sugar until it was sticky and shining. She had been busy jotting down recipes all day and exclaimed over the large jars of home-made pickles and exquisitely shaped smaller jars of mustard and red-currant jelly with beautiful writing on the labels. Arthur followed her gaze,

"Everything alright for you m'dear?"

"Everything's lovely." Marjorie was, in fact, surprised at how much she was enjoying herself;

she had been quite nervous about Christmas at Savron Pinder House, but had tried to keep this hidden from Crystal. Arthur passed her a dish of steaming potatoes,

"Help yourself, Marjorie, but leave plenty of room for tomorrow's feast – all good home-made stuff. Anything we couldn't grow, make ourselves or get locally came in a hamper from Fortnum's. Your good health and a Happy Christmas!"

In the red room Arthur switched on the television set but was furious when he saw that the screen was fuzzy and the black and white picture kept revolving round and round in the most irritating way. He raised his arm,

"Arthur, don't you dare bang the top of that box. Don't you dare."

His arm stayed suspended in mid-air as Constance's voice rang out across the room. He looked at her.

"I mean it. You'll break it; just wait for a minute and I'll go and call Bowman."

Arthur's eyes followed her across the room and the moment she disappeared round the door the flat of his hand came down smartly on top of the television set. By the time Constance re-appeared, followed by Mr. Bowman, the set was working perfectly and Arthur's face a picture of innocence.

Crystal and Marjorie couldn't help themselves. They dissolved into fits of laughter as Constance stared suspiciously at her husband who continued to look as if butter wouldn't melt in his mouth. The incident was funnier than anything they saw on the television all evening.

CHAPTER TWENTY ONE

Swinging his stick, Arthur reached the Church steps first, closely followed by Crystal, while Constance and Marjorie, arm in arm, sauntered slowly behind. Arthur made a hook with his elbow and smiled at Crystal who slipped her hand through his arm and walked with her grandfather up the steps to the Church door. Constance squeezed Marjorie's arm,

"Look at him, proud as a peacock walking into Church on Christmas morning with his beautiful granddaughter on his arm." She turned to Marjorie, "You don't know what you've done for us, bringing Crystal to stay; thank-you so much."

The morning so far had been all bustle and excitement with 'Happy Christmas' ringing out through the house. Vera and Alice had come in from the village to help Mrs. Bowman with the breakfast and preparation of vegetables for lunch and then they were to go home to spend the rest of Christmas Day with their families. Marjorie insisted that she and Crystal could help with the clearing up and Constance had agreed, but only if she did too. Everyone had been secretly creeping in to the red room, adding to the pile of presents, wrapped and shining – red, gold, green, silver – silently waiting for the afternoon opening ceremony. Arthur had

215

stood at the door breathing in the beauty of a day as bright, crisp and golden as the previous one

"Let's walk to Church. What do you say, Connie, are you game?" Constance looked concerned for her guests,

"Well, Marjorie may feel she would rather ride…."

"Marjorie feels no such thing," said Marjorie, presenting herself booted and ready to go.

Still pink with a combination of bracing morning air and the pleasure of his granddaughter's company, Arthur collected service books and hymn sheets, shaking hands with old friends and introducing Crystal to all and sundry – most of whom she already knew.

"…..don't think you've met my granddaughter have you….? I say, come and meet Crystal. She's my granddaughter…."

The vicar, Peter Kempton, warmly squeezed both of her hands in his and smiled,

"It's lovely to see you my dear – and looking so……..well."

She smiled back at the kindly man who had been such a help to her through her painful, tragic experiences; so much so that she had felt moved to start attending services and had derived a great deal of strength and comfort from her growing faith.

Constance and Marjorie arrived and the four of them made their way up to the pew on the left at the front of the Church, still chatting to people as they went. Crystal was thrilled to see Matthew Graham, Minty and Minty's Gran sitting halfway up the Church with some of Rob's family. She waved to them and mouthed, 'see you afterwards.'

Coats were removed and papers shuffled, but at last all was still as they waited in hushed silence for the service to begin. Reverend Kempton walked forward in crisp white cassock and the congregation rose. Everyone expected him to start speaking, but instead he looked to the back of the Church as though he was waiting for someone.

There was a loud clang as the door, which had been quietly shut, opened again and everyone turned to watch the group enter, collect hymn books from an agitated sidesman and make their way up to the front of the Church. Crystal was sitting next to Arthur at the end of the pew nearest the aisle, so she was able to observe clearly the stately progress of Isobel Lynton-Bell up to the pew at the front on the right. She was followed by Claude, Geoffrey, Eleanore, William and Rosemary. Isobel obviously wanted to sit near the aisle so she stood to one side while the others passed her by and sat down. Then she turned and sat, and, when she was quite comfortable, inclined her head towards Reverend Kempton indicating that the service could begin.

Crystal could feel Arthur fidgeting with irritation. When he had realised who it was coming up the aisle of the Church with the regal bearing of the Queen Mother, he had muttered to Constance in what he thought was a whisper,

"I thought the old witch was dead."

Then, when it was obvious that she was determining when the service would begin, his tutting was audible enough to cause sniggering in several pews behind. Isobel also heard and turned her head. She saw Crystal and her eyebrows shot up. When she realised that her granddaughter was sitting with Arthur and Constance, her lips formed a thin line of disapproval.

Crystal kept her eyes firmly fixed on Reverend Kempton throughout the service, but was aware of Isobel looking at her more than once. She pressed her lips together to stop herself from smiling during the sermon which was all about love coming down at Christmas and the importance of forgiveness.

At the end of the service she hurried down the aisle to find Minty and was caught in the general throng of people making their way towards the door. Outside in the bright sunshine she kissed and hugged Minty, Matthew and Martha, wishing them all a Happy Christmas.

"Ooooh, watch out there's trouble brewing," Minty was looking in the direction of the church door and Crystal turned to see Isobel staring at her, muttering something to Eleanore who was clearly feeling very uncomfortable and trying to placate her mother.

"...no I will not speak to Constance; neither will I meet your other daughter. I have three granddaughters and that is quite sufficient." The old woman's words rang out in the frosty air and several people, stopping in mid-conversation, turned to look at her. Arthur was glaring at Isobel, and Constance had placed a restraining hand on his arm. Eleanore threw an apologetic look towards Constance, whose answering smile indicated that it was alright, she understood; then walked towards Crystal. She kissed her on the cheek and squeezed her hand,

"Happy Christmas, darling," she lowered her voice, "I'm sorry about that. I think she sees you as a link with the Elliotts and it's a link she doesn't want, also she....well never mind. Have a lovely day; I know you will."

She walked back to where her mother stood waiting impatiently and together the Lynton-Bells made their way down the Church steps. As Isobel passed Crystal she stared straight ahead, refusing to look at her while Crystal, feeling quite unmoved by the old lady's rudeness, took the opportunity to study her profile. She could see Geoffrey in the sharpness of the features, particularly the nose, and Evelyn in the sparse frame and stately bearing. Eleanore's elegance and Claude's affability were clearly from somewhere else in the family as was Bette's liveliness.

Crystal stood watching them go and wondered again what the problem was between the two women.

"Wicked old troublemaker" Arthur had come to stand beside her and stared after the group who had reached the bottom of the steps and started to climb into two very large cars waiting there for them.

Arthur grunted then, all bluff, good humour again, turned to summon his little party,

"Come on, girls, lunch awaits."

Tucking Crystal's hand firmly under his arm he muttered, "Mustn't let anything spoil today, especially that little pint-sized tyrant. Onward we go." he led the way down the steps to where Bowman was waiting with the Rolls Royce. As they all climbed in he explained that he had taken the precaution of arranging for Bowman to collect them from Church as they had to save plenty of energy for the rest of the day. He winked at Constance, his boyish good humour firmly re-established, and

Crystal wondered what surprises were in store for them.

Lunch was superb – a traditional Christmas dinner with all the trimmings and certainly the best that Marjorie and Crystal had ever tasted. After the last mouthful of pudding was consumed, Mr and Mrs. Bowman were called in and had to stand, pink with pleasure and embarrassment, while they were profusely thanked and their good health toasted.

As promised, Constance, Marjorie and Crystal hurried down to the kitchen to help with the clearing up, in spite of protests from Mrs. Bowman, and then Crystal carried coffee and petite fours into the drawing room.

"When do Mr. and Mrs. Bowman have their Christmas dinner?" she asked.

"They will be getting it ready right now," replied Constance and then, as if reading her mind added, "We would be more than happy for them to join us on such a special day, and have invited them to do so more than once, but they always refuse. Their discomfort would rob the meal of its pleasure and festivity for them; I'm afraid the old Edwardian class thing is taking a long time to die."

Crystal sipped her coffee thoughtfully, then noticed that Arthur was getting impatient again, hovering anxiously by the window. He stroked his moustache and looked pleadingly at Constance, obviously concerned that if he chivvied everyone along, he was in danger of getting the sharp edge of her tongue again. She took pity on him,

"As soon as you have finished your coffee, Arthur and I would like you to join us outside for the first part of the gift-giving ceremony.

Intrigued, Crystal and Marjorie wrapped up warmly and followed their hosts across the crisp grass and down towards the stable block. Arthur was not so much walking as bouncing with excitement and whispered something in his wife's ear. She turned and gestured to her guests,

"We're going to the garages first. This way."

They veered to the right and soon found themselves in front of a block of four large garages. Arthur waited until they had gathered round then turned the handle on the door and slowly lifted it up, rolling it in under the roof. Inside was something under a green cover with a huge red bow on top.

"Come on then, Crystal, take off the cover and let's see what it is." She stepped forward and tugged the light material which came off easily, revealing a small, shiny car underneath. It was dark blue and, she guessed, brand new; looking more closely she saw 'Hillman' written on the back with 'Imp' underneath. She touched it but couldn't speak.

"Do you like it?" Arthur was peering at her, enjoying every moment.

"It's wonderful," Crystal breathed.

"Look, here's the card." Arthur grabbed an envelope that had been sellotaped to the windscreen and handed it to her. She stood, turning it over in her hand then staring back at the car. Was it really hers?

"Open it…open it."

"Arthur…dear…" Constance put her hand on his arm.

After a moment or two Crystal carefully slid open the envelope and took out a large card. Inside it said,

To Crystal,

Wishing you the happiest Christmas ever,

Your loving mother,

Eleanore.

"From Eleanore!"

"Yes, my dear," Constance walked round the car and hugged Crystal, "She has arranged for you to have driving lessons too."

"Oh…I…" She looked at Marjorie, who was beaming and nodding,

"You knew it was something like this, didn't you? I just can't believe it…"

Arthur was looking anxiously out of the garage door to where the sun was just setting, casting an orange glow across the sky.

"We should move on….there's something else." He carefully shut the garage door and they all made their way to the stable block.

Already stunned, Crystal watched her grandfather open the top door of one of the loose boxes and whistle softly. Within seconds, a horse's head appeared over the top of the door. It was jet black with bright, alert eyes, a star shaped patch on its forehead and ears pricked forward. The eyes looked straight into Crystal's and the mare gave a small whinny, tossing her head as if welcoming her new owner. She had a halter on, so Arthur was able to open the door and lead her out, stopping her in front of Crystal where the little mare nuzzled her. Crystal put out her hand and stroked the soft, velvety nose; she opened her mouth to say something, but all that came out was a sob and she realised that she was shaking and tears were streaming down her cheeks.

"Oh good Lord....I say....." Arthur was nonplussed, but Constance stepped forward and hugged her granddaughter.

"Lead her round, Arthur, let Crystal see how she moves."

With Constance on one side of her and Marjorie on the other Crystal watched with shining eyes while the little jet black mare danced round the cobbled yard, Arthur proudly showing her off

"By golly....she's a spirited little mare.....see how she steps out.....look at the way she carries her head.....what do you think, Crystal eh?"

He brought the mare to a halt in front of his audience, two of whom had been shouting encouragement, but it was the third he wanted to hear from,

"Eh, Crystal?"

Crystal slowly reached out and stroked the mare's nose again,

"She is so beautiful....so beautiful."

She moved forward and buried her head in the glossy, black neck, gently stroking her mane.

"She's called Star apparently....named for the mark on her forehead. You can change it of course....she's yours."

"Crystal looked at the mare, then at her grandfather and grandmother,

"Star sounds lovely. Thank-you both so much."
She led Star back into her box and reluctantly
closed the top door.

Arthur didn't stop talking all the way back to the
house. 'Crystal can keep the mare at Monk's
Manor.....she could enter shows...may even
encourage Eleanore up into the saddle again to ride
with her round the fens...used to be a fine horse-
woman....what fun they would have." He paused
and turned to Crystal, lowering his voice, "Would
love to keep the little mare here, but... bit tricky
with Mary...anyway all set up at Monk's
Manor....Eleanore has a stable all ready and plenty
of grazing. The car...well that would be better kept
at Maple Cottage for Crystal to use every day, when
she's passed her test of course...' and so on. He was
full of plans for the future and delighted to have
made his granddaughter so happy.

When they had all settled down with tea and
Christmas cake round the fire in the red room it was
time to open some of the parcels under the tree.
Arthur was delighted with the leather wallet that
Crystal had bought him; and the warm, pale lemon
scarf, knitted for him by Marjorie in very thick
wool, he declared was exactly the right colour to go
with his new overcoat. Constance loved her long,
dusky pink chiffon scarf; and the leather, fur
trimmed gloves in dark brown she said would go

beautifully with a long leather coat she had just bought for herself. Marjorie was absolutely overjoyed when she opened a very large box to reveal a brand new knitting machine; and Crystal, having received so much already, was amazed when she saw that there were several more packages under the tree with her name on.

They watched as she opened the first of these and took out a pair of jodhpurs, followed by hacking jacket, boots, white shirt, stock, hat and riding whip in the other packages. After she had thanked them profusely, Arthur 'found' one more little box wrapped in gold paper lurking under the tree. He watched while she opened it and took out the most beautiful gold stock pin – his special present to her. She was overwhelmed and blurted out,

"You have given me so much…..what I've given you doesn't seem like anything in return."

Constance held up her hand,

"You are here with us – that's the best gift we have ever had." And for once Arthur couldn't speak.

They had a relaxing evening watching a little television then playing Scrabble at which Arthur kept inventing words, insisting they were real and only unknown to the others because they hadn't travelled as extensively as he had. Crystal found his antics amusing, which gave him the encouragement he needed to redouble his efforts, but Constance very soon reached the limit of her patience and, as they were all yawning, suggested it was time for bed. Arthur readily agreed and got up from his chair as if he had just remembered something,

"Yes, you're right m'dear. Off to bed, Crystal we need you bright-eyed and bushy-tailed in the morning; up good and early ready for another surprise."

CHAPTER TWENTY TWO

Crystal was taken aback when Vera brought, not just a cup of tea in the morning, but a message saying that she was to dress in her new riding outfit which had been laid out ready for her in the adjoining bathroom. Crystal did so and was not at all surprised that it all fitted perfectly, guessing, correctly that Marjorie had had a hand in that.

At breakfast Arthur could scarcely contain his excitement, looking at his watch, then leaning back in his chair and staring out of the window as though he was expecting to see someone coming down the drive. He would then look at Crystal's plate, willing her to hurry, but not daring to say anything, aware of his wife watching him from the other end of the table. Constance laughed,

"Arthur, tell Crystal please and put us all out of our misery." He leaned forward,

"Well, the thing is, m'dear, we've arranged for you to go hunting today. They're meeting here for their stirrup cup – always used to in the old days, so it didn't take much persuading to get them to come here again for their port and mulled wine – then you're all going to charge off over the fens. What do you think, eh?"

Crystal was overjoyed and, unable to eat any more breakfast, went with her grandfather to the stables where Jim had already saddled Star, gleaming and shaking her head in the frosty air, impatient to be off.

"Weather's held for us then, Jim,"

"Yes, Sir," he stroked Star's mane and looked at Crystal,

"It's a lovely little mare you've got here, good natured, but sparky with it – beautiful creature."

Star nuzzled him with her nose in answer to the compliment and Arthur stroked the mare's neck,

"Yes indeed. She took a bit of finding, but it was worth it."

Jim held Star steady while Crystal mounted then adjusted the stirrups and girth. She thanked him and rode out of the stable-yard with her grandfather at her side and as they rounded the corner of the house they were greeted by a sight that Crystal knew she would never forget.

In coats of black or red, leather boots and snow white stocks, the riders meandered about, greeting each other and filling the frosty air with shouts and barks of laughter which mingled with the baying of hounds all running around, sniffing the grass with their tails held aloft. Mrs. Bowman, Vera and Alice were weaving in and out, handing up glasses of port or steaming cups of mulled wine. The horses pawed the ground impatient to be off, their breath pluming out against a clear blue sky, while Marjorie and

Constance walked about chatting to people, shielding their eyes against the bright sunlight.

"Here we are." Several heads turned as Arthur led Star up to the Master and introduced Crystal to him.

"Glad to have you with us, m'dear. I understand we have someone detailed to look after you,"

He half turned and at that moment Crystal saw Matt riding up to them on one of the hunters from Manor Farm. So that's what Constance had meant with her reference to the name Graham and another surprise.

"Yes, you can be sure Crystal will be safe with me." He winked at her, "Just like old times, eh?"

She felt relieved to see him and to know that he would be with her on her first experience of hunting. Matt looked at Star and gave an admiring whistle,

"Wow, pretty little mare!" He smiled, "you've been spoilt, young lady."

Crystal looked round again at the riders enjoying their stirrup cups in the morning sunshine and thought what a mixed group they were, of varying ages and sizes, but all speaking with the clipped, upper class accent she now associated with Rosemary and some of her other newly found relatives. Suddenly she became aware of someone staring at her; it was that strange feeling as though the hairs on the back of her neck were transmitting a signal. She turned and found herself looking straight into the eyes of a very handsome young man, a little older than her. She felt herself blushing and looked away immediately. Before she could look back the Whipper-in was rounding up the hounds and they were all preparing to leave, the air ringing with goodbye's and 'thanks a lot....see you later.'

She and Star trotted down the drive next to Matthew then across the road and up a muddy track. They were soon tearing across the open country-side behind the excited hounds that seemed to think they were pursuing a fox.

Crystal had a secret dread. She knew that it was traditional for first timers at a hunt to be blooded. One of the girls she had met at the shows during the days when she was riding Bluebell, had told her excitedly about having the severed foot of the first caught fox of the day wiped across her forehead. She had felt so proud of this badge of honour that she hadn't washed her forehead for several days. Crystal didn't feel the same at all. She had no wish to experience this ritual and was a little unsure about how she felt regarding the killing of foxes.

She needn't have worried. The hounds seemed incapable of following a scent for long enough to find the wily foxes and spent a great deal of time running in circles after a chase across open ground before charging off again, a sea of waving, vertical tails pursued by horses and riders.

Star was a dream ride and Crystal already loved her. She was eager and responsive, giving her new rider such a feeling of confidence that a bond of trust was quickly formed. There was only one slight accident, but help was at hand in the person of the unknown young man who Crystal had noticed just before they had moved off that morning.

It happened as they were approaching a low fence which most of the riders had already cleared easily. Crystal and Star had jumped a couple of fences and some ditches with no problem so Matt, obviously confident that they could manage this one, had jumped over and galloped off. Crystal spurred Star on but then, for no apparent reason, the mare faltered and Crystal toppled over her head and landed with a bump on the ground.

She scrambled up unhurt and was glad that she was almost last in the field at that point. She held Star's reins and picked up her hat which had fallen off then, glancing up, saw the young man looking down at her,

"Are you OK?"

"Yes. I was lucky. I didn't fall awkwardly." Blushing furiously, Crystal brushed some grass off her jodhpurs and put her hat back on. The man was still there.

"Come on, try again. I'll go first." He urged his mount, a beautiful hunter, up to the fence and looked over, "there's nothing there. Your mount probably just thought she saw something and balked. They do sometimes, don't they?" He smiled and watched Crystal mount Star.

"Come on, I'll go first." And without waiting for an answer, the man cantered a few steps away and waited for Crystal to catch up. She did, then turned and followed him over the fence. They both cleared it perfectly and the man looked back, making sure she was alright before galloping over the field to catch up with the others. She galloped after him, more disturbed by the memory of the smile that had lit up his whole face than she was by the fall.

It was an amazing day; they caught absolutely nothing but all returned in the late afternoon sunshine glowing with an inexplicable sense of achievement. Matt accompanied Crystal down the drive to Savron Pinder House.

"I thought I'd better see you safely home, since I failed in my duty earlier in the day. I was told you came off at the fence in Low Bridge Meadow and young Charlie Fairlawn helped you over. I'm sorry I wasn't there for you – never occurred to me you'd have trouble with that one."

"It's OK," Crystal reassured him, "just one of those things and I wasn't hurt. I've had a brilliant day."

Arthur was standing on the steps looking anxiously up the drive as they arrived back. He walked forward to greet them and, after they had said goodbye to Matt, they walked Star round to the stable where Jim was waiting to attend to her. Crystal would have like to do it herself, but felt sure Marjorie and Constance would be waiting to hear all about the day.

During supper, a traditional Boxing Day buffet of cold turkey, ham, salad and baked potatoes, they were all comparatively quiet, aware of something very special coming to an end. After coffee in the red room, Constance asked if Marjorie and Arthur would mind if she and Crystal disappeared for a few minutes. They both said of course not and sat dozing in front of the television while she slipped upstairs with her granddaughter.

Constance led Crystal into her bedroom, beautifully furnished in pale cream and gold with an enormous four poster bed in the centre.

"Sit down, darling. I have something I want to show you."

Crystal perched on an ornate double sofa near the window and Constance opened a drawer, taking out a large white album. She sat next to Crystal and, turning the pages, showed her pictures of the family while they were growing up, many of them Jack and Eleanore, her father and mother. There they were playing in the woods, at picnics on the lawn or partying in the Orangery, two beautiful, vibrant, happy people smiling at each other or laughing into the camera.

Crystal looked for a long time at her father Jack's images, focusing on his face, as if by staring hard she could somehow get to know him just a little, probe beneath that warm, open, smiling face and touch the heart beneath. She put out her hand and gently traced the outline of his face with her finger, letting it rest finally on his mop of dark, curly hair. She was too moved to speak and Constance understood. She spoke softly, shaking her head,

"If the photographs were in colour you would see that his dark brown hair was shot through with red – like mine and yours, only his was more subtle."

She squeezed Crystal's hand and they both felt a deep love and connection with one another and the handsome face smiling up at them from the photographs – son to one and father to the other. Constance sighed,

"He and Eleanore were meant for each other; it seems inconceivable that they should have been kept apart by Janice Wetherall's wicked scheming and lying. She cheated me out of the loveliest daughter-in-law I could ever have wished for." She smiled, but it was a smile tinged with sadness, "I wanted you to see these so that you can try and understand why you are so special – you are the product of the true love between two lovely and very special people."

She closed the book and replaced it,

"I have given instructions that you are to have all the photographs of your parents when I am no longer here," she smiled, "Come along now. Let's go and rescue Marjorie; you never know what tales Arthur will be telling her." And she led the way back down the stairs.

Before she went to bed, Crystal crept quietly along to the kitchen and found Mrs. Bowman just finishing up for the day. The breakfast things were ready to carry through in the morning and she was folding the last tea towel, preparing to hang it on the radiator to dry.

"Hello, my dear. What brings you down here?"

"I just wanted to say thank-you for everything. You've worked so hard and made it all so lovely for us. Your food is delicious."

Mrs. Bowman's cheeks were flushed,

"It's no trouble, Miss; a pleasure in fact when the folk we are looking after are as appreciative as yourselves. And I have to say it's a tonic for Bowman and me to see the master and mistress looking so happy. It's not my place to say anything and maybe I shouldn't but….." Mrs Bowman hesitated and a worried frown creased her forehead. Crystal waited for her to go on, but at that moment Constance came bustling in and stopped when she saw Crystal.

"I was just thanking Mrs. Bowman. I didn't think there'd be time in the morning."

"Splendid idea; what a thoughtful girl you are Crystal." She turned to the housekeeper, "What do you think of my granddaughter, Nelly? Isn't she lovely?"

"That she is Ma'am; right lovely."

They both smiled as Crystal bid them goodnight and made her way up the stairs wondering what it was that Mrs. Bowman was going to say to her. What could it have been that made her so agitated that the tea towel, instead of being folded neatly and put to dry on the radiator, ended up twisted and crushed in her hands?

CHAPTER TWENTY THREE

1964 – 1967

"Happy New Year!"

Marjorie and Crystal raised their glasses to each other and sipped the bubbling liquid – sparkling wine pretending to be champagne – but it was a gesture and just right to reinforce their positive thoughts towards the New Year stretching ahead of them. Without George, Marjorie was still struggling and felt as though she was learning to walk again having had one of her legs amputated.

The pain of Giles' death haunted Crystal day and night; it sometimes seemed that not an hour went by when she didn't think of him. The holiday in Italy had been a welcome distraction and the fairy-tale Christmas they had spent at Savron Pinder House had done a lot to lift their spirits and make them feel as though they were not alone; they often talked about the magical experience,

"Were we really only just down the road? It was like another world."

They were pleased that whatever the year held in store for them, Arthur and Constance wanted to keep up the contact they had established – in spite of some problems with Mary.

It was during these first few days of January that Crystal made an important decision about her future. She had a day off from the shop, having drifted back again after Christmas to help with the Sales, and went for a walk. She took the familiar route along the village street and then down the fen road; but before turning the corner, she reached the low wall that surrounded the little school and leaned on it to watch the children playing in the sunshine.

Suddenly she knew that that was what she wanted, and by the time she got back to Maple Cottage she had revived her dream of being a teacher. Marjorie was very supportive, particularly as Crystal decided to apply to the local Training College, and by April they had heard that she had been accepted and would start in September.

In the Spring Rosemary married Gerald Bull, a wealthy farmer who owned a lot of land in the neighbouring village and, to her surprise, Crystal received an invitation to the wedding. She asked Eleanore's advice about whether she should go or not, mindful of the potential problem with Isobel, and she was reassured,

"Rosie wants you there, darling. She is such a down to earth soul, bless her, and bears no animosity towards either of us for what happened, even though she loved Giles dearly and misses him dreadfully. She takes the attitude that what's done is done. You can't undo the past and she now has a sister whom she wants at her wedding. As for Granny Isobel, Rosie is about the only one of us who can handle her and she'll take no nonsense from her, so please do come if you would like to."

Talk of the past reminded Crystal of Eleanore's promise to tell her about the problem between her two grandmothers; also, any mention of Giles always upset them both, so partly as a distraction from that, she said quickly,

"You were going to tell me about the trouble between Constance and Isobel."

Eleanore, brought back from thoughts of her beloved dead son, agreed that now would be a good time and the two of them settled down in the drawing room with a pot of tea and plate of biscuits.

"My father, John Lynton-Bell, was Scottish and a very dashing, handsome man, vibrant – positively tingling with life. When he fell in love with Isobel Hunter they had to run away to get married – apparently she was not considered to be good enough for him; according to his family, he was supposed to marry the daughter of another wealthy land owner. It was all arranged, but there was just one problem – he didn't love her. My mother is from much lowlier stock; she was in fact the daughter of the local blacksmith, but, as I said, she and my father fell madly in love and ran away to marry.

They moved here as they were given Manor Farm by my father's Uncle, who did approve of their love and felt sorry for them; John's father had done what father's often did in those days to sons who didn't toe the line, he cut him off without a penny. Anyway they settled here, we children came along and John made a success of the farm. It was a fairly happy marriage – in fact a very happy marriage at first; I know my mother seems austere in old age, but she was a very spirited lady and could be great fun. She has always had a sharp tongue and I think maybe was too conscious of the fact that she isn't from the same social class as my father. I know it sounds ridiculous, but these things mattered much more years ago.

Anyway as you know, our family became very friendly with the Elliotts at Savron Pinder House. Again it was very much the way of things then – families of the same class stuck together. There were all sorts of functions and gatherings and my mother started to suspect that John and Constance were having an affair. Arthur was often away on business, whereas my father's work was here on the farm so he was always around. There is no doubt that Constance and my father were attracted to each other and I think my mother was aware that Constance is of the same social class as my father; she probably had a bit of a chip on her shoulder about it." Eleanore paused and smiled, "You know the whole business of class is not something you bother, or even think about, if you have it – it's effortless, like breathing, but Isobel was very aware of Constance's breeding and her jealousy made her behave badly towards her.

This had the effect of making my father, whose manners were impeccable, apologetic for his wife's behaviour and solicitous towards Constance, all of which fuelled my mother's jealousy. We children would hear her sometimes fly into fits of rage which did nothing to endear her to my father and would have driven a weaker man into the arms of another woman. We are all as certain as we can be that they behaved honourably, but we don't know for sure how they felt about each other.

Anyway there was never any evidence of an affair as such, but when my father died, mother said that she had found some letters to him from Constance and that these are conclusive proof of their infidelity. She won't show anyone and no-one knows where they are, but every so often she makes reference to them and uses them as her reason for never speaking to Constance again. We just don't know what to think. Are there any letters? Or is this something my mother has invented because it vindicates her bad behaviour for so many years, behaviour that drove a wedge between the families. If she was wrong then all that was for nothing.

Constance has maintained a lady-like silence on the subject, though we are sure that she would talk to my mother and put things right if she got half a chance. But again, you see, if my mother relents and talks to Constance and it is obvious she is innocent, it still puts her in the wrong. We just don't know about the letters, but Bette and I think that if they really prove our mother's suspicions were correct, she would have shown them to someone by now. So there you have it – impasse."

Crystal did go to Rosemary's wedding, first of all to the local Church and afterwards to the reception held at a very smart Farmers' Club in Cambridge. The whole scene was a fascinating blur of men in top hats and tails, and ladies in expensive-looking pastel outfits with matching meringue-like creations balanced precariously on their heads. Rosemary, large and pink and very happy, seemed perfectly suited to the robust, florid-looking man at her side; Crystal could see them down the years, surrounded by their brood of stalwart children, if not exactly cherishing, at least content with each other until death parted them.

"Now that's a strange and very enigmatic look you have on your face,"

Startled, Crystal turned and found herself staring straight into the gentle, grey eyes of Charlie Fairlawn, and the embarrassing incident at the Boxing Day hunt flashed before her. She blushed and was, for a moment, lost for words, so he continued,

"Don't you remember me? Think mud and a sore backside." He smiled.

"Yes...yes, of course I do," she stammered, "It was just a bit of a surprise seeing you again."

The room was filled with squawks, shouts and barks of laughter, getting louder as the champagne flowed freely into the rapidly emptying glasses. Clipped, upper class voices shattered the air with a noise like breaking glass; Crystal could see Charlie's lips moving but couldn't hear what he was saying. He indicated a door and she felt herself being gently propelled towards it, his hand under her elbow.

She found herself in a room with a lot of windows all looking out onto a beautiful garden; it was like a conservatory but more substantially built. There were a few people sitting around, talking quietly and Charlie indicated a comfortable, chintz-covered chair into which Crystal gratefully sank; Charlie sat opposite her, putting his drink on the small table between them and leaned forward, studying her, his arms resting casually on his knees.

"Now where were we? Oh yes, the enigmatic look on your face. I was going to be corny and say penny for them but they looked as though they might be worth a good deal more."

He was smiling and Crystal thought it was the most engaging smile she had ever seen apart from….no, don't think about Giles.

"Oh…you know, just musing really. I suppose, in a nutshell, I was thinking how well suited Rosemary and Gerald seem to be. But before I share any more thoughts with you, I think we should introduce ourselves."

Charlie leaned back and made a little pointed steeple under his chin with his index fingers, lacing the rest together.

"I know who you are; I made it my business to find out after our muddy encounter on the hunting field." He leaned forward again, "And I'll bet you know who I am." Crystal laughed, and he held up his hand,

"No don't say anything, because if I'm right I claim a prize. When the wonderful array of food out there is reduced to a sorry wreck in the middle of the room, all the witty speeches have been delivered and the bride and groom warmly toasted almost to destruction, a band will start to play. When that happens I claim the first dance. If you didn't discover my name after our encounter, I will disappear, never to be seen again. What do you say?"

Crystal suddenly felt mischievous,

"What about a middle course? Supposing I didn't discover your name, but would like to know it now?"

He thought for a moment,

"No, sorry, no middle course." He looked at her, grinning and she had to give in.

"OK." She held out her hand, "How do you do, Charlie Fairlawn."

He gripped her fingers in his,

"And how do you do, Crystal Morris…."

At that moment the door opened,

"Come on, Charlie….the car….you know…"

Charlie got up,

"I'm needed out there – balloons and tin cans tied on the back of the wedding car, that sort of thing; remember, though, the first dance is mine." He turned to go,

"Did I actually agree to your prize? I don't think I did." Crystal looked at him and he stopped, his face becoming very serious,

"Oh, you will though… please say you will."

Crystal was impressed by his sincerity and laughed,

"Yes, I will, Charlie Fairlawn."

He looked relieved and a smile spread across his face again as he darted back and quickly kissed her hand, looking deeply into her eyes as he murmured,

"Till later then."

Crystal danced more than once with Charlie Fairlawn and discovered that he was Gerald's nephew. She also learned that he was managing one of the farms for him, was passionate about horses and wanted nothing more than to own his own farm and stables,

"One day, Crystal, my dreams will come true; I am prepared to work hard to make sure they do."

He made her laugh and, as Eleanore drove her home later, Crystal found herself thinking about Charlie Fairlawn, his dark brown curly hair, sincere greyish blue eyes and lovely smile, and she believed that he would indeed make those dreams come true.

CHAPTER TWENTY FOUR

All through that spring and summer, Crystal gradually found a sort of peace she thought had been denied her for ever. She knew that she would never stop mourning Giles, loving him in a very special way, but she also knew she had to make a life, had to – for her own and Marjorie's sake. She had to live because it's what Giles would have wanted. 'Always in my heart' she thought 'he's always, always in my heart.' And she knew he always would be.

She worked at the shop during the week and hurried down to Monk's Manor in the evenings to look after Star, sometimes going for a short ride down the fen roads, cantering beside the soot-black fields and enjoying the sunsets splashed across the evening skies. At the weekends Eleanore would go with her and they relished each other's company, talking, laughing and getting to know each other. As she had predicted, William had left Eleanore and Monk's Manor soon after Rosemary's wedding and was living with his sister, Janice, in the neighbouring village.

The effect of his departure on Eleanore was to release her from some restraining bonds; she discovered a new lease of life and revelled in her freedom. She loved Crystal's company and occasionally both women would go together to visit Giles' grave, standing side by side, holding each other's hands, lost in their own private worlds of grief from which they knew they would never fully recover.

In September when she went to college Crystal entered a world different from any she had previously known. She had chosen the all girls training college in Cambridge, only twenty miles from Savron Pinder, so that she could easily visit Marjorie and Eleanore at weekends. She had the little car – luckily she had passed her test at the first attempt – so that would make travelling easier than if she had to rely on public transport. She would be living at the college during the week and the fact that she was not going far away made the goodbyes much easier than they would otherwise have been.

"Don't you dare start worrying about me," Marjorie admonished as she helped Crystal to pack, "You know perfectly well that I have a good life here and want nothing more than that you should enjoy yourself and get as much out of this experience as possible."

Eleanore was just as positive,

"My darling, I hope you have a lovely time at college and I look forward to hearing all about it when I see you. I shall miss you, but I shall look after Star for you and we can ride when you come home. God bless you."

She watched her daughter climb into the little car and waved until it disappeared round the bend in the drive.

Crystal settled well, made friends easily and enjoyed her work. She had always thought of Cambridge as a magical place and was even more convinced of this now that she was seeing it from an entirely different perspective. She made the most of all that was on offer and sometimes stayed at college at the weekends instead of travelling home so that she could go to parties and hang out with the other students.

The college girls tended to be popular with the undergraduates as male students outnumbered females, so there was no shortage of invitations out. Her new friends quickly got themselves boyfriends and were surprised when Crystal didn't.

They couldn't understand it as she was so attractive, but didn't seem to want to get involved at any level. When they teased her about it

".....you can take playing hard to get too far you know, Cryssie...."

"Yeah, who are you waiting for, Prince Charles?"

She just laughed it off. She was popular with the male students but always insisted that they were just friends; if anyone tried to take things further she found herself recoiling. The stone – that hard lump inside her that had formed when Giles died – was still there. It wouldn't go away; and many of the young men became intrigued by the beautiful girl who joined in the fun but remained a little aloof. An air of mystery grew up around her, compounded by the fact that she occasionally disappeared at weekends. She was fun, good company, but impossible to get close to and those who tried were kindly, but firmly, rebuffed.

In many ways Crystal blossomed. She discovered that she had a talent for the Arts; English and Drama were her main subjects, but she also studied Dance and the visual Arts, spending time at the Fitzwilliam Museum and getting involved in some of the student productions. These activities, plus her work, about which she was very conscientious, kept her busy and often several weekends would go by without her visiting Savron Pinder.

She kept in touch with both Marjorie and Eleanore by telephone and frequently asked after Arthur and Constance. Eleanore told her that they were well as far as she knew, but that she hadn't managed to see much of them as quite often when she telephoned it was Mary who answered and Connie and Arthur were not available. She was told that they were out and would ring back later, but they seldom did, and Mary would tell her next time that her parents must have forgotten,

"….so sorry, Eleanore, but they are getting on a bit, you know. They seem to need a fair amount of extra rest these days. I'll see what I can do."

On the rare occasions that she did manage to visit Savron Pinder House, Eleanore was impressed by Mary's change of attitude towards her parents. She had become very solicitous of their welfare, tucking rugs around their knees and getting Mrs. Bowman to make sure they had plenty of hot drinks. But Arthur and Constance seemed the same as always, in fact they both looked a bit fuller in the face as if they had gained a little weight. It suited them; they did, however, seem a little more tired than Eleanore had known them to be previously, but she had to agree with Mary, they were getting older and couldn't be expected not to show signs of old age. She was glad that their eldest daughter seemed to be taking such good care of them and even more pleased and surprised when she learned that, since the Christmas of 1963, Mary had kept in close touch with Emily and her husband.

"I am very hopeful that they will come and visit soon," Constance said, as she saw Eleanore out after one of her visits.

As she walked home, Eleanore reflected on the family she had known for so long. She thought back to the good times they had all had when they were young but shivered as she remembered the devastating effect on them all of Jack's death. It had been terrible for her, but dreadful for them too. There was no doubt that he had been the shining star of the family and their hope for the future continuation of Arthur's business. Mary had always been a little difficult; not the eldest child, which would have suited her bossy nature, or the youngest; but stuck in the middle between her elder brother, whom everyone seemed to adore, and her younger sister who used her dimpled cuteness to wind everyone round her little finger, getting her own way in everything.

Emily had shown a talent for dancing, something she had inherited from Constance, and a great deal of money was spent on dancing lessons for her. Constance even had a dream of setting up a dancing school at Savron Pinder House by knocking together some of the upper rooms, but that idea never came to fruition as Emily announced one day that she was giving up dancing. Then, at seventeen, she had rocked the family by running off and secretly marrying Jed, the son of the man who brought the fair to the village green every year.

'What a to-do that was,' Eleanore thought as she turned off the foot path and started down the drive to Monk's Manor, remembering, as if it was yesterday, Arthur's fury and Constance's tears of sorrow and disbelief. Jed with his black, shining curls, gold earring, dark skin and flashing eyes, a red handkerchief knotted at his neck above white shirt collar and shiny black waistcoat. He could balance expertly on the merry-go-round, swaying in time with the huge machine as it undulated in circular motion carrying its cargo of brightly coloured, grinning horses. He would lean against the painted body and smile his dazzling white smile at a girl as she moved up and down, clinging to the twisted pole in front of her. He was well known as a rogue and would often disappear behind the caravans at the end of the evening with the silly girl if, flattered by his attention, she had been unable to resist his charms.

Emily and her friends had only gone to the fair for a bit of a lark at the end of an evening out,

"I say what fun! Look, let's go on those horsy things."

And they had, squealing their way around in mock terror. All except Emily who had sat still on her horse, staring into Jed's eyes and he, for once, wasn't grinning his Jack-the-lad, cock-sure grin, but just stared back. When the ride came to an end they still held each other's eyes, and Emily had told her friends to go home without her.

"And husband number two wasn't much better," thought Eleanore, shaking her head as she let herself into her quiet home.

Minty's wedding in the autumn was great fun. Crystal and Lottie, Minty's ten year old cousin, were the only two bridesmaids and were dressed in pale green satin. Minty, for once, managed to shed her tom-boy image, looking radiant in white as she walked down the aisle on Matt's arm, and he was glowing with pride as he gave away his only daughter to a young man he obviously liked and admired. The reception was held in the village hall which rang with music and laughter far into the night. It was homely, old fashioned and wholesome and Crystal loved every minute, glad for her friend and just a little envious of her happiness.

CHAPTER TWENTY FIVE

The Christmases of 1964 and 1965 were very different from the magical experience of 1963. The first was spent quietly – just Crystal and Marjorie together, accepting invitations to drinks with kindly neighbours, tramping across frosty fields to work up an appetite and dozing in front of the fire. The next year they managed to get to Norfolk in Crystal's little car and enjoyed a riotous time with Granny Morris, Madge and an assortment of relatives on George's side of the family. In 1966 they went to Eastbourne on the train. Grandma Bates was very ill and it meant a lot to Marjorie to be able to spend some time with her mother, a decision she never regretted as the old lady died the following spring.

Crystal knew how hard it had been for Eleanore to visit Arthur and Constance, and when she had tried to do so during a weekend home in the autumn of 1964 she had met with the same rebuff – "I'm so sorry, my dear, but my parents are resting."

It was therefore with some considerable surprise that in the spring of 1965, while home for the Easter holidays, she was called to the phone by Marjorie saying that Mary wanted to speak to her. She and Marjorie had just finished a day of spring cleaning and were looking forward to a hot meal, during which Crystal had promised to entertain her mum with tales of her latest teaching practice; an experience from which she was still trying to recover.

"Are you sure?" She mouthed.

Marjorie covered the receiver and whispered, "Yes. It's Mary Elliott and she wants to talk to you."

"Hello…it's Crystal here."

"Hello, my dear. How are you?"

"I'm very well thank-you" Crystal made a face at Marjorie, then listened as Mary continued,

"I was wondering if you would like to come to tea – shall we say Saturday? My parents would love to see you. The old poppets are getting very frail and I'm sure it would mean a lot to them. So what do you say?"

"Well….yes..Thank-you…"

"Good. About half past three then. We shall look forward to it."

Crystal replaced the receiver and stared across the room at Marjorie who had one eyebrow raised, waiting to hear what it was all about.

"And they say a leopard can't change its spots! She sounded as nice as pie and has invited me to tea on Saturday."

"And you're going?"

"Well, yes. I'd love to see Arthur and Constance again. It just seems so weird, her inviting me."

Crystal's hand suddenly flew to her mouth, "Oh, I'm sorry, Mum, I didn't ask if the invitation included you."

Marjorie waved her hand in the air,

"Don't you worry about that. It's you they will be delighted to see. Perhaps I'll be able to come next time."

So Crystal went to tea at Savron Pinder House that Saturday and was quite surprised by the change in her grandparents. They were indeed starting to show their age and seemed to have lost some of the sparkle and bounce that had been so apparent just over a year before. Like Eleanore, she was impressed by Mary's care of them and watched with some surprise as she saw to their needs and made sure they were comfortable.

And so it was that these visits, now begun, became a regular feature of her college holidays until she left in the summer of 1967. Mary would call and invite her to tea, sometimes with Marjorie, and Crystal was sad to see that the old couple, of whom she was very fond, were indeed deteriorating very fast.

Savron Pinder House

Spring 1967

Arthur sat by the big window in the blue drawing room with a rug over his knees staring out at the familiar scene stretching before him in the bright spring sunshine. It was the middle of the morning and the distant water of the lake shimmered at the end of the rolling lawn; in the wood snowdrops had given way to a carpet of golden and pale lemon daffodils. He sighed. He used to relish days like these, coaxing Constance into her coat and outside to tramp around the grounds inhaling huge gulps of air and trying to identify the birds that flew through the branches above their heads.

But this was the third spring now that he hadn't been able to get out like he used to. He just felt so blessed tired all the time, so lethargic. He would no sooner get across the threshold than he'd want to be back indoors again sitting down. He kept getting appalling headaches and the soles of his feet were painful, even went numb some of the time; it took all the pleasure out of walking. 'What a plague is old age,' he thought, shifting his weight in the wing chair. 'And poor old Connie's so tired this morning she isn't even up yet'.

"Here you are, pops, I've brought you some tea." Mary entered the room smiling brightly and put his favourite cup down on a small table where he would be able to reach it quite easily. She adjusted the rug around his knees then pulled up a chair and sat next to him in the big bay window.

"Pops, I hate to bother you, but there are several financial matters that need your attention. Do you feel up to it?"

Arthur frowned. If only this damn muddle would clear from his head; he just couldn't think straight these days.

"Do you think they can wait, love? Perhaps this afternoon."

Mary smiled and patted his hand,

"Of course." She got up to go and stood looking down at him, one hand resting on his shoulder,

"There is a solution you know, pops. Have you thought any more about what I suggested?"

"Well, yes I have Mary, but I really need to talk to your mother. Is she up yet?"

"Bowman's just taken her some tea. I'll go and see how she's feeling." She dropped a kiss on top of her father's head and went out of the room, closing the door quietly behind her.

Power of Attorney, that's what Mary suggested; she wanted him to give her power of attorney, then she could take all the financial burdens off his shoulders. He sighed again. It did seem like a good idea. Funny thing that – Mary's attitude towards them both since they had started to show significant signs of old age. She had always been a bit impatient with them before. Quite sharp and bossy. They used to call her the sergeant major; but since they had needed more attention she had been much nicer somehow, kinder, more tolerant. You would have thought it would have been the other way round. Ah well. She already ran the house-keeping side of things, of course, had done so for years, so maybe this wasn't such a big step, Power of Attorney. And he had to admit, he rarely felt like tackling things these days, just too damned tired all the time. Still, it felt like giving up his last bit of independence and Arthur was reluctant to do this,'Never was one to give in,' he thought as he strained his ears, wishing he could hear sounds of his wife approaching.

Upstairs, Constance sat in bed drinking the tea that Nelly had brought her, hoping that perhaps it would make her feel like getting up. The tiredness these days was chronic and the headaches almost unbearable. Thank goodness for the pain-killers James had given them. And the strange patches on her arms. A form of dermatitis, James said, but the cream did seem to be doing some good. She had never known anything like it, but then she had never been seventy seven before.

And poor Arthur, he was feeling the same; there was no doubt about it they were just getting old. Next year was Arthur's eightieth birthday and she did so want them both to be well enough to celebrate it in style. Perhaps they could have a big party…..perhaps all old quarrels could be put behind them before it was too late. Dear, dear Arthur. If anybody knew how to forgive and forget it was him. What a wonderful example he was and how lucky she was to have him.

She leaned back on her lacy pillows and thought again about that difficult time, the time that had been painful for all of them when she and John Lynton-Bell had realised they were in love with each other. She sighed. That was the amazing and terrible thing about love, the wonderful, totally awful thing. You didn't ask for it to come. It descended and gripped you, shook you like a dog with a rabbit, took over lives and threatened to turn your world upside down. It couldn't just be denied, it changed everything; and all you could do was decide what to do about it. It had to be faced because one thing you couldn't do was pretend that it wasn't there.

She and John had faced it and decided they had to walk away from each other. Too many people would get hurt; their love just could not be because they both knew that they couldn't build any kind of happiness on other people's misery, particularly people they cared deeply about.

And Arthur had known. He had seen her struggle, felt her pain and loved her through it, so relieved, so thankful that she had chosen him and the family. She had been rewarded by a long and happy marriage to a man who adored her too much ever to mention the past or hold it against her in any way. They had helped each other through the pain that Emily had inflicted on them and then the agony of Jack's death.

Constance heard her door open and tried to raise herself up from the pillows but her shoulders ached with fatigue. She turned her head and saw Mary coming towards the bed. She was smiling and kissed her mother on the cheek.

"How are you feeling, Mums?"

"Very tired, dear."

"Well, you just stay there for as long as you like. I'll get Bowman to bring you some lunch up on a tray." She patted her mother's hand and Connie tried again to sit up,

"No…come on now. You lie still until you are feeling better." Mary gently eased her shoulders back onto the pillows and Connie sighed again. She felt tears of frustration spring into her eyes,

"Dear, dear. This is so silly….so silly." She dabbed her eyes with a hanky.

"It's not silly at all. You know what the doctor said – plenty of rest and to be sure to take the medicines he left for you. Bowman will bring them up with your lunch. Now you lie still and rest. Maybe you can get up for a while this afternoon."

"Where's Arthur?"

"He's downstairs. He's fine, just sitting in his chair reading a book." Mary walked to the door and blew her mother a kiss before letting herself quietly out into the passageway.

Constance looked around at the bedroom she had shared with Arthur for so many years. It was beautiful, big and light and airy. It was looking especially bright these days as Mary had insisted on re-decorating it every year for the past three years. The walls were pale blue and the ceiling a sort of dove grey,

"So good for softening the effects of the bright early morning light," Mary had said.

When Constance had questioned the need to decorate it again, Mary had justified it by saying that she wanted it to be as lovely as possible for them as they obviously needed to spend more time there these days. She had even insisted on doing it herself, a fact which surprised both Eleanore and Crystal when they had visited and been told all about it.

Constance turned over in bed and sank down further into its warm softness. This was new too; gone was the old four poster with its rich canopy,

"...it's blocking out all the light," Mary had said, and in its place she had installed an expensive and very comfortable king size bed

"...you both deserve the very best at your time of life."

It was so strange, Mary's change of attitude towards them, strange, but welcome. How lovely that she had turned out well in the end, and it all seemed to stem from that Christmas she had spent with Emily and her new husband. The break must have done her good. In fact she and Arthur had been pleased when Mary had gone to stay with them again for several long weekends after that, and now there was even talk of Emily coming to see them. How lovely that would be...they could meet her new husband at last....patch up all the old quarrels before it was too late...yes...that would be lovely. With thoughts of her younger daughter floating around in her head, Constance fell asleep.

It wasn't until much later in the day, early evening in fact, when the bright spring sun had set and twilight shadows stretched across the lawns that

Constance sat next to Arthur in the bay window. She reached across and held his hand. He had just gone through Mary's proposal with her and she had to admit it made a lot of sense.

"I think we should do it, dear, but do you really have to bother with the formality of Power of Attorney? Just give her control of the finances and keep an eye on things from more of a distance so to speak; I hate to think of you worrying about money all the time. We know there's plenty there from the sale of the business, it's just a matter of ensuring that it's well managed and I know it bothers you not being able to keep on top of it like you used to."

Constance had never had to concern herself with financial matters, that had always been Arthur's domain, as running the house had been hers. In 1964 they had both changed their wills to ensure that Crystal, their beautiful granddaughter, the living link with Jack who they didn't previously know existed, would benefit substantially when they died. Mary and Emily would, of course, inherit the house as well as some money, but quite a large sum of money was to go to Crystal. They were not entirely happy about giving half of the house to Emily as they knew only too well that she would want to convert her share to money; and money ran through her fingers like sand, but they had to do it as she was their daughter and must be treated fairly.

They could only hope that Mary's sense would prevail, particularly now that the two sisters seemed to be getting on so well together. They would have to sort it out themselves. It was just a shame to be thinking like this as they had so hoped to enjoy many more years of active life in reasonably good health. They both had longevity in their backgrounds with parents who had lived into their late eighties and even nineties. Arthur's grandfather had famously made it to a hundred and one and had still managed to get out and about.

That evening they felt well enough to sit at the table and, while enjoying some broth that Mrs. Bowman had made for them, they told Mary of their decision. She was obviously delighted,

"I think you are doing the right thing. I shall set it all in motion with Mr. Bradford at Bradford, Fisher and Dawson's tomorrow morning and I will, of course, keep you informed about any transactions that I make."

She looked from one parent to the other and smiled broadly.

CHAPTER TWENTY SIX

May 1967

James Robertson stood at the window gazing out onto his garden as he drained the last few drops of his morning coffee. It was lush and green; the tulips had finished, but his eyes came to rest on a glorious clump of forget-me-nots, pale blue jewels sparkling in the sunlight, so welcome after days of rain.

"Well, it may be a blessed nuisance at times, but the garden certainly does benefit from a drop of rain."

He put down his cup and picking up his old, battered leather bag, called upstairs to his wife,

"I'm off then," but she didn't hear him above the sound of the hoover. No matter; he let himself out knowing that she would expect him to be gone, and that she knew exactly what time he would be home. His habits hadn't changed much for the last twenty years. He threw his bag into the back of his old car and then hesitated. He sniffed the air.

'No, dammit, I'll walk. It'll do me good."

He retrieved his bag and set off in the direction of Savron Pinder House. The handle creaked, metal on leather, and James smiled,

"I reckon you and I will both just about last the course; yep, you'll see me up to retirement."

Then he looked round, hoping nobody had actually seen him addressing a tattered, brown medical bag.

His progress through the village was punctuated by calls and waves; women hanging out their washing,

"Is it going to rain again, Doctor? If it is I'm wasting me blessed time!"

"No, don't think so. Set fair for the rest of the day now."

He was called to admire rows of tiny green shoots in one of the cottage gardens; Sid was hoeing carefully between them and James could see that the crop this year would be as impressive as ever.

He had known these people for most of their lives; he knew their families and they knew him well enough not to try any malingering; he was sure to find them out. He was their doctor, they trusted him and he had earned their respect over the years.

He reached the end of the village and had only a short walk until he came to 'Squire's house.' There was no question of Arthur riding about the village on his bicycle now; those days were gone for ever. No, he and Constance were fading fast; all sorts of aches and pains now; old age – what a bugger. He turned into the drive and watched two squirrels chasing each other across the parkland and up a nearby tree. Yep, his mind was made up. He'd be retired by this time next year and then he could really get to grips with the garden.

'Might even build that summer house Jean has been on about for so long.'

He stopped as he rounded the bend and was struck again by the magnificence of the house he saw before him.

"What a place! What a beautiful place. And what times we've had here."

He walked on remembering the fine dinners with gleaming silver and sparkling crystal – the opulence of it all. And Constance. What a woman! There was gossip once about her and John Lynton-Bell. Mind you, would have been surprising if someone hadn't fallen in love with her; truth to tell he'd been a little in love with her himself, worshipped her from a distance – his best friend's mother, a beautiful, unattainable older woman who floated past him on a cloud of perfume, causing him to blush and stammer if she looked at him or asked even a simple question, a woman who only knew him as Jack's best friend. Ah, well. All changed now. Poor souls. It comes to us all and they do seem to be getting worse;

'Didn't like the look of Arthur's skin last time I saw him. Bit jaundiced; cirrhosis? Too much of the old scotch in the evening? No, surely not. Still, he didn't look too good that's for sure. Bit of a shame to be ailing now just when they've discovered a granddaughter they never knew existed. A daughter, born to Eleanore Lynton-Bell and fathered by Jack Elliott. No wonder she's a stunner.

James crunched over the gravel and up the steps, turning as he did so to look at the lake, gleaming in the watery sunlight; and he remembered the times that he and Jack, three years his junior, had climbed trees and made rafts to paddle out onto the water, shouting and laughing, thinking that those days would never end.

He rang the bell and waited

July 1967

"Mum…I'm home."

Crystal crashed through the door, staggering under the weight of several bags which she dumped unceremoniously in the middle of the floor. Marjorie appeared at the living room door and welcomed her with a hug.

"Cup of tea please, Mums. I'm parched."

"Are you sure you don't mean black coffee?" Marjorie eyed her daughter, guessing correctly that the previous evening, her last at college, had been devoted to some serious celebrating.

"Oh no, absolutely not! We've been sloshing that back all morning."

She grinned and flopped down at the dining room table.

"Tea it is then." Marjorie smiled, raising her eyes to heaven as she made her way out into the kitchen.

A few minutes later she set Crystal's favourite mug down in front of her and sat in the chair opposite.

"So a bit of an end-of-college-days celebration last night was it?"

"Just a bit."

Crystal sipped her tea, one hand on her forehead.

"So you won't be wanting any of the sparkling stuff I've got in the fridge then?"

"Tell you what. I'll drag this lot upstairs, throw myself into a lovely hot bath and then we'll see, shall we?"

They grinned at each other, both glad that Crystal was home and that they had something to celebrate – the amazingly quirky good fortune of the location of her first teaching post.

She had gained her teaching certificate with honours and had also managed to secure a job at the local primary school. It was one of those strange co-incidences that rarely happen in life. She had applied for a couple of posts and had attended one interview for a job teaching juniors at a school on the other side of Cambridge, but narrowly missed securing that. She wasn't too disappointed as there was something about the ambience of the school, a sort of coldness in the atmosphere, which she didn't like very much.

What she really wanted was to teach in a little school like Savron Pinder. She knew they were doing some outstanding work, particularly in the Arts, under a new and very dynamic head teacher, but she didn't think there was any chance at all of a vacancy occurring there just at a time to suit her. She was therefore astounded when Marjorie had rung her at college to say that she knew for a fact the junior teacher was leaving in the summer. Crystal had wasted no time but applied immediately and, after a rigorous but enjoyable interview, had been offered the job.

October 1967

Jon looked at Crystal and blinked, then he carried on looking, his eyes unblinking through steel-rimmed spectacles, and she thought, not for the first time, how much he reminded her of an owl, a baby owl, wise beyond its years and on a quest for more knowledge. She smiled at him and then looked back at the project work he had just presented to her – pages of it – "Methods of torturing people in the Middle Ages." And all with graphic and bloodthirsty illustrations.

"Your work is amazing, Jon, but why does it always have to be so gruesome?"

He carried on staring, "What's 'gruesome,' Miss?

"Well, it means to do with blood and pain, that sort of thing."

"I don't really know. My father often brings stuff home that's a bit 'gruesome' and we talk about it."

Jon's father was a scientist at one of the laboratories in Cambridge; his mother was charming and his baby sister adorable. Crystal was quite sure that there was nothing really, intrinsically sinister about Jon's obsession with the gory aspects of any topic they covered. She had spoken to his parents about it and they had agreed that it was more than likely just a passing phase; the work was carefully researched and beautifully presented.

She sent him back to his place and peace reigned in the class room as thirty children pored over their topic books, all keen to produce their best work. She liked this new method of teaching and really believed that it was best for the children. They pursued their own lines of enquiry within a given framework; it stretched the brightest, giving them plenty of scope, and left the teacher with time to help those of lower ability.

The afternoon drew to a close and Crystal made her way home along the village street, thinking how strange it was to be teaching in the very school where she had once been a learner, then she smiled at the thought, realising that she was still very much a learner.

She let herself into Maple Cottage, made a cup of tea and sat down in one of the comfortable chairs in the sitting room. Marjorie was out at a WI meeting and for Crystal an evening of marking and preparation stretched ahead. Tomorrow was Friday and she promised herself an evening ride on Star. Unfortunately Eleanore was away for a fortnight making the most of the last sunshine that Italy had to offer before the winter set in. She had gone with Rosemary who was happily pregnant and preparing for the arrival of her second child the following spring. Her first, a robust little boy called Gerard, had arrived just before Christmas in 1964 and was staying with Gerald's mother while Rosemary took a break with Eleanore.

Crystal had been so busy with her new job that she had hardly seen anything of her mother since August when they had spoken about Arthur and Constance and shared with each other their concerns for the elderly couple. The invitations from Mary had stopped abruptly and no-one seemed to know what was happening at Savron Pinder House. It was rumoured that both Alice and Vera had been dismissed but there was no way of knowing for sure as Mary made it impossible for them to go there, saying that her parents were not well enough to receive visitors.

Crystal frowned as she washed up her cup; something just wasn't right. She settled down to her work, but the niggle at the back of her mind wouldn't go away.

CHAPTER TWENTY SEVEN

It was nearly lunch time the following day when Jane Langham, the Head Teacher, crept quietly into the class room and whispered in Crystal's ear. The buzz of noise stopped as the children strained to hear what was being said, but they couldn't and had no idea why their teacher suddenly rushed from the room leaving Mrs. Langham sitting at the desk in front of them.

When she reached the tiny room that served as a medical room, staff room for three teachers and an office for Jane, Crystal was greeted by an extremely agitated Nelly Bowman, standing by the window and twisting a large handkerchief in her hands.

"Oh, my dear, I am so sorry to come here like this, but I didn't know what else to do or where to go. I know that Mrs. Cowper's away at the moment and I just have to talk to someone and with you being their granddaughter and all I just thought...." Her eyes filled with tears and she blew her nose to try and stifle a sob.

Crystal took her arm and helped her to a chair.

"Mrs. Bowman, calm down and tell me what's wrong."

Nelly was rocking back and forward in the chair and suddenly broke down completely, sobbing, wiping her eyes and saying that she was sorry over

278

and over again. Crystal waited until the older woman was able to speak and became increasingly horrified by what she was being told.

"Oh, I don't know, Miss, I really don't, but I have to speak up. I just hope I'm not speaking out of turn…"

"Mrs. Bowman just tell me what's wrong."

"Well yesterday lunchtime, Squire was downstairs in the drawing room and Mrs. Elliott was still in bed – which is often the case these days – anyway I took some lunch up to her and she looked proper poorly. She's gone a sort of yellow colour and she was scratching these sores on her arms; poor pet, it upset me to see her like that. I tried to leave her the tray but she didn't want it, so I took it back down to the kitchen then went to find Miss Mary. I just felt she ought to know that her mother seemed to be getting worse. I went out into the hallway and saw that she was on the telephone…well I didn't like to interrupt, so I was about to go back to the kitchen and wait for a few minutes when I couldn't help overhearing what she was saying."

Nelly stopped speaking and Crystal, seeing that she was about to start crying again, put her arm gently round the plump, shaking shoulders,

"Go on, Mrs. Bowman, what did you hear?"

Nelly composed herself and continued,

"Well, I thought it was strange, but probably wouldn't have said nothing about it if it wasn't for what Miss Mary did to me afterwards."

The tears threatened again as the memory of the previous day's event came flooding back. Crystal waited patiently until she finally had the whole story. It seemed that just as Nelly Bowman was about to return to the kitchen she heard Mary say,

"It's working. The plan's working." Then, at that moment, she had turned, seen Nelly and glared at her with a murderous look on her face.

"It was terrible, honestly Miss Crystal, I've known her for years and never seen her look like that."

Flinging down the receiver, she had stepped across the hall, taken hold of Nelly's shoulders in a vicious grip and shaken her back and forward like a rag doll. When she finally let her go, she had ordered her out of the house, both her and Mr. Bowman. Just like that.

"I couldn't believe it! She was shouting that I was creeping round spying on her. She called Bowman, give us both some money and said we was not needed any more."

This induced a fresh bout of weeping with much blowing of her nose; while Crystal stared silently out of the window. She turned back to the figure huddled in the chair,

"Where are you and your husband staying?"

"Well, we was given enough time to pack our things and we went up to my sister's in the village. But the worst thing is, Miss Crystal, we never saw Squire before we left and as we was going up the drive there was this ambulance coming down ringing its bell. I just don't know what's happening."

As the poor, distraught woman sobbed into her handkerchief, Crystal became aware of the noise of children released into the playground for their pre-lunch run around.

She assured the agitated house-keeper that she had done exactly the right thing by coming to her, and even managed to calm her considerably before sending her on her way

"Try not to worry, Mrs. Bowman, I'll think of something and I'll get in touch with you as soon as I have any news."

Watching Nelly tie her headscarf under her chin, Crystal realised that she had no idea what that something would be. She felt a gentle pressure on her arm,

"Truth to tell, I've been worried for quite a while," the older woman shook her head and the skin underneath her chin wobbled, "something's just not right...hasn't been for some time now....I don't know."

Shaking her head again, she made her way across the playground and out of the gate.

Crystal watched her go, her mind churning, how strange that Nelly's parting words should echo so exactly her thoughts of the previous evening. 'The plan is working." What plan, and who was Mary talking to?

Even as she asked it, she was horribly certain that she knew the answer to the last question.

CHAPTER TWENTY EIGHT

"Well that's your lot dispatched into the playground."

Jane breezed into the room and stopped abruptly as she saw Crystal's face,

"Oh, my dear. I thought I'd better come and get you as the poor old duck looked so agitated. I gather from the expression on your face I either did exactly the right or absolutely the wrong thing"

"Oh....er...yes. Thank-you for that, Jane. You did the right thing; it was very kind of you. Oh dear."

"Right. Cup of tea for you and then you can tell me all about it."

Jane made the tea then listened as Crystal told her why Nelly had come and went on to share with her some of the reasons why she had been concerned about her grandparents for some time.

"So what do you think is happening? Are they just manifesting the sort of illnesses you would expect people to get in old age? Could the house keeper be imagining things? The plan she overheard being referred to doesn't have to be anything sinister, you know."

Jane was so down to earth; talented, but with her feet firmly on the ground and listening to her Crystal felt more confused than ever.

"I know. There's just something I can't quite put my finger on."

Jane thought for a moment then made a decision.

"Look. It's Friday afternoon. I can easily go and sit with your lot and do my paperwork while they get on with those amazing project books they are doing; you are so well organised that they all know exactly what to do. Then for the last hour Meryl can take them out to games with her class. You go down to Savron Pinder House and demand to know what's going on. Crystal, they are your grandparents; you have a right to know."

Crystal gave her boss a grateful look and thought again how lucky she was to work for such a person. Jane was silent for a few moments then frowned,

"But didn't you say Mary seemed to be treating her parents much more kindly than she had previously?"

"Well yes, she has but….I know it sounds weird….it just doesn't ring true somehow; it's like watching a show."

Crystal was almost surprised herself to hear what she was saying, but she knew it was true. That was exactly how Mary's little shows of kindness had struck her – as just that, little shows with no substance. She got up and absent-mindedly bent down to pick up Jane's empty cup. The head took it from her,

"Leave that and get down there; find out what's going on – and don't let Mary bully you."

Ten minutes later a group of children watched in surprise as their teacher walked out of the school gate and disappeared round the corner at the top of the road. She strode purposefully in the direction of Savron Pinder House then hesitated when she reached the top of the drive where her courage almost deserted her. What if Mary flew at her in a rage? Could she really handle this situation on her own and should she even be trying? If only Eleanore were here. Then suddenly Arthur's face was there in front of her – boyish, flushed and happy – just as it had looked so often during that wonderful Christmas; and Constance too, so kind, beautiful and elegant. The thought of these two very special people suffering gave her the courage she needed and she continued on down the drive and up the steps to the front door.

She was about to ring the bell when she heard a voice coming from inside the house. One of the drawing room sash windows was open very slightly at the bottom and it was through this that Crystal could hear Mary shouting. She crept nearer and flattened herself against the wall.

"…You must come up to your room. You are not well enough to be sitting up like this. You should be in bed in your own room…"

She strained her ears and managed to hear Arthur's reply though his voice was very faint,

"Mary… leave me…I will not go to bed. I want to see Connie. Where have they taken her? Where's Bowman? Tell him to fetch the car round…."

Crystal kept her body flat against he wall but moved her head so that she could see into the room. Arthur was sitting in his chair while Mary, red in the face, was towering over him, tugging at his arm.

"Father, will you do……"

Crystal didn't wait to hear any more but hurried back to the front door and pulled as hard as she could on the bell, not stopping until Mary flung open the door. At first her face looked the same as it had a few moments before, red with anger and frustration, but as soon as she saw Crystal her expression softened.

"Crystal….I'm so glad to see you….I'm at my wits' end. Mother has been taken to hospital and father's being very difficult….do come in, perhaps you can help me."

She had lowered her voice almost to a whisper; her hand was at her throat and her eyes, full of concern, suddenly looked a little damp with tears as she blinked at her niece.

Crystal followed her to the drawing room where Arthur was still slumped in his chair. He looked up as they entered and Crystal was shocked by his appearance. He was painfully thin and his skin had a strange, yellowish tinge to it.

"Now, father, look who's come to see you; it's Crystal. Maybe she can persuade you that you would be better off upstairs in bed."

Before Arthur could say anything, Mary turned her back on him and drew Crystal to one side,

"Honestly, I'm so worried. I'm all on my own and I just don't know what to do."

Mary and not knowing what to do didn't belong in the same sentence. She was using the soft voice again; a sound which bore no relation to the harsh, grating rasp that had jarred Crystal's ears through the open window a few minutes earlier. There were tears in her eyes which she made a great show of brushing away with the back of her hand. Stage managed – that was it – the whole thing was being stage managed for her benefit. Out of the corner of her eye Crystal saw Arthur raise his hand and it fluttered in the air like a little bird,

"Want to see Connie," he mouthed, his voice scarcely more than a hoarse whisper.

"Father, you can't." Mary spoke firmly and sounded to Crystal as though she was addressing a naughty and rather dim child. She turned to her visitor again and, covering her mouth with her hand, whispered,

"You can see, Crystal, can't you that he's not well enough to go anywhere." She looked back at her father, raising her voice,

"Crystal agrees with me. You have to go to bed and stop being so tiresome."

Arthur slumped in the chair and Crystal suddenly felt herself boiling with rage. She wanted to tell Mary that she certainly did not agree with her and then take this vicious, manipulative woman by the shoulders and shake her until her teeth rattled. She wasn't afraid and could easily have stood up to her, but something stopped her. She was to wonder about this many times afterwards and be eternally thankful to whatever power it was that restrained her that day. She just knew instinctively that, in order to find out what Mary was up to, she had to play along with her, keep her on side.

Mary was speaking again,

"He hasn't been up to bed for several nights; claims it was because he wanted to give my mother chance to get a good night's sleep, but I'm just concerned that he isn't getting enough sleep himself."

The crocodile tears were in evidence again and Crystal took the opportunity to ask what was wrong with Constance.

"Gastroenteritis the doctor says. She's been vomiting and had very bad diarrhoea."

Staying completely calm Crystal moved across the room and knelt down by Arthur's chair. As she expected, Mary followed her, affecting concern, but clearly unwilling for even a few words to be exchanged without her knowledge. Ignoring her aunt, Crystal took her grandfather's hand in both of hers and looked into his eyes.

"Grandfather, you do seem unwell and in need of rest. Don't you think you would be more comfortable upstairs in your bed?"

Arthur tried with difficulty to focus on Crystal's face and muttered,

"Can't get there, Crystal. Can't manage the stairs. Could sleep on the sofa in the morning room"

"Oh but, father, you can! We will help…"

Crystal leapt up and cut Mary off in mid-sentence,

"I'm sure we could make the sofa comfortable for him." She opened her eyes wide, looked directly at her aunt and smiled very sweetly, then turned back to Arthur,

"We will make up the sofa in the morning room as a bed for you as long as you promise to do everything Mary tells you. She is doing her best to make you better and you must behave yourself and be a good boy for her."

'Forgive me…please forgive me,' she thought as she squeezed her grandfather's hand and prayed that she would get an opportunity one day to explain and apologise.

"Yes…yes, of course, Crystal's right. Then when you're feeling better you can go back upstairs," and, tight-lipped, Mary started towards the door.

Still with the smile on her face Crystal said,

"I'm sure Mrs Bowman will fetch some blankets. Shall I call her?"

Mary hesitated,

"Oh…er…no, it's alright, I'll fetch them, Bowman's busy at the moment."

'Yes,' thought Crystal, 'busy crying her eyes out at her sister's house because of your vicious treatment of her, you malicious, lying woman.'

But, keeping her expression bland, she helped Mary to get Arthur to the morning room and settled as comfortably as possible on the sofa there.

As they crept quietly out and pulled the door shut behind them, Crystal asked,

"Has the doctor been?"

"Oh yes. Dear James has paid regular visits. He came down this morning and it was then that he insisted we call an ambulance and get mother into hospital as she had started vomiting. He thought it was gastroenteritis – which has since been confirmed by the hospital – and is worried about her becoming dehydrated; she is in the best possible place at the moment. It's just old age, you know,

Crystal, we have to expect this, upsetting though it may be."

Crystal turned away, unable to be certain that her resolve to play along with her aunt would hold if the false tears were squeezed out again. They walked to the door and she managed a smile as she said,

"Well, bear up, Mary, and let me know if there's anything at all I can do to help."

"No, there's nothing, thank-you, dear. It was a godsend you coming down here this afternoon, but I can manage now. Don't worry about me"

The smile she directed towards her niece would have appropriately graced the features of an early martyr, preparing to be burned at the stake; and with the singe of burning flesh in her nostrils, Crystal strode up the drive, hands and teeth clenched.

She made her way quickly to The White House half way along the village street and rang the bell. Jean Robertson opened the door, looking both surprised and pleased to see her standing there. She smiled and continued to dry her hands on a spotless white towel, but the smile changed to a look of genuine concern as she saw the expression on her visitor's face.

"Why, my dear, whatever's the matter? Come in, come in."

Crystal followed the kindly, grey-haired doctor's wife down the passageway and into a warm kitchen, filled with the smell of baking. Jean carefully folded the towel over the rail at the front of the Aga and reached for the kettle.

"Tea, I think. You look as though you have seen a ghost."

"Is Doctor Robertson at home?"

"Not yet, dear, but I'm expecting him any minute. Is there anything I can do for you?"

"No, not really, but thank-you for asking."

Crystal smiled and thought that, as the wife of a country doctor, Jean must be used to this situation. She was a lovely lady who did a lot for the village, particularly the WI, and Marjorie spoke very highly of her. She handed Crystal a flowered cup and saucer,

"Sit down, my dear. I know James won't be long; surgery finished ten minutes ago but he does occasionally like to stay chatting with some of the old boys. He's known them since they were all children here together."

They both sat down. Crystal, on a squashy sofa near the window which looked out onto the garden, noticed again the warmth and comfort of the kitchen. A large, pine table stretched the length of the room, and a dresser along one wall was loaded with blue and white china; a black cat slept peacefully on a red blanket in a basket placed near the warmth of the huge, cream Aga.

Jean Robertson pushed herself gently backwards and forwards in a rocking chair. She was the epitome of a kind, gentle country woman, content with her lot, and looking forward to the day when her husband could retire and they would be able to spend more time together. She had no particular desire to travel far, having all that she needed on her own doorstep. Her only child, a son, had followed his father into medicine, becoming a GP, and he lived with his wife and baby daughter in the next village where he had his own practice. Jean's main hope for the future was for a baby brother or sister for the existing grandchild, then her world would be complete.

Her kindly eyes rested on the beautiful, young woman curled up on the sofa in front of her, clearly very agitated, but trying hard not to show it. 'What a lovely girl she is and what a lot she has had to come to terms with in her short life. The strange circumstances of her birth and the tragic death of the brother with whom she had, in all innocence, fallen in love. How the hearts of the village people had gone out to her, particularly as they had got to know her and appreciated what a fine person she was turning into.' She knew for certain that the parents in the village were delighted that Crystal was teaching at the school. ''Breeding will out,' as my mother used to say.'

Crystal sipped her tea, appreciating Jean's quiet presence and the fact that she asked no questions, but just sat, gently rocking. Like many of the village women, Jean had no time for, or indeed interest in, the fashions of the day. She wore sensible, comfortable slippers, a greenish tweed skirt and a pale grey twin set. Her grey hair was plaited and the plaits then wound up on top of her head. She wore no make up, but her pink and white skin was soft and scarcely wrinkled; it was a lovely face, made beautiful by the gently twinkling grey eyes that looked steadily across the room and made Crystal think of wisdom, strength and kindness.

The back door flew open and James Robertson burst into the room in a flurry of fresh air and with a scattering of autumn leaves around his heels. He dumped the old brown bag on the edge of the table and removed a pair of worn leather gloves which he slapped down on top of it.

"What ho there, Crystal. Good to see you, girl. What can we do for you?"

Before she could answer, Jean, raising her eyes to heaven, got up, removed the bag and gloves and placed them carefully on the floor near the wall, under a row of pegs. Reaching up she took her husband's scarf and the coat, which he shuffled off into her waiting hands, and hung them carefully on one of the pegs above the bag and gloves. It was clearly a familiar routine.

"Sit down, James, and I'll pour you some tea, then I shall go into the sitting room where I have something to attend to and Crystal can tell you why she has come."

She busied herself with topping up the tea pot, then after filling a mug with 'Dad' written across it – no flowered cup for James – she quietly left the room, smiling and winking at Crystal just before she closed the door. James paced up and down, slurping tea and looking out of the window onto the garden,

"Rum sort of day – definite nip of autumn in the air this morning. And how are you, old girl?" He had bent down and was stroking the black cat, causing her to stretch her limbs and arch her back with pleasure at his attentions. Finally he sat heavily and noisily on one of the kitchen chairs, leaned back and looked directly at Crystal,

"Now what brings you here to see me this afternoon, my dear?"

His presence completely filled the room and Crystal suddenly felt very unsure of herself. Exactly what was she going to say to this man who had known Arthur and Constance – indeed most of the people in the village – for so many years? What could she say?

"I...I'm just really worried about Mr. and Mrs. Elliott....my grandparents."

It still felt odd, calling them her grandparents; she experienced a sudden rush of pride, a sense of belonging, and she was aware that everyone in the village knew the story – that's how it was in villages. James let out a sigh and slumped forward, his arms on the table,

"Yep...a sad, sad business. I took one look at Connie this morning and knew she had to go straight to hospital. I shall be keeping a close eye on Arthur too, you can be sure of that."

"But what's wrong with them?"

"Well, Connie's got gastroenteritis and I think Arthur's just getting old. Too many miles on the clock....comes to us all."

"But why is he that strange colour?"

"Don't know, my dear," James didn't like to say that he thought Arthur may have been indulging in a little too much alcohol; after all it was understandable – not being able to get about much and with a fair bit of sadness in his life one way and another. Still, he didn't want to actually say as much to Crystal; she was obviously very fond of the grandparents she had only recently discovered. He looked across at the sad expression on her face and his heart went out to her.

"Tell you what; I've got to go to Addenbrook's in the morning for a short meeting. Why don't you come along and I'll arrange for you to see Connie." He stood up and continued,

"But in the meantime I want you to go home and get a good night's sleep. Doctor's orders"

Crystal thanked him and walked over to the door.

"I'll pick you up at nine o'clock. OK?"

That evening Crystal rode Star fast and furiously along the track beside the fen road before bedding her down for the night. She listened to the rhythmic chomping as the little mare crunched her way through a bucket of chaff and carrots; then crouched down and stroked her neck,

"I will find out what Mary's doing to my grandparents," she whispered into the soft, velvet ears; and realised that Star, in the soft evening twilight of the quiet stable, could, at the moment, be her only confidante. What she didn't realise was in what incredible and strange way fate would deliver the revelation she needed.

CHAPTER TWENTY NINE

Constance looked awful; skin as pale as parchment but with a yellowish tinge, sunken eyes and wisps of dry, lifeless hair framing her thin face. She tried to smile as she saw her grand daughter approaching her bed, but pain turned it to a grimace. Crystal sat down and, trying not to betray the shock and dismay she felt at the change in this once beautiful woman, she took the tiny, bony hand that crept across the blanket towards her and whispered,

"How are you feeling, darling?"

Her voice shook and the question was stupid, but what else was there to say?

"Oh, pretty groggy," Connie's voice was a barely audible croak; she gripped Crystal's fingers and beckoned to her with the bony fore finger of her other hand which trembled in the air then dropped back on to the blue hospital blanket.

Crystal leaned towards her and felt warm breath on her cheek as Connie murmured,

"Don't forget, my darling, the photograph album is yours....... and some of my best jewellery..."

"Oh, Grandma, please don't talk about that. We'll have you out of here in no time, you'll see."

Crystal could feel the tears pricking the back of her eyes as she squeezed the thin hand and tried to smile. She was still holding her hand as Connie's eyes closed and her head slipped sideways onto the pillow. Crystal could no longer stop the tears which now coursed freely down her cheeks and onto the blanket. She felt a hand on her shoulder and realised that James Robertson had crept quietly up behind her.

"Come on, sweetheart, let her sleep."

Reluctantly Crystal stood up and released the tiny hand, laying it gently on to the blanket. She looked once more at the face on the pillow then turned and followed James down the ward and out into the sunshine.

That evening when the phone rang and Marjorie told her Dr. Robertson wanted to speak to her, Crystal knew exactly what he was going to say. Constance Elliott, her beautiful, beloved grandmother, had died that afternoon.

It was Wednesday afternoon and rain battered against the classroom window, thrown by the unseen hand of the wind which rattled drainpipes and whistled around the chimneys. The children were rattled too, fractious and fidgety. Crystal clapped her hands,

"All of you sit down – now! Kenneth stop splashing water and come right away from the sink – NO – don't even think about flicking your wet hands at Mary or you will lose your playtimes for a week! Stephen you made the mess on the Art table so you clear it up; perhaps Hannah will help you. Ralph, if you shout across the room once more you will go and stand outside the door……now when I count to three I want to see everyone in their places with their project books in front of them.

After a slow count and much scurrying, order was restored and Crystal sank gratefully into her chair wanting nothing more than a peaceful end to a trying day in a week fraught with sadness. The children sat in exaggerated 'good' mode, arms stiffly folded, backs unnaturally straight and scarcely breathing as they looked with wide innocent eyes towards their teacher, waiting for praise.

They read out their work in turn and Crystal gave it as much attention as she could, but her mind kept slipping back to the trauma of her grandmother's death. The shock and sadness in the village, her own pain and grief, Mary's unbearable efficiency – 'Best get the funeral over and done with as soon as possible.' At least she had been over ruled on that. Eleanor, who much to Crystal's relief had arrived back on Saturday night, insisted that it could not be organised quickly as there were people who would want to come from other parts of the country – maybe even a few old friends from abroad. It couldn't be for at least ten days. Tight-lipped, Mary had reluctantly agreed, so the funeral was scheduled to take place the following Wednesday. She had also, rather oddly, tried to insist that her mother should be cremated and it was Arthur who had stepped in on this one. Grief seemed to give him the confidence to stand up to his forceful daughter as he reminded her that Constance would lie in the family plot already designated for them in the Church yard. Red-faced and furious he had told her that he had no idea where the cremation nonsense had come from and he would hear no more of it.

"…..and it was the Romans who first had central heating which they put under their floors and it warmed them up. They also used to lie down when they ate their food and they wore togas which looked like sheets wound around them. They made all the roads straight"

Ralph stopped reading and looked up expectantly, waiting for Crystal's reaction. She praised him then invited questions and comments from the rest of the class. Jon put up his hand and Crystal's heart sank,

"Yes Jon. What bloodthirsty observation are you going to delight us with this afternoon?" All eyes turned towards him and a few children tittered. Jon blinked and looked round, relishing his role as the supplier of ghoulish information guaranteed to liven up any topic under discussion. He cleared his throat and spoke slowly and deliberately, unaware that this afternoon's titbit was destined to change the course of so many lives.

"No blood this afternoon, Miss Morris, and it's not really about the time when the Romans were here," the dimples when he spoke were engaging and his stare unblinking as he looked towards his teacher,

"But I did find out that the United States Ambassador in Rome suffered chronic arsenic poisoning when, over a period of two or three years, lead arsenate dust gradually fell from the paint in her bedroom ceiling. You see, lead arsenate was used in the paint. The effects of this sort of poisoning are that people get sick and have diarrhoea or they get pains and stuff in their feet and sores on their skin and then they die. Some doctors think they just have gastroe…"

Crystal was sitting very still, scarcely breathing, staring across the room at the little boy who was proudly aware that he had his teacher's full attention.

"Jon are you sure….are you very, very sure that what you are saying is correct?"

"Yes, Miss Morris. My dad brought home a book called "Poisons and Poisoners" and it's full of stories all about people who've murdered other people with poisons. There was one…."

Crystal was trying to control her shaking.

"Thank-you, Jon, you may sit down now."

She noticed with relief that it was time to send the children home and, keeping her voice as steady as she could, she went through the dismissal procedure.

Outside the school gates the children were astonished to be overtaken by their teacher running along the wet pavement, while they shuffled, heads down under hoods and umbrellas, dragged by impatient mothers.

CHAPTER THIRTY

Crystal was still panting when she arrived at The White House to be greeted and ushered inside by the unflappable Jean.

"He's in the sitting room, my dear – I assume it's James you want to see – just give me your wet things then I'll take you through.

James lowered the newspaper and removed his glasses. He didn't speak until Crystal had finished the whole story then let out a long breath, tapping his folded glasses against his chin.

"And you think a post mortem will show that Connie died from chronic arsenic poisoning."

He got up and walked to the window, deep in thought as he stared out, still tapping his glasses against his chin. Crystal spoke quietly.

"I'm sure of it. Several things did strike me as odd, but I didn't really think any more about them, now it all adds up. Why did Mary insist on decorating the bedroom so often, doing it all herself and using only paint supplied from London by Mickey? Why did she remove their lovely old four poster bed with the canopy over the top? Why was she so insistent that Arthur should go back up there to sleep even though he couldn't manage the stairs? Why did she want her mother's funeral to take place so quickly and why did she suddenly suggest cremation?"

James put down the glasses, went across to a tall bookcase near the window and took down a large, leather-bound book which he started to shuffle through, then he read:

"The effects of arsenic poisoning........chronic exposure.....more difficult to diagnose....numbness and pains in the soles of the feet.....severe head ache....nausea, vomiting, diarrhoea.....hepatic and renal damage.......skin lesions which look like other forms of dermatitis."

He closed the book and looked at Crystal as the seriousness of what they were suspecting dawned on them both.

Suddenly James Robertson, solid, comfortable country doctor coasting quietly along to retirement, leapt across the room feeling more animated and alive than he had done for years. Something inside him twisted as he thought of pain being inflicted deliberately on the beautiful woman who had so charmed him in his youth.

"By God, we'll take this one right to the wire," he muttered as he pulled open the sitting room door with more force than was needed. He turned back to Crystal,

"Can you come to Addenbrook's with me this evening....now?"

"Well…yes."

"OK. I'll call the hospital, then you call Marjorie and tell her you'll be home later. Jean….Jean…" he was through the door and shouting for his wife.

Ten minutes later Crystal and James were heading towards Addenbrook's Hospital as fast as his battered old car would allow.

"I've arranged for us to see the doctor who issued the death certificate and the Coroner. Your part, Crystal, is to tell your story as clearly as you told it to me. I will insist that, as the Elliott's family doctor for so many years, I am not satisfied that Connie died of natural causes and I think we've got enough for the Coroner to order a post mortem. Mary and Emily will squeal like crazy, of course, but they can protest until they are blue in the face, there will still have to be a post mortem if the Coroner says so."

"What happens if I'm wrong?" Crystal spoke very quietly; James turned to her and smiled,

"Don't weaken now – don't even think about that. We'll worry about that when it happens. It's got the ring of truth, Crystal….it has the ring of truth." And they drove on in silence.

The Coroner did order a post-mortem to be carried out on Constance Elliott's body and the morning following his dash to the hospital with Crystal, James paid an early visit to Savron Pinder

House to inform a furious, and now very frightened, Mary of the procedure. He also told her that he would be taking her father into hospital 'for observation and a few exploratory tests' and indeed he had scarcely finished speaking when the sound of the ambulance bell could be heard.

Luckily Arthur had been unable to make it back upstairs again and had in any case, over the past months and due to his consideration for his wife's comfort, been exposed to less of the arsenic dust than Connie as he had frequently – unknown to Mary – slept in the spare room.

Once in hospital he was given a course of injections of Dimercaprol, an antidote to arsenic poisoning which had been developed for use in the Second World War, and he seemed to be responding well to the treatment. He was sitting up in a chair beside his hospital bed when James and Crystal arrived to tell him the post mortem revealed that Connie had died as the result of chronic arsenic poisoning. Crystal held her grandfather's hand and was full of admiration for the courageous way he behaved in the light of such dreadful news. She felt that he had to be told the truth and shared with him the full story of the poisoned paint. He looked stunned and sat very still with his back straight, staring out of the hospital window.

"Good God. All the fuss she made about getting that special paint from London. Apparently only Mickey, Emily's new night-club owning husband, could supply us with paint good enough for our bed room. What a load of pretentious tosh! And to think I trusted her with all our financial affairs"

Crystal was sad to see the old man's eyes fill with tears as he swallowed hard and stared back out of the window again. He was in such pain as the result of the betrayal and she was reminded of the lines from King Lear –

'How sharper than a serpent's tooth it is
To have a thankless child.'

But suddenly Crystal's heart sank further as she thought about what her grandfather had just said and the awful truth dawned on her. This wasn't Mary on her own; Mickey and Emily were involved too – of course they were – and if through Mary they had had access to her parents' money…..

"We have to go now." She patted Arthur's hand and kissed the top of his head. "You get plenty of rest and I'll come back and see you soon."

She looked at James in a way that she hoped would signal she needed to talk to him urgently and smiled again at her grandfather before turning to walk out of the room.

"Yes…yes, of course. You rest up, old chap and we'll be back to see you in no time."

James followed her out and on the way back to Savron Pinder in his car Crystal spoke to him of her fears that not only had Mary, Emily and Mickey plotted to kill the old couple and make it look like natural causes, but they had probably emptied their bank accounts too. She remembered hearing Mary boast, after one of her visits to London, about Mickey acquiring two more clubs and she had a horrible suspicion that she now knew where the money for these had come from.

It was some time after the event that Crystal learned of the undignified circumstances of Mary's arrest. She was in a taxi, apparently trying to escape to Mickey and Emily in London, and had almost reached the gates of Savron Pinder House when a police car blocked the way. Seth White, sweeping the pathway at the top of the drive as he always did on a Wednesday morning, was startled and had to jump out of the way as the black car, with blue light flashing and the siren at full blast, suddenly swept round into the drive. He leaned on his broom and stared open-mouthed as Mary was bustled out of the taxi, kicking and screaming hysterically. He was the centre of attention at the pub that evening as he tried to remember exactly what she had said,

"Sounded something like 'it's not just me…..it's my sister and her husband….they're not going to get off scot free…they're guilty too….GET YOUR

HANDS ORFF ME!' Kicked off good and proper she did until one of the policemen said if she didn't calm down she'd be had for assault as well as murder."

Murder! The locals took a long draught of their drinks then all started talking at once, gradually piecing together the story and realising the awfulness of the tragedy that had occurred in their midst. They shook their heads in disbelief. Things like that just didn't happen in Savron Pinder.

Mary, Emily and Mickey were arrested on suspicion of murder and fraudulently obtaining money from Arthur and Constance. They were released on bail awaiting trial during which time Emily and Mickey disappeared back to London and Mary buried herself in Savron Pinder House.

The gates were locked most of the time and Crystal had no idea how she was surviving. Eleanor tried several times to make contact with her, but she didn't answer the phone. It was only Mr. Willis from the shop who was allowed to drive down once a week with provisions and he came back with tales of Mary's increased levels of dishevelment.

"Looks like a mad woman, she does. Hair hasn't seen a comb for days and as for the house and grounds – well. Can't hardly get me van down there for all the weeds…..cobwebs round the windows….terrible, just terrible."

There was much tutting and head-shaking as the village people listened but felt powerless to intervene. They stood chatting on the pavement,

"Twill be a good thing when it comes to court. Get it sorted – she'll get what's coming to her and no mistake; be put away for the rest of her life for what she's done, I shouldn't wonder, and serve her right. Poor Squire and his wife didn't deserve to be treated like that. What a way to end up when they've never done no harm to anyone"

Such unfairness didn't sit well with them and they were still muttering as they turned and made their way homeward, stunned by what had happened and feeling somehow tainted by it all.

It was several months before the case came to court, but Crystal was there with Eleanor on 23rd March 1968 to see them tried and sentenced. She looked across at Mary who stood twisting a sodden handkerchief in her hands and looking genuinely sorry for what she had done. Emily, heavily made up, swept into the court room and stood glaring defiantly at the judge while Mickey, standing next to her and still resembling a gangster, also appeared unrepentant. It was with a sinking heart that Crystal learned he had indeed spent all the money he could lay his hands on from the Elliott's accounts and in the process had over-stretched himself and had been declared bankrupt.

When he left the hospital Arthur went into a convalescent home. He was still quite weak from the effects of the poisoning as there was a limit to the amount of Dimercaprol he could be given at his age. The court case generated a lot of interest, and it was impossible for Crystal to shield him from the details of this as they were reported extensively in the papers, both locally and nationally. Whether from the shame of seeing his family business plastered all over the local press; the effects of the poison, or a broken heart at the loss of his beloved wife and the betrayal of his two daughters, it was uncertain, but three months after Connie's death, Arthur suffered a massive heart attack and died in the night.

Crystal had visited her grandfather as often as she could and brought a great deal of comfort to the old man during the last weeks of his life, but she had no idea, until she sat in the offices of Bradford, Fisher and Dawson that he had met with his solicitor and changed his will. Numb with shock, she learned that her grand father had made her his sole beneficiary and, as a result, she was now the owner of Savron Pinder House.

PART TWO

Home To Roost

CHAPTER THIRTY ONE
May 1968

"And so you see, there's no money left."

Jonathan, the young solicitor cleared his throat and looked down at his shoes, shiny and black, just right with the grey pin-striped suit, but an ill match for the pale sheepskin jacket. He turned towards Crystal, looking both earnest and apologetic as he adjusted his glasses and coughed again. He was trying so hard to be the 'country solicitor,' working out how his father would handle this situation.

"It isn't your fault,"

Crystal said and sighed as she looked again around the deserted stable yard. There wasn't a sound and weeds grew up between the cobbles. Jonathan suddenly felt embarrassed; good gracious, he mustn't allow a client to feel sorry for him. Of course this lovely young woman's situation wasn't his fault, he was simply informing her of the facts and he must be as business-like as possible. He took a couple of paces away from her and removed his glasses which he waved in the air as he spoke,

"You know, we can remedy this, Miss Morris. Your best option will be to put the place up for sale; there's no market at the moment for properties of this size as private houses but where you would do well is if you sold it to a company for offices. The other very good use for a place like this would be as a conference centre…." He was pacing about now, getting into his stride, "….very much the thing of the future, conference centres; an attractive venue in the country where companies can send their employees for a training week." He paused and looked around, sucking in his breath over his teeth, then waving his glasses enthusiastically towards the rolling lawn and lake,

"Ooh yes…maybe even get in a swimming pool and a mini golf course."

He stopped as he saw Crystal's face. She was staring at him in horror as she visualised Savron Pinder House chopped up into little offices or re-fashioned into a conference centre, knocked about until the original beauty of the place was completely obliterated. Jonathan tried again,

"Of course, you wouldn't want to live here," he gave a bark of nervous laughter, "You'd rattle around like a pea in a very large pod." He stepped towards her and replaced the glasses,

Tell you what, I'll go back to the office and draw up….

"Mr. Bradford."

"Jonathon, please….call me Jonathon."

"Jonathon….." Crystal paused and looked at the young man standing in front of her, his dark hair falling over his eyes as he spoke. He was trying so hard to please her, to say the right thing, and failing miserably. She felt quite sorry for him, but spoke firmly,

"Jonathon, please don't draw up anything. My grandparents' home will not be turned into offices or a conference centre. I have absolutely no idea what I am going to do or how I'm going to do it, but the moment I need your help again I'll phone."

Jonathan looked crestfallen, defeated, and Crystal felt even sorrier for him. She smiled and, as if reading his mind, said,

"Jonathan, you have given me good advice. It's exactly what your father would have said and anyone with any sense would be doing what you have suggested. I am probably being very foolish and may get myself into all sorts of trouble, but take comfort from the fact that none of it will be your fault and you will be able to say, 'if only she had taken my advice…..'"

Jonathan blushed,

"Now you're laughing at me."

"No, I'm not. Believe me, I'm not. I mean it when I say you will most probably have the opportunity to laugh at me."

They looked at each other, Jonathan very sure that he would never laugh at this beautiful, determined young woman and Crystal wondering how she could forgive him for making her feel so old.

"Please call me if there is anything else I can do for you."

Crystal assured him that she would before they shook hands and she watched the young solicitor depart, picking his way through the overgrown grass.

She walked slowly over to a mounting block just outside the stable yard and sat down on it. From there she could see the front of the house, the lawn – or what used to be the lawn but now looked more like a hayfield – and the glittering lake just beyond the woods. The windows of the house were filthy and the paint on the frames starting to peel. One of the Orangery windows was cracked and the topiary balls lining the path from the house to the hedge that marked the boundary between the family garden and the huge rolling lawn beyond were now just overgrown clumps of green.

She heard a bang behind her as a sudden gust of wind blew the top half of one of the stable doors against the wall and it hung there, swinging back and forward. The place was in ruins; everywhere so horribly neglected that, as she walked over the cobbles and absent-mindedly closed the door, Crystal swallowed the lump in her throat and fought back the tears. How dare she? How dare Mary let this beautiful place go to rack and ruin? She turned again and looked across the desolate, depressing scene.

'Maybe I should sell it and let it be turned into offices or a conference centre….maybe that really is the only responsible course to follow. After all, I've no money….what can I possibly do?'

She sat down again on the mounting block and then, as she stared at the scene before her, an idea started to form and take shape in her mind. The vision slowly unfolded before her, and as it began to crystallise she realised it had been lurking there at the back of her mind all the time; that it was the reason she had had the courage to turn Jonathan away. It was crazy, but just thinking about it made her feel better, so much so that when Eleanore appeared, full of concern for her daughter and expecting to find her depressed and in despair, she found instead a girl full of hope with shining eyes.

"What's happened? I thought you were seeing the solicitor and getting advice on the best way to deal with this poor old place." She paused, looking again at her daughter's face, "I didn't imagine it would be a particularly happy situation. Honestly what a mess. It's enough to make you weep."

"Yes and it almost did." Crystal looked up at her mother, "until I had an idea."

Eleanor sat down on the block and Crystal stood up, moving a few paces away before she turned to her mother,

"We can make this place live again."

She pointed to the stable yard,

"Livery…..and a possibly a Riding School…..." She waved an arm excitedly towards the house,

"A Ballet School….you know just like Constance always wanted." Then she turned to the vast expanse of green sweeping down to the lake and indicated the place where it flattened out just before meeting the woods,

"….And there….a theatre!

Eleanore was taken aback. This was not what she had expected, but Crystal had been through so much, it was little wonder she was behaving rather strangely. Realising she would have to handle this one very carefully, she stood up and joined her daughter where she was standing gazing out and now seeing something very different from the ruin before them. She put her arm around her,

"Darling, we don't have enough money for such a grandiose scheme. I can't sell Monk's Manor, even if I wanted to, because of the terms and conditions on which I inherited it…"

Crystal was surprised and touched by the fact that her mother even considered such a step in order to help her, and gently touched her arm;

"Eleanore, I don't want you to give me money," Crystal was smiling,

"I want to do this myself....for Connie and Arthur. I shall go to the bank and get a loan. It has to be possible."

Her face was still shining and so full of hope that Eleanore hadn't the heart to deflate her, though she thought it would, in the long run, be the kindest thing to do. What a ridiculously impossible dream, but she looked again at her daughter and, in spite of herself, couldn't help admiring her for dreaming it.

"Come on. Let's go and get some tea. I think Star wants to see you."

August 1968

"And so you see, I think it really is a viable business proposition for you and a good investment for the bank's money." Crystal sat back and waited. Her hands felt hot and clammy and there were beads of perspiration on her upper lip. She glanced up and saw that the old fashioned windows – ones that lodged against a metal frame when you pulled a loop of string – were open, but the design of the window meant that the draft, such as it was on a sunny day in August, all seemed to go up towards the ceiling.

Looking down and taking his time, Mr. Morrison also leaned back and pulled out of his pocket a large, clean white handkerchief on which he blew his nose. It wouldn't do to let this earnest young woman see even the ghost of a smile on his face. He had worked at Young's Bank for nearly forty years, as Manager for the last ten, and he really thought he had seen every kind of crack-pot and dreamer in that time – but it seemed there was always room for one more. He put away his handkerchief and leaned forward.

"So, Miss Morris, (they had already exchanged pleasantries about the similarity of their names) you want to borrow ten thousand pounds to set up a stable and ballet school at Savron Pinder House – then perhaps build a theatre in the grounds."

"Yes, and you see….."

Samuel Morrison held up his hand,

"No more, please. I have understood your presentation perfectly; I just wanted to summarise it in one simple sentence – to put it in a nutshell, so to speak."

The combination of sunshine and light emitted from a single overhead bulb encased in a milky glass shade made gleaming patches which darted about on his bald head as he shook it slowly from side to side.

To her shame and embarrassment Crystal could feel hot tears pricking the back of her eyes. She looked away and swallowed hard; of course it was ridiculous. She had, with Gerald's help, spent the whole summer holiday putting together a plan that she hoped would impress the Bank Manager enough to lend her the money she needed and instead she had just made a fool of herself. She could, if she was honest, see her scheme through the eyes of this experienced banker and it did sound crazy. Of course he wasn't about to lend such a huge sum of money to a girl. She closed her file and stood up, holding out her hand to Samuel Morrison,

"I can see that you are not impressed by my idea; thank you so much for your time" she was speaking in what she hoped was a dignified manner then turned and, in her haste to be out of the room, moved a little too quickly and caught the edge of her file on the chair. The contents emptied themselves all over the floor and as she knelt down to retrieve them, Crystal was mortified to see a tear fall onto her arm. Samuel, who had stood up to shake her hand, came round the table to help her gather up the jumble of papers. He was embarrassed as he saw the tears trickling down her cheeks and wished he hadn't been so ready to pretend to blow his nose earlier to hide his amusement. He would have liked to offer this lovely young woman a clean handkerchief. In fact he felt a bit of a heel and these feelings were compounded when she looked up, apologising profusely, then said,

"How silly of me…..how very silly of me to believe I could…and coming here, wasting your time. It was just…. I wanted to do it for my grandfather… and Connie of course."

To her surprise, Crystal found herself guided gently back into the chair and was very soon sipping a cup of tea which magically appeared from somewhere after Samuel had stuck his head round the office door for a moment. There was also a box of tissues and, waiting until she had blown her nose, Samuel Morrison leaned forward then said, very quietly,

"Why don't you tell me about your grandparents."

So she did, all thoughts of formal presentations gone as she spoke from the heart, thinking she was just fulfilling his curiosity. What she didn't know was that Samuel Morrison's only grand daughter had been killed in a road accident when she was five years old. As he listened to Crystal's story it was his turn to try and hide his emotions. How proud he would have been if Felicity had turned out like Crystal; how wonderful that she wanted to honour her grandparents in this way.

By the time she'd finished he had decided to lend her the money, but he was at great pains to point out that it was a business arrangement. A certain amount had to be paid back each month and the rate of interest was agreed. The whole sum had to be repaid in seven years or the bank would possess the house.

Crystal was overjoyed. "Oh yes, I'm sure I can do it. You see I shall keep my job on for a while until we start to make enough money for me to give it up and Marjorie will move in with me as Eleanore is selling Maple Cottage and investing the money from the sale in the project and…"

"Yes…yes so you said in your plan."

Samuel stopped her, unwilling to try and unravel again how this girl managed to have two mothers, both falling over themselves to look after her; but he was smiling this time. He stood up; they shook hands and they arranged a day and time when all the paperwork could be dealt with. He wished her luck hoping, as he watched her bounce out of his office heading for the main door and the warm summer sunshine, that he hadn't just made one of the biggest mistakes of his career; and wondering how he was going to explain his decision to the young, super efficient new boss at head office.

'There's no fool like an old fool,' he thought as he drained the last dregs of cold tea from the bottom of his cup.

By the time the new term started, work had already begun on the restoration and transformation of Savron Pinder House. Marjorie and Eleanore had been only too willing to do some of the necessary groundwork while Crystal carried on at the school, so by the middle of October the house and grounds had been cleaned, cleared and tidied.

"The canvas has been prepared…." Crystal thought as she walked quietly from room to room enjoying the sense of order and the fresh smell of polish that greeted her, then, gazing out at the newly mown grass and trimmed hedges, she finished the sentence in her head,

"….And now the real work can begin."

She felt what could only be described as a bubble of joy inside her as she leapt out of bed each day, full of energy, buoyed up and carried along by the love and support she was receiving from those around her, and time passed in a blur of activity.

She was amazed by the willingness she found in others to work hard for the cause. Mr and Mrs Bowman had knocked on the door of Maple Cottage one evening saying they had heard a rumour that 'things were happening down at the big house' and begged to be allowed to be part of it all. Crystal had hugged them both and said she wouldn't dream of trying to do it without them, if they still wanted to be 'part of it all' when they heard what it was she was planning. They drank tea and listened carefully as she outlined her ideas and by the time they left to return to Nelly's sister's it was agreed that they would move back in to Savron Pinder House at the weekend.

She had no trouble finding people to help with the practical tasks of cleaning the house and clearing the grounds; and Nelly and Sam proved to be invaluable as Crystal took her first steps as an employer. With their local knowledge they helped her to weed out the idle, the curious and the gossips from those with a reputation for hard work and a genuine desire to help.

And so it was against this background of orderliness that the real work did indeed begin and again Crystal was amazed. She was venturing forth into, what was for her, unchartered territory but found that doors opened every where she turned. What she didn't know, of course, with her youth and inexperience, was the infectious quality of her enthusiasm and the fact that she energised those around her making them want to become part of the dream she was building.

Home To Roost

PART THREE

Home To Roost

CHAPTER THIRTY TWO

May 1970

Manor Farm,
Savron Pinder,
Cambs.

Dear Signor Vitelli,

I have seen several of your photographs and I'm impressed. I am an Art dealer with offices in London and I wondered if you have any more examples of your work you could send me; I feel sure we could do business together. I also have associates in Paris who I am sure would like to see your photographs.

Would you perhaps be interested in coming to London? I could meet you at the airport and you would be welcome to stay as a guest at my family home in the country. I have enclosed my business card with this letter and look forward very much to hearing from you.

Yours,

Philippe Lynton-Bell

Milan.

Dear Mr. Lynton-Bell,

I thank-you for your kind letter and am both pleased and flattered by your interest in my work. Your name is not unknown in Milan and commands respect already in the art world here

I have enclosed some photographs which are examples of my latest work – I hope you find them pleasing.

I would indeed like to take advantage of the kind offer to visit your country and to stay with you and your family while I decide what to do. All things English are of great interest to us here and I am intrigued to see your Carnaby Street in swinging London. I have booked my flight and will land at Heathrow Airport on Saturday 14th July at ten o'clock in the morning. Please tell me how to find your offices or arrive at your country home.

I very much look forward to meeting with you,

Yours,

Mario

Manor Farm,
Savron Pinder,
Cambridgeshire.

Dear Mario,

Delighted to hear of your imminent arrival here in London. I will come to Heathrow and meet you myself. When you have reclaimed your bags, come through to the arrivals area where my driver will be waiting for you with a sign bearing your name. He will see to your luggage then guide you to my car and we will drive immediately to the country house where my father lives. It is in a delightful village called Savron Pinder which is about fifty miles from London; I think you will find it very quaint and I hope you will enjoy the ride through our English country side.

I feel sure we can do profitable business together.

Yours,

Philippe

July

Heathrow Airport

The flight had been uneventful. Mario looked out of the tiny window onto wet tarmac and smiled; he had heard about English rain. As the plane taxied slowly towards the terminal, he opened his wallet and took out a small black and white photograph. He looked at it for a few seconds and smiled his lop-sided smile – 'the lovely English girl; the one who got away.' He was struck again by the young woman's beauty, evident even in a quick snap but, of course what wasn't captured, what he could only see now vividly in his mind's eye, was the remarkable, deep-red colour of the hair. He put the photograph carefully back into the wallet and prepared to set foot in England for the first time in his life.

Philippe sat in his car and waited. He watched through the tinted window for the arrival of his guest, leaning back against the black leather seat; he was intrigued to know what this promising, and obviously very talented, photographer looked like, but it wouldn't do to seem too eager.

As Bateman, the chauffeur, approached with their visitor, Philippe got slowly out of the car and held out his right hand. This was firmly grasped by a man considerably taller and more solidly built than himself. While pleasantries about the flight were exchanged, Philippe noted that his guest was smartly dressed in a soft, black leather jacket and pale trousers. He allowed Bateman to put his luggage in the boot, but refused to relinquish the camera bag he had slung over his shoulder. Courteously, Philippe made room for it next him on the seat and, with both men settled, the car purred slowly out of the airport and headed east.

"Your country-side is very beautiful – but wet."

Philippe laughed, "Yes, I'm afraid we do get a lot of rain. Still it does make for 'a green and pleasant land.'" He paused, and then continued, "I am finding it quite hard to acclimatise as I spent my childhood in France."

"Why was that? I thought you were an English country gentleman."

Philippe looked out of the window and didn't respond, so Mario said, quite gently,

"Did your parents move to France?"

"My mother did and took me with her. I didn't see my father again until quite recently."

He turned towards his visitor and continued, "My father is an English gentleman, my mother is French."

As he spoke Mario looked more closely at his host and thought that he did indeed have about him the look of a Frenchman. His features were quite sharp, the nose finely pointed, but it was his small mouth with thin lips that betrayed the Gallic influence.

Philippe turned back towards the window wondering how this stranger had got under his defences so quickly. He hoped that his tone, without being rude, had indicated that he didn't want to talk any further about his family background. His life with his mother, Marianne, and her artist lover, after he had been unceremoniously snatched from Manor Farm as a child, had been far from happy. The fact that it had become intolerable after that relationship broke up and she moved him and his two step sisters in with Georges was not something he was prepared to talk about to anyone.

He was independent now; his own man, and he had formed, if not a close, certainly a tolerable relationship with his father after many years of estrangement. Geoffrey was a bit of a cold fish; if he was honest Philippe could see that his father's nature would not be conducive to sustaining the interest of a passionate Frenchwoman like his mother, but he and Geoffrey had certainly become friends over the last couple of years so he really didn't want to rake up what had happened between his parents so long ago.

Mario sensed his companion's reluctance to talk about his childhood and thought it might help if he divulged a little of his own. He spoke slowly and chose his words carefully.

"Perhaps you were quite lucky to know your mother. Mine died when I was very small and I lived with my father and his mother. I have no brothers and sisters and my father was too busy to spend much time with me. My grandmamma was the strongest influence of my childhood."

As if by mutual agreement, both men felt they had revealed enough, and the rest of the journey passed in talk about the Art world until they reached Savron Pinder. Mario sat forward, his eyes drawn to two large, new-looking pillars made of pale stone, marking the entrance to a drive which obviously led to a house of some importance. There was an engraved, brass plaque on one of the pillars but it was impossible to read the name as the car sped past.

"What's down there?" He asked Philippe as he leaned back against the black leather.

Philippe smiled, "That, Mario, is Savron Pinder House and there's quite a tale to tell about the place; a dramatic story – straight out of a crime novel – and there have been some interesting changes made to the place in the last couple of years; all down to a cousin of mine who lives there now. But look, we're here."

The car had reached the other end of the village where it turned into a driveway flanked by grey stone pillars, much smaller and older looking than the ones leading down to Savron Pinder House. It drew slowly to a halt and the men prepared to alight.

"This is Manor Farm; I will tell you the extraordinary tale of Savron Pinder House over a pre-dinner drink. First I think we both need to freshen up and you have to meet my family – or what's left of them."

It wasn't possible for Mario and Philippe to talk before dinner as Geoffrey and Claude were eager to find out more about their visitor from abroad. While sipping a very dry martini, Mario responded to their questions and found himself wondering about these two gentlemen. Claude seemed affable enough, an avuncular character, almost a stereotypical Englishman with a fresh, quite boyish complexion, watery blue eyes and a shaggy grey moustache that wagged back and forward when he talked.

Geoffrey, his brother and Philippe's father, was so different from him in looks and build that it was hard to believe they were part of the same family. His body was angular and his features sharp with a beaky nose similar to Philippe's, but larger. Mario glanced again at his new friend, who was listening intently to his father talking about horses, and thought that the refinement of his features must have been the French mother's influence for, although sharp like his father's, they were much more delicately formed.

"Do you ride, Mario?" Geoffrey fired the question across the room and fixed him with a piercing stare which was quite disconcerting.

"No....no, I'm afraid I've never had the opportunity."

"Well, we shall get you up on a horse while you're here."

Philippe drew on the small cigar he was smoking and tried to suppress a smile. Claude guffawed, but before anyone could speak again, the door opened and a maid entered the room looking flustered,

"I beg your pardon, Mr. Geoffrey, but your mother says she will come down to dinner this evening. She's on her way now"

The maid went out quickly, closing the door behind her, leaving the announcement in the centre of the room like an unexploded grenade. Claude, Geoffrey and Philippe leapt to their feet; sherry was poured, a window was opened just a fraction and a chair moved over to it – 'not too close, Claude,' Geoffrey admonished, pulling it back slightly and adjusting the cushions. Other cushions were plumped and the three of them stood with their eyes on the door. Mario rose slowly and noticed that the informal atmosphere which had prevailed a few minutes earlier had evaporated. The three other men were standing stiffly as if to attention, hands behind their backs, drinks abandoned.

Suddenly the door burst open again and as the maid turned, putting out her hand to assist the newcomer into the room, Mario heard a sharp voice,

"For goodness' sake, girl, leave me alone. I'm not an invalid," and an old lady walked in as briskly as she could manage, while prodding the carpet with a walking stick. She stopped then snapped,

"Claude, shut that window and move my chair away from it; I shall catch my death if I sit there."

Her eldest son immediately did as he was told while the old lady turned her gaze towards the visitor. Geoffrey stepped forward,

"Mother, this is Mario Vitelli, Mario, my mother, Mrs. Isobel Lynton-Bell. Do you remember, Mother, we told you about him; he is here to do some work with Philippe?"

"Of course I remember. I'm not stupid. Step a little closer please, Signor Vitelli."

Mario did as he was asked and held out his hand while smiling straight into Isobel's eyes.

"I am very charmed to meet you, Mrs. Lynton-Bell; thank-you so much for having me to stay."

Isobel looked at him for a few moments and said nothing. If Mario had found Geoffrey's stare disquieting it was nothing compared to that of his mother's bright, beady glare. Everything about her was tiny, sharp and bony; and her shiny black taffeta dress only served to accentuate her bird-like frame. After a few moments she released his hand and made her way towards the re-positioned chair muttering to her grandson as she passed,

"Yes...very pretty...very pretty indeed. Should cause quite a stir in that strange world you inhabit, Philippe, especially among the young ladies,"

Sitting heavily down in her chair, she suddenly gave a bark of laughter which took everyone by surprise.

Dinner was announced and, as they went in, Philippe managed a whispered aside to Mario, warning him not to mention Savron Pinder House.

The meal was a strained affair as the old lady's whims had to be constantly ministered to while she prodded her food with sharp, pecking movements, interspersed with comments, opinions, questions and observations fired across the table like little bullets. Afterwards, Claude and Geoffrey excused themselves to attend to final duties about the farm before nightfall; May, the maid, returned for Isobel and Mario was left alone with Philippe who made straight for the brandy bottle.

"Phew. I'm in need of this," He turned towards Mario and held up the bottle, "what about you?

"Yes, certainly; I will join you." He accepted the brandy, relieved that his detachment from this family meant that his need was not as desperate as Philippe's.

"Is she always like that?" He asked as both men sat in chairs opposite each other and Philippe lit a tiny cigar.

"I'm afraid so. Luckily, because she is 84 years old, she spends most of her time in her rooms upstairs; it was in your honour that she graced us with her presence this evening. As you can see she exerts a lot of influence on the entire household; everyone jumps even before she comes into a room."

"Why did they fuss with the window and chair if they knew she wouldn't like it?"

"Because if they hadn't, the first thing she would have demanded on entering the room would be for the window to be opened and her chair moved closer to it. With Grandmother Isobel it is impossible to guess what she will and won't like. Yesterday's balm is today's poison. And talking of poison, I said I'd tell you about the dramas surrounding Savron Pinder House."

"I can't wait to hear."

While Philippe told Mario about the murders that had occurred two years previously, Isobel Lynton-Bell struggled into bed, cursing old age and infirmity, then lay there, also reflecting on things of the past. She looked across the room to where the black taffeta frock hung on the front of the wardrobe. It was her favourite; John had loved her in that frock. He had said once it had made her look small and dignified, though every scrap of dignity had vanished when, in the next moment, he had picked her up, twirling her round while she clung to him laughing. Her eyes filled with tears as she remembered her beloved husband, so cruelly taken from her by death – just like the old Queen's dearest Albert. And like the old Queen, she too had vowed she would wear black for the rest of her life.

Still, at least it was death that had got him and not that scheming Connie Elliott. Oh no, even though she had tried to lure him away with her fancy upper class ways, her soft voice and fluttering eye-lashes, she was sure in her heart that her John had stayed faithful to her. But she had never forgiven Connie.....even so, she wouldn't have wished that dreadful death on her. Poisoned by her own daughters and that good for nothing night club owner. Isobel grunted. If any of hers had tried to pull a stunt like that she'd have taken a stick to their backs and beaten them senseless. Too soft with them when they were young, was Connie, and she had paid a high price for that indulgence.

The old lady turned over in bed, her joints aching, and thought about her children. Poor Evelyn – a miserable life and dead before her time. Geoffrey and Claude – both hopeless with women; Geoffrey seduced by that dark-eyed French piece then abandoned; Claude twisted round the little finger of that devious house-keeper. It had been a pleasure to throw her out, and no mistake; and it was just as well to have Claude back, making himself useful round the farm.

She thought about Eleanore, the beauty of the family, and sighed. Much good her looks had ever done her! Taking up with that Elliott lad and producing the red-headed minx who had caused the death of Giles, her favourite of all the grandchildren. And they had expected her to welcome the girl! No chance; even though the whole village seems to have gone gaga over her because she has transformed Savron Pinder House. Huh!

And now Eleanore's divorced from that strange fish she married – by all accounts that had something to do with the redhead's appearance on the scene, reminding them all of her dalliance with

Jack Elliott. What was the matter with them all? The marriage vows just didn't seem to mean anything any more. Mind you, there was Bette. Ah yes, little Bette. A sweeter, lovelier child she couldn't have wished for; their little afterthought, conceived in such joy that time John took her away to reassure her that it was she he loved, not Connie; that she had no need to be jealous.

That was one in the eye for stuck up Constance Elliott – left with that bumbling idiot of a husband, the self-styled squire of Savron Pinder. Squire, my eye! Riding around on his bicycle like Lord Muck! But she had her John back, and they had little blue-eyed Bette to remind them of their love for each other – married now to her soldier and bringing up those two girls to be little ladies. Pity of it is that she's always so far away.

Isobel turned over again and thought of her other grandchildren. Rosemary, Eleanor's girl, her eldest grand-daughter; yes, she had a lot of time for Rosemary – more sense than the rest of them put together. Rosemary had given her Gerard and Julia, the great grandchildren, lively as crickets the two of them – good reason to get out of bed the days they visited, even though they wore her out.

Then she thought of Clive, another oddball, more to do with his father's family than hers she felt sure. Strange, though, the way he had suddenly gone missing, oh well, good riddance to him – a missing person nobody missed at all; it would be a sorry day if he ever turned up again.

The old lady turned over once more and felt that sleep was now, mercifully, not far away. She closed her eyes and her thoughts turned to the two young men sitting downstairs. It had been odd, Geoffrey's boy turning up again like that almost two years ago with his artsy-fartsy ways and fondness for flowered shirts and velvet jackets, though he made a bit of a show of playing the young country gentleman when he thought it might do him some good and win him a few points with his father.   Still, it made Geoffrey happy to have him around after not seeing him for so many years – what a flighty piece that wife was and no mistake. And now an Italian staying; she smiled, 'that one spells trouble if ever I saw it.' Finally she slept.

CHAPTER THIRTY THREE

Dressed casually in jeans and a royal blue shirt, Mario hovered near the dining room door. The table was laid for breakfast but there was no-one there.

"Do go in, Sir. Mr. Philippe will not be long, I am sure."

The voice came from behind him and Mario turned to see a very pretty girl standing there with a tray. He moved aside, apologising for blocking her way, and then followed her into the room. She smiled at his uncertainty and tactfully indicated a seat,

"What can I get you Sir? Bacon.... eggs.... tomatoes… fried bread….?"

He held up his hand, laughing,

"No, no, no! I have heard about these English breakfasts, but no…thank-you. For me just some bread and a little jam – if you have cherry jam that will be perfect. Also some coffee with hot milk"

'My, but she's pretty,' he thought again as she leaned over the table arranging the china and cutlery, her blond curls just brushing her shoulders, neat figure with small, firm breasts and good legs.' Her cheeks dimpled as she smiled at him again. 'Such a lovely face – clear blue eyes and a flawless complexion; what do they call this – English Rosebud?'

"I'll bring your breakfast, Sir."

The girl left the room, her colour heightened a little as she was aware of the scrutiny she had received from their good-looking visitor. He watched her go,

'Mmmm. Too tiny to be a model, but perfect for photographic work.'

As he hoped she would, the girl returned before anyone else appeared for breakfast, and while she laid his simple meal before him, Mario took the opportunity to find out more about her. She told him that her name was Lisa Willis and that she had always lived in the village as her mum and dad ran the village shop.

"How long have you been maid here?"

She laughed, "two weeks. I only do this while the full time maid is on holiday. I am going to secretarial college in September."

She had stopped arranging the table and was looking directly at Mario, for some reason keen that he should know she was out to better herself. Not for her a life stuck away in Savron Pinder.

Before he could ask any more questions, Philippe came quietly into the room and sat down.

"Good morning. I trust you slept well"

He turned to Lisa, "My usual croissant and black coffee please, Lisa."

She inclined her head slightly then left the room and Mario noticed that Philippe seemed unaware of her charms.

"So, Mario, What would you like to do today? There is not much excitement in an English village on a Sunday, but we'll do our best for you."

Mario dipped his bread into his coffee and, as he thought of Lisa, decided that the day had already provided quite an exciting start. He had no way of knowing that the discovery he was to make later that same day would provide even more excitement than he could ever have predicted.

Philippe showed his guest around the farm. The weather was much improved as the rain of the previous day had given way to watery sunshine and a fresh summer breeze. Mario saw Claude ambling around one of the fields with the farm manager and Geoffrey waved as he walked a fine-looking horse towards a paddock.

Lunch was served at one o'clock precisely and it was, in spite of being the middle of the summer, roast beef and all the trimmings.

After lunch Philippe smiled at his new companion who was lolling back in one of the comfortable drawing room chairs drinking a small cup of black coffee with one hand resting on a very full stomach

"I'm afraid it's always roast beef on Sunday, no matter what the weather; families like mine are sticklers for tradition. I found it strange when I first arrived here as the way we ate in France was very different." He didn't add that sometimes any food at all was a bonus if Marianne had remembered to shop or wasn't too preoccupied to bother preparing a meal.

"Yorkshire pudding.....in Italy we have polenta....quite similar."

"Well, you will have a chance to walk off some of that Yorkshire pudding as I have arranged for us to go and visit my cousin at Savron Pinder House."

Mario brightened. He had been fascinated as he had sat far into the night while Philippe re-filled his glass and regaled him with a story that could have come straight from a book. His cousin had fallen in love with her brother – without knowing he was her brother. The brother had died in a car crash and no-one was sure if it was an accident or suicide; then she had uncovered her aunt's plot to kill both her parents – the girl's grandparents – and get their money. It was too late to save the old couple, but the grandfather had hung on just long enough to change his will and leave everything to the girl. Phew! No wonder they call the English eccentric! Now the girl, against all the odds and everyone's advice, had developed the property and created a livery stable and ballet school which was putting sleepy little Savron Pinder well and truly on the map. Apparently there was even talk of a theatre being built in the grounds Crystal....yes, that was her name Crystal Morris – or was it Elliott? And why did she have two mothers? It was at this point of the story that the brandy or tiredness, or both, had taken over and the two men had decided to leave the rest until another time.

The brisk walk along the village street provided the opportunity for Philippe to explain Crystal's background and clarify her connection with the Elliott's and indeed his own family. By the time they had walked the length of the newly resurfaced drive and crunched over the gravel, admiring the stunning beauty of the house and its grounds, Mario couldn't wait to meet this unusual young woman.

Philippe pressed the newly installed large, white bell button and the door was answered by a plump woman in a white pinafore.

"Hello, Nelly. Crystal is expecting us."

"Yes, that's right Mr. Philippe. She's just popped down to the stables, you can go down and meet her if you wish; you know the way."

They crunched past the front of the house, turned left and then right through a new brick archway and into a smart stable yard. At first it appeared empty, but then Mario saw her. She had her back to them as she had come out of one of the stables, but turned to continue a conversation with someone still inside. That hair…it reminded him of…then she turned. Seeing Philippe, she smiled and Mario found himself looking at the girl in the photograph he had carried in his wallet for the last seven years.

"Crystal, my darling girl,"

Philippe opened his arms wide and rushed forward, embracing his cousin then leading her towards Mario keeping one arm lightly round her waist. "I have someone here who is simply dying to meet you."

"Crystal shook hands with Mario and felt disturbed at the touch of his hand. There was something vaguely familiar about him. Had they met before somewhere? Or maybe he just reminded her of an Italian film star she had seen in some movie. 'He's certainly very good looking,' she thought as she led both men back to the house.

Nelly brought them tea and Philippe talked about the transformation that had occurred at Savron Pinder House. Mario noticed how relaxed they seemed in each other's company and how proud he was of his cousin's achievements as he stood in the centre of the room, his enthusiastic discourse punctuated with much arm-waving.

"She was advised to turn it into offices or a conference centre, but she was having none of it;

and so it is, as you see before you, a thriving livery stable and successful ballet school. If you were here from four o'clock onwards every afternoon or all day Saturday, you would encounter a procession of pink-clad giggling little girls running up and down the stairs. If you ventured up to the top floor you would tremble before the terrifying Madame Verbiere barking out her orders at the now silent and obedient little girls. If you had a horse, my dear Mario, you could not do better than to keep it here for Crystal runs the best livery stable for miles around. She is also building a theatre down near the lake so that the besotted parents of the afore-mentioned little ballerinas can come and watch their ducklings being transformed into cygnets before their very eyes." He paused and looked adoringly at his cousin before continuing, "She has breathed life into these old stones."

Crystal laughed and threw a screwed up napkin at Philippe,

"Go on with you. I've only been able to do it all because I've had so much help, and because I have marvellous people working for me. Jenny takes care of the stables and Uncle Geoffrey is always on hand to help and advise us…"

"…As long as Grandmother Isobel doesn't know he's doing it!" Philippe added and the cousins exchanged a meaningful look.

"Where does the Old Witch think you are this afternoon?" Crystal asked, every trace of the smile gone from her lips.

"Oh, she doesn't even know we're out. She came down to dinner last night and ruined Mario's first meal here, but she's stayed in her rooms all day today. You know what she's like; it's a bit like having a deadly spider lurking in the corner, you never know when it's going to scuttle out and bite someone."

Crystal did know what she was like. Isobel had appeared at both her grandparents' funerals and she remembered glancing up through her tears and noting with anger the utter contempt with which the old lady had regarded Arthur's internment. But it had been with fury that she had seen the tiny, malevolent smile hovering around Isobel's lips as, a few months earlier, she had watched Constance Elliott's coffin being lowered into the ground.

"Anyway to return to my cousin's achievements," Philippe continued, "she is being far too modest. The whole thing has been damned hard work and it's a credit to her. Perhaps she'll tell you all about it while you're here, Mario."

"I would like that very much," the Italian murmured, smiling across the room at Crystal who looked away quickly, embarrassed by what she had seen in his eyes.

Mario was both intrigued and amused. He could scarcely believe that fate had delivered him the opportunity to become acquainted with the beautiful redhead he had seen on the beach all those years ago; the one who had got away, the girl who had shown no interest in him whatsoever. He had carried her photo ever since, hoping that he might find her. He knew that he had not betrayed his astonishment at seeing her; he also felt sure that she was vaguely aware that they had met before, but couldn't be sure. She seemed a little unsettled, slightly off-balance.

At that moment the tension in the room was broken as the door opened and a tall, fair-haired young man burst in.

"Charlie!" Crystal leapt to her feet as the newcomer strode across to where she was and kissed her lightly on the lips before turning to greet Philippe who made the necessary introduction,

"Mario, this is Charlie Fairlawn. Manages a farm locally. His uncle is married to Crystal's half sister. It all sounds a bit incestuous, I'm afraid." Philippe saw Crystal's face and, realising what he had said, wanted to bite out his tongue; he wouldn't hurt his cousin for anything. Their respective odd connections with the family at Manor Farm had provided a strong bond between them. They were close friends, allies, and Crystal was one of the few people who knew why it could never be anything else. To stop herself from thinking about Giles and to cover Philippe's obvious embarrassment, Crystal slipped an arm around Charlie and turned towards Mario,

"Charlie has been a tower of strength to me these last two years; I simply couldn't have done it without him."

They were smiling into each other's eyes in a way that made something twist in Mario's chest. He swallowed and murmured,

"Well...good for you, Charlie" before turning to look out of the window.

At Philippe's insistence, Crystal showed them round the house and grounds. It was indeed impressive and on the way back to Manor Farm Mario said as much. He also asked,

"What is the relationship between the Charlie Fair...house? And Crystal?"

"Fairlawn...Charlie Fairlawn. I think he more than anyone else has helped her to come to terms with the Giles business and move on. She'll never forget him, of course, but with Charlie she is, shall we say, coming to life again"

As they turned in to the drive and walked in silence towards the Manor, Mario felt sure that he could work a much swifter and more effective cure on the beautiful woman he had met again that afternoon.

Much later that evening, Crystal walked down to the stables to do a final check on the horses. Every box was full and she watched Jenny give each inquisitive nose a quick pat or kiss before she shut them up for the night.

"Bye, Crystal. See you tomorrow."

"Yes. Bye, Jenny"

She walked back up to the house and looked over towards the lake where the scaffolding was holding up the half built theatre. The builders would be back in the morning and Madame would complain bitterly about the noise disturbing her lessons.

Back in the house Marjorie brought Crystal a cup of tea while she looked over the accounts before going up to bed. All seemed to be well and they were on track for repaying the loan to the bank in five years. She smiled at her adoptive mother as she closed the books and perched for a few minutes on the arm of her chair. They both looked out of the window into the gathering dusk. The trees of the little wood were silhouetted against the sky and the water of the lake shone in the moonlight.

"Are you sure you didn't mind leaving Maple Cottage?" Crystal asked, not for the first time.

"I'm quite sure as I've told you before, so there's no need to ask again. Helping you to run this place...being useful...it's given me a new lease of life. Now go on with you, up to bed. Tomorrow will be busy like all the days here."

In spite of being tired, Crystal couldn't sleep. She was disturbed. July was always difficult as it was Giles' birthday month; that and the anniversary of the accident which caused his terrible death were two humps she had to crawl painfully over every year. They still affected her profoundly and probably always would. She had been to his grave that morning and remembered again the vow she had made there all those years ago. She was still sure she would never marry and she would unravel the mystery surrounding the accident.

She thought of Charlie and how important he was becoming in her life. She had meant what she'd said that afternoon; all the achievements would have been impossible without him and she cringed at the memory of her initial naïve ideas about how to borrow money from the bank. It was Charlie who had rescued her by persuading his uncle Gerald, Rosemary's husband, to help her put together a business plan. There had been so many problems and Charlie had always been there to help her overcome them. When she was in despair, he lifted her up and would never let discouragement get the better of her.

Their friendship had grown and deepened over the last two years and she was beginning to worry now about hurting him. She suspected he may be falling in love with her, unaware of the vow she had made, and was not sure how she was going to deal with this. In fact she wasn't at all sure about how she felt. If it were not for the lump inside, the door that she felt sure had closed for ever, would she have found in Charlie the sort of love that lasts a lifetime?

Then suddenly she sat bolt upright. The memory of a dark-haired, dark-skinned man ambling along a beach in Italy swam in front of her eyes and married itself to the man she had met that afternoon. He was older – seven years older – and smarter; and his English was better, but it was definitely him. Mario – yes that was the name she had heard called across the sands. The beach photographer from Torre de Mer was here in Savron Pinder! She lay down again to sleep, feeling sure that almost recognising him must have been the reason why she had felt so unsettled in his presence that afternoon.

It was just after three o'clock the following afternoon when Philippe unlocked the door of his London flat and led Mario inside. The décor was ultra modern, white and cream with touches of black, and everywhere was utterly spotless. Philippe indicated a bedroom leading off the sitting room,

"You can have that one, Mario, and you are welcome to stay as long as you want. I feel sure you are going to be very successful and if you stay in London you will want a place of your own, but until then….." He paused and Mario was about to thank him when Philippe held up his hand, "…..actually, there is something I should tell you, because you will find out anyway and when you do you might not want to stay"

Mario sat down as Philippe continued,

"I live here with my partner; his name's Julian. We share the other bedroom."

Mario had guessed as much from his observation of Philippe's mannerisms and his obvious immunity to Lisa's charms.

"I have no problem with that….but I…"

"You very much like the ladies. Yes, I had noticed."

CHAPTER THIRTY FOUR

For the rest of the week Mario was introduced to artists, editors of fashion magazines, boutique owners and musicians. The scene was as bright and glittering as he had been led to expect. Everywhere the boundaries were being pushed back; people were experimenting and he found himself in the middle of a heady explosion of colour, sound and creativity. He suddenly became aware of being in the right place at the right time and knew he could blossom here as a photographer; Philippe was just the person to introduce him to all the right people.

It was Saturday; Crystal and Charlie were standing under the stone archway leading to the stable block and listening carefully to Mario who had just presented them with an idea.

"It would be perfect, just perfect." he concluded looking at Crystal and hoping that she would agree. She had to admit the offer was tempting. A fashion shoot at Savron Pinder House would be good publicity for the place and help to attract future business both for the ballet school and the stables as the house and grounds would be shown off to their best advantage while providing a back drop for the models. There was also the added attraction of good money to be made. Mario had stressed that the magazine, one of the prestigious glossies, could afford to pay very well and Crystal was keen to ensure that the loan was paid back to the bank on time – the future of Savron Pinder House, her own and Marjorie's futures, all depended on it.

"What do you think, Charlie?"

"I don't like the idea at all. It would be very disruptive and quite tacky, not in the spirit of what you are trying to achieve here Crystal."

Crystal felt irritated by Charlie's response and the look of disapproval on his face. What was his problem? She found that she already liked the idea very much; it would be fun and if she was honest she had to admit that there had been very little fun in her adult life. It had been all work and very little play since she had left College.

Her job as a teacher at the village school had been challenging, and then when she had taken the plunge and immersed herself in renovating and developing Savron Pinder House, the demands on her time and energy had left little room for fun. She knew this was largely her own fault; that she used work as an excuse not to think about the awful things that had happened to her, the terrible attempted rape by Clive, who had thought she was his cousin, but discovered she was, in fact, his half sister; the trauma of Giles' death and the horrific murders of the grandparents she was getting to know and love.

It was Charlie who had provided the bright spots in her life over the last two years. When the pressures got too great he had taken her out to dinner and sometimes dancing; they had talked and laughed and she had returned home feeling relaxed and able to face whatever problems occurred the following day. So why was he now, the man who had been her rock and continual source of encouragement, standing there looking so disapproving of what was potentially a perfectly good money making scheme?

She turned to Mario,

"Thank-you for thinking of us, Mario, I'm sure there are other places you could have recommended to the magazine. I like the idea very much. When would you start?"

"A week Monday, if that suits you."

"That would be no problem at all."

Mario leaned forward, "Perhaps I could come down tomorrow and discuss all the arrangements with you."

"Yes, of course, come for tea – about three o'clock."

Crystal turned,

"Charlie…."

But before she could ask if he would like to come too, he turned and, without a word, walked away across the lawn.

"Well, really….! I'm sorry Mario; I don't know what's come over him."

"It does not matter."

Furious, Crystal turned again towards Charlie's retreating back and continued to watch until he had disappeared down the drive. She was unaware of the slow smile that spread across Mario's face.

The shoot went well. Crystal set aside the blue drawing room as a changing room and was fascinated by all the weird and wonderful garments modelled by the stick thin girls who draped themselves around the grounds as instructed by Mario. She found herself impressed as she watched him crouch and click, moving around the girls with authority; a perfectionist, totally committed to and involved in the moment. She was mesmerised by his energy as she watched from the sidelines and suddenly became aware of her unfashionable jeans and baggy sweater. How must she look to him amongst all these exotic creatures and why did it suddenly matter?

This feeling of dowdiness was made worse when, just before he left on the last day of the shoot, Mario leaned forward to say goodbye and pulled a piece of straw out of her hair. As the glittering, chattering girls piled into the transport that had been provided, they talked excitedly about the party they were all going to that evening; and when Crystal closed the door the silence of the house, usually a source of peace and comfort now seemed to unsettle her further. She ran upstairs and pulled open the door of her wardrobe. There were a few of the zany clothes she had worn at College, but they were already out of date and lacked the style and quality of the beautiful things she had seen over the past few days. She threw them back in the wardrobe in disgust and as she did so saw, right at the back, the powder blue dress she had worn at Giles' twenty first birthday party. Angrily she shut the door; this was not the time to think of Giles.

She stared at her reflection in the mirror and tried to see what Mario and those girls must have seen. The red curls bobbing around her shoulders were wild and untamed; she was fashionably slim but her figure was always hidden beneath the practical clothes she chose for the life she lived. There was no reason to dress up and she had been far too busy over the last few years to bother about what she looked like. If she needed to look smart for a meeting with the bank manager or to conduct interviews she simply pulled out a suit she had left over from her post college job hunting days. She had been only too happy to stop wearing make up and had laughed with Jenny about the horses not minding. She had been happy, but as she stared at the reflection frowning back at her, she felt that, at only twenty six, life was passing her by.

She was still in this strange mood, which Marjorie noticed but decided not to comment on, when the telephone rang just as they were finishing dinner.

"Hello Crystal. It's Mario."

She could feel her heart starting to beat faster and blushed as she realised she had been thinking about him.

"I just wanted to thank you so much for letting us use your beautiful grounds for our photo shoot." He paused and she was completely tongue-tied.

"Are you there?

"Yes….yes…it was no trouble….very interesting to see the girls and…" she stopped, realising she was babbling stupidly and was sure she could hear a smile in his voice when he spoke again.

"I'm staying in London to see a film on Saturday afternoon and wondered if you'd like to come. I'll meet you at the station. We can grab a bite to eat afterwards and then both travel back to Savron Pinder together. I've promised Philippe I'll come down and spend Sunday at the Manor. He likes to see his father but is very wary of the old lady and says that my presence helps to make it more bearable for him. What do you say?"

By the time she put the phone down Crystal had agreed to go up to London on Saturday and as she walked back to the dining room she convinced herself that it was nothing – just a film and a meal, nothing at all. She was irritated to find herself thinking of Charlie and even feeling a little bit guilty. How ridiculous! She and Charlie were friends; and anyway he had walked away and she hadn't seen or heard from him all week. She didn't need to feel guilty because of Charlie, she told herself.

The film was Antonioni's "Blow Up" and Crystal loved it. She teased Mario about seeing himself as the David Hemmings character and he smiled.

They emerged from the darkened interior of the cinema into the sunlight and stood for a few moments blinking on the pavement.

"Let's grab an early meal, then, if it would amuse you, we've got time to drop in on a party before we catch the train for Savron Pinder,"

"Yes…fine."

Crystal was enjoying herself. She had stepped confidently down from the train earlier in the day knowing that she looked good. Her efforts trawling round the shops in Cambridge then at the hairdresser's were more than rewarded by the look in Mario's eyes as he had walked to meet her.

"Phew, what have you done to yourself? You look amazing!"

"Oh just a new dress and a hairdo, thought it was about time to change the image a bit...you know..."

She tried to sound matter of fact, but was basking in his admiration, and hoped she wasn't blushing. The dress was a black and white mini shift and she had had her hair cut into a bob. She would have liked it even shorter but knew that she could never achieve Mary Quant sleekness with her curls. Still, at least it was now styled instead of a wild, woolly mane.

During the meal Mario talked a little about Italy and the grandmother who had brought him up. He had obviously been a solitary child and, as she listened, Crystal got the impression that he was quite lonely.

"What started your interest in photography?"

"My father" Mario paused and laughed, "he had no time to spend with me and one year when he had to go away on business again instead of taking me on holiday, he bought me a camera. I was...as you English say....hooked from then on. So my father's guilt present determined my future." He paused again and looked into Crystal's eyes, "I am going to be a very good photographer."

"From what Philippe tells me you already are."

"Yes, but I will be the best. Come let us leave now."

He put up his hand to summon the waiter and accidentally tipped over a glass that was still half full of cola. It spilled across the table and some of it came into contact with the sleeve of his immaculate white shirt. He jumped up and demanded a cloth, speaking in Italian and obviously upset by the incident. Crystal waited quietly while the stain was removed and couldn't help thinking that Charlie would simply have laughed and dabbed at his sleeve with his handkerchief.

Mario calmed down and Crystal deliberately dismissed all thoughts of Charlie as she followed him out into the evening sunshine.

Candles glowed around the edges of the darkened room, casting eerie shadows against the walls; flames flickered as music pulsated and bodies moved slowly to a rhythm of their own. It was hot and exciting, the air full of laughter, and Crystal was aware of a strange pungent smell as she allowed Mario to lead her through the swirl of kaftans and long bare limbs to a small area just big enough for him to turn and take her in his arms. As they danced, she leaned against him, swaying, with her eyes closed and when he kissed her she responded eagerly and passionately, aware that she felt more alive at that moment than she had for a very long time.

It was Mario who pulled away first and, tipping her chin with his fingers, looked into her eyes with an amused, almost detached expression on his face. She longed for him to kiss her again and closed her eyes, but instead of the touch of his lips she felt a hand on her arm. Opening her eyes she saw Philippe standing next to them.

"Crystal….Mario….I didn't expect to see you here."

He was frowning and Crystal, normally delighted to see her cousin, found herself irritated by his presence. She loved her cousin dearly but wanted to remain in Mario's embrace, to experience again the ecstasy of his kisses. Instead he led her to the side of the room then disappeared to the kitchen to get them some drinks.

"I didn't know you would be here with Mario."

Philippe was shouting to make himself heard above the music and was still frowning. 'And why should you know?' Crystal thought, still unable to shake off the feeling of irritation, 'You are my cousin, not my keeper.' But keeping her voice devoid of expression she said,

"He asked me to go to the cinema; we went to see a film called 'Blow Up'"

Philippe seemed uninterested in what they had done but asked, as Mario rejoined them,

"Are you going back to Savron Pinder tonight?"

He was looking intently at Mario who told him that they were catching a train later in the evening.

"No need. Bateman is meeting me here with the car in about half an hour. I'll be glad to give you a lift. He was smiling now and engaged Mario in a conversation about a deal he had made earlier in the week while Crystal wandered a few steps away sipping her drink, furious that her evening had been spoilt by Philippe's arrival.

"Oh, hello there. Aren't you the girl with that fancy pad out in the sticks?"

By the light of several candles on a nearby mantelpiece, Crystal could make out the face of one of the models who had been at the shoot the previous week and with her were two other girls she hadn't seen before.

"It is, isn't it? Crystal."

Crystal glanced over to where Mario and Philippe were deep in conversation and sighed.

"Yes....yes, you came and did a photo shoot at my place."

The girl, who was dressed in a mini of orange and purple swirls, with a pair of skin-tight, shiny black boots reaching up to her thighs, turned to her two friends and screeched,

"You should see it! It's absolutely fab. and she owns it!"

She turned back to Crystal, her eyes shining with admiration. One of the other girls, dressed in a long flowing kaftan and wearing a headband around a mass of untidy black hair, looked disdainfully at Crystal while allowing a curl of smoke to escape from her nostrils.

"Doesn't impress me, darling. All property's theft as far as I'm concerned," and with that she turned and drifted away.

"Take no notice of her. She's loopy." The girl in the orange swirls pulled the other girl nearer and shouted,

"honestly, it's a terrific place and she's brought it back from being practically derelict. We were there for the Haspars shoot last week with that amazing new Italian photographer..." she froze and the shriek suddenly got louder, "Oh my god! There he is!... And he's coming over....."

The other girl, also mini clad and booted and looking so similar to her friend they could have been sisters, stared as Mario approached the trio.

"Wow, what a stud!"

Mario smiled at both girls before taking Crystal by the hand and leading her out into the cool night air. She could feel their envious eyes following her progress across the room and at that moment she was walking on air.

The journey home was, for the most part, silent. Crystal sat between Mario and Philippe aware of a tension between the two men that she hadn't noticed before. She was angry. Why did Philippe have to muscle in on their evening? What was he up to? At twenty six she was old enough to look after herself and though she had never fallen out with Philippe before, she would not allow him to set himself up as some kind of protector. There had been so much unhappiness, tragedy and then sheer hard work in her life that maybe, just maybe it was time for a little happiness; and she did indeed feel happy, excited and alive again.

Quickly pushing all thoughts of Giles to the back of her mind she glanced up at Mario. His body felt warm and vibrant next to hers and a tingle of excitement shot through her like a charge of electricity when she felt him reach for her hand. He gently rubbed her fingers with his thumb as he started to talk to Philippe about a contract he had received that week. Crystal closed her eyes and leaned back against the soft leather of the seat, oblivious of everything except Mario's gentle touch.

CHAPTER THIRTY FIVE

The next morning Crystal was busy helping Jenny at the stables; as owners arrived to ride their horses she chatted to them, making sure they were happy with the service she was providing and ironing out a few minor problems. After lunch she strolled down to the half built theatre and wandered around inspecting the latest work making a note of one or two things to talk to the foreman about in the morning. It was all the same as usual and yet everything was totally different. She felt as though the bubble of excitement inside her would burst, in fact it already had and she felt sure everyone must notice that she was different, she had a secret; she was in love. Everywhere she looked Mario's face was there in front of her; she could still feel the touch of his hand, the thrill of his lips and she just couldn't wait to see him again.

On the way back to the house she did a detour to the stables for a final check on the horses. Jenny was just finishing for the day and all was in order.

"Did you manage to sort out the problem with the feed for Anna Gray's pony?" Crystal asked, as her stable manager gave the chestnut mare she was stroking a final pat on the nose.

"Oh yes, no real problem at all. It's being delivered tomorrow. Mrs Gray was fine about it."

Crystal was only half listening; what she really wanted to do was to shout out,

"Jenny, I'm in love!" And race around the stable yard like a demented child.

"'Bye, then."

"'Bye Jenny. See you tomorrow."

The stable yard was empty and the only sound was the soft stamping of horses, muffled by straw. Glancing idly round, Crystal noticed that a bucket had been left out by the wall. It didn't really matter but, still in her dream world, she wandered absentmindedly over, picked it up, opened the door of the only empty loose box and put it inside. The fresh, newly laid straw rustled beneath her boots and the sweetness made her pause for a few seconds just to enjoy its fragrance.

She had her back to the door and was suddenly conscious of movement in the straw behind her; as she swung round and saw Mario it seemed the most natural thing in the world that he should be standing there. Without a word he reached out and pulled her towards him, kissing her until she was weak with desire. She felt his hand on her breast and didn't want him to stop; but suddenly she pulled away, shaking with emotion. She looked at Mario and, though the light inside the stable was dim she was sure she could see that strange smile hovering around his lips again. She fastened the buttons of her blouse, feeling suddenly confused and shy, embarrassed now by the strength of the feelings that had made her want to lie with him in the fresh straw beneath their feet. She turned away and spoke with her back to him,

"Mario, I'm sorry...... I have to be sure......."
She turned back,

"My life has been very far from normal."

"Yes, Philippe told me.... your family... your... er... brother."

"Yes, you see, I never expected to feel this way about anyone.... ever. I have to be sure that it means something," Mario stepped towards her and took her in his arms again, kissing her very gently,

"I understand. I will wait. I hope you didn't mind me coming here; I was just out getting some fresh air and I very much wanted to see you..." And it was at that moment Crystal became aware of Marjorie standing in the doorway.

"I wondered how long you were going to be, Crystal." She addressed her daughter, ignoring Mario, and Crystal, for the first time that she could remember, felt angry with her adoptive mother.

"Not long," she pulled Mario towards the door, "but perhaps now that you have come down here you would like to meet Mario, the man who took me out yesterday."

Marjorie glanced at the Italian, then looked back at her daughter as she said,

"We have already met when he came to the door a few minutes ago. I'll see you back at the house," then she turned and walked away. Crystal was furious; what was the matter with everyone? – First Charlie then Philippe and now Marjorie behaving oddly around Mario.

"Mario, I'm sorry…."

"It's OK. Perhaps I had better go now. I will call you." And he too disappeared out of the stable yard and up the drive.

Crystal stamped angrily over the gravel, threw open the back door and sat down to pull off her boots. As she tugged at them she thought about Marjorie and felt some of the anger draining out of her. They had both been through so much and had always given each other love and support; but still…. She must be allowed to grow up….to live her life and no-one was going to stop her from……from what?

She walked into the sitting room and found Marjorie quietly knitting in a chair by the window. She looked up,

"Shall I tell Nelly to get the supper now?"

"Yes….please."

Marjorie put down the knitting and left the room. Crystal waited a few moments then followed her out and went upstairs to wash and change. As she brushed her hair, she looked at the face staring back at her – the girl with everything….the girl with nothing. Where was she going to and what really mattered in her life? She had thought she knew, but now everything had changed.

Later she was still troubled by these strange thoughts as she sat at the table with Marjorie, saddened by the tension between them. It had never been like this before and she hated it. Couldn't Marjorie see the wonderful thing that was happening to her and why wasn't she glad? She watched her eating, the woman who had brought her up as her own, and for the first time she saw her as a woman, the comfortable, kindly mother she had loved all through her childhood; the woman to whom she was attached by love and gratitude, but not by blood.

She couldn't imagine that Marjorie had ever felt the passionate love for George that Crystal felt for Mario. She thought of Eleanore and Jack, of their overwhelming love for each other that was the very reason for her existence and realised she was truly her mother's daughter. She was sure Eleanore would understand about Mario.

After supper, the atmosphere was still far from comfortable, so Crystal made an excuse and went to bed early, wondering, just before she fell asleep, if love was always this painful.

But even Eleanore's reaction wasn't what she had hoped for. She had felt so sure that her real mother, the woman who had known the earth shaking passion of true love, would understand exactly how she was feeling. And sitting under the apple trees in the old orchard at Monk's Manor the following afternoon sharing a pot of tea and some cake with her, she opened her heart and waited for her mother's enthusiastic response.

Eleanore was silent, sipping her tea and gazing into the distance for a few moments thinking about the suave Italian she had met during the photo shoot at Savron Pinder House. Cautiously she said,

"He's certainly very attractive, darling, and has quite a worldly air about him. Do you think he feels the same about you?"

"Oh I think so….well, I hope so. I don't see how he could kiss me the way he does if he doesn't love me."

Eleanore was silent again knowing how wrong that reasoning could be. Unknown to Crystal, while she had been checking the horses and dealing with the builders that morning, Marjorie had phoned and spoken to Eleanore about her misgivings regarding Crystal's sudden infatuation with the Italian,

"I know she's twenty six, Eleanore, but in some ways…emotionally… she's still only about sixteen – and has missed out on her teenage years. There's something about this Italian that I don't trust – he's just too charming. What I'm afraid of is that if we try to tell her, it will only serve to drive her further into his arms. I can already sense that she is feeling irritated with me for not welcoming him more enthusiastically, but I just couldn't. He arrived last evening and went down to the stables to see her and …oh I don't know, I just found him a bit creepy…calculating. The trouble is she can't see it."

"Oh dear! I'm so glad you phoned. She wants to come and have tea this afternoon, probably to tell me all about him. Forewarned is forearmed…I'll be very careful what I say and I won't let on we've talked. The way she's feeling that will make her think we're ganging up on her. Not easy this one. Thanks again for the call, Marjorie. I'll do my best."

"I'm sure you will, dear. If anyone can say the right thing, it's you. I think she may be at the stage where she believes that no-one else has ever felt the overwhelming passion she is feeling at the moment – certainly not George and me – but perhaps in her eyes you and Jack came somewhere close. Though

George and I had our moments, and we certainly loved each other very deeply."

"I know you did, my dear. Crystal really doesn't yet know how the world works and I fear she may have some painful revelations ahead – as if she hadn't had enough already. The trouble is, Marjorie, I don't think there's anything we can do to save her from them."

"No, I think you're right. We'll just have to be here when we're needed."

Feeling saddened by Eleanore's lukewarm response to her revelation, Crystal picked up the tea things and followed her mother back to the house. They walked in silence and as they turned right out of the orchard onto the path leading to the back door she glanced to the left towards a group of out buildings. The first was the garage where Eleanore kept her car; it stood open, the sun gleaming on the bonnet of the little red Mini Cooper that she used for whizzing around the villages and into Cambridge to attend her Art classes. She had started to paint after Giles died and found some comfort and a focus for her life in this pursuit. She was surprised to discover that she did indeed have talent, so when William left she plucked up courage and enrolled for a course at a College in Cambridge, a move she had not regretted as it had opened up a whole new world for her.

For the first time Crystal saw that, attached to the garage, was an identical building which for some reason she had never really noticed before. The door was shut – had she ever seen it open? She wondered what Eleanore used it for, but was not interested enough to ask; and when they reached the kitchen door they parted more frostily than ever before in the short time they had known each other. Crystal marched up the drive, staring straight ahead, unaware of her mother's eyes, so full of love and concern, following her until she rounded the bend and disappeared from view.

'So, as long as I'm towing the line….as long as I'm doing exactly what everyone expects of me, then everything's OK! Don't I have a right to my own feelings? Maybe it's childish looking for approval and maybe I just have to accept that everyone isn't always going to applaud everything I do. My feelings for Mario are so strong…how can they be anything other than real?'

Crystal marched along the road between Monk's Manor and Savron Pinder House willing herself not to dwell on Eleanore's reaction to her declaration of love for Mario. Was she too old to remember how true love felt? Was this the same woman who had loved her father so passionately that she had risked all in one night of love? Why should she be denied the same experience? Suddenly she thought of Giles and wavered for a moment... but no. The vow was never to marry, not to stay a virgin for the rest of her life, so maybe she and Mario could vow to be true to each other for ever, perhaps live together and build a wonderful future on their mutual passion...

By the time she reached the back door and kicked off her boots she had made a decision.

CHAPTER THIRTY SIX

The rest of the week went well and Crystal immersed herself in work to make the time pass more quickly; she seemed to be buoyed up, carried along by an extra burst of energy that she knew could only come from her feelings for Mario. His face was everywhere – in the stables, the half built shell of the new theatre and there in front of her just before she went to sleep at night, murmuring his name into her pillow.

Even Madame's problems with the ballet school seemed easier to deal with than usual. Her protestations of not being able to coax her talented little protégés to the heights of which she knew they were capable with all the banging and sound of big machinery down by the lake were met with a smile from Crystal and an assurance that she would adjust the men's hours so they didn't coincide with the lessons. All was possible in this brave new world that, for her, had acquired an exciting and wonderful dimension.

She was in love and just had to pass the time until she could see him again. On Wednesday evening he phoned,

"I want to see you again."

"Yes…oh yes…this weekend?"

Crystal gripped the phone, her heart beating wildly, shaking with excitement. She was sure he would be visiting as he did most weekends to conduct business with Philippe or just keep him company at Manor Farm.

"Ah…no…so sorry, this weekend I have to stay in London. But next weekend I come and perhaps we spend time together on Sunday…?"

"Yes…yes, of course."

They talked for a while about what they had been doing, Crystal asking him questions just to keep him on the phone so she could hear his voice, not wanting to ring off.

"I must go, Cara….until a week on Sunday."

"Yes…yes…a week on Sunday." Crystal hesitated then said softly, "I love you."

There was a pause before he answered and it was a barely audible,

"Yes…ciao, Cara..." and he put down the phone.

Another whole week after this one! An eternity! Had she really told him she loved him? She went hot and then cold. Had that been the right thing to do? Had he been so moved that he had been unable to respond in the same way? He would though, when they were together again and she let him see that she was ready to love him in the way he wanted, to give herself to him completely.

On Sunday Marjorie got ready for Church as usual and raised her eyebrows when she saw that, ten minutes before they usually left the house, Crystal wasn't dressed.

"I'm not coming to Church today…I'm feeling a little unwell."

"Oh."

Marjorie picked up her gloves and quietly let herself out of the front door. She felt sad that Crystal was missing Church again as she had done quite a lot recently; it had been such a source of strength through all her troubles.

When she had gone Crystal felt a bit guilty about lying but dismissed this as she locked herself in her bathroom and set about her plan. She opened the bag of things she had bought from the chemist in Cambridge and carefully applied the oozy paste to her face. She lay on the bed to let it dry, feeling her skin go taught and trying not to smile, as it said on the instructions that it would work better if it didn't crack. It dried to a grotesque, chalky mask that pulled her skin tight and when she looked in the mirror she laughed, reducing it to crazy paving before washing it off.

She waxed her legs then set about filing and painting her nails. She had noticed that Mario liked women to be well groomed; it was important to him, and she wanted to look her best, wondering as she applied the red paint to her fingernails what the horses would make of it, and wrinkling her nose at the strange smell of pear drops. It was a whole week before she could see Mario, but that would give her time to work on her appearance, something she had never done before.

She lay on her bed again while the nail varnish dried and her thoughts strayed to Marjorie and the grey, stone Church halfway along the village street.

She remembered the first time she had gone to a service there, prompted by a suggestion from George, even though he didn't himself attend. She saw him quite clearly, one foot on the spade as he paused while digging the garden soon after they had arrived at Maple Cottage,

"It might be a good idea for you to go along to the Church, love, you know, give it a try."

He had resumed his digging and the following week Crystal had taken up his suggestion, turning the old twisted handle and walking through the heavy oak door. How strange everything had seemed; the musty smell, and the words, chanted and sung with such confidence by the sparse congregation but scarcely comprehensible to her ten year old ears. Something, she didn't know what, had drawn her back week after week in all weathers. She remembered meandering along the village street on hot summer's evenings and relishing the cool interior of the old building after the heat of the dusty road outside; and then in winter, running fast, wrapped in her riding mac, her feet pounding the pavement and her breath pluming out in the frosty air.

When Reverend Kempton had suggested attending confirmation classes she had done so, cycling down to the Rectory on her bicycle every Saturday morning until the day when, dressed in a new, shining white frock lovingly made for her by Marjorie, she was confirmed into the Church of England. She remembered feeling exhilarated and somehow special as she had raced along the grassy track on Poppy that afternoon.

"Are you all Holy now?" Minty had asked, irreverently. She attended Chapel every Sunday with Matthew and Gran, except at Christmas when they made an exception and went to Church, but she only went because she had to. She had no choice in the matter as Martha had made clear when she had tried to rebel.

"No, of course not, I've just made a special commitment, that's all."

"What, to be good for ever?" Minty looked scornful.

"No, but I shall try and be a good Christian."

She had meant it too. And both when she had felt deserted by Giles, and then when he had died, she had spent many hours sitting quietly in the old grey building, gathering strength, talking to God and sometimes Reverend Kempton, and it had helped. She really did believe in God, in spite of all that had happened and was sure she had felt the everlasting arms lifting her and carrying her along until she was strong enough to walk again. She had clung to her faith in the darkness and each time had been pulled through to light on the other side.

Marjorie had only found her faith after George died when Crystal persuaded her to go along with her one Sunday morning,

"Come on, Mum, it can't do any harm and you may find some comfort,"

And Marjorie did, making it a regular part of her life ever since.

She had often seen Mrs. Dean, her old village school Head Teacher, there in her pew on Sunday mornings – such an admirable and upright woman. Crystal thought again how strange it was that her own life had revolved so much around that little school as both pupil and teacher, and what a wonderful send off they had given her when she had left soon after moving into Savron Pinder House. She remembered saying goodbye to little Jon, with his owl eyes, looking so important because some facts that he had unearthed had provided the clue to the treachery at Savron Pinder House where Mary,

Emily and Mickey had plotted to kill her grand parents.

'Oh well, all in the past now. Time to grow up.'

Crystal leapt off the bed and stared at herself in the mirror. She raised her hands and flapped the now dry crimson nails, admiring the way they shone in the light. That afternoon she had planned to go and see Minty who she felt certain would understand about Mario. She walked over to her wardrobe and chose a new pair of jeans, tight fitting, not baggy like the ones she usually wore, a black silk shirt and a string of white beads with matching looped earrings. They were made of white enamel and swung as she moved her head. She applied make up with care, foundation, eyeliner and mascara and finally blusher to accentuate her cheek bones; then brushed her thick, red hair, still shorter than previously and in as much of a bob as she could achieve with her mass of curls.

She ran lightly down the stairs, calling to Nelly to say she wouldn't require any lunch but to tell Marjorie that she would be home for dinner, then pulling on a pair of smart boots, she set off down the drive and across the fields to where she knew a short cut that would take her to Rob and Minty's farm on the outskirts of the village.

Minty's dream of life had so far come true. Rob farmed in a modest way and she kept chickens and bred rabbits, just as she had always wanted. In November 1965 their first child, Bobby, had been born and in January 1968 Frankie, their second boy had come along. The two friends hadn't seen as much of each other as they would have liked, what with the demands of motherhood and Crystal's total preoccupation with Savron Pinder House, though they knew they would always be there for each other when needed.

Minty hadn't been surprised to get the call from Crystal saying she would like to see her. Village gossip was beginning to intimate that the visiting Italian was causing a bit of a stir in more ways than one.

CHAPTER THIRTY SEVEN

If Minty was surprised by the way her friend was dressed, the level of make-up and the flashing red nails, she didn't let on, but busied herself making some tea in the kitchen that Rob had so lovingly renovated for her, painting the walls and making the cupboards himself. She carried the tray through into the sitting room, comfortably furnished with two chairs and a squashy sofa covered in bright flowery material; it had been in the best parlour at Pook's Farm and Minty had been touched when Gran had said she could have it. She and Rob were saving and one day they would buy a new one, but meanwhile this suited them well, especially with the boys being so young. She was determined the house would always be a home, never a show place and both she and Rob were happy with the lived in feel of their little farm.

Crystal played with the boys, helping two year old Frankie with his building bricks; and then reading a story to four year old Bobby who listened with huge eyes and a thumb stuck firmly in his mouth. She looked up when her friend entered and couldn't help thinking how much motherhood suited her. Entirely comfortable in her world of children and animals, Minty looked the same as always; coarse, brown hair, as unruly as its owner, a few freckles peppering her nose and dressed in old baggy jeans and one of Rob's shirts. She put down the tray and flopped onto the sofa, scooping up little Frankie on the way and pressing his head against her shoulder where he snuffled, his podgy arms wrapped tightly round her neck.

They drank tea and when both boys fell asleep, Frankie against his mother's chest and Bobby in the corner of the sofa, Minty looked at her friend and asked,

"What's up Cryssie?"

Crystal told her all about her feelings for Mario, that she was sure he felt the same and how happy she was. Her friend was silent for a moment,

"The fact is, Crys, you didn't look the picture of happiness when you walked in and you don't now. So what's up?"

"Oh it's just...well I am happy, absolutely ecstatic, but my relationship with Mario seems to have caused rifts with others in my life. Charlie is hardly speaking to me, Marjorie disapproves and Eleanore was quite distant when I told her. They just don't understand; anyway, I came to see you, I knew you would....you know...understand."

She finished lamely and waited for Minty to tell her not to bother with what anyone thought or said, or didn't think or say – after all she was a free spirit, her best friend through all her troubles. But Minty didn't say anything. Crystal stared at her,

"What?"

Minty hesitated, then spoke quietly and gently, not in her usual way at all.

"Crystal….are you sure you can trust this man? Only there have been rumours…"

Before she could finish, the back door opened and there was the sound of footsteps in the kitchen.

"Hello, I'm home."

It was Rob. They heard him filling the kettle and before either woman could speak, he continued, shouting through to the sitting room,

"It's getting colder out there, Mints, not like August at all….and guess what? I've just seen that eyetie creeping off down to Lot's Barn with Lisa Willis to get his leg over again, I'll be bound …in London all week then down to the country at the weekend for a roll in the hay…"

He wandered into the sitting room and stopped speaking, a red flush creeping slowly up his neck as he saw the frozen, horrified expressions on the faces of his wife and her oldest friend.

"Oh, God, Cryssie, I'm sorry…"

"Just shut up, Rob"

It was Minty who spoke, staring at Crystal, her eyes full of sympathy. Crystal leapt to her feet,

"You must be mistaken, Rob, you can't have seen him....he stayed in London this weekend....I must go."

Minty jumped up, still clutching a dozing Frankie,

"No, Cryssie, don't go...not like this. Stay and talk. Have another cup of tea."

But her friend was out of the door and halfway down the path, just conscious of Minty calling Rob a tactless lump and her husband's protestations that he didn't know Crystal was there.

He was wrong...of course he was wrong! She knew Mario was in London. He wouldn't lie to her...he absolutely would not lie! So why were her feet taking her towards Lot's Barn? She had to go...she had to see for herself that there was no-one there – or if there was it was someone else with Lisa Willis. Of course he wasn't there ...whoever Rob had seen it wasn't Mario. There were loads of boys around the village with dark hair.

She knew Lisa Willis, the daughter of the local shop keeper, had known her since their school days; a pretty blond girl who had liked to play kiss chase and was told off by Mrs. Dean for showing the boys her knickers (and a bit more, only Mrs. Dean didn't know that) behind the outside lavatories. She knew

Lisa was still very pretty as she had seen her around the village and according to local gossip she was off to secretarial college in September.

Lot's Barn was isolated; it belonged to Manor Farm and was used to store dry straw for the cattle in winter. Crystal kept staring straight ahead as she approached the large black building, then crept cautiously around to the door which was open just wide enough for her to squeeze through. Her feet were silent on the dusty floor and she couldn't see anything as her eyes tried to adjust to the dim interior after the brightness of the chilly day outside. She stood still and blinked, aware of the smell of fresh straw.

Suddenly, to the left and a little way forward, she heard the straw rustle and, looking round, she could just make out the shapes in profile of two bodies locked together. Mesmerised, she was incapable of movement but stood, rooted to the spot, as a shaft of sunlight filtered through a hole in the barn roof and its path of dancing dust led straight to the couple in the straw. It shone on Lisa's pale leg, curled around the man's body, on the man's tanned, gleaming torso and dark hair, on the profile that was unmistakably and cruelly Mario's.

Silently Crystal turned and left the barn, the sound of Lisa's moans of ecstasy rising to a crescendo and following her out of the door.

On Wednesday when Mario phoned, Crystal asked him in a bright, cheery voice how his week was going. She listened with rapt attention as he told her all about the new contract he had secured with one of the most prestigious magazines of the day, work for which had kept him in London, and away from her, the previous weekend. She murmured in a suitably husky voice,

"I can't wait until I see you on Sunday. Let's have a picnic in the boat house by the lake; I'll get Nelly to pack us up a hamper of delicious food and a bottle of champagne."

Mario sounded delighted,

"Until then, my darling. The hours will drag very slowly until I am with you again. Ciao, Cara."

On Sunday Marjorie wasn't surprised when Crystal told her that she wouldn't be going to Church again and, pulling on her gloves, walked down the drive on her own. She was still saddened by the change in her daughter and mystified by something she had detected, a sort of hardness, a steeliness that had hovered around her all week. She was unreachable and Marjorie was further perturbed when Crystal had renewed the nail polish on Saturday, painting on an even more garish colour, and now, this morning had appeared after breakfast,

397

plastered in makeup and dressed in an extremely short mini skirt with a top that left little to the imagination. She had a feeling that Mario would arrive very soon after she had left the house...oh dear...

With a heavy heart she walked steadily along the village street to the Church where she hoped to find some solace.

Crystal made her way to the kitchen where Nelly had just finished clearing away the breakfast things,

"In about half an hour Mr. Mario will be here. If I'm not in the house he will be expecting you to direct him to the boat house by the lake. Could you tell him to come to the stables first please, Nelly. Tell him it's important as there's something I have to show him before we go to the boat house."

"Yes, of course, Miss."

Crystal left the kitchen and Nelly put the last of the plates on the large dresser that stretched along the length of one of the walls. Oh dear...what on earth had happened to the lovely, bright young woman who had worked such miracles in this old house? Who was this painted creature that had taken her place? She and Bowman had sat many an evening hoping and praying that the Italian would disappear back to where he had come from and leave their young mistress alone. He was no good, they were sure of that, but Crystal, normally so level headed, just couldn't see it. She'd lost her head, no doubt about it. Oh the damage a handsome face and winning smile can do! Like the yanks in the war…coming over and turning the heads of the local girls…caused many an upset. How glad she had been that she'd had Bowman, her rock through the years. Still poor miss Crystal had had such a rough life in many ways, no time to be a young girl and find out what some of the boys can be like…Ah well, we must keep going and just hope for the best. She reached into the larder for the cold ham to slice for lunch.

The clean straw in the stable had been freshly laid and Crystal stood in the corner, watching the door…waiting. She had one hand behind her back and knew she had to keep it there, hiding what was in it until just the right moment. She didn't have to wait long before she heard his shuffling approach and saw his smile as he looked over the top of the stable door. His eyes grew wide with admiration.

"Wow you look…amazing…so different."

He paused,

"So, my darling, what are you doing here? Nelly said you have something to show me."

Still smiling in the lop-sided and slightly quizzical way that she had thought she loved, he walked in and stood in front of her, resting his hands on her shoulders, looking deeply into her eyes. She wondered then why she had never noticed before how controlled and calculated everything about him was. Nothing was spontaneous. Crystal smiled back and allowed him to kiss her.

"So…what is the mystery? You show me then we go to the boat house." He bent to kiss her again, but Crystal drew back and said, in the huskiest voice she could manage,

"Oh no, darling, I thought you might like to take my clothes off here and roll around in the straw….after all that's what you like, isn't it…?"

His smile vanished and she continued, aware of the hard edge in her voice,

"You see…I saw you last Sunday with Lisa…there in the straw at Lot's barn…"

He tried to smile again,

"Oh but, my darling…" And it was at this point she snapped

"Don't you dare…don't you DARE 'my darling' me you lying, cheating bastard…"

She brought the whip out from behind her back, slashing him viciously across one side of his body then the other. The end of it caught him just under his eye and he raised his hand to where a drop of blood was already starting to run down his cheek. He looked terrified and backed away.

"You mad woman…mad woman…"

"Get out…GET OUT…" she screamed as he ran through the door.

Crystal threw down the whip and stood in the stable shaking, as the sound of Mario's retreating footsteps rang on the cobbles outside.

It was an hour later when Marjorie ventured down to the stables. She knew from Nelly that Crystal had been into the house and that there had been a lot of door banging and thundering footsteps before she had disappeared out again,

"I can't be sure, Madam, but I'd try the stables if I was you. That Italian was here, but he left in rather a hurry."

"Yes I know." Marjorie smiled but didn't say anything to Nelly about Mario hurrying past her on the drive, head down, with one of his spotless handkerchiefs clutched against his face. She changed out of her Church clothes and walked slowly, hoping she had given Crystal enough time on her own, but thinking that whatever had happened her daughter might be glad of someone to talk to.

Star was tethered in the yard and Crystal was brushing her, fast and furiously, her hand clutching the body brush banging against the little mare's shining black coat and sweeping down then up again, her whole body keeping time with the motion of her arm. Marjorie stood and stared at her daughter's back and as her hand came up again to the little mare's withers she noticed that the nail polish had gone and that she had scraped her hair back into an elastic band where it sat on her head like a giant red flower.

"So, he's gone then…Mario."

Crystal didn't look round but carried on brushing.

"Yes, he's gone. And you needn't worry he won't be coming back."

Star winced when the brush hit her side again, then looked round as the rhythmic grooming stopped; she felt the full weight of her beloved mistress against her side and flinched as the brush clattered over the cobbles.

"Oh, shit…"

With her forehead against the mare's warm flank and arms flung across her back Crystal's body shook and she started to sob.

In three quick steps Marjorie was at her daughter's side, turning her away from the startled horse, hugging and soothing her just as she had always done.

Marjorie didn't ask any questions; she felt sure that the full story would emerge when Crystal was ready, but the two women sat in companionable silence that evening, Marjorie pleased to have her daughter back, but knowing that it would take some time for her wounds to heal, and Crystal just feeling numb and confused, not really ready to deal with what had happened. She did venture to ask Marjorie one question,

"Mum, did any one ever betray you?"

Marjorie stopped knitting and looked across the room,

"Oh, yes,"

Crystal looked surprised,

"What happened?"

"Well, it was a long time ago, when I was still at school. I was just fourteen…it was in the days when you stayed at your village school until you were fifteen and then left. There wasn't any Secondary school then. Anyway I was really sweet on a boy called Gregory and we had started walking out together. Then I saw him one day kissing a girl called Monica Bradshaw behind the bike sheds." Marjorie paused.

"What did you do?" Crystal prompted. Marjorie smiled and looked a bit sheepish,

"I put a dead mouse in his lunch box."

Crystal gave a bark of laughter…her mum…Marjorie…doing something like that?

"Did he know it was you?"

"Well, he wouldn't have done except that Monica saw me and told the teacher. I had to sit on my own to eat lunch for the rest of the term, but it was worth it; especially as George saw what had happened and, when no-one was looking, dipped the ends of Monica's plaits in the inkwell. There were great blobs of ink all over her gingham dress; he was never found out, but I guessed it was him and he admitted it years later when we were engaged." She paused again and a wistful look came into her eyes. "Dear George. I think that was when I first fell in love with him; he was so kind."

"Not to Monica Bradshaw, he wasn't!"

Marjorie laughed,

"No, but always to me…always to me."

They were silent, lost in their own thoughts for a few minutes, then, yawning, Marjorie declared she was ready for bed."

"Yes me too." They started towards the door and Crystal laughed again,

"Gregory…honestly Mum…how could you fall for someone with a name like Gregory!" And Marjorie was so glad to see her smiling.

CHAPTER THIRTY EIGHT

January 1971

The metal bucket clanged on the cobbles, the sound reverberating through the cold, clear air; horses peered over the tops of their stables, ears pricked forward, heads shaking, snorting out great plumes of smoky breath from flared nostrils. Time for a feed…time for a gallop in the sunshine over frost-white ground. They stamped on straw covered floors, impatient to be free.

Crystal breathed in, filling her lungs with air and enjoying the sharp sting in her nostrils, the tingle on her cheeks which she knew would be glowing red by this time; she loved the winter weather in all its crisp coldness and was always happy to spend some time on mornings like these helping Jenny. She turned and looked down towards the lake to where the new theatre stood gleaming in the sunshine. Half hidden by trees, it blended in beautifully with the surrounding wood and landscaped lawns – how proud her grandparents would have been, how Connie would have loved helping her with the preparations for the grand opening in the spring. She looked again round the stables, every one of them occupied, and could just imagine Arthur standing there, hands resting against the yellow waistcoat stretched across his ribs, staring around with shining eyes.

'Good lord, Crystal….this is wonderful, truly wonderful. You've made the old place live again. Well done girl!'

And in her heart she answered him, 'it's for you, grandfather…you and Connie – and it just happens that I love it too.'

"Crystal, can you come and look at young Freddie Brown's pony. It may be my imagination, but I think his fetlock's a bit swollen."

Jenny's voice pulled her back to the present and she hurried along to the loose box at the end of the yard.

Walking back to the house for breakfast half an hour later, she looked again at the new theatre; it had been hard work keeping the builders on schedule but worth it as the project had come in almost on budget; nothing short of a miracle and mainly due to Rosemary's husband, Gerald, and, to everyone's surprise, Marjorie.

Since helping her to put together a business plan, Gerald had continued to monitor Crystal's accounts once a month, helping her with forward planning and ensuring that the loan was repaid in regular instalments to the bank. She also employed the services of an accountant, but it was Marjorie, not her, who liaised with him on a weekly basis. After years of running a house-keeping budget, she had discovered that she was able to transfer the skills with which she had efficiently managed the modest amount given to her each week by George into being able to keep track of the large amounts coming in and going out of Savron Pinder House in connection with the stables, ballet school and the building of the theatre.

"Have you always been good with figures?" Crystal had asked when it became clear that, although she herself had the vision, drive and creative ability to bring about the changes at Savron Pinder House, balance sheets just swam before her eyes and bored her silly. To Marjorie they were fascinating and she unravelled them in seconds, spotting errors that Crystal knew she would have missed.

"I suppose I have really, though, of course, girls weren't encouraged to excel at arithmetic at school in my day; we were judged by our ability to hem a handkerchief and do beautiful blanket stitch, and I suppose I just fell in with what was expected of me. I do remember once feeling really exhilarated when a new teacher with some strange ideas came to the school and suggested that we should run our own tuck shop. We did, and I managed the money side, ensuring that we made a profit." She paused and smiled, "That, and being asked to do a recorder solo at the village music festival were the highlights of my school career."

Crystal had long been aware that Marjorie was musical and would have loved to have piano lessons as a child, but such luxuries were out of the question in a household where Grandpa Bates had barely earned enough money as a signalman to make ends meet. It had therefore been with great pleasure that Crystal had purchased a piano and organised lessons for her mum as a thank-you for all her hard work at the end of their first year in Savron Pinder House. She had presented them as Christmas presents and could see that Marjorie was absolutely delighted, in spite of her many protestations that they couldn't afford such things and that Crystal shouldn't spend money on her when she had such plans and dreams. Marjorie loved her lessons and Crystal found it soothing to hear her play in the evenings while she watched the sun set over the woods and lake.

She paused and looked back towards the stables, remembering that fateful Sunday in August when she had whipped Mario and watched him run out of the door. She couldn't really believe she had done it but she wasn't sorry. Minty had laughed when she had told her,

"Serves him right, cheating bastard, you struck a blow for women in more ways than one. Good on yer"

But Rob had shaken his head in disbelief,

"I sometimes think you're a bloody nutcase, Crys. He could have had you up for assault."

Minty snorted,

"Yes, very likely, drag the whole story out and risk getting beaten up by the village men with Reg Willis in the lead baying for his blood. I should think he knew better than that and if he didn't his Froggy friend would have put him straight. Oh, sorry, Crys. I forgot you're close to your cousin again."

And it was true. Following the discovery of Mario's cheating with Lisa Willis, he had stopped coming to Savron Pinder at the weekends and Philippe occasionally visited her, rekindling their friendship as though nothing had happened. They didn't talk about Mario but Crystal realised that when he had seemed disapproving of their relationship it was because he knew what the Italian was like and had been trying to look out for her.

She had also been surprised by how quickly she had recovered; it was as if seeing him in his true colours had turned the love she had thought she felt for him immediately to something akin to hatred, like milk going sour. She despised him; the very thought of him was repulsive and she was amazed that that could happen so quickly. She felt whole again and strong; and didn't have to go through anything like the agony she had felt on losing Giles; the two experiences were as different as any two things could possibly be.

Eleanore, too, had understood when Crystal had gone to see her soon after the painful event. Sitting at her easel in the orchard painting, she had listened patiently while Crystal told her what had happened; to her surprise she also found herself confessing to her mother how much of a fool she felt. Eleanore had put down her paint brush and looked steadily at her daughter, the young woman whom she loved almost more than she could say.

"We've all done it, Crystal, believe me. We've all lost our heads and hearts to the wrong sort, someone who is bound to hurt us. Sometimes we break the kindest heart in the process, someone we have perhaps overlooked; and many women, of course marry the attractive rogues, condemning themselves to a life of misery. So you're not alone, my darling, not by a long way….and you don't have to apologise to anyone, not me or Marjorie or Philippe…or…"

She seemed about to say another name but stopped. She had read her daughter's mind because Crystal did indeed think that she owed an apology to the people who shared her life and who she felt she had treated badly during the time of her infatuation with Mario. For she knew now that that was exactly what it had been, an infatuation that had taken over her life and impaired her judgement. She was curious about her mother's past – had she come close to not experiencing the great love she shared with Jack? Was he the kind heart she had risked breaking and if so, with whom?

She watched Eleanore carefully applying paint to canvas and realised that this was not the right time to ask that question, as she had a feeling that it may be just a little more serious than Marjorie's experience with Gregory. She was also sure she knew the name that Eleanore hadn't said, and her mind strayed instead to thoughts of him.

Since the day he had turned his back and walked away from her as she had stood agreeing to Mario's photo shoot in the grounds of Savron Pinder House, Crystal had scarcely seen Charlie. She was sure he still managed the farm for Gerald and found herself hoping that he would be there when she paid her monthly visit to go over the accounts. She did see him once getting into his car just as she was arriving and almost called out to him, but she stopped herself though she didn't know why. She didn't think he had seen her and had been surprised by the effect the sight of him had on her. She was startled by his good looks – why had she never noticed before how good looking he was, how very attractive in every way? She missed him; she missed the fun, the laughter, the way he had always been there when she needed him.

She had seen him at Christmas when Gerald and Rosemary had invited her to a party, but he hadn't spoken to her and by the time she had made up her mind to go and talk to him she was too late as he was deep in conversation with the new District Nurse who had just moved to the area, a pretty girl with dark hair and bright, shining eyes.

Crystal reached the back door of the house, pulling off her boots before letting herself into the warm kitchen where Nelly was preparing breakfast. Bacon sizzled, filling the place with its wonderful aroma, and two pieces of toast popped up in the automatic toaster. Crystal helped herself to one of them and buttered it, sitting down at the long green table and gazing out onto the kitchen garden, kept so beautifully by Mr. Bowman.

She loved the kitchen, the big clock that ticked steadily away day and night, the old green dresser stacked with china, the huge fridge that hummed away in the corner just like the one at Pook's farm from where she and Minty had taken huge jugs of cloudy lemonade to fill their glasses on hot summer's days. She loved the old flag stones on the floor and the blue and white china that they used every day, replacing any pieces that got broken from junk shops.

She knew that Nelly loved it too, but occasionally pulled her leg, threatening to install a beautiful new one with a range of Formica cupboards and work tops that were all the rage now. She had pretended to be serious, saying that it would be labour saving, only to be told by an indignant Nelly that her labour didn't need saving and what there was left of it she was quite happy to use doing the things she had always done and that if she had any cause for complaint, she would soon speak up and say so…Crystal had laughed and held up her hands to stop the tirade before retreating to safer ground.

Helping herself to the second piece of toast, she wandered towards the door,

"It'll be on the table in two minutes tell yer mum….when I've had time to make more toast!"

Crystal smiled and walked purposefully towards the stairs. It was Monday, usually a busy day, but she had just made up her mind to do something quite radical.

CHAPTER THIRTY NINE

When she arrived at the farm – square, red brick and, like its owner, solidly built, all was quiet; she went round to the back door and almost bumped into Gerald as he was coming out; his face lit up when he saw her,

"Now you're a sight for sore eyes on this bright winter morning," he gave her a hug, squeezing her tightly against his scratchy tweed jacket, then released her to extol the virtues of the day,

"Grand morning, Crystal," he banged his sides, just as Arthur would have done, and gazed around his immaculate yard, "good for the winter crops, this – the sort of day when you can get a lot done around the place. Big shoot, Saturday…everyone coming…you don't fancy a blast at some birds, do you?"

Crystal laughed,

"No thanks, Gerald…not quite my scene."

"Oh…pity."

He looked at the young woman standing in front of him and thought again what an absolute stunner she was. Heard some nonsense about an Italian, but couldn't make head or tail of it…always thought she and young Charlie might…oh well, you never can tell.

"What brings you here, m'dear?" He suddenly looked concerned, "No problem with the accounts is there?"

"No, not as far as I know. I've just brought along some things for Rosemary…you know…for her charities…it's just a few clothes I don't want anymore. I thought…"

"Yes…yes, of course," Gerald laughed," I think she's saving whales this week along with an assortment of furry animals – and the aged of course. Got to give them a leg up."

He opened the door and yelled,

"Rosie…company…Crys is here for you."

He banged the door shut again but not before Crystal heard the sound of a child crying from somewhere inside the house.

"Well…must get on, Crys. Good to see you girl. Meet as usual this month?"

"Yes, of course." She watched him as he crossed the yard, solid and square, his peaked cap firmly on his head, arms swinging; and she smiled, thinking of the farmers in the books she had used with the children she had taught. There was one who had looked exactly like Gerald, round face, florid complexion, and she remembered using this to explain stereotyping, assuring them that farmers didn't really look like that.

The door opened,

"Come in, my dear, come in. Chaos as usual."

She followed Rosemary into the kitchen where two year old Julia was sitting in her high chair, banging a spoon on a plate. She was watching, fascinated, as it stuck in the gloopy porridge then suddenly flew up, spraying a little of the mixture into the air. She gurgled.

"Julie…no…no banging. EAT the porridge. Oh gawd, what a mess."

From somewhere just outside the kitchen door came a different banging.

"Gerard…stop running that car into the skirting board or I shall wallop you again! In fact you can get outside with it." Rosemary disappeared for a moment then returned, a red pedal car dangling from one hand and dragging a protesting six year old with the other. She hurried past Crystal and pushed both into the yard,

"Now stay where I can see you, there's a good boy." She grabbed the kettle and filled it. "He got the wretched thing for his birthday and wants to pedal it round all the time. He'd sleep in it if we let him. No, Julie…please put the food in your mouth, not around the room."

Crystal sat down, removed the spoon from Julia's hand and proceeded to feed her.

"Oh, Crys, you are a love. Thanks. Whoever decided nannies need a day orf should be strangled… and why in the name of all that's holy don't the village girls want to be maids any more? All off to college or the shops in Cambridge to work; I'm having the devil of a job finding anyone."

Crystal made sympathetic noises then indicated the large bag she had dumped near the door.

"I've brought you a few things, you know for the charity shops." She hoped the mini skirts and other garish items would raise a bit of money, but wasn't ready yet to reveal the real reason for her visit.

Rosemary made coffee and she and Crystal chatted in relative peace as Julia ate with some contentment now that she had the attention, if only partial, of an adult; and Rosemary could, as she leaned against the sink, monitor Gerard's progress around the yard with the occasional glance out of the window. She asked her half sister about progress down at Savron Pinder House and was pleased to learn that the theatre was on schedule for a spring launch. Like everyone in the village, she was impressed with Crystal's achievements and proud of what she had done for the family.

"Ma's got some paintings in an exhibition in Cambridge in the summer. I'm so pleased for her,"

"Yes, I know. I've seen them, they're awfully good; she's always daubing away when I go to see her."

Rosemary looked directly at Crystal,

"I'm so glad you two found each other; she thinks the world of you, you know."

"And I of her," Crystal murmured, glancing quickly away.

She looked back again as Rosemary turned and banged on the window, beckoning to Gerard and shouting 'no, not round the corner…' mouthing the words in an exaggerated way, her gesture and expression showing her son that she meant it. What a practical, down to earth friend and ally Rosemary had turned out to be ever since the day they had met. Her no-nonsense approach to life provided the rock that both Eleanore and Crystal needed at times. Crystal asked about the rest of the family.

"Oh, you know, poddling on as usual. Uncle Geoff loves having Philippe around and grandmother Isobel is in remarkably good health – 86 this year, you know. She's as cantankerous and unpleasant as she ever was, but I just don't put up with it. As soon as she starts on about her sons' disastrous marriages, Mum throwing herself away on Dad or 'that stuck up she-devil, Constance Elliott,' I just shut her up by telling her that if she utters one more word I shall take Gerard and Julia away and never bring them to see her again. That does the trick as she dotes on them – and Bette's two of course."

"Yes, how are they?" Crystal asked quickly, eager to move the conversation on away from talk of Isobel's birthday, remembering that it was precisely that occasion ten years earlier which had brought Giles home from university and led to their first meeting. She knew without Rosemary saying it that grandmother Isobel would also rail against her, given half a chance, as she still hated her, blaming her for the death of her favourite grandson.

"Oh they are all fine. Tommy has retired now, Charlotte is engaged and Daisy is doing a Fine Arts Course at Oxford. Bette was such a tower of strength to Ma through her divorce from my father. I know they only stayed together for me at the end and most of the time I wished they hadn't bothered. The atmosphere was terrible." She glanced out of the window before continuing, "I go and see him occasionally, but I rarely take the children; he has retired now and potters about the bungalow doing nothing much while that witch of a sister of his, Janice or Wendy or whatever she calls herself now, just moans all the time about anything and everything. She's full of bitterness, but it's her own fault. Lying, devious cow."

Crystal smiled, remembering the sad story of deception which had changed the course of her parents' life, and wondered if it had occurred to Rosemary that, but for Wendy Wetherall's lies,

Eleanore would not have married William and she would not have been born. Probably not, as Rosemary didn't probe deeply into issues, preferring to deal with things as she saw them and she could always be relied on to tell it just as it was.

Crystal plucked up courage and took a deep breath,

"I was also wondering how….."

She didn't get the chance to finish her question as the door flew open and Gerald appeared,

"Rosie, bring Gerry in will you, I've got a tractor coming round to load up some bales from the barn...don't want him squashed flat do we." Rosemary raised her eyes to heaven, wondering why Gerald couldn't have brought him in, 'put in the compartment labelled 'woman's work' I suppose,' she fumed silently as she turned to fetch her son.

Gerald scooped Julia up from the high chair, where she had been happily looking at a book since she had finished eating, and, much to her delight, started throwing her up in the air.

"Gerald I should stop that if I were you or you'll have her breakfast all over you, she's just finished eating…"

Rosemary disappeared and returned almost immediately with Gerard under one arm, screaming because the car had been left at the back door.

"Oh for goodness sake!"

She dumped him down and he promptly ran to his father, wrapping himself around his legs and burying his face in cavalry twill which muffled the screams. Julia was returned to Crystal and Gerald miraculously pacified his son by producing a pop-gun from the pile of toys in the corner. All thoughts of the red car forgotten, he happily pushed the cork on the piece of string into the metal end and popped it out again, laughing each time, while Gerald helped himself to some coffee.

"So delivered your rags and bones to the queen of charitable causes then, Crys?"

He smiled across the room at their visitor and Rosemary ignored him. He sat down,

"What have you two been jawing about? All the family gossip, I'll bet – the old witch at Manor Farm and the slightly younger witch currently residing with your Pa at that palace of fun down the road – Ha!"

Rosemary looked exasperated,

"Yes, very funny, Gerald." She turned to the sink and started to wash her cup and saucer.

Gerald barked with laughter and, taking a gulp of his coffee, addressed his wife's back,

"Ah but have you told her the piece of good family news yet, eh? No I'll bet you haven't…"

Rosemary stopped washing the saucer and her back was so still it seemed to freeze. She turned and tried to say something but it was too late, Gerald was in full flood,

"The good news, Crystal, is that our Charlie is marrying the District Nurse! Pretty thing she is…bit of a whirlwind romance…but they've fallen madly in love and have set their hearts on a summer wedding…good eh? So you'll need to get some glad rags for the occasion. Well, must get on."

He slapped his hands on his knees and leapt up, ruffling his son's hair as he made for the door,

"See you at lunch time, Rosie; remember I'm off to Cambridge this afternoon. 'Bye, Crystal, good to see you." And he breezed out.

There was silence in the kitchen apart from the pop of the toy gun. Rosemary was slowly drying the saucer, wiping the tea towel carefully round its edge and looking intently at Crystal.

"Are you alright, lovie?"

Crystal forced a smile onto her face and answered brightly,

"Yes…yes, of course…it's wonderful news…I…I'm so pleased for them. Where are they planning to live?"

She listened while Rosemary explained quietly that they were renovating one of the old houses in the village,

"It's called Baron's Manor…in a terrible state, but it's what they want to do…"

She trailed off. The air between them was still and it was almost a relief when Julia let out a scream so Rosemary could retreat into mother mode, leaping across the room to grab the pop gun from Gerard and giving him a sound whack on his backside for firing it in his sister's face.

Crystal stood up and made her way carefully to the door,

"I must go; thank-you for the coffee and chat. I'll see you soon. 'Bye."

"Bye Crys." Rosemary stood amid the chaos watching her go, and Crystal hurried out of the door, anxious to get away from her sister's sympathetic stare.

She drove her little Hillman carefully back along the road and into the drive of Savron Pinder House feeling numb and wanting only to bury herself in the mountain of work that waited for her. She would not allow herself to give form to the half-baked notion she had been nurturing all morning; a bubble of something somewhere inside her had been pricked and she didn't want to think about it. Charlie was getting married so he was no longer…no longer what? As she got out of the car she felt as though, for the second time in her life, she had lost something of great value that could never be returned to her.

Banging the car door she walked resolutely down towards the theatre to speak to the builders.

CHAPTER FORTY

The opening of the theatre in the spring was a great success. Everything was perfect from the plush red and gold seats in the auditorium to the finishing touch, the one Crystal had commissioned and supervised with great care: over the shiny new glass doors was a sign in blue and gold bearing the name, "The Elliott Theatre."

A band played as a troupe of pink-clad, giggling girls tripped lightly across the lawn down to the shining new building with Madame bringing up the rear, barking out orders in French as she went. The Mayor of Cambridge and his wife were safely ensconced in the front row and a hush descended over the auditorium as the lights went down and everyone looked expectantly towards the stage.

Each dance was announced by a different girl and their efforts were loudly applauded by proud parents with shining eyes. Crystal had also managed to persuade a local comedian, a group of musicians and two singers to perform as well which injected just the right amount of variety into the programme. Afterwards everyone gathered on the lawn for refreshments. A marquee had been erected and Bowman had arranged for lights to be strung in the trees at the edge of the wood where they twinkled and shone, reflected in the water of the lake in long strings of colour.

"That was wonderful! Well done, my darling. All your hard work has paid off."

Marjorie removed her shoes and looked at Crystal, her eyes full of admiration for her daughter's achievements. Crystal sat in a chair by the window, just as Arthur used to do, and gazed out to where Bowman and a group of men were clearing away the last of the chairs and tables. The lights still glowed in the trees, jumping a little in the breeze that had sprung up towards the end of the evening.

"Rain before long, I think. Weren't we lucky with the weather? It was just right."

Marjorie stood behind her daughter, aware that she hadn't said a word since they had got in, and rested a hand gently on her shoulder. There was something wrong; she had said as much to Eleanore earlier in the day and she had agreed, but they were both sure it had nothing to do with Mario,

"No, no. Crystal is a very strong character; from the moment she saw for herself the duplicity in that man she despised him."

As Eleanore took a sip of her tea they had both looked over to where their daughter was chatting and laughing with the Mayor. Always able to behave impeccably no matter how she was feeling, she radiated joy, genuinely pleased, over the moon, with the way things had gone; it was just that she seemed to have lost some of her bounce. Eleanore was unsure whether or not to share something with Marjorie; she hesitated, then made up her mind,

"Rosie came to see me the other day and I told her of our concern about Crystal. Rosie being Rosie just gave me a withering look and said, 'of course the poor little mare's mopey; it's because Charlie's getting married. Honestly, Ma, don't you notice anything?' Do you think she could be right?"

"I think she may well have hit the nail on the head," Marjorie had replied quietly, "and there's absolutely nothing we can do about it."

On July 22nd Charlie Fairlawn married his nurse, Faye Wright, and two villages rejoiced. Crystal had to smile and nod in agreement as, everywhere she went, the virtues of the pretty young woman and that handsome young man from the farm were extolled.

"Isn't it lovely, him finding someone like that!"

"A real love match they say. They hadn't been seeing each other for long before they got engaged. I should think the families are delighted."

And, of course, they were. Crystal had stared at the piece of stiff white card on the mantelpiece with its crinkled gold edge and embossed, black writing all loopy and shiny, and she knew she couldn't go.

"Damn, damn, damn..." she stomped around the stable yard all alone and wondered how she could have been such a fool, a blind, stupid fool to take for granted, overlook and lose a man like Charlie. Why did it take someone else falling in love with him to show her what she had missed? How perverse and stupid...

She could imagine how proud and delighted his parents would be on the day. His lovely dad, such an erudite scholar and still lecturing at the university in Cambridge, making his speech with eyes full of love and admiration for his only son, so different from him, yet building a life successfully in his chosen field. His gentle mother would be the perfect hostess for the day while his sister and friends would make sure all the traditions were observed.

She banged her fist on the stable wall as she remembered him leaving the room at Gerald and Rosemary's wedding to go and tie cans and balloons to their car. She could see again, so clearly, the expression of genuine concern in his eyes when she had hinted she might not agree to dance with him. Now he would always be dancing with someone else and there was no way she could sit and watch as Charlie and Faye waltzed into their new life together.

Eleanore made sympathetic noises when Marjorie rang her on the morning of the wedding to say that Crystal had a very bad cold and they were therefore unable to attend,

"I understand," she said. And she did.

Crystal tried to avoid hearing about the wonderful honeymoon and only gave a cursory glance towards the scaffolding outside Baron's Manor every time she passed. Work was progressing and her secret dread, the thing she really didn't want to hear, was that their first child was on the way. It could surely only be a matter of time. She thought of Minty and Rob, of evenings spent contentedly in each other's company, planning the future; she saw again Frankie's podgy arms around his mother's neck. She thought about Rosemary and Gerald, sparring their way through life, but rooted in each other, family photographs on the grand piano in the sitting room, anniversaries... weddings...She thought of Giles and the vow made at his grave, of her silent promise to Connie and Arthur to make Savron Pinder House live again. She had done it, but at what cost? She felt as though all the natural, normal things of life had been denied her forever.

No, this wouldn't do! It was a bright autumn evening, she pulled on a coat and walked quickly down towards the stable yard, stopping to turn and drink in the beauty of the old house; then her eyes swept over the immaculately kept lawn down to the woods and lake. She celebrated again in her mind the success of the theatre – there would be more shows and a special Christmas spectacular. She turned and looked at the nodding heads of the horses watching her, ears pricked forward and wisps of their night time hay trailing from their mouths.

She still had Savron Pinder House; this was her home, this was her world and she must look positively at what she had got instead of hankering after the impossible. She had, at this moment, no idea how close she would come to losing everything she had worked for.

CHAPTER FORTY ONE

March 1974

Looking back, as she did many times in the years to come, over the events of that fateful night at the beginning of March – her birthday month, the year in which she would become thirty, Crystal could never work out why she had woken with a snap, at once wide awake, in the way that she had.

She remembered that it had taken her a while to get to sleep which was unusual for her. She had lain awake thinking about her forthcoming birthday and, something she found far more exciting, the fact that the loan would be paid off in just over a year. She was justifiably proud that the development of Savron Pinder House, a project which had initially seemed impossibly grandiose, had succeeded. She had had the ideas, but knew that without the help of people like Marjorie and Gerald she couldn't have done it.

And Charlie, of course. Charlie, who had been such a source of inspiration and a tower of strength and whom she had taken completely for granted until it was too late. How could she have allowed herself to be swept off her feet by that Italian opportunist and in doing so lose someone of true worth? She had noticed that work on Baron's

Manor seemed to have finished, but she hadn't seen either Charlie or Faye around the village for a while, not that she joined in a great deal with social events as work occupied most of her time.

The theatre was a great success, hired throughout the year by travelling companies, much to Madame's annoyance as she would have liked it to be for the exclusive use of her little protégés, protesting that the visiting companies 'ruined ze stage floor' for her ballerinas. Crystal pacified her by having it specially cleaned and resurfaced twice a year, an expense easily offset against the money brought in by the ticket sales for the productions.

She tossed and turned for a while, trying not to think about Giles or go over again in her mind how good her life had been with Charlie in it, and eventually she slept.

Her eyes snapped open and she was suddenly wide awake. She lay blinking in the darkness; what time was it? Why had she woken? She lay very still listening to the wind whistling around the house, shaking the windows making them creak and shudder. Then she heard it, almost imperceptible at first above the sound of the wind, but it was definitely there, a strange, unfamiliar roaring noise. Then the crackling...she snapped on her bedside light and saw wisps of smoke curling up from under her bedroom door.

Leaping out of bed she bounded towards the door, flung it open and froze in horror as she saw flames licking around the banisters at the top of the stairs. Marjorie! Crystal ran across to the door opposite, opened it and felt weak with relief to see that her mum was not there. She must have got out. She looked towards the stairs and realised at once that they were impassable; coughing and spluttering she ran back into her own room and shut the door. Gasping, she leaned against it. Smoke was starting to fill the room. She ran to the window, undid the catch and flung it open knowing it was her only chance.

She climbed out onto the stone balcony that ran the whole length of the front of the house and, shutting the window behind her, looked down to the gravel drive below and then at the wisteria clinging to the old grey walls and weaving in and out through the little stone balustrades of the balcony.

It was her only chance and, praying that the ancient creeper would hold her weight, she climbed over the balcony and started to make her way down. She had only gone a few feet when she felt it start to peel away from the wall,

"Oh God…no!" She was falling…

"Let go and jump…I'll catch you." It was a voice in the darkness…a familiar voice, a voice from somewhere in the past. She let go and landed on the gravel, held up by a pair of strong arms.

"Come on, round to the back. The fire brigade's on its way."

Even as he spoke, Crystal looked up the drive and saw two red engines roaring towards them. Nelly and Sam Bowman stood shivering in the darkness and Crystal looked round for Marjorie. Still coughing and spluttering, she turned to Nelly,

"Where's mum?"

"I don't know dear....I don't know....Oh terrible business...terrible!"

Tears were streaming down her face as she turned to Bowman for comfort and Crystal stared in horror towards the house which the firemen were already spraying with water. She screamed and ran forward,

"My mum...my mum is still in there..." she was restrained by one of the firemen, then felt again the arms of the man who had saved her, holding her back. Tying a handkerchief over his nose and mouth a fireman hurried towards the burning building,

"I'll do what I can,"

And he disappeared in through the back door. Crystal stood sobbing, still held by the man who had saved her, but thinking only of Marjorie. Where was she? She wasn't in her room, so surely she must have got out. She must be safe. She would appear any moment with words of comfort for everyone like she always did. The fireman came out again, coughing and spluttering. He looked towards his colleagues and slowly shook his head.

"NO….NO…NO!"

Crystal clung to the man who had saved her and sobbed until she thought her heart would break.

It was as if a great, dignified, ancient oak under which she had sheltered from the harm of all life's storms had been felled; Crystal couldn't describe the pain of losing Marjorie in any other terms. She had always been there, her best friend, the mum that many of her friends wished they had. She used to joke, telling her that if she had made her up from a kit she couldn't have done any better and Marjorie would flap her hands, muttering,

'Oh go on with you, you silly,' all pink confusion .

And now she was gone, leaving a great void in her adopted daughter's life.

As she sat under an apple tree in the orchard at Monk's Manor, Crystal wondered if it was because Marjorie had adopted her that they had such a strong bond. She was chosen, a gift, a precious gift, Marjorie had said many times, and then it had been Crystal's turn to be embarrassed, calling her a soppy date, but pleased nevertheless. How glad she was now that these things had been said, that they had known for sure how much they had loved each other, before it was too late.

As soon as they told her where the body had been found Crystal thought she could see what had happened. Unable to sleep, Marjorie had gone downstairs for a cup of tea and carried it through into the red room as she often did. It was warm in there, as Bowman always left the fire in such a way that she was able to coax it into life. She would put on a light and read while she drank her tea. Then when she felt drowsy she would return to bed after first making sure the fire was safe.

But on that terrible night she must have nodded off in the chair and been unaware of a piece of coal falling onto the rug. 'Easily done,' the fireman had said, shaking his head sadly. What a horrible, tragic accident. Crystal felt the tears starting down her cheeks again as they did every time she thought about it. It was just so unlike Marjorie, completely out of character for her to be careless in any way. Still, nobody's perfect, maybe her age...?

Crystal thought again about the house, the beautiful house, the front looking almost the same as always but the back charred and wet with wisps steam still rising occasionally from pieces of blackened wood, even after two days. Oh dear God, the beautiful house. She was still waiting to hear whether the damage was so bad that it would have to be pulled down. She covered her face with her hands and tried to stifle a sob. It was all unreal, a nightmare.

The grass near her feet rustled and as she drew her hands slowly down her face she saw him standing there. He pulled up another of the old striped deck chairs and sat down. She had known he would come.

"How are you feeling?"

'As stupid questions go that one's a prize winner,' she thought but just said,

"Oh, you know, pretty numb…devastated in fact."

She turned away, unable to look into the gentle grey eyes, hoping he wouldn't hear her heart hammering inside her chest.

"I'm sorry about…Marjorie."

"Yes."

There was silence between them until he spoke again,

"Gerald said to tell you that he will go over the place with the insurers and let you know the result of their assessment…so you can rest and recover for a while."

"Thank-you."

She tried to smile; it was kind of him to bring the message. He stood up,

"I must go. I hope you feel better soon and that things work out with…you know."

"Yes."

He turned and Crystal watched him go…back to his wife at Baron's Manor.

"Charlie!"

He stopped and took a few steps back again; she had to ask him,

"Yes?"

"What were you doing at Savron Pinder House in the middle of the night? Why were you there?"

She didn't add that if he hadn't been there and called the fire brigade from the phone box at the top of the drive, as well as saving her; the house would most definitely have burnt to the ground and she would have sustained an injury when she had jumped from the balcony. He hesitated,

"I went for a walk across the fields behind the woods."

"Walking! At two in the morning? What on earth for?"

"Oh, you know, couldn't sleep." He glanced at his watch,

"I must go."

"Yes, you said."

As he walked back up through the orchard he was aware that there were two important things he hadn't told her, one to do with the fire and one that could affect the rest of their lives. There was so much he just couldn't say as he stumbled between the trees away from the woman he loved.

CHAPTER FORTY TWO

"Well the good news in all of this, my dear, is that the house can be saved."

Gerald pushed himself squarely back into one of Eleanore's kitchen chairs and took a large gulp of coffee.

"Straight forward insurance job…clearly an accident…no question…piece of coal falling out of the fire. Happens all the time, according to the fire chappies. You'll have to tell Bowman to douse all fires before retiring in the future. Of course what really makes a difference to the old place is the fact that the fire brigade got there so quickly. Most of the damage is located around the back of the house – mainly the kitchen and the red room. Huh…afraid it's the black room now. Still we'll soon get it sorted. Still can't fathom who it was who called the fire brigade at that time of night - any idea? "

Crystal muttered something about someone in the village, reluctant, for some reason, to tell Gerald about his nephew's strange nocturnal wanderings.

He finished the rest of his coffee in one gulp and got up looking across the kitchen at Crystal as she slumped in the chair, staring straight ahead, eyes glazed, and wondered if she had taken in what he had said. Poor little mare. He thought his news might cheer her up, but there was none of the old sparkle. The fire and losing Marjorie were certainly going to take some getting over and no mistake. He looked towards Eleanore who came to the rescue,

"Thank-you, Gerald. We'll be in touch."

"Yes, do that. We can talk re-building...soon have the old place ship-shape again. Good thing the stables and theatre were untouched."

He stood awkwardly for a moment before disappearing through the door and out into the sunshine. It was the eighteenth of March, the day before Crystal's birthday, and one of those bright, golden days that sometimes occur in spring, making everything in nature believe that winter's over; a belief only too often dashed by bitingly cold April weather. For Crystal it was a mockery. She had walked down to Savron Pinder House and wept bitter tears to see the charred bits of brick, wood and tile thrown in stark relief against the blue sky. She had heard Gerald's words and knew she should be pleased, but all she felt was numb, a dull ache that wouldn't leave her day or night. So Savron Pinder house could be saved. She should be delighted, she should be relishing the challenge of building it up again, but she felt no interest in it whatsoever. She had no energy left and really couldn't face it.

She walked through into the sitting room at Monk's Manor and curled up in the corner of the sofa. The new doctor from the village had been to see her and was pleased to say that there was no sign of damage to her lungs either from smoke or fire.

"Getting out so quickly was a lucky escape..."

Crystal had burst again into floods of tears on being told that and had sat sobbing. Why hadn't Marjorie had a lucky escape? Through her sobs she had heard the young doctor talking quietly to Eleanore, telling her that the state of shock would probably persist for some time and there was no easy remedy. Just time.

Crystal was grateful to her mother for realising that no birthday celebration was possible. Eleanore had passed her a small package at breakfast time and, opening it, Crystal had gasped at the pair of exquisite crystal earrings lying there inside the velvet box, a perfect match for the pendent. She felt tears pricking behind her eyes as she looked across the table to where her mother sat, unable to speak.

"Don't wear them yet. One day will be the right time, but not yet."

Crystal nodded. Thank God she had put the pendent into the bank along with the best of the jewellery that Connie had left her. That at least was safe and hadn't perished with the rest of the things in her bedroom.

She pulled on a pair of Eleanore's old jeans and a shirt and together they went for a long walk down

442

the fen in the afternoon. Eleanore was easy to be with. Having borne so much pain herself, she seemed to know when to speak and when to be quiet and the silences between them were not uncomfortable.

Crystal had to get through Marjorie's funeral and she was dreading it. The good weather persisted with bright sunshine, warm on their backs, mocking the solemn proceedings. Crystal would have preferred it if rain were being hurled against her by a fierce, strong wind. She wanted to be lashed by the elements – how much more fitting that would have been. There would have been some comfort in that. She got through the whole thing, feeling as though she were lifted and carried along by some unseen arms. She was even able to bring some comfort to others, and there were many as Marjorie had been well liked by all; but it was afterwards in the privacy of her own room that she was burned again by memories of the dear person she had lost.

CHAPTER FORTY THREE

May 1974

"Well, Ma, it's going to take longer than a month or two."

"I know…I know. It's just so difficult to know what to do to help her."

Eleanore and Rosemary were sitting together in Rosemary's drawing room furnished with large, serviceable, very comfortable, pieces of furniture that perfectly reflected their owners. Dainty chairs and cabinets full of exquisite china would have looked as incongruous in this household as they would in a stable. They were talking about Crystal, Eleanore sharing with her elder daughter her concern about her half sister's state of mind.

"She simply has no interest in anything or anyone. She won't even go and look at Savron Pinder House any more, won't think or talk about re-building it, but just mopes about all day, occasionally riding Star down the fen or sitting in the orchard reading a book. I'm at my wit's end. It's as if she wants to retreat from life and reality. I just can't reach her."

Eleanore sighed and took a sip of tea.

"I don't know what to suggest, Ma, I really don't."

Rosemary stretched her legs out in front of her, still relishing the long periods of peace and time to herself that were now possible with nine year old Gerard in a prep school in Cambridge and Julia, nearly six, happily ensconced in a very nice little private school in the next village. She looked at the clock on the mantelpiece,

"I've got to go and pick up Jules. If I get any bright ideas I'll give you a ring. But honestly, Ma, I think all you can do at the moment is just bide your time and be there for her. Something will turn up."

Eleanore followed her out of the room, not knowing how prophetic those words were or in what strange and utterly unpredictable way salvation would arrive – and with what consequences.

There was nothing at all remarkable about the evening at first. They ate supper as usual, washed and put away the dishes, then settled down in the sitting room, Crystal with a book and Eleanore with an art magazine. She was still managing to paint, finding solace and release in this activity. The door bell rang and the two women looked at each other; they weren't expecting anyone. Eleanore's forehead creased into a small frown as she left the room and Crystal heard the front door being opened followed by the muffled sound of voices.

When she appeared again a few moments later Eleanore had turned ghostly white and was striving to remain composed.

"We have a visitor, darling."

Her voice shook very slightly and, as she moved to one side, Crystal saw, framed in the doorway, an extraordinary looking woman. It was a warm evening but the woman was dressed in a grey costume reminiscent of fashion in the forties, though it was misshapen and not a good fit. On her head she wore a black felt hat from which wisps of untidy grey hair were escaping. She was thin, painfully so, and her gaunt face, a yellowish grey, was wrinkled, her cheeks hollow and her eyes underlined with dark circles. She and Eleanore both stood awkwardly until Eleanore, always mindful of the importance of manners no matter what the situation, politely invited the obviously unwelcome visitor to be seated.

There was an air of resignation about the woman, a weariness; she clearly cared little whether she stood or sat, but with a slight, almost imperceptible, shrug of her shoulders, lowered herself into the nearest chair. Eleanore sat too, uncomfortably on the edge of the sofa, and realised some introduction was needed though Crystal sensed her reluctance to bring this about.

"This is Janet Wetherall, William's sister." Her eyes flickered towards Crystal,

"And this is…"

"Crystal Morris – or Elliott – yours and Jack's daughter. Yes, I know."

So this was Wendy Wetherall…windy Wendy who had loved Jack and cruelly deceived him and Eleanore; the woman whose lies and deception had changed the course of so many lives was sitting here before her.

"How do you do…"

"Don't bother with all that. I'm not here to play parlour games." Wendy – or Janet as she now called herself – spoke in a low monotonous voice which complemented perfectly her drab appearance. Her whole demeanour was of someone who, for some reason, was almost past caring about anything at all. Crystal saw Eleanore's lips twitch and her face colour with anger at Janet's rudeness. She spoke coldly,

"You said you had something very important to tell us that we really should know…."

"…So get on with it then we can be rid of you!" Janet finished the sentence for her, rising as she did so and facing Eleanore squarely across the room. Her mouth twisted in what was supposed to be a smile, but it didn't reach her eyes and Crystal knew where she had seen that smile before. Involuntarily she gave a little gasp as she saw again the dark stable and Clive's evil face illuminated by a cigarette. Janet's eyes remained focused on Eleanore,

"Too much of a lady to be rude, eh, even to me, even after all I've done. Still too much of a lady...just like Jack's mother. Sorry business that poisoning...she didn't deserve that, nor Mr Elliott neither. Now your mum, hoity-toity jumped up madam with a tongue as sharp as a knife... Well I'd as soon slip her..."

Eleanore was on her feet, white with fury,

"Janet, please say what it is you have come to say. Tell us straight, with no more disparaging remarks about my mother – or any other members of my family – then leave this house."

"Fair enough, I asked for that." She sat down again and Eleanore also resumed her position on the edge of the sofa, her back straight and eyes, as cold as Crystal had ever seen them, fixed on Janet.

Janet now turned and looked at Crystal. Her head nodded slightly,

"Yeess...I'd heard you were a looker... but then you were always going to be, weren't you, with Jack as you dad and this lady as your mum. A lady...something I could never have been...how foolish we are when we are young....how full of self deluding nonsense."

Out of the corner of her eye Janet saw Eleanore twitch with impatience and, aware that she was in danger of being evicted from the house before she had accomplished what she had come for, she folded her hands in her lap and continued in the same grey voice.

"All right, I'll come to the point. I am very ill...dying in fact... and for some reason I feel the need to unburden myself... now...before it's too late. I know I've done some bad things, they can't be undone and I am not asking to be forgiven – I don't expect it,"

She looked defiantly at Eleanore and emphasised these last few words to show that she meant it. "I shan't rest easy knowing what I did...how my lies caused so much unhappiness and denied the time, short though it would have been courtesy of the war, that you and Jack could have had together. However, lies are one thing, murder is another."

She paused and the three women sat in silence; all attention was focused on her and she continued in a voice as matter of fact as if she were imparting some information about the weather. She was looking at Eleanore,

"Your boy, Clive, my nephew... bad lot that one...even his father can see it now... well he's back round here again, living in a caravan down the fen and still does a fair amount of snooping around

– as he always did. I have no idea how he makes his money, but I do know he hates this lovely lady here…"

She indicated Crystal,

"…hates her with a fearful passion. I don't know what happened between you in the past, but he's determined to have his revenge." She paused for a moment looking at Crystal,

"It's my guess he wanted you and you were having none of it." Crystal felt herself colour and she looked down quickly,

"Yes, I thought so. Must be in the blood. Anyway he's out to ruin you. I've overheard him talking to William but never took much notice until the other night. He had been at our bungalow drinking with his dad until quite late…to be honest, I'd had enough of him and I wished he would clear off. I saw him just before he went and there was something particularly sinister about him…I can't put my finger on it, but there was just something about the way he stood at the door and winked at William…and then he said,

'I've got something that'll wipe the smile off that little bastard's face.'

I didn't think any more of it, I was just glad to see the back of him, but I did wonder who they were talking about. Of course next day I heard about the terrible fire at Savron Pinder House and it set me wondering, so I paid him a visit at his caravan. I took him a few clean clothes and asked if he had any for me to wash. He threw me a bundle and there was a pair of trousers in it that reeked of petrol. He saw me screw up my nose and said he had spilt some when he was filling up his van.

Anyway, I didn't wash his things…took them straight to the police and told them what I suspected. I had no idea whether they would believe me or not, but apparently they had already had a visit from that Fairlawn chap, you know, good looking …married the district nurse and lives in that Manor up the village…" Eleanore's eyes flickered towards her daughter and Crystal squeezed her hands together to stop them from shaking.

"Apparently he was somewhere around the big house at the time of the fire – sounds a bit odd to me but there you are – and he was sure he saw a man running away. Didn't chase after him as he was more concerned about getting the fire brigade and that but… he said it bothered him afterwards and he just had to go and tell the police.

They took Clive's clothes but said it was going to be difficult to prove that he was there, though any small clues would be helpful. They examined them carefully and I wrote down the name of the make of the trousers as they are from a London tailor – quite prestigious apparently and not, they said, the sort of clobber owned by many people around here, especially some vagrant living rough down the fens"

Eleanore winced as Janet paused and took a piece of paper out of her handbag,

"Here it is, look 'Grieves and Horne. Jermyn Street, London.'"

Eleanore spoke quietly and asked,

"What colour are the trousers?"

"Dark brown; just as well really seeing the state of them."

Janet gave her peculiar half smile again and Eleanore snorted with disgust.

"What a slob he has become. I gave him those trousers donkeys years ago; they were a birthday present. I can't believe he is still wearing them."

Janet shrugged,

"It's all the same to me...but you're right he is a slob. You'd probably be hard pushed to recognise him now. Anyway the other thing they noticed was that there was a button missing. It's quite an unusual design, metal, with the tailor's name engraved around the outside. The waist band is wide and where there should be two there is now only one. They don't, of course, hold out much hope of finding it – needles and haystacks and all that – and it is more than likely that he lost it ages ago. He's not exactly the sort to sit and sew buttons back on, and he knows better than to ask me to do it. It was enough of a surprise to him when I offered to do some washing for him. When the other button goes we are fully expecting him to arrive at our place with his trousers held up by a piece of string."

She paused again and the lop-sided non smile flitted across her face, though she could see the pain that her description of the re-appearance of her eldest son was causing Eleanore.

"Anyway…there it is. I wanted you to know as I understand your other mum was killed in the fire…" Crystal swallowed hard and looked down at her clasped hands while Janet continued, "…bad business. He's an evil sod and he'll stop at nothing."

She looked back at Eleanore,

"I've done you wrong and, although it's hard for you to hear, what I've told you it's my way of trying to put things right."

With the ingrained habit of a life time of good manners, Eleanore started to say a quiet thank-you, but Janet stopped her abruptly, her voice rising for the first time. She held up her hand,

"Don't! Do not thank me. I told you I want nothing…no forgiveness… no thanks. I've made my bed and got exactly what I deserve. I shall live out what little time I have left with that miserable lump of a brother of mine shuffling around the bungalow littering the place with newspapers and

453

cigarette ash, and it just might bring me some small comfort to know that I've done what I can to stop my nephew from causing any more harm."

She paused again then looked at Eleanore with a strange expression on her face and said quietly,

"Between us, my brother and I have pretty well blighted your life – and for what? Don't ever thank me. If it were not for me, my stupid delusions of grandeur and blinding jealousy, Clive would never have been born. How clearly we see things in old age when death is staring us in the face."

Her voice was bitter and it was with a shock that Crystal realised she was, in fact, not old but must be about the same age as Eleanore. She looked across at her beautiful, elegant mother who had managed to remain composed even in the light of these revelations, and thought about Janet's words. She did indeed seem to be paying the price for her deceit.

Crystal waited for her to get up and leave, but instead she started speaking again.

"There is something else…and this is going to be even harder for you both to hear…but it's time it all came out in the open." She took a deep breath and ploughed on,

"It's about that accident back in the sixties when your youngest son…" she paused and glanced at Crystal "…and your brother…was killed when his car went off the road..." both listeners froze, and Janet was aware of the affect she was having on them. She continued,

"I know there were no other cars involved and as he'd had a drink and a bit of a shock, so I understand, the verdict was accidental death."

Janet paused again and looked from one to the other of the still figures in front of her before adding,

"I'm pretty certain it wasn't an accident."

Eleanore's hand flew to her mouth where it clamped itself tightly over her lips. Crystal rose and went to comfort her mother, or to be comforted, she couldn't have said which. Janet hurried on.

"That night, you hit Clive and threw him out because of the trouble his meddling had caused. He had no-where to go, so arrived at my bungalow blind drunk and wallowing in self pity. He was sick in the toilet then collapsed on my spare bed. As I was trying to remove his filthy shoes – he had already trailed mud right across my carpet – he kept laughing and, in his drunken stupour, slurring the words, 'snip... snip... snip...' while miming a cutting action in the air. Then his hand would fall and he'd start to laugh mumbling something about, '...it was so easy...just a little snip...snip...snip.'

I thought at first he was saying 'sip...sip...sip' and told him I was aware he'd had more than a sip or two that was for sure. He mumbled something about it being time that little blue eyed goody-goody got a bit of a shake up, then fell into a deep sleep. I was so disgusted with him that I didn't take any notice, but when he heard about the crash it had a profound affect on him. He turned and, without a word, walked out of the house. Disappeared. And I didn't see him again until a few weeks ago. I don't suppose it will make any difference to anything now after all this time, but it just made me realise how dangerous he is. If he did…"

Eleanore held up her hand,

"Stop…please…" she sobbed and reached for a handkerchief, unable to hear any more.

Janet stood up,

"I'll go now. No need for goodbyes, but you won't see me again."

Crystal went with her to the front door and stood on the step as the visitor went through the porch then turned back towards the house. It was dusk and a few lazy insects buzzed around the light which shone above their heads. Janet took a deep breath and looked for the last time at the beautiful garden then up at the lovely Manor, the life-style she had craved, but knew now could never have been hers. When she looked back at Crystal her eyes were almost kind.

"What terrible things we do and manage to justify to ourselves at the same time. You know, jealousy is a dreadful thing. It gnawed away at me, driving me on; and Clive was consumed by the jealousy he felt for his younger brother. It ate at him the way this cancer is eating at me. Don't mess your life up, girl. Think and talk right; be straight with everyone. You'll reap what you sow as sure as sparks fly upwards."

And with that she was gone, walking unsteadily down the path, her ill fitting suit, hanging loosely on her bony limbs.

Two weeks later the evening paper carried the news in just a tiny paragraph that Mrs. Wendy Lynton-Bell, nee Wetherall, ex-wife of Mr. Claude Lynton-Bell of Manor Farm, Savron Pinder, had died.

CHAPTER FORTY FOUR

Eleanore and Crystal were stunned, absolutely shattered by the visit and the extraordinary revelations it produced. Crystal had managed to hold back her tears until she had shut the door and returned to the sitting room, but then she and Eleanore clung to each other, crying quietly, until the older woman dried her eyes, stood up and made for the kitchen. She returned a few minutes later with some coffee and two large brandies and they sat talking over what they had been told.

"I don't think there's any doubt that it's all true. She had nothing to gain from coming here and you could tell that her lying days were over."

Crystal agreed with her mother and they both wondered what their next move should be.

"It's going to be just about impossible to prove that Clive set fire to Savron Pinder House...there's no evidence. Oh dear God how could he? How could he...? What an unbelievably evil...." She tailed off, realising that however awful Clive was he was still Eleanore's son. She didn't want to hurt her mother any more, but she needn't have worried. Eleanore spoke quietly.

"It's alright Crystal, you can't say anything I haven't thought a thousand times. How on earth did I produce such a creature? It does seem a rather

458

excessive punishment for marrying a man I didn't love. And where on earth will it all end?"

Crystal already loved Eleanore, but it was at this moment, seeing her so utterly dejected, that her heart truly went out to her and she made up her mind. Somewhere deep inside something stirred – her old fighting spirit perhaps, the spirit that had enabled her to get the better of Mary, Emily and Mickey; the drive that had overcome all obstacles in her way during the transformation of Savron Pinder House. She resolved then and there that it would end; that her elegant and beautiful mother would have some peace in her life at last.

She had never really believed that Giles had had an accident – he was too good a driver – and she utterly rejected the theory that he had committed suicide, a notion muttered behind hands at the time. No. As she had listened to Janet speaking, something deep inside her had said that this was true. She knew instinctively that it was true, that Clive was responsible for the deaths of both Giles and Marjorie; for that he would pay the price and she would not rest until he had. She had no idea how to bring this about...no idea at all. She looked at Eleanore and spoke softly,

"I'm going to get him, mother, I don't know how...but I shall..."

Eleanore looked oddly at her daughter, rose, crossed the room and kissed her gently on the forehead.

"Thank-you, darling. In the morning I will show you something which may help us. Come on, time for bed. We're both exhausted."

Crystal noticed there were still tears in Eleanore's eyes, but something had happened. In the same way that she felt a new determination that Clive would not only atone for what he had done but would never again get the better of them, so something had changed for Eleanore. It was only much later when she was trying to sleep, with the events of the evening running in her head like a film, that she realised she had called Eleanore 'mother' for the first time.

In the morning the sun shone and there was about the two women at Monk's Manor a steely resolve, a sense of purpose, the quiet strength of people who have been pushed to their limit and have had enough. Buffeted by fate, they had battled with situations brought about by circumstances beyond their control and now, suddenly, found themselves in a position from which they could fight back. Somehow they would bring the truth to light. Somehow.

Eleanore took a small key from the set of hooks by the door and together she and Crystal walked down past the orchard towards the garages. The door of the first one was open and the sun bounced off the bonnet of Eleanore's red and white Mini Cooper. She kept the car itself locked but never bothered much about the garage doors as the gate to the drive was always locked at night.

The second door, the one Crystal had sometimes wondered about, was shut as usual.

"Steel yourself, darling. What you are about to see will cause you pain, but we have to do it."

So saying, Eleanore walked towards the garage and inserted the tiny key in the lock at the centre of the handle. It was stiff and difficult to turn, but eventually it moved; there was rust between the handle and the door, but after banging it with a stick, Eleanore managed to wrench it open and lifted it, slowly sliding it into place just under the roof. Crystal walked forward to join her mother and together they stared in silence at the vehicle inside. As if in a dream, they both went towards it and gently touched the dusty red paint of the little car in which Giles had died. Crystal looked Eleanore.

"You kept it."

"Yes."

"Why?"

"I honestly don't know. I just had it towed in here after the accident, locked the door and never opened it again – until now."

She had been right, it was painful. Both women stood looking at this piece of the past and ghosts circled around them – the ghosts of the people they once were, and the ghost of that dear, precious person who had been so cruelly snatched from them. It was such a strange sensation, lifting the lid on the past; it all came rushing back but before they had a chance to wallow in grief and nostalgia, Eleanore brought them swiftly back to the present.

"Let's not touch it any more. We'll ring the police, show them this and tell them Janet's story."

And so it began. The two women worked tirelessly, amazed by their own strength; it was as if they had hit rock bottom and bounced back up again. They had nothing to fear for they had done nothing wrong. Before she died Janet had made a statement to the police which was corroborated – reluctantly – by William. The car was examined and nobody was surprised when it was discovered that the brake cable had been cut.

On the strength of this alone Clive was prized out of his caravan and arrested. It was not easy to prove that he had done it as he protested his innocence, accusing Janet of being a 'miserable, vindictive, lying old harridan.' Eventually, however, he confessed that it was him who had cut the brake cable, but he stressed that he had never meant to kill his brother, just shake him up a bit. He regretted the death.

"As if that makes it any better," Eleanore snorted when she heard.

It had not been difficult to bring the case to court in view of the fact that Giles had died, and in the light of the new evidence, but Eleanore had not wanted to be there to watch her son being tried. For some reason, though, she did want to see him, just once more; so before the arrest, she and Crystal had driven slowly down the fen in Crystal's Hillman.

They parked in sight of the caravan that Crystal suspected was his and waited. She had noticed it several times during her fen rides on Star and had wondered what sort of strange person lived there; but she had never seen anyone around it and shuddered now as she realised how close she had come to an encounter with the dreadful Clive.

It was filthy dirty and lop-sided with cardboard in one of the windows where glass should have been. Before long the door opened and a man emerged. He was wearing a pair of baggy, black trousers held up with string tied around a very thin waist, a dirty shirt that was once white and he had an old black scarf around his neck. The wisps of black hair on his head were peppered with grey and from his stubbly chin there hung the beginnings of a straggly beard. He walked round to the side of the caravan and stood with his legs apart as he urinated into the grass.

As he turned to go back inside he stopped for a moment and looked towards the car. Both women froze; it was as if he was staring straight at them for what seemed like forever; but it was, in fact, only a moment before he disappeared back into the caravan.

Eleanore couldn't speak as they drove back, torn inside by the sight of her eldest son, haunted by the thought that she had somehow failed him.

The next time they saw him it was a photograph in the evening paper of him being led away by two policemen. The headline read:

'Local Man Found Guilty of Manslaughter Jailed for Six Years'

There followed a detailed and sensationalised report of all the facts, dragging them up again from the past. People in the village were stirred up by this turn of events and everyone, of course, had an opinion. The bars at The White Hart were buzzing and trade hadn't been so good for years:

"I always said 'e were a bad lot, that Clive. Had no time for 'im."

"Fancy that! Cutting the brake cable on his brother's car, but didn't really mean to kill him! Huh, a likely story, but them magistrates have fallen for it. Should have been done for murder and put away for life if you ask me."

Crystal was very much of the same opinion. Six years was not long enough, not long enough to stop him in his tracks for ever and that's what she wanted. Still convinced Clive was also responsible for the fire at Savron Pinder House, she contacted the police again only to be told that there was no evidence to support this. And it was true. Charlie had seen a man running away, but who was it? There was nothing to lead them to Clive.

She couldn't give up and, abhorrent though the idea was, she had to go and look around for herself. Reluctantly she set off and it was with a heavy heart that she rounded the bend in the drive and saw, for the first time in weeks, the still, silent house. Two of the windows at the back had been boarded up and the hole where the kitchen door should have been also had wood nailed across it. She didn't allow herself to think, if she had she would have wept again at the sorry sight before her. Any furniture that could be salvaged was in store so what was left was just a shell, a sad empty shell.

Crystal forced herself to look around. If Clive had started the fire it must have been at the back door. That was where the worst of the damage had occurred; the flames had gone from there through the kitchen and the red room then along the passage and up the stairs. Most of the front of the house was relatively untouched; it would have been bathed in moonlight and a creature like Clive would have instinctively gone to the back to carry out his deadly deed in darkness. Trying hard to get inside his warped, criminal mind she thought there must be something…he must have used petrol, hence the smell on his clothes, so would he have thrown the empty can away? Surely he would. Startled by the ferocity of the flames he had created, he would have thrown it away before he ran off across the fields…

She crouched by the door, pretending to shake the contents of a petrol can over the threshold, then jumped back and hurled the imaginary can with her right arm as hard as she could. Following the arc of her throw with her eyes, she ran towards the kitchen garden wall, looked over and scanned the scene before her. Everything was overgrown with weeds and long grass, 'how swiftly nature takes possession again of anything we neglect,' she thought, and could see nothing but vegetation. She walked round to the arched entrance and went in. It was hopeless. There was nothing there except the wreck of a once immaculate garden where all kinds of herbs and vegetables had been cultivated.

Just for something to do, and with no real hope of success, she walked through the tangle of vegetation until she reached the point where her imaginary petrol can would have landed. Of course there was nothing there. She looked up and decided to continue across to the overgrown path at the other side of the bed, then follow the wall back to the entrance.

She'd only gone about a dozen steps when her foot hit against something and she stumbled. She turned and pulled the grass and weeds away to reveal a rectangular tin can. Lifting it up she laughed, remembering how the boys had always teased the girls about their lack of prowess when throwing a ball. In a sudden flash she saw Minty furiously chasing Rob when he had dared to mimic her 'girlie' throw and then she had spent hours practising so she could beat him. She never had. And Clive, of course, would have thrown the can much harder than her.

Feeling triumphant, Crystal carefully lifted the dirty piece of dented metal and took it to the police station, but was crushed by their lack of enthusiasm for her discovery. It was just a petrol can, a standard petrol can with the scratched remains of a well known company's name on the side.

"It could have been there for ages," the dour policeman said, clearly not very interested.

"Oh, I don't think so," Crystal replied indignantly, wishing that Bowman were there to respond to this idea of a stray petrol can just lying about in his beautiful kitchen garden. Partly, she suspected, to get rid of her the policeman took the can and said it would be examined, but couldn't resist adding,

"...Doubtful that we'll find anything after all this time."

He put it to one side, his eyes flickering back towards the paperwork he was obviously keen to get on with.

"Thank-you for your time," Crystal said politely without meaning it, and made her way back to Monk's Manor.

CHAPTER FORTY FIVE

"It's hopeless! Absolutely hopeless!"

She paced about the kitchen while Eleanore cooked the evening meal.

"There must be a way. How can we prove that it was him?"

Eleanore let her daughter fume, but felt powerless to help; they had reached a low point in their quest and neither of them could see a way forward.

They ate in silence and had almost finished clearing away the dishes when there was a knock at the door. It was the back door this time, the door that opened straight into the kitchen, and Eleanore hesitated, remembering the pain their last unexpected evening visitor had caused. The knock came again. Removing her apron and smoothing her hair, Eleanore walked forward and opened the door while Crystal stood watching, tea towel in hand.

He filled the doorway, dwarfing Eleanore, and had to duck slightly to avoid banging his head on the lintel as he stepped inside. Crystal felt herself go hot and her heart started to pound. She couldn't speak and quickly dried the last two dishes while trying to compose herself. Eleanore dealt with the pleasantries,

"How are you? How nice to see you…would you like some coffee…we were just about to have some…"

"No thank-you. I can't stop for long. I'm sorry for bursting in on you like this, but I just had to come…it's something quite important…"

"Well, at least sit down for a moment, if only in here."

He sat and Crystal felt him looking at her. She started to rub the draining board hard with the tea towel.

"Come and sit down for a moment, darling, and listen to what Charlie has to say."

She sat carefully to one side of him, feeling sure she would start shaking if he looked at her. He was facing Eleanore across the table, his arms resting lightly in front of him and Crystal noticed the light fuzz of golden hair on his tanned skin, the strong, capable hands lightly clasped, and his hair, thick and bleached by the sun, that curled gently at his neck. This amazing person had been her friend and could have been so much more if only she hadn't been so stupid. She looked down, knowing that he would turn towards her, afraid to look again into his gentle grey eyes. He started to speak and sounded quite nervous

"The fact is, I've found something that may be significant. I went back to the police station to see if anything else had transpired in connection with the fire and they did tell me about the visit of that Wetherall woman. I'm not sure whether I should have been told but Ronnie, the policeman on duty, was someone my Mother once helped. Long story, but as a favour, he told me all about the business with the trousers smelling of petrol and the missing button. He also said that you..." he turned to Crystal at this point and, in spite of being focused on what he was saying she felt something inside her turn over, "...went down with a petrol can you had found and that his superior, a rather tired sergeant counting the days to retirement, had been a bit dismissive."

He paused and reached into his right hand trouser pocket,

"Well...I hope I haven't stepped out of line here, but I couldn't resist paying a visit to the old house. I spent almost a day down there combing through all the grass and gravel around the back door. Ronnie had heard what you said to his sergeant about your theory that the fire was started near there and then the petrol can flung over the wall where you found it, so that's where I spent the day."

Crystal looked away, humbled by the thought of Charlie doing this for them. She could see him meticulously searching, refusing to give up until he found something...found something! She felt a sudden rush of excitement that was not directly related to his proximity. She looked up and leaned forward eagerly.

"So what did you find?"

His right hand had come out of his pocket and was clenched, knuckles resting on the wooden table top. He opened it and both women gave a tiny gasp as, resting in his palm, was a small metal button. Both Crystal's hands flew to her face while Eleanore leaned forward and gently lifted it towards her. She nodded and passed it to her daughter. With shaking hands Crystal slowly turned the button and read 'Grieves and Horne' engraved and visible, albeit faintly, around the rim. She put it carefully on the table and walked to the sink where she steadied herself against it, looking out of the window. She could hear Eleanore,

"Oh thank-you... thank-you, Charlie, so much...thank-you. Where exactly did you find it?"

She heard him reply, sensing his embarrassment at the effect his revelation had caused,

"Lodged in the gravel a few steps away from the back door...seems logical really that it must have given up the ghost when he hurled the can over the wall."

"What a one in a million chance – and you found it! Charlie, we can never thank you enough, can we Crystal?"

Crystal turned, looked straight at him and said softly,

"No, Charlie, we can't."

He got up quickly and walked towards the door,

"Must go…take care now and good luck. Hope it all works out."

"Oh it will now, thanks to you." Eleanore had followed him to the door, and added,

"You and your wife must come for dinner soon so we can at least try and thank you properly."

He looked embarrassed and Crystal was momentarily horrified until she heard him say,

"Fact is, it's a bit tricky at the moment…loads of work, you know."

"Yes, of course. Never mind. Take care now. And thank-you again a thousand times."

He smiled and was gone. The two women hugged each other, unable to speak then put the precious button carefully in a box on the mantelpiece. They talked far into the night as both knew they would get very little sleep.

Savron Pinder House was once again in the news as the extraordinary story broke and Clive received a life sentence for murder.

The little red car was never returned to Monk's Manor and Eleanore cleaned out the second garage,

"There you are," she said to Crystal as she finished, hand on hip, admiring her handiwork,

"Now there's somewhere for you to keep your Hillman Imp, though I can't imagine why you still hang on to that old thing. I'm sure you can afford something better now."

She smiled at her daughter, knowing full well that her reluctance to part with the simple little car had everything to do with the fact that she had given it to her. A first ever Christmas present to the daughter she thought she would never see. Crystal smiled back,

"It does me well enough."

But she was unsure about the clearing of the garage, not from a sentimental point of view; the little red car had served its purpose, waiting there all those years until just the right moment to reveal its vital secret; no, it was more a case that making a special place for her car seemed to symbolise permanence.

She was full of gratitude to her mother for taking her in so willingly after the fire. It had turned out to be an important time for them, a time when fighting for justice had bonded them more closely than perhaps anything else could have done; but it shouldn't be permanent, and in their hearts they both knew it.

Crystal also knew that she had to do something about Savron Pinder House; it was hers, her responsibility – but where was the enthusiasm? She knew she was letting everyone down, herself, Connie and Arthur, even Mr. and Mrs. Bowman who had been to tentatively enquire as to whether the old place was going to be re-built. But she just couldn't take the first step. Not for the first time in her life she was stuck in limbo and did what she always did when in that state; she walked or rode down the fen a lot. She noted in passing that Clive's terrible old caravan had been cleared away and all that was left was a patch of brown earth surrounded by long grass. It would soon grow over as though nothing had ever been there.

It was at the end of one of these rides when she was clip-clopping back up to the top of the fen road to join the village street, that she saw the District Nurse's car approaching. It slowed right down in order not to scare Star and Crystal was forced to look at the driver and raise her crop in a gesture of thanks. The girl inside smiled and waved in return; it was a pleasant smile from a plump, round face that wasn't Faye's. The girl was in uniform, but it definitely wasn't Faye. The car passed and continued on its way to one of the outlying houses down the fen and Crystal stopped at the junction, puzzled. Then it dawned on her. Faye had given up work as Faye was most probably having hers and Charlie's first child. She trotted Star back to her stable at Monk's Manor trying not to think about it.

But she had to find out and what better way than to ask Gerald. He would just tell her with no fuss. She had to see him anyway about the state of her finances, so she could just slip the question in quite naturally.

When she arrived at the farm she saw him across the yard struggling with a tarpaulin that was refusing to stay on some bails of straw. He was puffing and quite red in the face

"Oh hello, m'dear. Go straight in…I won't be a minute…must just get this stubborn… blighter… back… into… position." With every word he gave a tug, getting redder in the face by the second. "Damn it!"

Crystal plucked up courage.

"Isn't Charlie around to help you?"

Keeping hold of the tarpaulin with one hand, Gerald turned.

"You haven't heard the news then? Apparently they need time off for these things nowadays…no, Charlie won't be back until…."

The end of the sentence was lost as a tractor, instead of making a turn as it came to the fence at a corner of the nearby field in which it was working, crashed into it.

"What the hell is that sodding man doing?"

Dropping the tarpaulin and, now purple with rage, Gerald stormed across the yard towards the field.

"I'll come back another time," Crystal shouted, but was sure he didn't hear her.

She couldn't think of anything else. Would Charlie's child be a boy or a girl? What colour eyes would it have? Would it look like him?

She tried, she really tried to focus on the re-building of Savron Pinder House, but her heart wasn't in it and very little got done apart from some initial planning. People were disappointed…what would happen to the lovely little theatre? What about the stables? What a shame to let that beautiful place go to rack and ruin. Still, she's had a lot to deal with in her life and a body can only take so much.

CHAPTER FORTY SIX

A week after the tractor incident Rosemary visited Monk's Manor. It was a lovely afternoon and Eleanore carried the tea things out onto the lawn, shouting up to Crystal, who was in her bedroom, that it was ready. She finished brushing her hair, left her room, quietly shutting the door behind her, and made her way along the passage towards the stairs. She paused at an open window and looked down to where her mother and half sister were sitting in deck chairs talking. Their voices drifted up,

"...the tractor wasn't badly damaged, but Gerald was furious...puce with rage. It didn't help that Gerard insisted on playing crashes all evening with his train set until Gerald swore at him, which made me angry. He knows I won't have it. Poor old Gerald, he does get in a stew about things." Rosemary and Eleanore both laughed before Rosemary continued, "Anyway, Charlie is back now, thank God, and tractor man is well under control." She paused, "Does Crystal know yet...?"

Crystal walked quickly down the stairs, through the back door and over the lawn; she pulled up another deck chair and sat down. There was an uncomfortable silence and, thinking to put them out of their misery, she said quietly,

"Don't worry, yes I do know that Charlie and Faye are having a baby. I don't know whether it's been born yet, but I assume it has if Charlie is back at work. So," she added brightly, "What is it – boy or girl?"

Her mother and sister stared at her and no-one spoke, so Crystal dropped the forced brightness,

"It's OK, really. You can tell me. I know I shall have to get used to it."

Rosemary looked at Eleanore then back at Crystal before she said,

"My dear, what on earth are you talking about? Charlie and Faye...having a baby? Good grief how can they? They are getting a divorce! Faye has already left."

It was Crystal's turn to look startled,

"A divorce...? But Gerald said..."

"Oh dear God what now? What has Gerald been saying? Though I find it hard to believe that even he can get those two things muddled."

In fact, when Crystal thought about it what had Gerald said? He had left a sentence hanging in the air and her imagination had finished it for him. He heart was racing. She should be saying how sorry she was that the marriage hadn't worked out and all that, but she just listened as Rosemary continued,

"It's all very amicable. They have simply decided they have absolutely nothing in common and have to go their separate ways, though you'd have thought they could have decided that before they got spliced in the first place, wouldn't you? Expensive wedding and all that. Jolly good thing they haven't got any kids, I'd say. Mind you, divorce is becoming so commonplace nowadays, some of their friends have even sent them happy divorce cards! I ask you? Have you ever heard of such a thing?"

Eleanore said she hadn't then both women stared at Crystal who just sat back in her chair and laughed uncontrollably.

Half an hour later she lifted the telephone receiver and, with a shaking finger, dialled the number of Baron's Manor. When he answered she had to clear her throat twice before speaking and an hour after that she was standing on the step as Charlie opened the newly refurbished oak door of his beautiful old house and let her in.

They were both hesitant and nervous, as though meeting each other for the first time.

"Would you like a cup of coffee?" Charlie indicated a chair and took a faltering step towards the kitchen. Crystal smiled and, ignoring the chair, stood in front of him and put her arms around his neck,

"No, I wouldn't," she breathed and suddenly they were kissing, hugging, crying and laughing all at once. It wasn't until much later that they sat entwined on the sofa with a half empty bottle of wine on the small table in front of them.

"Crystal, I love you so much…"

She turned and looked into his eyes,

"And I love you, Charlie."

He held her tightly,

"I hope it's not too soon to ask this, but you will marry me, won't you?"

She laughed as she saw that he had the same anxious expression in his eyes as he'd had all those years ago at Rosemary's wedding when he had thought she might refuse to dance with him. 'What an attractive quality humility is' she reflected as she told him, no, it wasn't too soon to ask as they had already wasted enough time and, yes, yes, YES of course she would marry him!

"Oh, my darling, I'm so very happy for you!" Eleanore stood in the kitchen at Monk's Manor the following morning, her hands clasped to her face and tears glittering in her eyes as Crystal told her the news. In fact everyone reacted very positively.

"About time too! Everyone else could see you two were meant for each other." Minty flung her arms around her dearest friend then moved aside and Rob enveloped her in a bear hug. Not wanting to be left out of a hugging opportunity, Bobby and Frankie presented themselves to Crystal and as she kissed the top of Bobby's head she looked at Minty,

"You will be my Matron of Honour, won't you?"

"You bet! Wild horses wouldn't stop me."

But it wasn't wild horses that almost prevented Minty from carrying out this important duty for her friend. The wedding was arranged for the following August and by that time she was four months pregnant with her third child – hoping it would be the longed for little sister for her two boys, a girl she could call Arabella in memory of her mother.

Bobby and Frankie were roped in to be page boys, but Gerard declared himself too grown up for such things. Julia, however, was beside herself with excitement when she was told she would be a bridesmaid for Auntie Crystal and Uncle Charlie, begging to be allowed to wear a fairy dress covered in pink rosebuds with a pink bow at the back. Crystal had said she would see what she could do and smiled to herself, wondering how Rosemary would cope with this ultra feminine little girl she had somehow produced.

"…So I'd be very honoured if you would be my best man." Charlie paused and Gerald sat bolt upright in one of the chairs in his drawing room, a flush of pleasure deepening his already florid complexion.

"Really…good lord …well I never…I don't know what to say…"

"Well, 'yes' would be good, Gerald, unless you don't want to do it."

Rosemary chivvied her husband, shaking her head and smiling as he blustered on declaring that of course he would do it and the honour was all his.

Crystal had not gone with Charlie to the Bull's farm that afternoon as there was something very important she had to do – alone; something she couldn't put off any longer. Carefully she tied the small white card to the bouquet of flowers then walked slowly and purposefully through the village to the Church yard.

His grave was tidy and well kept – Eleanore tended it every week – and Crystal stood still before it reading again the inscription on the head stone. Yes, he did die too soon, taken by the stupidity and treachery of his evil brother. She knew Giles hadn't committed suicide and his couple of glasses of wine would not have caused him to go off the road. She made herself think again about the look he had given her just before he had left Monk's Manor and walked out of their lives for ever. She had thought for a while that maybe he was trying to tell her he was looking at her for the last time, that perhaps he was planning suicide as the only way out of their terrible predicament, but in her heart she had never really believed that. It just wasn't Giles. As she thought about it, she was more sure now that his look had been saying that somehow they would work things out; he was reassuring her they would find a way. She knew he would never have left her like that.

As she and Charlie were getting to know each other again, she was surprised to learn how close he and Giles had been as boys. They were best friends and, without thinking, when he and Crystal had been discussing the wedding arrangements, Charlie had blurted out,

"…of course Giles Cowper would have been my best man but as he…." He had stopped speaking and clapped his hands over his mouth, "Oh, lord, Crystal, I'm so sorry…"

"It's alright." She had reassured him, and realised then that she had to put things straight, in their proper place. She had, finally, to grow up.

She stood staring at the grave and thought about the vows she had made. She was glad she had discovered the truth about the car crash and Clive would be in prison for a very long time. That one was closed.

She thought then about the other vow and squeezed her eyes shut, forcing herself to bring Giles' face up, right there in front of her. He was smiling…it was OK. She opened her eyes and stared again at the smooth, green mound of earth, the earth that covered the man she could never have married, the man who would have been the most wonderful brother to her, but for the circumstances of their lives. Giles would have looked out for her and been there at her wedding to Charlie, giving her a brotherly hug and holding the rings that would bind his sister and his best friend in marriage.

"My brother…goodbye Giles…the dearest brother I could have had. How I wish we could have grown up together, but it wasn't to be. Things are as they are and, as my brother, you would never hold me to a vow based on something that could never have been."

She closed her eyes again and he was still smiling, it was a smile that said, 'go and be happy…I'm your brother, that's what I would wish for you.'

It started to rain as she placed the flowers on the grave and the drops were already washing away the words on the white card, the words that said,

'To my dearest brother, Giles, from your sister, Crystal. Until we meet again.'

She watched with tears running down her cheeks and mingling with the rain until the card was a soggy mass streaked with black; and she felt clean.

CHAPTER FORTY SEVEN

August 1975

It was a wonderful day from start to finish. She and Charlie made their vows to each other in the village Church, packed with family and friends; Peter Kempton, grey haired and ready for retirement now, had delayed his departure as Vicar of Savron Pinder so that he could perform this one last wedding ceremony. He hugged Crystal and told her that he couldn't think of a more fitting end to his working life.

Crystal had asked her uncle Geoffrey to give her away and he had been delighted to accept. She had been a little concerned that Claude might feel offended, but, in his good natured way, he had taken the attitude that it was Geoffrey, not him, with whom Crystal had had the most contact through the horses, so he was quite happy just to attend.

As she made her way steadily down the aisle of the village Church that had meant so much to her over the years, she glanced at Geoffrey, walking so proudly beside her, his arm as steady as a rock, and she saw that he was blinking back tears. Just for a moment she allowed the ghost of her real father to occupy that place and fleetingly the face from the photographs was there, the dark hair now greying slightly at the temples, the eyes smiling into hers.

She looked past Geoffrey, and Philippe, catching her eye, blew her a kiss. Yes, she was glad she had asked Geoffrey; there wouldn't be any other weddings in which he could play such an important role. Things are as they are.

Then the reception in a huge marquee on the lawns at Savron Pinder House was everything they could have hoped for. They had hired a firm of caterers, much to Nelly's disgust, as she had declared she was sure she could be trusted to produce a meal fit for such an occasion. Crystal agreed that, of course she could, that fact wasn't in question, but she had put her foot firmly down. She was not allowing it as she wanted her old friend fit and well for a very long time to come. If she exhausted herself who would be there to run the household for her and Charlie – and whoever else there might be living there in the future? Nelly understood, and at the hint of children, realised that she didn't want to do anything that would risk her not being around for these possible future events.

She was completely placated when Crystal had said, quite casually, that the caterers would, of course, need to be closely supervised and she was relying on Nelly for that. She had smiled as she had watched Nelly bustling about and had to have a quiet word with the head of the catering firm to explain why his staff were being bossed around by the elderly housekeeper, even promising that, if they could grin and bear it for the day, there would be an extra large tip for each and every one of them.

The sun shone all day, but a gentle breeze that stirred the trees in the wood and ruffled the surface of the lake, kept them cool as they celebrated well into the night.

Minty, past the morning sickness stage and glowing with health, kept her two boys in order and guided little Julia through her duties. She was happy with the colour scheme of cream and pale burgundy which suited them both; although Julia had been a little tearful at first until Crystal and Minty had managed to convince her that the burgundy rosebuds, sash and bow on her creamy, fairy tale confection of a dress were actually pink – a special shade of very dark pink – just as she had asked for.

Gerald's speech was admirable and delivered with so much confidence and so little blustering that even Rosemary was impressed.

When compiling the guest list, Crystal had checked with Eleanore to see whether she wanted William to be invited. She was pretty sure that his presence wouldn't be welcome and this was confirmed by a loud and uncharacteristic snort from her mother,

"No I don't! Good grief, he's nothing to us now, and my life has been so much better since he hasn't been in it." And it was true; Eleanore had blossomed, socially and with her Art work in a way that she never could have done with him around, sapping her confidence with his depressing negativity. "Anyway, darling, he'd probably be the one to stand up at that bit where you have to declare if you know any reason why these two people shouldn't be joined together, and start spouting off all the family history. We don't want to risk that, do we?"

The other and more major problem was grandmother Isobel. In the end they decided that, as Crystal's grandmother and a very old lady at that, she had to be invited, but they were confident she wouldn't attend. Crystal was still struggling to forgive her for her attitude at both Connie's and Arthur's funerals, but felt that maybe offering the olive branch in this way was the right thing to do – anyway, she wouldn't come.

Crystal didn't know it, but not only did the old lady declare that she certainly wasn't going to attend the wedding of that upstart, but she had tried to stop the rest of her family from going too. It was at this point that they had finally rebelled. Geoffrey, Claude and Philippe had looked at each other and told the old tyrant that they were most definitely going. She had thrown a tantrum and sulked in her room; then was further put out when, having contacted Bette, she learned that she would certainly be attending the wedding with her husband and daughters and would be staying with Eleanore at Monk's Manor.

Isobel Lynton-Bell continued to sulk and the three men discovered that it actually made very little difference to their lives, eventually wondering why they hadn't stood up to her before. Nobody pandered to her, and she was completely forgotten in the excitement of the day; only poor May, the maid, was left to cope with her bad behaviour.

It was therefore to everyone's astonishment that she appeared, dressed in her usual black and supported under the elbow by Bateman, just as Gerald was finishing his speech and receiving a well deserved round of applause accompanied by cat calls and whistles. These gradually died away as, one by one, the assembled group turned and saw the old lady standing by the entrance to the marquee. Eleanore and her brothers looked at each other, embarrassed and unsure what to do, but Rosemary stood up and walked purposefully over to her grandmother. She dismissed Bateman and led the old lady firmly by the arm to where an extra chair was already being placed at her table. She murmured a few words into her ear and glanced at

Eleanore, giving a quick wink, as Isobel, her face an inscrutable mask, stared straight ahead of her. Eleanore whispered to Crystal,

"Nothing to worry about, darling, if she plays up Rosie will march her out so fast her feet won't touch the ground."

Gerald toasted the bridesmaids, his eyes resting proudly on his tiny daughter who was sitting up very straight, her deep blue eyes solemnly reflecting how seriously she was taking her role for the day and blond, cork screw curls shaking as she looked around the room.

Much later, when all the formalities had ended and people were sitting quietly in groups chatting or swaying to the music of the band softly playing the last few melodies of the day to bring the proceedings to a close, Crystal stood in the centre of the lawn and looked up at the house. The setting sun was shining on the new sand coloured stonework, and glinting off the many windows surrounded with shiny new paint.

What a joy it had been to rebuild the place with Charlie at her side and how beautiful they had made it. She had deliberately replicated the blue drawing room and the red room using the best paints, wallpapers and fabrics that she could find. Nelly had supervised the refurbishing of the kitchen, still stoically rejecting anything in Formica, but allowing Crystal to persuade her to introduce a few labour saving devices such as an automatic washing machine in place of the twin-tub and even a machine that dried clothes. This last one produced a snort of derision from Nelly who declared it a waste of money as she would continue to peg her washing out on a line as she had always done. Crystal reminded her that it did sometimes rain, and there may be occasion for drying things quickly. Imagining a pile of warm dry nappies, Nelly was once again placated, especially as Charlie said the new things would be hidden away in a utility room.

Crystal had insisted that she and Charlie would have the main bedroom that had once been Connie and Arthur's, and it had been redecorated to look as it had when she had first seen it in rich creams and golds. A new four poster bed had been installed draped in cream and gold brocade, and it was here that she and Charlie would spend their wedding night; there was nowhere else in the world they wanted to be.

Crystal and Charlie's love had grown over the year as they had gradually got to know each other better. She still felt horrified when she thought about how she had taken him for granted at first and how she had very nearly lost him for ever. What an amazing person he was.

She asked him about his marriage and he told her that it was indeed as Rosemary had said. He and Faye had had to face the fact that they just didn't belong together, but he blamed himself more than her for the failure as he knew all the time that he could never love her. He was, and always had been since they had first met, in love with Crystal. He had a feeling that Faye had always known there was someone else, though they had never talked about it, but it had made him feel guilty and try even harder to make the marriage work. The trouble was they were both conscious of the effort and how false it was.

"That was why I happened to be walking past Savron Pinder House the night of the fire. I was wondering how to cope with my crumbling marriage and staring at what I thought might be your bedroom, thinking of you. The rest, as they say, is history."

She wandered alone through the woods and stood by the edge of the lake, still in her beautiful white wedding dress which rustled over the carpet of old leaves; gently she touched the crystal pendant at her throat and felt the matching earrings brush softly against her neck as she looked out across the water. Reeds whispered in the gathering dusk and she thought about the first time she had stood on that very spot with Arthur, looking out to where the reeds on that occasion were frozen into the surface of the lake. 'There will be skating again, Arthur, I promise you…there will be skating again.'

How she had missed them all today – Connie, Arthur, George and Marjorie. How proud and happy they would have been. She listened to the rustling all around and closed her eyes. They were there…all of them, even Giles, in the rustling of the wind. They would be there for ever in the memories of those who loved them and their stories would be told to those yet to come, the future generations whose voices would ring around these woods making Savron Pinder House live again.

Also by Sylvie Short:

Novels:

The Bubble published 2010

Starting Out published 2013

It Rained in Bora Bora published 2016

History:

Two Churches Together published 2014

Short Stories:

Short Cuts published 2013

Reflections and Stories;

Short Steps Along the Way published 2014

Short 'n' Savoury published 2015

Nine of Sylvie's short stories have been published by Cambridgeshire County Life.